RETURN TO LONDON

ERIN SWANN

YOU DON'T ALWAYS HAVE TO BE A LADY.

This book is a work of fiction. The names, characters, businesses, and events portrayed in this book are fictitious. Any similarity to real persons, living or dead, businesses, or events is coincidental and not intended by the author.

Copyright © 2020 by Swann Publications

All rights reserved.

No part of this book may be reproduced, stored in a retrieval system, or transmitted in any form or by any means, electronic, mechanical, photocopying, recording, or otherwise, without the express written permission of the publisher. Reasonable portions may be quoted for review purposes.

The author acknowledges the trademarked status and trademark owners of various products referenced in this work of fiction, which have been used without permission. The publication/use of these trademarks is not authorized, associated with, or sponsored by the trademark owners.

Cover images licensed from Shutterstock.com, depositphotos.com

Cover design by Swann Publications

ISBN13: 979-8556045286

Edited by Jessica Royer Ocken

Proofreaders: My Brother's Editor, Donna Hokanson

Typohunter Extraordinaire: Renee Williams

The following story is intended for mature readers. It contains mature themes, strong language, and sexual situations. All characters are 18+ years of age, and all sexual acts are consensual.

~

Want to hear about new releases and sales?

If you would like to hear about Erin's **new releases** and sales, join the newsletter at https://erinswann.com/subscribe. We only email about sales or new releases, and we never share your information.

~

Erin can be found on the web at https://www.erinswann.com

❦ Created with Vellum

ALSO BY ERIN SWANN

Why romance? Because we all need a chance to escape doing the next load of laundry.

We deserve a chance to enjoy love, laughs, intrigue, and yes, fear, heartbreak, and tears, all without having to leave the house.

If you can read my books without feeling any of these then I haven't done my job right.

Covington Billionaires Series:

The Billionaire's Trust - Available on Amazon, also in AUDIOBOOK

(Bill and Lauren's story) He needed to save the company. He needed her. He couldn't have both. The wedding proposal in front of hundreds was like a fairy tale come true—Until she uncovered his darkest secret.

The Youngest Billionaire - Available on Amazon

(Steven and Emma's story) The youngest of the Covington clan, Steven, avoided the family business to become a rarity, an honest lawyer. He didn't suspect that pursuing Emma could destroy his career. She didn't know what trusting him could cost her.

The Secret Billionaire – Available on Amazon, also in AUDIOBOOK

(Patrick and Elizabeth's story) Women naturally circled the flame of wealth and power, and his is brighter than most. Does she love him? Does she not? There's no way to know. When Pat stopped to help her, Liz mistook him for a carpenter. Maybe this time he'd know. Everything was perfect. Until the day she left.

The Billionaire's Hope - Available on Amazon, also in AUDIOBOOK

(Nick and Katie's story) They came from different worlds. Katie hadn't seen him since the day he broke her brother's nose. Her family retaliated by destroying Nick's life. She never suspected where accepting a ride from him today would take her. They said they could do casual. They lied.

Previously titled: Protecting the Billionaire

Picked by the Billionaire – Available on Amazon, also in AUDIOBOOK

(Liam and Amy's story) A night she wouldn't forget. An offer she couldn't refuse. He alone could save her, and she held the key to his survival. If only they could pass the test together.

Saved by the Billionaire – Available on Amazon, also in AUDIOBOOK

(Ryan and Natalie's story) The FBI and the cartel were both after her for the same thing: information she didn't have. First, the FBI took everything, and then the cartel came for her. She trusted Ryan with her safety, but could she trust him with her heart?

Caught by the Billionaire – Available on Amazon, also in AUDIOBOOK

(Vincent and Ashley's story) Ashley's undercover assignment was simple enough: nail the crooked billionaire. The surprise came when she opened the folder, and the target was her one-time high school sweetheart, Vincent. What will happen when an unknown foe makes a move to checkmate?

The Driven Billionaire – Available on Amazon

(Zachary and Brittney's story) Rule number one: hands off your best friend's sister. With nowhere to turn when she returns from upstate, Brittney accepts Zach's offer of a room. Mutual attraction quickly blurs the rules. When she comes under attack, pulling Brittney closer is the only way to keep her safe. But, the truth of why she left town in the first place will threaten to destroy them both.

Nailing the Billionaire – Available on Amazon

(Dennis and Jennifer's story) Jennifer knew he destroyed her family. Now she is close to finding the records that will bring Dennis down. When a corporate shakeup forces her to work with him, anger and desire compete. Vengeance was supposed to be simple, swift, and sweet. It was none of those things.

Undercover Billionaire – Available on Amazon

(Adam and Kelly's story) Their wealthy families have been at war forever. When Kelly receives a chilling note, the FBI assigns Adam to protect her. Family histories and desire soon collide, questioning old truths. Keeping ahead of the threat won't be their only challenge.

Trapped with the Billionaire – Available on Amazon

(Josh and Nicole's story) Nicole returns from vacation to find her company has been sold to Josh's family. Being assigned to work for the new CEO is only the first of her problems.

Competing visions of how to run things and mutual passion create a volatile mix. The reappearance of a killer from years ago soon threatens everything.

Saving Debbie – Available on Amazon

(Luke and Debbie's story) On the run from her family and the cops, Debbie finds the only person she can trust is Luke, the ex-con who patched up her injuries. Old lies haunt her, and the only way to unravel them is to talk with Josh, the boy who lived through the nightmare with her years ago.

Return to London – Available on Amazon

(Ethan and Rebecca's story) Rebecca looks forward to the most important case of her career. Until, she is paired with Ethan, the man she knew years ago. Mutual attraction and old secrets combine to complicate everything. What could have been a second chance results in an impossible choice.

The Rivals – Available on Amazon

(Charlie and Danielle's story) He was her first crush. That ended when their families had a falling out. Now, they are forced to work together on a complicated acquisition. Mutual attraction is complicated by distrust as things go wrong around them. A second chance turns into an impossible choice.

Clear Lake Series: The Clear Lake books follow the Bensons of Clear Lake as they deal with a disappearance in town which shatters the tranquility of their community and puts them in the cross-hairs of the local police chief.

Temptation at the Lake – Available on Amazon

(Casey and Jordan's story) Shot in the line of duty and on temporary disability, Jordan leaves the city for Clear Lake to recuperate. Getting back to one hundred percent was supposed to be hard, but she didn't count on the irresistible Casey becoming the devil pushing her to the breaking point. A fling with this devil becomes complicated when she gets pulled into the investigation of a disappearance in town. Has she started sleeping with a murderer?

CHAPTER 1

Rebecca

"Top priority," Smithers had said before he disappeared into the crowd—just the kind of assignment I needed.

I'd expected him to offer me a security escort when he handed me the small, blue case.

He hadn't.

Midblock, I arrived at the correct doorway and pushed in.

Not a single hair was out of place on the middle-aged woman who greeted me. "Good morning. Welcome to The House of Stafford," she said loudly as the door closed behind me.

She appraised me from head to toe. The crinkle that formed at the corner of her eye said she didn't find my business attire, especially in its current wrinkled state, up to the standards of her desired clientele.

"My name is Martha. How may I assist you today, madam?" she added dryly. The door to the street opening behind me drew her attention away.

"I need to speak with Mr. Stafford," I told her.

Her eyes returned to me. "I am afraid Mr. Stafford is a very busy man and only sees clients by appointment," she said with a haughty lift of her nose. She looked past me to the couple who had entered. "Now, if you'll excuse me."

I slid to the side, blocking her attempt to move around me. "If you'll tell Mr. Stafford that Rebecca Sommerset is here to see him, I believe he'll make the time."

Her huff was barely audible. "I'll be with you momentarily," she said to the others. Her smile faded. "I'll check with Mr. Stafford." The slight cock of her head and squint of her eye was more polite than an eye roll, but conveyed the same disdain.

The House of Stafford dealt in incredibly rare and expensive jewelry, catering to the equally rare, incredibly wealthy upper crust of society. The display case in front of me made the point. Large, exquisitely elegant necklaces with multiple large stones adorned black velvet mannequin necks. Nothing so lowbrow as a price tag was anywhere to be seen.

I shifted to the next case, which announced itself as *special*.

From the collection of the Duchess of Overdale.

It contained the most fantastic necklace in the store. The duchess had been a very lucky woman.

I moved aside for the bearded man in a suit and the woman wearing a black hijab. Middle Eastern royalty had the money to compete with London's upper crust for Stafford's services.

Stick-up-her-ass Martha returned from the back with a pasted-on smile. "This way, please, Mrs. Sommerset." She held open the employee door for me.

"Ms. Sommerset," I corrected as I passed her and went into the back.

She led the way around a corner and down a hallway.

William Stafford stood from his bench and greeted me with a gracious handshake. "Miss Sommerset, it's unfortunate that we meet under these circumstances."

I nodded. This was an unpleasant business. "Thank you for making the time for me."

"Thank you, Mrs. Marston," he told Stick-up-her-ass.

I waited for Martha to leave before pulling the large, flat jewelry box from my purse. With *House of Stafford* embossed in gold on navy blue leather, the box screamed expensive. If Smithers had thought it was the real thing, security would have accompanied me here.

Mr. Stafford accepted the case with both hands. "Your company called ahead, asking for an authentication. I understand you have some doubts."

I nodded. "We do." The necklace in the case I'd been given this morning had been determined by our in-house gemologist, Grinley, to be full of fake stones.

Stafford opened the case and gently lifted out the diamond-and-ruby necklace.

I hadn't chanced a look at it before arriving. Even if it was a fake, the stunning necklace took my breath away.

"One of our finer efforts." He started his examination at one end and shook his head multiple times as he progressed through the length of it. He examined the major stone suspended from the center. "What a pity. Miss Sommerset, as you suspected, this is an imitation." He shifted his jeweler's loupe to the next stone of the necklace. "The entire piece, not merely the gems."

My stomach churned. "Are you sure?" I asked without considering my words. Our in-house specialist was of the opinion that only the stones had been replaced, with good-quality imitations. Selling off gems and replacing them with fakes in the original settings was a well-known method of raising money for the idle rich who found themselves in need of cash.

He turned to me and scowled. "Why do you Americans insist upon being rude? Are you questioning my judgment, or merely my integrity? My great-grandfather created this piece for the duchess." He huffed. "Not this one, but the original."

I nodded. I deserved that. The House of Stafford was the premier jeweler in all of Britain, and their customers included the royal family. As the fifth Stafford to run the business, William Stafford was the go-to man in London for the best that sparkled.

"I'm sorry, Mr. Stafford, what I meant to ask is what makes you think the entire thing is a forgery?"

He handed me a 30X loupe with The House of Stafford engraved on it. "Check the clasp for yourself. What engraving do you see?"

It appeared I was going to get a lesson rather than an answer.

I leaned over and adjusted the light, checking both sides of the silver clasp. "What should I be looking for?"

"What do you see?"

I kept at it another ten seconds. This was a test, and I was failing. Turning the clasp over again, I rechecked the reverse side. "Nothing. It looks to be in excellent condition." It didn't appear to have the wear a piece this old should show.

"Exactly, Miss Sommerset." He reached over and pulled another piece from a black velvet mat. "Now check the clasp on this." He handed me a necklace with a simple stone and light gold chain.

In the magnification of the loupe, the initials came immediately into view. "H-S," I said.

He opened the folder to his left. "The duchess's necklace had such a mark, and it was verified…" He checked for a date on his paper. "We received it for its most recent cleaning two weeks ago." He slid over a small, close-up photo of the clasp with *HS* clearly visible.

I shook my head. "Could the clasp have been replaced?"

He slid over another photo. "Miss Sommerset, this house has been dealing with such issues for generations. This marking was verified on the fourteenth link of the chain when it was brought in to be cleaned." The photo also showed an *HS*. "Go ahead check the fourteenth link for yourself. I insist."

Clearly I'd pushed the boundaries with the man. I slowly counted links and checked the fourteenth, and then the one on either side in case I'd miscounted. "So the whole thing was replicated?"

He returned the photographs to the folder and closed it. "The entire piece, I'm afraid. The duchess must be beside herself."

"I'm sure she is," I assured him. I pushed the loupe across the table.

"You may keep that—to show your superiors, if need be."

Ten minutes later, the door to The House of Stafford closed behind me. On the noisy street, Stafford's words echoed in my head. *"The duchess must be beside herself."* But the duchess would be six-million-pounds richer when my firm cut the check for the necklace's insured value, and *my bosses* would be the ones beside themselves.

How had someone managed to recreate the entire piece in such detail that our inspection had only detected the fake stones, *and* substitute it for the real necklace in the last two weeks?

Three blocks from the tube station, I stopped briefly outside a small Indian restaurant. My feet had swollen from the long flight and were killing me. I should have put the heels in my carry-on and worn something more comfortable aboard the plane. The menu on the wall was just as I remembered from the last time Ethan had taken me here. I'd ordered the lamb madras—spicy and delicious. Swatting the distracting memory away, I continued on.

Everything about this morning was off. Since when did I rate being met at Heathrow by Mr. Smithers, the head of investigations? Short answer: since never.

He'd handed me the package I had in my purse with a three-sentence explanation and an address. *"Top priority,"* he'd said. *"Call me as soon as you finish."* A minute later, he'd disappeared with my bags in tow. At least I didn't have to schlep my luggage through the underground.

Top priority?

A vision from my past stopped me in my tracks. I rubbed my tired eyes to get a better look.

Ethan Blakewell?

It couldn't be.

It better not be.

The man glanced my way.

A truck came to a halt on the street between us, and he disappeared from view.

Had I imagined a hint of recognition on his face? It had been too fleeting to be sure of anything from this distance.

I hadn't seen him in five years, almost six now, and still the sight of him—or maybe just the thought of him—had jolted me. After straightening my shoulders, I walked on. I wouldn't allow him to intimidate me. I'd moved on. We both had.

The truck resumed its journey down the street.

I glanced over.

He was gone.

I clamped my eyes shut to clear the cobwebs induced by the long flight before opening them again and scanning the block. He wasn't there. Had I conjured him out of thin air? Had he been a mirage triggered by lack of sleep and walking past the restaurant?

That had to be it.

I glanced across the street one more time. No Ethan Blakewell.

Maybe I should have tried to sleep on the plane. I stopped to pull out my phone and dialed Smithers.

"Is it as bad as Grinley thought?" he asked immediately.

"No. It's worse."

"Take the results straight to the managing director. I'll talk to you after," he said before hanging up. Somebody was in a bad mood.

Report straight to the managing director? I'd never even been introduced to Joseph Cornwall, much less been to his office. Things on this side of the pond were much more formal than our San Francisco and New York offices. Here, someone in my position didn't get invited up to the top floor.

I puzzled the implications of this sudden assignment as I stepped onto the down escalator of the tube station.

～

Ethan

Becky?

As soon as the lorry pulled between us, I ducked into the bookshop, hiding from my past—hiding from her. I doubted she'd seen me.

"Can I help you find anything in particular?" a young woman's voice asked from behind me.

I turned and smiled back before picking up a thriller from the table. "Just browsing."

Her smile grew. "That's his latest. I quite liked it. Have you read him before?"

"Like I said, just browsing." I held up the book and turned back to the window in time to see Rebecca make a call on her mobile. For a moment I pretended to be reading the back cover while I watched her continue down the road.

Even in the business attire, I'd have known Becky Sommerset anywhere. She wasn't someone you forgot. It was the eyes—she had eyes that could look clear through me.

The bookshop lady was still nearby when I turned around.

I approached and handed her the book, even though I'd never read Michael Connelly. "I'll take this."

She beamed as she rang me up. "I'm sure you'll love it, Mr.—"

"Ethan, just Ethan," I filled in for her as I slid my card and paid.

She bagged the book and returned it to me. "I'm Claire. Stop in any time, Ethan."

I nodded as I exited and, after a glance across the road, turned toward the tube station in the opposite direction Becky had walked.

She had once brought out the best in me, but this morning it was quite the opposite.

What was Becky doing in London?

I strode toward the tube without having to face my failings from years ago. A few blocks later, I escaped into the underground system, pleased that I hadn't looked behind me once.

Instead of my usual hurry, I stood to the left on the long down escalator and let other fellows with less on their minds pass me by.

They said with time you forgot the one that got away. Becky had receded in my thoughts, but my reaction this morning spoke volumes. The saying was wrong. I'd not forgotten. I'd not recovered from her.

On the platform, waiting for the train, my mind drifted back to our time together—happy and carefree months before turbulence overtook my life, before I learned the truth about my parents. I dispelled the past from my thoughts when the voice over the speakers came alive. "Mind the gap."

When the doors opened and the crowd surged onto the train, I rejoined the present and left thoughts of Becky and Imperial College behind.

I checked my watch as the train got up to speed. I'd still make it in time for my lecture.

CHAPTER 2

REBECCA

When I started up the escalator to the surface, my phone buzzed that I had a voicemail waiting. Pulling out the phone, I found I'd missed a call from my mother. I started listening.

"Rebecca, you can't keep missing dinner with us, and at least have the decency to tell me instead of leaving a message."

So it was okay for her to rant at me over a voicemail message, but me leaving a message when she didn't pick up was out of bounds? This would take a call to smooth over, but not when I was this dog tired.

For the tenth time this year, I walked the short distance from the tube station to the tall building that housed our London offices.

After my ride in the elevator, I passed through the glass doors of Lessex Insurance.

"Good morning, Ms. Sommerset," Ginny said cheerfully as soon as she looked up. "How was your flight?"

"Peachy," was all the sarcasm I could manage after eleven mostly sleepless hours overnight in a noisy aluminum tube, followed by an immediate task for Smithers. I missed my bed in San Francisco.

The sarcasm rolled right off her. "Wonderful. Would you like a cup of tea to start?" The girl was nothing if not persistent.

The English were into tea, but give me a strong cup of java any day. "Nice one, Ginny."

"Can't blame a girl for trying," she said with her ever-present smile.

"I'm not so easily trained. Coffee, please."

"Sorry. The machine is still broken."

Of course it was. It had been broken last time I was here, and I seemed to be the only one in the office with good enough taste to want to use it.

"Hot water, then," I told her as I plopped down behind the shared desk I used when visiting London. I tried all the drawers, but came up empty in my search for the jar of coffee.

My bags were in the corner of the office, but I'd forgotten to bring any coffee with me. As soon as I sat, the torture devices masquerading as my shoes came off. The chair had to be adjusted. The last person here had set it to recline easily, which didn't suit me.

I needed the energy coffee would bring me before venturing upstairs—that and some makeup. It was my first invitation to the managing director's office and I would be bringing bad news.

When Ginny returned, she held the jar of instant coffee I'd been unable to find, along with my cup of hot water. "I saved this for you."

"Thanks a ton," I sighed.

"Larry wanted to throw it out."

"Of course he did." Larry Falwell was still pissed that I'd beaten him out for the promotion. His male ego couldn't handle being bested by a *skirt*, as the worm had called me behind my back.

"There is one other thing." Ginny's wary look could only mean bad news.

I shook my head. "Maybe later. I need to be up in Mr. Cornwall's office right away."

She ignored me. "Margaret, the new girl, well, she kind of let slip…"

I waited for the bad news.

"That you would be in the city this week."

"To who?" I corrected myself a second later. "To whom?"

"Mr. Stroud," she said sheepishly.

All I could do was hang my head and wish I hadn't gotten on the plane last night. One word with my ex-husband was a word too many. "How? Even I didn't know about this trip before yesterday." Mom had to have been his source.

"He called this morning. I'm so sorry," Ginny said. "She didn't remember the rules."

"Send her in."

Moments later, Margaret slunk into the office.

"What is the number-one rule of answering my phone?"

Her shoulders slumped. "Don't take calls from Mr. Stroud."

"The second?"

"Don't talk to Mr. Stroud."

"And the third?"

"If I talk to Mr. Stroud, don't answer any questions about you."

I waved her away. "Margaret, please remember them."

"Yes, mum."

"Get the door, please, will you?"

She might not have deserved me treating her that badly, but I certainly didn't deserve an interaction with my ex-husband, Wesley Stroud, because she had loose lips.

Just thinking of him made me queasy. Was I ever happy I'd kept my last name. I pulled my hand to my lap, realizing I'd reached for the scar on the back of my head.

After the door closed behind her, I put thoughts of my ex behind me and opened the gray envelope to read the letter again.

Miriam in the San Francisco Human Resources office had given it to me the day before I left. "I thought we should memorialize this conversation in writing," she'd said after handing me the ugly envelope filled with mushy words that hinted at an ugly outcome.

I pulled an antacid from my purse. They said I'd created a hostile atmosphere at work and needed to improve my interpersonal skills. The *or else* was implied instead of stated. HR people were all about platitudes and soft, mumbling words, up until the sharp knives they hid behind their backs came out.

How dare she?

The fact that I'd called Jackson out on his lie had been *his* fault for lying in the first place, not mine for pointing it out. If he'd kept his big mouth shut, none of it would have happened.

After folding the paper and reburying the notice at the bottom of my purse, I took a cleansing breath. Today was another day, and a "top priority" case was just what I needed to get the office focused back on my capabilities.

I was the best at what I did. That had to count for something.

∽

Ethan

The sign on the door said TechniByte IT Consulting Ltd., because we didn't want to advertise our presence here. Inside, I passed through security and made my way up the lift to the fourth floor and my office.

The new assistant in our section, Judith, was at her desk with another fresh, single rose in the vase. "Good morning, Inspector."

I leaned over to smell the pink rose. "Morning. How many plants do you have?"

"A bit more than three dozen—thirty-eight, actually," she answered with a smile.

"And which variety might this beauty be?"

"Constance Spry is its name. Quite pretty, I think."

"Agreed." I leaned over to sniff it once more. "Any messages?"

"Just one from your brother." She lifted the note and read from it. "He said he landed in New York. And I quote, 'He's fine. He's going radio silent, and don't sweat it.'"

I cocked my head. "Sounds like him."

"What does he do? You never said."

I backed away from her desk. "No. I didn't."

She nodded an acknowledgment and was senior enough here at the Metropolitan Police Service—the Met—to know better than to ask again.

Once inside my office, I powered up my computer and both screens. My email didn't contain anything urgent enough to deal with before class, so I opened my binder of notes for the lecture and started my review.

The room would be filled with the same several dozen denizens of this outpost as yesterday—a mixture of good notetakers and bad, alert and dozing eyes, those trying to learn and those trying to show off. It was the last category that bothered me. Trying to embarrass or trip up the instructor was the goal for two of them. Preparation was my best defense.

If I'd been given the latitude to fail a few of them out of the lecture, I would have by the second day. But the higher-ups had made it clear that *all* the attendees would be getting the benefit of my experience with the US National Cyber Investigative Joint Task Force in Washington. Expelling them from the lecture wasn't my prerogative.

The Yanks had things to learn from us, and it was equally true that we had things to learn from them. That was the purpose of my lectures.

Judith poked her head in the door. "You don't want to be late."

"So says you."

"So says the chief," she corrected. She had a point. Chief Inspector Harcourt seemed to care more about punctuality than anything else—*tight ship* and all that other rubbish he'd learned in Her Majesty's Navy. The three pips had gone to his head. Some of my job always entailed buffering between him and the blokes doing the work here. We were off in a separate building specifically because these computer types were a different breed than those inhabiting New Scotland Yard.

I gathered up my material and took the lift down to the third-floor lecture hall.

CHAPTER 3

Rebecca

I made my way to the restroom with my purse. The bags under my eyes couldn't be helped, but after a few minutes with my makeup, I decided the image in the mirror was work-worthy. Opening the larger of my bags in the office, I retrieved a set of heels one inch lower and a half size larger. My feet thanked me as I gathered my purse with the fake necklace inside and took the elevator to the top floor.

Mr. Cornwall's assistant, Emily, ushered me in as soon as I arrived.

Cornwall himself stood and checked his watch before rounding the desk to shake my hand. "Rebecca, isn't it?" he asked.

His assistant had probably looked that up for him.

I nodded. "Yes, sir."

He motioned me to one of the chairs facing his desk while he returned to his seat. "No disturbances, Emily."

"Yes, sir." She closed the door behind her.

Cornwall steepled his hands. "Is it as bad as Grinley said?"

I took out the box containing the necklace and opened it on his desk. "It's worse, sir."

"Accusing the duchess of substituting the stones is not going to go well," he mused. "But I can't very well let six million waltz out the door based on propriety."

"Sir," I ventured. "I don't think you understand the issue."

His brow creased. "Then perhaps you should enlighten me, Sommerset." The shift to my last name didn't portend well.

"It's not just the gems, sir."

He raised a hand to stop me and shook his head. "Nonsense. We've seen this a dozen times before. These members of the peerage are all alike. One finds herself in need of funds and sees selling off the stones as the easy way out."

Emily opened the door after a single knock.

Cornwall looked over. "I said I didn't want to be disturbed."

"Sir, the duchess is here to see you."

That simple sentence made his jaw drop. "Bloody hell. I'll be just a minute."

An older, well-dressed woman floated past Emily. "Joseph, are you trying to avoid me?"

Cornwall rose from his seat. "Never, your grace."

She approached his desk.

I rose from my chair as Emily scooted out and closed the door.

"Your grace," Cornwall started, "this is Ms. Sommerset, from our San Francisco office." He made San Francisco sound like it was a sewer somewhere. "Miss Sommerset, her grace the Duchess of Lindsley."

I did my best curtsy and repeated Cornwall's greeting. "Your grace."

She took the seat next to me. "I see you have the necklace here." She pointed at the open box. "I told your man Smithers it had to have happened in the loo." She looked at me. "I fainted for a second in the loo, and that's when it had to have been pinched."

I sat and nodded to her. She'd looked straight at me, and her honesty was easy for me to confirm. She really thought the necklace had been snatched in the bathroom.

Cornwall didn't look convinced. "We're still assessing things."

She wagged her finger at Cornwall. "Nonsense, Joseph. I sent it to Stafford to be cleaned two weeks ago. It was fine then, and we only picked it up from his shop the afternoon of the event." She shifted to me again. "And when I took it off at the end of the evening, the scratch was gone."

"What scratch?" Cornwall asked.

She leaned over and snatched the necklace from its case. "Here. The second ruby over. My mother scratched it with her diamond ring, by mistake, years ago." She held the stone in question and pointed it at him and then me. "See? No scratch. This isn't my necklace."

Cornwall started, "As I said—"

She cut him off. "Don't bloody put me off, Joseph. I know you've already been to Stafford's shop. What did he say about it?"

Cornwall had the look of a cornered animal and nodded to me.

I shifted my attention to the duchess. "Mr. Stafford confirmed that the entire piece is a forgery."

She smiled and turned on the managing director with a pointed finger. "See, Joseph? The blokes counted on me not noticing and getting away with the theft. Probably figured we wouldn't catch on for a year or two, and they'd be long gone."

Cornwall swallowed. "We'll look into it."

"I tell you," she continued, "there's an epidemic of this. The same thing happened to Elizabeth Haversom. You and the Met should get a handle on this right away."

Cornwall nodded.

"Now that you've had confirmation of what has happened, I'll expect a check in the morning, Joseph."

Cornwall had a deer-in-the-headlights look to him.

The duchess placed the necklace back in its box. "And I'll need to take this as well."

That woke Cornwall out of his trance. "You can't."

The duchess straightened up. "I can't very well show up at the next function and admit that it was stolen. What would people say? And, that would alert the thieves that we're on to them, now wouldn't it?"

Cornwall's face regained some of its color. "I can't authorize both a payout and this temporary replacement, is what I meant."

She closed the lid on the box and scooped it up. "Shall we say half, then? And I'll take this, for the time being?"

Cornwall was trapped, and he knew it. "We'll need to keep this confidential while we investigate."

She stood. "Of course, Joseph. I'm bloody well not yelling this from the rooftops. Can you imagine?" Now she was into image-conservation mode. She turned and stopped at the door. "You will keep me informed of your progress." It came out more as a command than a question.

Cornwall nodded. "Your grace."

A few seconds later, the door closed and we were alone again.

"Why didn't you tell me?" Cornwall demanded.

"I tried to." I wasn't letting this be my fault. "It wasn't her switching out the gems."

"I find her description of events hard to fathom." He stared at me with the unstated question.

I answered it for him. "She told the truth."

"You sure?"

"Absolutely." Determining things like this was what they paid me for, and I was good, really good.

He rubbed his temple. "This makes three now."

When more of an explanation didn't follow, I asked, "Three what?"

"The Haversom incident she mentioned was a brooch pinched at a party two months ago—same thing, an exact replica switched. And Amalgamated Insurance told me they also had a jewelry payout a few weeks ago. This has got to stop. We can't afford to have losses like this very often." He pointed at me. "Smithers said you were the best we had."

I swelled with pride and didn't know what to say.

"You've got to find the buggers and stop this."

That burst my balloon. "Me?" Now I could see how this would go. Smithers had been given an impossible task and nominated me as the sacrificial lamb for when it failed. "I don't think we can handle this alone." He had to face the facts now instead of later, regardless of what Smithers had told him.

He half laughed. "The duchess said she thought the Met should get involved. She has much more influence with them than I do, so I'll make it her job to get them on board to help you."

He'd just removed my one excuse, lack of resources. Working with what we Americans called *Scotland Yard* and still not putting a quick end to this would strike a stake through my career for sure.

"You're excused. Go see Smithers and work up a plan."

I stood. "This could require significant resources."

"You have my complete support. Whatever you require." He waved me away like a fly on his desk.

I found Smithers in his office one floor down from Cornwall.

The door was open, so I peeked in.

He looked up. "Sommerset, come in."

I took the chair he motioned to and smoothed my skirt. "I just finished with the managing director." I used his title because I wasn't sure of the etiquette on this floor.

"Report," he said.

"First, Stafford's assessment of the piece was worse than Grinley's."

A wrinkle formed on his brow. "You said that."

"The chain, the settings, the stones—it's all a replica."

The wrinkle increased. "Not the gems alone? That's very odd."

"Not if the theft was meant to go undetected. The copy was substituted for the original during a very narrow window."

He nodded slowly. "So you don't buy Cornwall's theory that the duchess herself replaced the gems?"

"Not likely. If she commissioned the replica, why bring the switch to our attention just days after the original had been verified at the jewelers? It doesn't make sense. She would have waited until next year."

He wrote something down on the piece of paper in front of him. "What else?"

"Cornwall got a visit from the duchess while I was there. He's assigning her to get the Metropolitan Police to cooperate on the investigation."

He laughed. "That must have been something. I had to pick up the necklace from her. She was in a mood to knock heads."

"He agreed to pay her half the insured value immediately."

Smithers shook his head. "Just because her husband has a title, we have to change all the rules." His tone was even harsher than his words.

I sighed. It was an argument the Brits could have among themselves. "I wasn't expecting to be in today. I'm still on west coast time."

The crinkle around his eyes indicated he wasn't pleased to hear me say that. "Go get some rest then. We'll pick this up in the morning. By then I expect the duchess will have gotten the Yard's attention."

I rose slowly. "Thank you, sir."

Back in my office, I had one imperative that wouldn't wait another minute—dig through my bag for some flats before heading out.

Waiting for the elevator to leave for the day, I opened the baggie in my purse's inside pocket and brought it to my nose. Breathing in the new-car smell from the tiny piece of scented cardboard, I envisioned the company car that would come with the promotion I hoped to get at the end of this assignment.

∼

ETHAN

AT THE LUNCH BREAK, I GOT A NOTE TO VISIT MY CHIEF INSPECTOR, WHO'D LEFT MY lecture early.

I heard him on the phone before I reached the doorway. "Damned aristocracy. We should have shipped them all off to Australia with the convicts."

I waited for the call to end before moving to the door. He had lifted the top off a sandwich to examine it.

He looked up. "Bloody cheese and cucumber again. Is it too much to ask for a little meat in a man's lunch once in a while?"

I didn't sit or attempt an answer.

He replaced the bread and picked up the sandwich, waving it toward the chair across from him. "Sit down, Blakewell."

I did as commanded and waited for him to finish chewing. "Did you have a comment about the lecture?"

He shook his head and slid a piece of paper across the desk before taking another bite from his lunch.

I took the paper, which had a name on it: *Superintendent Maxwell*.

"Just because some old lady lost a bauble, they want us to drop everything."

The *they* he referred to could only be somebody up the chain of command that the chief didn't dare talk back to. I stared at the paper without comment. When the chief was in a mood, it didn't pay to interrupt him.

"We have more than forty knife crimes and millions in e-crime every day, and we're supposed to drop everything because a shiny bauble goes missing."

I waited again for him to finish chewing. "How do I fit into this?" My specialization didn't have anything to do with jewelry theft.

He pointed at the paper. "He requested you for this. Be at his office tomorrow morning in New Scotland Yard and meet your team."

I sat up. "Why me?"

He chuckled. "They…" He let the sarcasm drip off the word. "…didn't think I needed to know." He bit into his sandwich.

I pointed out the obvious timing issue. "I have two more of the US cyber lectures scheduled."

He shook his head while chewing. "That will have to wait. You're on this now."

When he showed more interest in his lunch than me, I folded the paper and stood to leave.

"And Blakewell…"

I turned.

"You're assigned to the Specialist Crime Directorate for the duration of this. You report directly to Superintendent Maxwell. Do me proud."

I nodded and left with more questions than answers. SO10 was the old-timer's shorthand for the covert operations group that had since been designated SC&O 10.

After the lunch break, my lecture delivery wasn't as good as it should have been. The words *covert* and *partner* kept coming back to me.

Back at my desk at the end of the day, I did a quick internal records search on the Superintendent. Arriving unprepared was not my style. Maxwell, I learned, was third-generation Scotland Yard, and his list of accomplishments had been long up until he'd been assigned to covert operations five years ago. I didn't have access beyond that.

One case stood out. It had involved an international case with the Yanks. The name in the file turned my stomach when I read it.

Covington.

It was a name I'd hoped to never again see.

"I am a Blakewell, and bloody proud of it," I said under my breath.

A covert assignment with an unnamed partner, and important enough to put my lectures on hold, was something I wouldn't have guessed in a million years. And, I was reporting directly to a superintendent in covert operations.

Maxwell requested me.

CHAPTER 4

Rebecca

My sister Lizzy's place was the perfect place to stay when doing a temporary stint in the London office. It was nice, as units in this city went—not nearly the place I had back home, but the location in Kensington was convenient. Access to a kitchen and laundry didn't suck, but the main draw was being able to visit with my sister. Too bad she was in New York for work this week.

I'd managed to stay awake until almost dinnertime and then eaten a microwaved meal from her refrigerator before crashing into bed.

I was up the next morning before first light. It would take a few days to get my body acclimated to London time.

Since exercise had always helped me adjust after a long flight, I suited up for a run. I'd need to stop by an ATM for some UK currency. My only five-pound note joined my phone and ATM card in my pocket for my stop at City Caffeine, which seemed to be the only coffee shop to open early in this town. The unit key went in my tiny shoe wallet.

The street outside Lizzy's building was better lit than my street back home. I looked both ways before starting my run. It took three blocks before I limbered up. Spending what seemed like an entire day in that airline seat had taken its toll. The company didn't splurge on first class for me, and I'd been saving my miles for a vacation trip.

I was fairly winded by the time I rounded the corner to the ATM.

∼

ETHAN

I HADN'T BEEN TO THE NEW SCOTLAND YARD FACILITY OFTEN, AND I FOUND Superintendent Maxwell's office with a modicum of difficulty, yet arrived only five minutes late. I knocked.

He looked up. The man was older than I'd envisioned. I'd heard of some of Thomas Maxwell's exploits, but never met him.

"DI Blakewell," I said as I entered.

He rose and checked his watch before offering his hand across the desk. "Welcome to the section, Blakewell."

We shook. "Thank you, sir."

I noticed my name on the folder in front of him.

He tapped the folder. "Impressive list of accomplishments."

I nodded. "Thank you, sir."

"None of this will help you in this next assignment, however. Covert operations is quite a different beast."

"I understand that."

"Before we start, you need to decide if you're up to it. It can get a bit sticky when people you know socially are involved."

I nodded.

"When you wear a uniform on the street, it goes without saying that a friend is not likely to come up to you and admit being involved in anything nefarious. But over a pint at the pub, while you're hiding the fact that you work for us, he just might let slip something you have to act on."

He rubbed his temple and continued. "When I started out in this, I met up with an old mate from school. Very popular chap, he was. I had to nick him when he bragged about how easy it had been for him to embezzle from his employer." He sighed. "Needless to say, that cost me more than one friendship."

The warning was clear, but I couldn't see how it applied to me, and if someone I knew was breaking the law, that would be their fault, not mine.

"Are you willing to accept the consequences?" he asked. "Because when you go into an assignment like this, there's no turning back."

"I'm looking forward to it, sir... the challenge, I mean."

"Just thought I'd warn you."

I had to ask the burning question. "If you don't mind me asking, why was I selected for this?"

He tapped the folder with my name on it. "You made inspector quite quickly."

"I feel I earned it, sir."

"Your brother is Lord Charles Blakewell, and your parents the Duke and Duchess of Lassiter?" He didn't mention my sister, Kelsey.

I nodded, already feeling the blood drain from my face. If this was going to be about my family and my connections, it never went well within the Met. "That is correct, sir, but I've never played upon my family name. I'm *second* in line. My brother and I are twins, but he was firstborn, which makes him heir to the dukedom. I'm merely the spare."

He smiled. "No need to be defensive, son. It's your family tree that makes you perfect for this assignment."

I blew out a breath of relief. "How so?"

"What did Chief Harcourt tell you about this case?"

"Nothing, sir." Repeating the chief's disdain for the command structure making the case a priority wouldn't do me well. "Missing jewels or some such."

"Try ten million pounds of missing jewelry and not a clue how it's being done."

I couldn't hold back my slight gasp at the size of the heist.

"Some very influential people have been targets, and they are not happy."

I waited for him to echo my chief's complaint that the victims were getting special treatment due to their titles.

My phone rang. I declined the call without looking at the number.

"This, however, is secondary to the mayor's main concern."

If this had reached the level of the mayor, it was major.

"We want our city to maintain its status as the financial hub of Europe and the premier safe destination for wealthy expatriates and visitors," he continued. "A series of high-profile jewel thefts would tarnish that reputation."

Now the problem came into view, and it wasn't a bunch of whiny British socialites, but a fear of what would happen if the rich from around the world didn't feel comfortable here.

"The economic impact of a perception that London has become unsafe would be incalculable."

My phone rang, and again, I declined the call. "And what part can I play in the inquiry?"

He smiled. "We need someone who has the name and family connections to fit in and mingle with the target crowd."

I felt myself deflating. That explained it. I'd been chosen because of my family. He wanted me to be undercover in my parents' world.

My phone started up again.

He sat back in his chair. "Be back in an hour to meet your partner." He waved me away. "Go ahead. Get the blasted phone." He closed the folder on his desk. "Molly will find you a desk."

I moved to the hallway. The number was one I didn't recognize. "Blakewell," I answered.

"Ethan M. Blakewell?" the caller asked.

"Yes."

"I'm calling from St. Lucia's Hospital. There's been an accident and a patient is asking for you. Do you know a Rebecca Sommerset?"

The words hit me like a punch to the gut.

CHAPTER 5

Ethan

Downstairs, I didn't have time to requisition a vehicle. This called for a siren and lights. I caught one of the blue and yellow candy cars pulling away from the curb, put my hand up, and stood in front of him.

The constable jammed on the brakes and opened the door, clearly thinking he was about to arrest me for impeding a police officer. But before he could, I rounded to the passenger door and flashed my credentials. "DI Blakewell. Get me to St. Lucia's Hospital. Now."

A puzzled look came across his face. "But I—"

"Now! With siren and lights, or Superintendent Maxwell will have your head."

It had been a bluff, but Maxwell's name got the young constable moving. We weaved our way rapidly through traffic toward the hospital.

"What's this about?" he finally got the nerve to ask.

I read his name patch. "Victim interview, Ayers."

We arrived without hitting anybody, which seemed a bit of a miracle the way the young man was driving.

"Thank you, Ayers. You may resume your duties," I said before closing the car door and dashing to the entrance.

Flashing my credentials got me swift answers as to where Rebecca was. By comparison, the movement of the lift up to the third floor was incredibly slow.

A constable stood outside her room, scrolling through his mobile.

"DI Blakewell," I said as I looked inside. I gasped. It was empty. "Where is she?" I asked, already dreading the answer.

"Downstairs, sir. Getting an X-ray or something."

"How bad was the accident?"

He put his mobile away. "No accident, sir. It was a mugging. I'm waiting to take her statement."

The hallway was suddenly colder. "Was she hurt badly?"

"I think that's what they're trying to assess." He looked at me quizzically. "If you don't mind me asking, sir, why a DI for a simple mugging?"

"All I know is I got the call."

Because of who Becky was to me, would have been the honest answer, but that brought me right back to Chief Harcourt's complaint. A duchess has some jewelry pinched, and she got special treatment. An American tourist got mugged, and I show up, a detective inspector. It was all in who you knew. The difference was that the duchess meant to work the system, and I didn't believe Becky did.

That she'd asked for me, though, started an itch to know more. It had been five long years, yet the memory of her was fresh.

"Tell me what we know so far," I said.

A few minutes later, I had the simple time-and-place facts the constable knew—the 9-9-9 call, the scene of the attack, and the ambulance pickup—but no more.

~

Rebecca

"It hurts," I told the nurse. "A lot. Can I have some aspirin?"

She squeezed my hand as the gurney rolled down the hallway. "Aspirin isn't allowed with head wounds. You'll have to ask the doctor about Paracetamol. Light often aggravates these things. Try keeping your eyes closed. That will help."

I did as she suggested, and although it wasn't a radical change, it did help.

"What's your name?" I asked the angel who had been taking care of me.

She touched my arm. "Susan."

The noises weren't helping either. To dull the ache in the back of my head, I concentrated on the most soothing thing I could think of: warm, tropical waves lapping against the beach.

I heard the elevator doors close, but decided to keep my eyes shut for the remainder of the journey.

It was several minutes before all the jostling stopped.

"Is she ready for questions?" a man asked.

"Give us a minute," my nurse told him.

I raised my arm a bit as I felt her reattaching the pressure cuff of the automatic blood pressure monitor.

"Thank you, Susan."

"You can thank me by not trying to pull out your IV tubes again."

"Deal."

The motorized pump started up, and the cuff squeezed.

I canted my head to the side and opened one eye to watch the reading. All I knew was too high was bad, and too low was worse. One hundred and ten for a top number didn't seem too high.

As the pressure slowly released, the bottom number appeared: sixty-five.

I closed my eyes again, relieved. I'd watched enough hospital scenes on TV to know that crashing blood pressure led to bad things. *Code blue* they called it on television, at least in the US.

"Okay, but make it short," Susan said.

I opened my eyes to see a policeman on my left, but closed them again when the brightness in the room felt piercing.

"Ms. Sommerset, I'm Constable Smythe. Can you tell me what happened this morning?"

I trembled, pulling the memory out. "I was at the ATM getting some cash. There were two of them all of a sudden. I was getting my card back when he hit me." I pulled my right hand up to touch the side of my head where it hurt.

"Stop that," Susan said as she grabbed my wrist.

I opened my eyes to see her. "Sorry."

When I turned back to the constable, another man was by the door. I couldn't see him clearly. I closed my eyes against the light again.

Susan guided my hand back to my side.

"You were at the cash point, and he hit you," the constable said.

I started again. "As soon as I got back up, the big one shoved me against the wall. I hit my head, and then they ran off."

"How much did they take?"

"I was withdrawing two hundred. I had five in my pocket—I don't know about that."

"She had a fiver in her jacket," Susan told him.

"Two men?" he asked.

"Yeah, one maybe six feet. The other shorter, maybe five-three."

"Hair color, eye color, any identifying marks?"

I shook my head lightly. "It was dark, and they had hoodies. Caucasian, I think. That's all I could tell you."

"Clothing?"

"Dark color is all I can say. The street was dark."

"Would I be correct in guessing you're from the States?"

I nodded. "San Francisco."

"Visiting?"

"Business trip. I got in yesterday." I could hear him writing.

"And where are you staying?"

"My sister's place."

"Address?"

"Ninety-seven Landon Garden, Kensington."

"And do you have a mobile number we can use to reach you if we have more questions?"

"It's a US number." I recited my cell number.

"Very good then, Ms. Sommerset. That will be it for now. Inspector, do you have any questions?"

"Maybe after she rests a bit and the doctor has been by," Susan said.

Another man spoke softly. "Yes, ma'am." The voice was soothing, almost familiar. The blood pressure cuff started its noisy squeeze again.

I went back to visualizing the surf and lost track of time.

∼

"Good morning, Rebecca. My name is Dr. Patel," came a voice from the darkness.

I opened my eyes briefly to see a man with a clipboard.

"Susan tells me you're experiencing some light sensitivity."

I nodded.

"That's not unusual in cases such as these. You've had quite a bump on the head. Do you have any allergies to medication?"

"No."

"Then we can start you on Paracetamol. In the states you call it Tylenol." He took my hand. "Squeeze as tightly as you can."

I did.

"Very good. Now the other hand."

We repeated it on the other side.

"Now I'm going to ask you to open your eyes and count the lines on this piece of paper."

"Three," I told him after opening them long enough to see the clipboard.

He started with the day of the week, and asked a series of mundane questions.

"The good news," he began, "is that the CT scan doesn't show anything to worry about."

I smiled through the pain at the first good news of the day. "Can I go back to work?"

"Not so fast. I understand that you did not lose consciousness after the incident."

I nodded. "Yeah... No, I don't think so."

"I still suspect you may have suffered a concussion. You're traveling alone, Susan tells me."

I nodded. "Uh-huh. My sister is out of town."

"Then we'd like to keep you overnight for observation. It's not advisable for you to be alone during the first twenty-four hours in case things get worse."

"I'll be watching over her," another man's voice said.

I opened my eyes to see the outline of a man in a suit walking into the room. My view of his face was blocked by the doctor.

"And you are?" Dr. Patel asked.

"Ethan Blakewell," he said.

The voice registered with me just as he moved past the doctor. "Ethan?"

"Yes, Becky, it's me."

Ethan

I'd told the superintendent as I left that I'd been called to St. Lucia's because of a close friend's accident.

He hadn't said anything other than to call him with a progress report, so, while the doctor took Becky through the concussion protocol, I'd called him to say I wouldn't be back in today.

When the doctor said Becky couldn't be left alone, there was only one thing to do—I stepped up to watch over her.

"What are you doing here?" she asked.

"I asked if you knew anyone in town, and he's the name you gave me," the nurse said.

"Oh," Becky said. "I guess I forgot."

I took her hand and held it. "I'm here for you."

She closed her eyes and nodded.

"You need a day of rest," the doctor told her before turning to me. "Are you willing to take responsibility for her?"

"Absolutely," I answered.

The doctor and nurse excused themselves, and I was alone with the girl I'd avoided just yesterday.

I squeezed her hand lightly, and she smiled. "You shouldn't have been out alone at that time of the morning."

"You didn't have to come."

"As you Yanks would say, wild horses couldn't have kept me away."

"That's nice of you. But really, I'll be okay."

I let go of her hand. "Are you trying to get rid of me?"

Her eyes stayed closed as she shook her head slowly. "You must have things to do."

The nurse returned with a small paper cup with tablets and a glass of water. "Here's your Paracetamol."

Becky opened her eyes to take the tablets, and after she did, she even smiled when her gaze turned to me. Too soon, she closed her eyes and lay back again.

"We'll send you home with enough for two days," the nurse said. "If you need any beyond that, don't go to the chemist for more. The doctor wants to see you back instead."

"Got it. Two days," Becky said.

"And, no alcohol while you're taking this medication," the nurse added, looking at me.

"I'll see that she behaves," I told her. I patted Becky's leg.

She grimaced, and I couldn't tell if it was from pain or my statement.

CHAPTER 6

Rebecca

Leaving the hospital, I put a hand up to shield my eyes from the sunshine.

"Here." Ethan held out a pair of sunglasses.

They helped. "Thanks. Why did you come?"

He pulled me by the elbow toward a taxi. "Because you needed me."

I climbed in as he held open the door for me. "Ninety-seven Landon Garden, Kensington," I told the driver.

The driver punched a button on the meter, and three pounds lit up in red numbers.

Ethan climbed in and closed the door. "Thirty-eight Trevor Mews."

"No. Landon Garden," I insisted.

"You're coming with me to my place."

"You can't tell me that."

Ethan smirked. "Yes, I can. I'm responsible for you, and you told the doctor your sister was away."

I ignored him. "Driver, please take me to ninety-seven Landon Garden."

"No," Ethan said.

The driver shook his head. "When you two figure it out, let me know. Until then, the standing rate is thirty quid an hour."

The meter had already started ticking higher.

Ethan glared. "I'm responsible for you, so you're coming with me or going right back inside the hospital."

I gritted my teeth.

"Besides you only have five pounds on you, and that won't be enough."

The driver tilted his head my way. "The gent's right. A fiver won't get you to Landon Garden. So, are you going with him, or getting out?"

"Okay already… You win."

The driver pulled into traffic.

I hadn't remembered Ethan being this pigheaded before. "You weren't this mean in college."

"Because you weren't this stubborn. Perhaps you don't understand the system in the UK. I took responsibility for your safety leaving the hospital, and I don't fancy the authorities blaming me for negligence when your health falters."

"My health falters? Don't be ridiculous. I'm perfectly able to take care of myself."

The driver merely glanced in the mirror with the hint of a smirk.

I kept my eyes out the window and ignored Ethan.

We wended our way through the streets without any further words for several blocks.

"What?" I asked when I glanced back in Ethan's direction and caught him looking at me.

"Oh, nothing," he said before looking away.

It was another block before I gave in to my curiosity. "Spit it out. What were you looking at me like that for?"

He smiled. "I was going to say you look as lovely as ever, Becks."

"Thank you." I couldn't prevent the heat that grew in my cheeks with his use of my nickname from years ago. "You look fine too, but don't let that go to your head."

"Never." He probably even meant that.

Two blocks later, the cab pulled to the curb.

I waited while Ethan settled up with the cabbie. He'd been right that my five pounds wouldn't have gotten me back to Lizzy's place.

Ethan opened the door and extended a hand to help me out.

Depending on a man wasn't my style, so I didn't take it. But the glare of the sun hit me as I stepped out. I misjudged the curb and tumbled forward.

Before I hit the ground, strong hands grabbed my waist and jerked me upright. The force of it pulled a grunt from me. The sunglasses fell and made the trip to the sidewalk with a clatter.

I turned, squinted against the brightness, and ended up flat against Ethan's chest to steady myself.

"That's what I was afraid of," he said as he continued to hold me.

The feel of him against me told me loud and clear that my subconscious feelings didn't match my snarky words. "You can let me go now."

"Are you sure?"

I nodded. Staying in his arms for even a few more seconds would be dangerous.

"If you two lovebirds are done, close the door," the cabbie shouted.

Ethan released me.

My traitorous body instantly missed the contact. I'd have to read up on self-hypnosis or some other way to teach my subconscious how I felt about the man now.

Ethan closed the cab's door before picking up the sunglasses.

I took them with more grace than I'd been showing him so far. "Thank you."

"This way." He led me to the door, opened it with a key, and stood aside for me to enter first.

My running shoes squeaked as I crossed the marble floor to the elevator. Once inside it, he reached past me to push the top-floor button, naturally.

"Penthouse?" I asked.

"There are only five floors in this building. I prefer to think of it as the terrace level."

Upstairs, the door he opened revealed an apartment stunning in its size.

His phone rang just after he let me in. "Blakewell," he answered. "No, sir, not today… Sorry, sir, it can't be helped." Ethan continued on the phone, urging me farther inside. "She's out of the hospital, but I have to watch over her today… Possible concussion. Yes, sir, I took responsibility for her today."

We reached the kitchen, and I leaned against the island for support.

"Yes, tomorrow," he said before clicking off the phone.

I really needed to get back to work. "Can we just get whatever you need so we can go over to my sister's place? I need to get changed and go in to work."

He looked at me like I'd grown a second head. "What part of *'day of rest'* didn't you understand?"

I took a breath. Arguing with Ethan had always been a difficult thing. "I have a really big case I need to get started on. It's…it's something I was assigned by the managing director himself yesterday, and it can't wait." It was the key to my promotion.

He went around me to the refrigerator. "Water or juice?"

"If I drink your stupid juice, can we go after that?"

"Do you prefer orange or apple? I don't remember." The crinkle reappeared. *His tell for a lie.* I bet he remembered I liked apple.

"Whichever."

He pulled out apple juice, collected two glasses, and poured some for each of us.

"So you did remember."

"Lucky guess."

I tried batting my eyes at him when he looked my way. "I really can't be out today; the managing director will kill me."

"What's his name?"

"Who?"

"Your boss. The guy who's going to kill you?"

"He's my boss's boss."

He drank another slug of the juice with raised eyebrows and a hand gesture for me to continue.

"Cornwall. Joseph Cornwall. He's in charge of the whole London office." I sipped my juice when that seemed to satisfy him.

He picked up his cell phone. "What company?" he asked before sipping more from his cup.

I'd guessed wrong about him being satisfied. "Lessex Insurance."

His laugh forced him to spit up some of the juice, followed by a cough. Most of it went back into the glass, and only a little hit the counter. "You're kidding? Who works for a company that advocates *less sex*?"

I'd become immune to people making fun of the company name. "It's one word, Einstein, like your county Essex with an L in front. And, while we're talking ridiculous names, what country names a dessert *spotted dick*? It sounds like the late stage of an unpleasant disease."

He chuckled, typed on his phone, and then scrolled. "Personally, I agree with you, but you wouldn't catch me walking into a building that says *Less Sex Insurance*. Somebody wasn't thinking." He scrolled his phone some more. "Who wants to ensure less sex?"

"And what does it say on the building you work in?"

"TechniByte IT Consulting Limited." He punched something on the phone screen and put it to his ear.

The company name made sense, since he'd been a computer genius in school, compared to me.

"Managing Director Cornwall, please," he said into the phone.

"What are you doing?" I demanded, grabbing for it.

He pulled it out of reach. The man could be annoying that way.

He turned away from me. "No, miss, calling back will not do. This is Detective Inspector Blakewell with the Metropolitan Police Service. Please put Mr. Cornwall on the line. Now, or I shall be forced to send a car to collect him."

I shook my head—a mistake, given my headache.

"Mr. Cornwall, DI Blakewell Metropolitan Police here. This will only take a moment. I have one of your employees here with me, a Miss Rebecca Sommerset…"

I couldn't see his face as he lied like nobody's business.

"No, she's not in any trouble. Quite the opposite. She was the victim of a mugging early this morning… Yes, sir, she's recovering. She was seen at St. Lucia's and has been discharged. I have her with me for some questions…"

I tapped his shoulder, and when he turned around, I motioned for him to give me the phone, to no avail. I stomped my foot.

"She insists that you need her back into work, and that, sir, is the problem… Yes, sir, it's possible that the same mugger may have attacked an MP this morning, and I'd like to have her assistance for the remainder of the day and a portion of tomorrow."

I walked around the island, frustrated by the lies Ethan wove—lies that would come back to bite me when the managing director found out.

"She seems a very devoted employee, sir. Would you please instruct her to stay here and assist me?" He offered me the phone.

I stepped back like it was a red-hot coal.

Ethan moved forward with a Cheshire Cat grin, held up the phone, and set it on speaker. "Mr. Cornwall, you're on speaker with Miss Sommerset."

Cornwall's voice boomed. "Sommerset, stay there with the inspector and provide whatever assistance he asks."

"I will, sir," I told him.

Ethan's grin expanded, and he turned away again with the phone. "The MPS thanks you, Mr. Cornwall. I expect to release her back to you tomorrow afternoon at the latest, and one more thing, Mr. Cornwall."

"Yes?"

"This is a matter of the utmost sensitivity. You are not to discuss this with anyone. I repeat, not anyone at all outside of myself."

"Understood, Inspector."

I shook my head at his audacity.

"Very well then," Ethan said. He hung up with a quick goodbye and turned back to me with a smile.

I held my yell at bay until the call ended. "You can't just lie like that to my managing director. You're going to—"

He tapped on his phone. "Calm down." He kept tapping.

The stress was making my headache worse. "I need some of those pills."

He set the phone down. "It's not time yet."

I paced to the other side of the island. "I can't believe you just did that."

He located a towel and started to wipe the countertop. "I fixed your problem. A simple thank you will suffice."

"You're going to get me in so much trouble." My phone beeped on the counter, and I picked it up. "What did you do?"

"I sent a text to your mobile, so you have my number and can yell at me later, when you're feeling better and can use full volume."

"Oh." I turned off the phone.

He pointed toward the room with the windows and couches. "Now, go sit down and calm yourself, Becks. You no longer need to go in to work today."

"Don't call me that." Becks had been his special nickname for me back at Imperial College.

"Why not?" That evil smirk reappeared. "You used to like it."

I had liked it, a lot—actually more than a lot. It had been a name that meant I was special—special to him. That had been a wonderful period in my life, but that time had passed. "That was then, and this is now. We're not friends anymore. You're just my kidnapper."

He pointed to the other room again. "Go. Doctor's orders. Relax today, remember?"

I sighed and gave in. The other room was open, airy, and light with today's uncommon lack of clouds. After toeing off my shoes, I took a seat on the sofa and curled my legs under me. The room was bright enough I had to shield my eyes.

The sound of champagne being popped came from the kitchen area behind me.

Ethan appeared with the sunglasses and a flute in one hand. He sipped from the flute in his other hand.

I took the sunglasses, but not the flute. "No alcohol, remember?"

He sat next to me and held the glass out again. "Sparkling cider, no alcohol."

I nodded and couldn't hide my smile. "You did remember."

He tapped his temple. "Becks, you are a very memorable lady." He certainly was turning on the charm.

I took the glass and looked away. Those light blues had always been able to look right through me and capture me for days. "Stop calling me Becks, and nobody ever calls me a lady."

That was certainly the case at work. I'd been called a lot of things in my quest to get ahead and be the best I could be, but *lady* was never on the list. Evidence in point, the HR reprimand letter in my purse.

The bubbles from the sip I took tickled my nose. "But thank you." When I glanced back, Ethan's smile had grown. I stared out the window to break his hold on me.

"Glad I could do one thing right." He stood and left the room.

Taking in the space, I was struck by how different this was from the small place he'd occupied with a roommate when I'd seen him last at Imperial College. IT consulting had to pay well.

He returned with a laptop, which he opened as he sat.

I put my glass down on the side table. "Hey. If you can work, why can't I? Let's go get my laptop."

Ethan looked over. "Becks, you really need to learn to relax."

I saw the opening. "If you take me to get my laptop, I'll stop talking and let you get your work done."

He ignored me and tapped on the keyboard.

"Why is the sun out today? It's usually cloudy in this town."

No response.

"Seattle is pretty much the rainiest city in the US."

That got a grunt in response.

"Did you know London has almost as many rainy days as Seattle?"

A slight shake of his head was all that comment warranted.

I finished my sparkling cider and contemplated a different tack, since being mildly annoying wasn't working.

After putting down the glass, I went for the jugular. "Why didn't you call?"

The narrowing of his eyes as he turned to me said my question had come out meaner than I'd intended.

CHAPTER 7

Ethan

She wasn't playing fair. She'd asked the question I couldn't answer—I wouldn't answer. It had to stop.

I slammed my computer closed and stood. "Get up."

She looked at me with a mixture of surprise and regret.

"We're going to your sister's flat."

"Sorry," she said softly.

Sorry didn't cut it after what I'd been through. "You can sit there and take a quiet nap, and I do mean *quiet*, or come with me. Which will it be?"

She sprang up, teetering a bit.

I grabbed her arm to steady her.

After a deep breath, she looked up. "I got a little lightheaded for a sec." She looked down at my hand still holding her arm. "I'm okay now."

I pulled my hand back. "Day of rest, remember? Don't you dare fall down and make it my fault."

She huffed. "Consider yourself relieved of responsibility for me. I've been looking out for myself since I was eighteen, and I don't need you, or any man, to take care of me."

I nodded. "I understand, but that's not how it works in the UK."

She gave me an exaggerated eye roll as she put her hands on her hips. "And what's different here?"

"Here a gentleman honors his responsibilities. I committed to looking after you, and I intend to follow through—with or without your cooperation." I turned and started toward the door. "You coming?"

She followed. "This isn't over, Ethan Blakewell."

I strode for the door. "It is if you want to get to your sister's flat."

I didn't know if she was referring to our current argument about her health or what had happened between us before she left, but I wasn't about to ask. I wasn't discussing either.

The sound of her footwear squeaking on the floor behind me told me she'd given up the fight.

I pulled open the door and let her pass.

"Thank you, kind sir," she said with syrupy sweet sarcasm.

After pressing the button for the lift, I tried to defuse things. "Did I tell you how lovely you look?"

The door to the lift opened, and we started down before she glanced over and answered, "Yes, once."

"Let this be number two then," I said with a smile.

She smiled back—the same smile that had broken me years ago—and our truce was in place.

Downstairs, I handed her the sunglasses again before we exited to the road.

She gave the cabbie the address of her sister's flat.

As the taxi started through the midday traffic, every glance I stole in her direction had my mind venturing back five years. Could I have done anything then to have prevented what we went through?

I'd asked myself this question numerous times. The choice had been forced on me, and I'd made the only decision I could. I'd sacrificed our future for the sake of my family. The Blakewell name had to carry on.

"Hey, Mr. Glum, what's bothering you?" she asked.

Careful to look away, I said, "Nothing." I turned back with a smile and took a chance. "I'd like to know what you've been up to the last five years."

She looked out the window. "I thought you weren't into talking."

"I guess I deserve that… I was suggesting listening."

It was another two blocks before she reached over to touch my leg. "Buy me dinner, and I can do most of the talking."

"Fair compromise, I reckon."

"You reckon? Really?"

"Isn't that an American colloquialism? Did I say it wrong?"

"Your American needs a little work. I'm from California, not Texas."

The taxi pulled to the side in front of an apartment building, and I arranged with the driver to stay for fifteen minutes.

She let us into the second-floor flat, and I followed her to a small bedroom in the back.

"This is my room," Becky said. "I'm over here pretty often, so it's easier to leave things than carry a lot back and forth."

"Sensible." I didn't point out that it indicated she'd been in town numerous times without attempting to contact me.

The room was very utilitarian: a bed, chest of drawers, wardrobe, and desk. No paintings or posters—not even family photographs.

"That's me, a sensible girl," she said as she sat down at the desk and opened the laptop. "Thank you for getting me safely home. Now you can run along and let me get some work done."

I didn't budge. "Pack up your things. You're coming back to my flat."

"I like it better here. I promise to rest up."

"Would you like me to call your managing director again and say you're not cooperating?"

"Sure. Like you're really going to complain to him that I won't go back to your apartment with you."

"I can be more diplomatic than that. I'll just explain that I am very disappointed in your lack of cooperation."

She stood and picked up the laptop. "Okay, already. You know lying your way through life like that is going to get you in trouble. In my country, impersonating a police officer is a crime."

"Good to know."

"Have you become a habitual liar?"

"Right now, I can be entirely truthful when saying I'm disappointed in your lack of cooperation."

"Right. And you're with Scotland Yard. One truth and one lie still adds up to a lie."

I checked my watch as she gathered her laptop, phone, handbag, and chargers.

"And some clothes," I added, earning another eye roll.

∼

After an afternoon of computer work with ever-increasing yawns, Becky got up from the table "That was a long one."

"What?"

She stretched her arms over her head, which accentuated her bust. I averted my eyes.

"An assignment I had to complete." She walked her empty juice glass to the kitchen and returned. "I'm going to take a quick nap before dinner."

"Good plan. You must be tired."

She nodded and wandered to the guest bedroom I'd shown her earlier. "Bushed."

The door closed behind her.

Four hours later, she hadn't emerged. Evidently *tired* had been an understatement.

I turned down the thermostat for the evening and retired without waking her.

CHAPTER 8

Rebecca

I woke early the next morning. I hadn't been able to stay awake late enough to have Ethan take me to dinner. That was my fault. If I'd taken a nap midday instead of trying to stay up and work on my computer, I'm sure I would've been awake at dinnertime. But the Fernandez case had taken all afternoon.

As I slipped out of bed and padded into the attached bathroom, I finally noticed the opulence of Ethan's place—marble countertops, a glass-encased walk-in shower, a separate bathtub, and two toilets.

I examined the appliances again. Holy shit, the second one was a bidet. I had no idea how to use it and wasn't about to learn. How did you dry yourself after anyway? And if all this was for a guest bathroom, what did the master bath have? A hot tub, a swimming pool?

An IT consultant sure did live a privileged life. A guest room with an attached bath was the kind of place a lot of people only got to see on television. Yet here I was, partaking as his guest. Or, perhaps I was his prisoner in this gilded cage.

I stepped into the luxury of the multi-showerheaded, glass enclosure. After some experimentation with several of the handles, I got it set. Turning in the bliss of the warm spray, I decided even a gilded cage was perfectly fine this morning. A few minutes of decadent procrastination wouldn't hurt anything, and it felt so good.

Ethan had promised Cornwall I'd be free to go to work this afternoon, so this confinement would soon be over. A successful end to the high-profile jewelry theft case would clearly overshadow that stupid HR letter and make my move to the corner office at Lessex a breeze. I couldn't wait to get started.

As I ran the shampoo through my hair, the bump on the side of my head felt even bigger than yesterday, but it couldn't be, right? Maybe the swelling around it had gone down. Rinsing off, I pictured my name on the door of my new office on the top floor of our building. The woman who'd saved the company millions of pounds would certainly deserve it, wouldn't she?

When I stuffed yesterday's clothes into the bottom of the suitcase I'd brought, I stopped at the sports bra. I'd worn a sports bra all day yesterday, something I never did. Ethan had already been a bad influence on me.

Normally, if I exercised, I was religious about showering and changing back into work clothes, to get back to what mattered. *Lazy* wasn't ever an adjective I wanted attached to me. I was determined to get ahead in my career, and so far, things had fallen into place.

I found Ethan in the kitchen when I emerged. He looked up from the paper. "How do you feel this morning?"

"Finally human," I told him. "Sorry about dinner last night. The jet lag."

"No worries, Becks. I understand how difficult jet lag can be."

He'd just given me a tidbit about himself without realizing it.

"Go to the US often?"

"On occasion."

That wasn't very specific, but at least he'd answered a question—and he hadn't lied.

He stood. "Our breakfasts are staying warm in the oven." He started bread in the toaster. "And fresh toast is only a minute away. Sit."

"What can I do to help?"

He motioned to the stove. "Teapot on the cooker, juice in the fridge."

I poured tea and OJ for him, and apple juice for myself.

He brought the overflowing plates from the oven.

I'd forgotten how much there was to a full English breakfast. At least he'd remembered my aversion to blood sausage.

The toast came after I took a seat.

"So, missy," he said in his version of a Texas drawl. "What was so all-fired important about your work yesterday?"

"Back to trying Americanisms again?"

"Did I get it wrong?"

"No, that was good." I sipped my juice and started cutting my fried egg. "It was an interview video I had to analyze."

He lifted a forkful of baked beans. "Go on."

"I'm an investigator at Lessex. My specialty is determining truthfulness or deceit."

He swallowed. "You always were a bit of a human lie detector."

Between bites, I nodded. "It's what makes me good at my job. Take yesterday as an example. It was an interview of a fellow whose dry cleaning business had burned to the ground."

"And you suspect something is amiss?"

"I flagged four questions in the interview where I think he gave misleading answers."

He sat back. "You think?"

"More than that. It's not an exact science, but I'm pretty certain."

"And what does that do for Less Sex Insurance?"

I ignored the jab. "I give that kind of information to the detectives on the ground. They dig up evidence relating to the specific lies after I narrow it down. We'll confront him with it, threaten to make it all public, and usually we end up settling the claim for pennies on the dollar."

"But isn't setting fire to your own establishment a crime?"

I chewed my latest mouthful before answering. "Yes, but insurance is a business. We don't get into the punishment aspect of it. There's no payoff there. Plus, if word got around that we aggressively prosecuted our own clients, pretty soon we wouldn't have any. Clients, that is. We don't have to gather all the evidence that he's guilty, just enough to infer it, and his fear does the rest for us."

"That sounds wrong to me. You should turn him in to the police."

"Not my decision to make."

"It's still morally wrong."

"The people I work for are worried about the bottom line. I'm very good at what I do. They pay me, and those sorts of decisions are someone else's to make."

He shook his head. "The people I work for think criminals should pay the price."

I picked at my meal amid the sudden awkwardness between us.

He'd pointed out a moral flaw in my job, and I couldn't refute the logic, but like I'd told him, I didn't make the rules. I merely worked within them.

Eventually I pushed away the plate. "This was a bit much for me."

"I thought you Yanks said breakfast was the most important meal of the day?"

I stood and carried my plate and juice glass to the sink. "Some people say that."

He followed with his dishes and reached around me to put his plate in the sink. "What do you say?"

I could feel the heat of his body as he brushed my arm. The simple contact short-circuited my brain for a second. "What?"

"I said, what is your opinion on the subject?"

"I don't know." I realized I didn't have an opinion on it. I'd been treating meals as something to get past to get back to my work. "I don't spend much time on breakfast."

He put a hand on my shoulder. "Becks, what was the best breakfast you had last week?"

I couldn't think straight when every time he touched me, it brought me back to our time together. I moved away and took the OJ pitcher to the fridge. "I don't know." I couldn't remember having anything beyond oatmeal and yogurt.

"Maybe you should slow down a little and enjoy more."

"More breakfasts?"

"More of life."

"Sure." I shrugged. It was time to change the subject. "What's on the agenda for the rest of my confinement?"

"That's what you think of our time together?" He turned away and walked toward the other room.

"It was a joke. You told Cornwall I couldn't go back until the afternoon."

He spun around. "I promised him to have you back no later than the afternoon. There's a difference." He pointed toward the door. "Go to work. You have criminals to let off the hook."

"I didn't mean it like that." I'd dug a monstrously deep hole for myself. "It has been good to see you again, Ethan."

He backed up. "I promised the doctor I'd watch over you for the twenty-four hours after your injury, and I have. Go make money for your company." He threw a bill on the table. "For your taxi," he said and walked around the corner.

It was a fifty-pound note.

"Thank you," I called after him. I went back to the guest room, made the bed I'd slept in, zipped up my suitcase, and gathered my computer and my purse. With my full load, I returned to the front door. "Thank you for everything, Ethan," I called.

"Certainly, Becks."

His use of the nickname gave me hope that we could talk again after he'd calmed down. "You still owe me a dinner."

He rounded the corner and surprised me by taking hold of my shoulders. "Do I?"

With my hands full, I couldn't give him the embrace I wanted to. "I reckon you do."

"I may disagree with what you do at Less Sex, but it hasn't changed my affection for you." With those words, he gave me a peck on the lips, released me, and opened the door. "After you."

I exited in a daze. Just a simple kiss, and I was weak-kneed. He followed me and called the elevator.

I didn't know how to recover. "You don't need to—"

"A gentleman," he interrupted, "sees a lady to her taxi."

Once I'd pulled away in the taxi, I replayed the scene in my head a dozen times.

He'd kissed me, and I'd stood there like an imbecile—like a frigid imbecile is more like it—and not given him back any of the affection he'd admitted he held for me.

I stomped my foot against the floor of the cab in frustration.

"You okay back there?" the driver asked.

"Yeah. My foot was going to sleep."

The driver shrugged.

Ethan had said he had affection for me.

How did that translate from Brit-speak to American?

It didn't matter. I was free of him now. Work and my promotion beckoned. He would only be a distraction I couldn't afford.

He'd been a mistake five years ago, and he would be an even worse one now. I wasn't a silly college girl anymore. Now I was smart enough to put my career first.

I wouldn't make my mother's mistake.

Rummaging in my purse, I pulled out the plastic bag and sniffed the smell success would bring—my brand-new company car.

Ethan

I found Molly at the New Scotland Yard building, and true to Maxwell's word, she had located a desk for me. With nothing better to do, I logged in on the computer and continued where I'd left off with my last case at the TechniByte building.

Maxwell arrived with tea in hand. "How is your friend this morning?"

"Well enough to go in to work."

"Good. Because I need you here today. This case is top of the stack, and I already had to reschedule our meeting with your new partner to get things started. Another delay wouldn't be good."

His meaning was clear. Personal time off had not been the right way to start with him.

"It won't happen again, sir."

He eyed me warily. "Good to know. Ten o'clock, conference room C." A second later he was gone.

Good going, Blakewell. Get bumped up to a high-profile case the mayor is watching, reporting directly to the superintendent, and go missing the first day. Whatever goodwill I'd started with, I'd more than used up, and the case hadn't even begun yet.

CHAPTER 9

REBECCA

When I exited the elevator at work, Ginny took all of two seconds to ask the question. "How are you? Mr. Smithers said you got mugged."

I rolled the suitcase behind me to my office. "Yesterday was sort of rough, but I'm okay today. Thank you."

Margaret, the employee who couldn't be trusted to remember the rules about my ex-husband, appeared. "That must've been terrible. Did they catch him?"

"Not that I know of."

"Smithers said you were at Scotland Yard helping them. What's it like?"

Ethan's lie was going to get out of hand very quickly if I didn't control this. I put a finger to my lips. "I'm not allowed to say."

Both girls' eyes went wide. They probably envisioned a James Bond scenario instead of being cooped up in Ethan's apartment all day.

"Why not?" Margaret asked.

I pasted on my stern expression. "This isn't something we can talk about. Mr. Cornwall himself was sworn to secrecy. Perhaps you'd like to ask him."

Margaret seemed to decide that answer was good enough and scurried off.

"Keep an eye on her. This can't be discussed," I whispered to Ginny as soon as Margaret was far enough away.

"I will. And Mr. Smithers wants to see you."

"Figures." He could wait a few minutes.

I powered up my computer and navigated to my email. Letting it pile up was never a good idea.

The fifth message down was another from my dipshit ex. *What do you think?* the header read.

After a deep breath, I highlighted it and hit the delete key before the text even got a chance to display on the screen. The message could go to hell, along with every other thing related to Wesley Stroud. I'd vowed to not waste another second of my life on him, and it was a promise I intended to keep.

The remaining messages only took a few minutes to read.

Smithers was at his desk when I went upstairs. "How are you feeling, Sommerset?"

"Better." I touched the back of my skull. "Good thing I have a hard head."

He nodded at my joke. "Perhaps you shouldn't be out alone at the cashpoint in the dark."

It took me a second to recognize the Brit-speak for ATM. "So I've been told."

"We're due at New Scotland Yard at ten to discuss the Lindsley case."

"The necklace?"

"Yes, and our brooch as well, if they're tied together."

"Did they send over the police reports?"

Smithers leaned forward on his desk. "This will need to be handled differently than we would normally operate."

In my experience, different hadn't resulted in better. "How different?"

"To start with, there aren't any police reports."

Normally that would preclude us paying out, but apparently not now. "Why not?"

Smithers shook his head. "That's their call."

Evidently when a duchess was involved, the rules changed, and written police reports didn't matter. Cornwall's agreement yesterday to give her three-million pounds to start with had made that clear.

"So the investigation is only starting now?"

"Publicity of the thefts, or even an inquiry, is to be avoided at all costs. That's the directive."

The answer was oblique, and went against everything we knew about safeguarding valuables. If the way a thief chose his targets, or his mode of entry were publicized, many of the potential victims would alter their habits and at least slow down the thefts.

"Got it. No leaks."

"I hope not. This matter got all the way up to the chairman yesterday, and Cornwall is running scared. He needs this solved before it becomes a bigger problem. Do you understand?"

"I understand." Cornwall would sacrifice me in an instant to save himself if this went sideways. On the flip side, it would gain me an important ally for my promotion if I helped solve it.

I'd always risen to the task in the past. I just had to concentrate and power through this problem to a successful conclusion. Everything had a solution. All I had to do was identify the liars to get a start on it.

Smithers tapped his finger on the paper in front of him. "One other thing. A good outcome on this means getting the necklace back, intact."

I gulped. "That's not likely, sir. Only an idiot would try to sell a recognizable piece like this intact."

He nodded. "I was going to add that getting the gems back, so the necklace could be reset without anyone being the wiser, would also be an acceptable outcome, but anything less would be undesirable."

That bar was maybe a rung too high even for me. "Maybe you should put Paul on this, then. He might be more capable on this task."

"Rubbish. You're the best we have. Cornwall and I both have faith in you, and you have whatever resources you may need at your disposal."

That eliminated any out on this. Even if I believed I was the best in the company, I recognized that Zander Paul was his favorite. The fact that he insisted on putting me on it meant he, too, thought the outcome might not be rosy.

Smithers wouldn't sacrifice Paul on this, but he would be more than happy to sacrifice me.

"We will be meeting the team the superintendent on the case has put together."

The mention of a superintendent of police was a good sign; this wasn't being handed off to some rookie detective.

"I agree," Smithers continued, "with the approach he wants to take, and you'll be an integral part of his team. But to be clear, the Met is taking the lead on this, not us."

With the duchess applying pressure on Scotland Yard, I doubted they would give Smithers, or me, even the slightest say in the investigation. I'd learned early on in dealing with law enforcement agencies that it wasn't in their DNA to pay much attention to outside players such as us.

I put the happy spin on it. "I'm sure we'll all get along fine, sir."

"I'm counting on it. One more thing."

"Yes?"

He tapped his desk. "I don't expect this assignment with the Met to take up all of your time. When they don't need you, I expect you back here to help us. With Ronald and Albert out, it's just you and Zander for a while."

I nodded. "Of course." Cornwall had seemed to imply that this cooperation the Scotland Yard took priority, but I wasn't about to debate it with Smithers at this point.

"Meet me downstairs at nine thirty for the ride to the Yard." With that he was done with the discussion.

~

OUTSIDE A LITTLE WHILE LATER, I SQUINTED AGAINST THE BRIGHTNESS OF THE SUN AND solved the problem with the aviator-style sunglasses Ethan had insisted I keep for the time being. They weren't my style, but they cut the glare.

The ride to New Scotland Yard started out a quiet one. Smithers had made a point of saying we wouldn't discuss business in the presence of the cabbie.

"How's the head feeling?" he finally asked.

I tapped the sunglasses. "I'm a little light-sensitive, but otherwise fine, thank you."

He nodded.

My phone sounded its "Too Much Heaven" ringtone with my mother's name on the screen. I silenced it, but the song started again as soon as I got it back in my purse. "Excuse me," I told Smithers. "My mother. She'll just keep calling until I answer."

He smiled and shrugged. "It happens to all of us."

I accepted the call.

My mother started as soon as I got the hello out. "What's this about you missing dinner again? We planned on the opera as well." No surprise there; she always did. "And I invited that nice young man, Bobby Jenson, along as well. You remember him—Harvard MBA."

I remembered Bobby all right: stiff as a board and almost as talkative.

Lately, you'd think matchmaking was her passion instead of opera. Every visit was the same. She would start with, *"I took the liberty of inviting that nice young man…"* Some of them were nice, but I had a career to advance, which is where she and I didn't see eye to eye.

"Maybe next time," I told her to avoid the argument that would follow any lesser commitment on my part.

"I'm holding you to that, young lady. He won't stay on the market forever."

"Mom, I said I had to be here in London on a big case." I'd left her a voicemail when I'd gotten the call to come here.

"Should I tell him next week instead?"

"I don't know exactly when I'll be back."

"You shouldn't be putting your job ahead of your family, Rebecca. It's not healthy." Her use of my full name meant I was in the doghouse. Again. "When will you be back?"

She always couched her matchmaking as me visiting family. I was fine with doing that, but not so much with the blind dates she kept setting up for me.

"I don't know how long it will take. It's important, and—"

"That's not right, them taking you away for so long."

"The cases take as long as they take, Mom."

Smithers held his hand out for the phone. "May I help?"

I wasn't making progress with her, so I handed it over and put my fate in his hands.

"Mrs. Sommerset," he began. "My name is Smithers. I'm your daughter's supervisor in the London office of Lessex. She is working an extremely important case for us. It's a class double-A supersecret with national implications."

I slapped my hand over my mouth to keep from laughing. We didn't have any such designations.

"I'm not at liberty to say any more," he continued. "You have my assurance that we will send her back to the States at the earliest possible time… Yes. Very nice chatting with you too, Mrs. Sommerset." He handed the phone back to me.

"Mom?" I asked.

"He seems nice," Mom said.

"Yes, he's a very nice man," I replied.

That pulled a smirk and a nod out of Smithers.

"Is he single?"

I looked away. "No, Mother."

"Pity."

Luckily it was loud enough in the cab that Smithers didn't seem to have heard her impertinent question.

"I'll call tonight when I know more about my schedule," I told her.

"I'll have to come to you if you refuse to come home."

With that, I said goodbye.

"Thank you," I told Smithers.

He nodded. "We all have a bit of that in our lives."

∽

While waiting at Scotland Yard, I decided on a little fence mending and sent my mother a text.

ME: I'll be back for a dinner as soon as possible. Kisses and hugs.

We received visitor's badges, and a woman named Molly arrived to escort us upstairs.

I checked the time on my phone. Ten o'clock precisely.

We were shown into a small conference room on the third floor.

Shortly after we took our seats, Molly returned with a partly balding man in tow.

His voice was low and gravelly. "Superintendent Maxwell," he said as he extended his card to Smithers and they shook.

The three of us exchanged cards, names, and shakes all around before sitting.

"Would you like water, or tea, perhaps?" Maxwell asked.

I followed Smithers' lead and demurred.

"That'll be all then, Molly," Maxwell said. "Just get the inspector off that computer of his and in here."

I wasn't seeing a team here yet from their side.

"Have you explained the operation to her?" Maxwell asked my boss.

Smithers shook his head and sat back. "No. It's your show. I thought I'd let you lay it out."

"Very well, then." Maxwell nodded. "As the mayor sees it, this could turn into a major issue for the city. We can't have those who can afford to wear expensive jewelry feel unsure of their safety, or the safety of their belongings, in our city."

This made perfect sense. If the rich decided to abandon London for Paris, Rome, or Barcelona, it could be an economic catastrophe for London. My episode yesterday had proven London wasn't as safe as I'd thought, and I wasn't even in the category the mayor was concerned about.

Maxwell pointed at both of us. "Everything about this needs to remain hush-hush. We don't want any talk getting loose, even after we catch this bugger."

I nodded.

"You can count on our discretion," Smithers told him.

"Good. I'll hold you to that." His eyes narrowed as he took a breath. "As a result, this will be an undercover operation. No police interviews, no police searches, no reports, nothing. When we're done here, there will be no trace that this even happened. That means…" He pointed at Smithers. "No records of this whatsoever on your side either."

Smithers nodded. "Understood."

"So, the plan is simple." He pointed at me. "Sommerset, you and my team will start attending the functions where we believe the thefts are taking place."

It was a surprise to hear they had a theory as to where the thief was operating.

"And figure out who this bugger is."

I brought a hand to my mouth to keep from laughing, and turned it into a cough. *Go to functions, watch, and figure it out* wasn't a real plan.

Maxwell picked up the phone and dialed. "Molly, I don't care what he's doing, just drag the inspector in here."

"How many of us will there be undercover?" I asked.

Maxwell held up two fingers.

My jaw dropped. "That's a little light."

"Less chance of detection that way," Maxwell replied. "Just you and the inspector on the inside, and the inspector can call on support as required."

The door opened behind me.

"Finally," Maxwell said. "Here's our member of the team, Detective Inspector Blakewell."

I couldn't have heard him right. I turned.

Ethan stood in the doorway.

CHAPTER 10

Ethan

Becky?

I did my best to hide my surprise and closed the door behind me. Now there was no turning back.

Superintendent Maxwell had told me he was partnering me with an outside psychological consultant, but I never would have guessed he meant her.

"Inspector, good of you to join us," Maxwell said. We have Mr. Smithers and Ms. Sommerset, from Lessex Insurance."

Having controlled my shock, I nodded to both and took a seat opposite the girl who'd once destroyed me. I'd had a hard enough time spending twenty-four hours with her, and now I was partnered with her on this job? How was that fair?

Maxwell slid a folder to each of us. "This is the information we have at the moment. The inspector is on this case because he has family connections that will allow you to attend the events where we believe these thefts are taking place."

Becky cast a wary eye at me. I'd kept my family background from her—and everyone else at university—lest it contaminate my relationships.

"And Ms. Sommerset, I'm told you are rather adept at ferreting out truth from falsehoods when questioning witnesses."

"So, you want us to interrogate suspects informally?" Becky asked.

"Pardon her, Superintendent," Smithers said. "She's American and doesn't understand the situation."

Maxwell waved him off. "No worries. Your forthrightness is appreciated in this instance, Ms. Sommerset. I would say *interrogate* is a strong word. How do you feel about *engage* in conversation?"

Becky didn't respond, clearly not feeling so good.

"My wife packed me a ham and cheese sandwich for lunch today," Maxwell told Becky. "Is that true?"

Her gaze fell on him. "I wasn't watching you. Say it again."

"As always, my wife packed me a ham and cheese sandwich for lunch today," he repeated.

"That's not true," she said. "Most likely."

Maxwell pointed at her. "That right there is the talent that will allow this to succeed."

Smithers smiled. "I told you she was good."

I joined his smile. My Becky was good, which in the end, would be bad for me. If she could see the person speaking, she was unmatched at detecting a lie.

She caught my reaction, and the glint in her eye said she liked it.

Maxwell took charge. "So, let's go over what we know. Two pieces of expensive jewelry were stolen under similar circumstances."

Smithers raised a finger. "There may be a third as well. From industry contacts, we heard that Amalgamated had a large loss that may be related."

"Who was the victim?" I asked. We'd only heard about the two.

"At the present time, that is all I know," Smithers said.

"We have from the duchess that she fainted in the restroom at a party, and that's the only time she can think of that it could have happened," Becky told us. "Additionally, we know that the necklace went into the jeweler to be cleaned two weeks before the event, was verified by him to be authentic, and delivered to the duchess the afternoon of the party. When she returned home after the party, she noticed a discrepancy in the necklace and called our company. We then collected the item and had it checked."

During her monologue, I watched the woman more than listened to her words. She was focused, determined, and confident. Becky had come a long way since our time at Imperial.

Smithers picked up where Becky left off. "I personally took possession of it from the duchess, and we've confirmed that the entire piece is a forgery, not just the stones."

They went over a few more details, but all I noticed was how Becky reacted to and analyzed all the information she was given. When she'd mentioned she was an investigator yesterday, I hadn't paid enough attention.

"Inspector," she said, addressing me. "How are your family connections going to open the doors so we can talk to these people?"

I looked to Maxwell, who answered for me. "DI Blakewell doesn't bandy this about, but he is the son of the Duke and Duchess of Lassiter." Maxwell's finger traveled between Becky and me. "He can get himself invited to any of these functions, can't you, Inspector?" His gaze shifted to me.

"Most likely." My mother would drool at the prospect of getting me to attend more of her society functions.

When I glanced in Becky's direction, I could read the surprise in her eyes. I'd only supplied vague answers and steered the conversation away whenever my family had come up in the past. I'd skirted her lie-detector on purpose by changing the subject rather than giving responses.

"Where was the event held where the duchess thinks the switch took place?" Becky asked.

"Rainswood Manor," Maxwell said pointing at me. "His family's estate."

With those words, a lead weight descended on my chest and stole my breath. *My parents' home? It couldn't be.*

CHAPTER 11

Rebecca

The meeting ended abruptly with a simple, "I'll leave you two to puzzle it out," from Maxwell.

Ethan and Smithers stood to leave as well.

I grabbed up the few papers we had, folded them, and stashed them in my purse before I followed the two men to the elevator.

On the way down, I whispered to Ethan, "Did you know about this?"

He didn't answer.

I followed Smithers and Ethan outside without another word. Apparently the building affected both men's vocal cords.

Once outside, Smithers turned to me. "The managing director and I look forward to the successful conclusion of this…" He waved a finger in a circle. "Episode." He shook Ethan's hand. "Inspector, I'll leave her in your capable hands." He turned and disappeared into the crowd.

Ethan turned the opposite direction. "I fancy a walk in St. James's Park."

I hurried to follow. "And I fancy a direct answer to my question."

He kept walking.

I grabbed his elbow.

He turned, and with a hand at my shoulder, ushered us to the side of the building. He backed me against the wall. He looked both directions before his lips moved close to mine.

The power of his presence overwhelmed me for a moment. I hadn't asked for a kiss, just an answer. I closed my eyes.

"A public street is not the proper place to discuss this," he said softly.

Blinking my eyes open, I nodded, ashamed that I'd misread the situation.

"We are going to the park. No arguments." A second later he was walking again, and I moved to catch up, silently.

When we finally crossed Horse Guards Road into the park, he spoke. "I knew the case involved jewelry."

"I knew that much too," I told him.

He looked over and smiled, motioning for me to walk with him toward the lake. "But I didn't know I'd be partnered with you."

I let out a relieved breath. "Good. For a moment I thought—"

"You thought I'd requested you?"

"No. Not that." I realized it hurt that he hadn't. But that was stupid. How would he have known to ask for me in the first place?

"Then what?"

"I thought I was losing it." I threw up my hands. "Forget it. It's nothing."

He pulled me to a stop by my shoulder. "Tell me, Becks."

Once again, contact with him interrupted my thought patterns. "I'd have been disappointed in myself if I couldn't tell yesterday that you knew we'd be partnered together."

He shook his head and raised his hands. "Becky, you're unbelievable." He started down the path again.

I caught up. "What?"

He stopped again. "This was the problem before. I'm not a damned lab rat for you to analyze every minute we're together. If you want to practice your mind-reading games on others, be my guest, but not me. If you can't cut it out, this will never work, and we should tell Maxwell right now."

My eyes went wide. "You can't. I need this. I really need this. Can't we just forget I said that?" I put on my best puppy dog face.

He held up a finger. "One condition."

"Name it." I cocked my head for the answer.

"I just did. When you're talking to me, do whatever you have to, but turn off that lie-detector game that's always running in your head."

"I can do that. If it helps, yesterday I thought you were lying about being with Scotland Yard when you called Cornwall."

He laughed. "You could have asked instead of assuming I was a lying arsehole."

I walked with him a few steps. "I guess I was too wrapped up in what was happening to me, but I got it wrong."

His hand at the small of my back urged me forward. The touch felt familiar and oddly right.

Another burning question needed to be asked, so I blurted it out. "Why didn't you call?"

That stopped him. "I changed my mind." His face hardened. "Two conditions. No dissecting the past. We need to focus on the case."

"Was I too clingy?" I'd had a hundred thoughts on what had gone wrong with us, but never one that resonated.

He put that finger up again. "This is exactly what I'm talking about. I'm not playing twenty questions with you. Didn't I just say the past can wait?"

"Sorry," I said, catching up after he started off again. Controlling myself with him was going to be harder than I thought. Was I really that bad? That was another question, but one I didn't verbalize.

"The case..." He quieted as we passed a couple going the opposite direction. "...is what we need to focus on, not past mistakes."

The words gave me hope. Maybe he thought not calling had been a mistake.

"How do you plan to meet with and interview the guests at the party to determine what happened?" I asked. "Do we have a list?"

"Very simple," he said as he checked behind us. "You and I have reignited our acquaintance—"

"Acquaintance?" I asked with a smirk.

"Okay. Passion."

I swallowed hard. I hadn't seen that coming. *Passion* was a big leap from *acquaintance*.

"You returned to London. We met again. Things sparked between us, again. So we're going to be attending the next several events as a couple."

Five years ago I would have given anything for him to say that. Now, not so much. "*Now* you want me as your girlfriend?"

He nodded. "What's so odd about that?"

"You don't even like me."

He stopped me and held my shoulders. "How can you say that?"

I couldn't keep up with his logic *or* the constant starting and stopping.

"Because…" I couldn't finish the sentence.

"It's not what you think. One day you'll understand, but I want you to know that I've never forgotten you."

"But…"

"I'll tell you what." He raised that finger again. "This one time, you are allowed to play your ninja mind game and tell me if you believe me."

I nodded.

"I carry deep affection for you, Rebecca."

I watched, and all my instincts told me it was the truth. One-hundred-percent true. "I believe you." But I still needed a Brit-speak-to-American translation for the phrase. "What exactly does that mean?"

"I said no twenty questions. We're done." He raised his hand to my face and his mouth was on mine in an instant, claiming me.

I pulled back a little. "What are you—"

He laughed. "That is the reaction we can't have." He looked both ways before speaking again. "Our cover story is we're passionately in love." I noticed he'd added *love* to the *passion* in his previous description. "We need to sell it. If you can't handle that, we shouldn't start this, and I need to get a professional who can."

I nodded. "I think I can." I needed this job to end in success. And, although I had no right, the idea of another woman's lips on his made me oddly jealous.

He sighed. *"Think* isn't good enough."

"I know I can." But his kiss had ignited memories I'd kept bottled up for the last five years—dangerous memories.

∽

Ethan

She'd had an amateur reaction to my kiss, the kind that would blow the case.

"Let me guess, you want to have practice sessions?" she asked.

"I don't need them, but maybe you do," I said softly as I pulled her toward me again.

This time her lips met mine willingly for a soft, short kiss.

I controlled my urge to push the boundary, to show her exactly how I felt, to test her limits. Instead, I kept it a gentle public display of affection.

Her tongue darted out to trace her upper lip as I pulled away. "I'll be just fine when this starts."

I wrapped my hand around her waist, and we started walking again. "It already has. We're on a date." Twenty yards later, he said, "Be casual, and check out the guy by the tree to your left."

She glanced that way.

"Don't forget to smile," I told her. Mine was genuine, as the heat of her against me brought back memories of our past.

She smiled another of her beautiful smiles and whispered in my ear, "Who is he?"

The man stood by the tree with a camera, which sported a lens a foot long.

"One of the paparazzi. He mostly hangs out either here or Hyde Park."

She pulled herself closer to me. "Is that why we're here?"

I leaned down to give her a quick kiss, just a taste. "You're as smart as you look. That, and we need to talk without anybody nearby."

Her gaze as she looked up at me was to die for.

I truly wished I had her gift for discerning deception—was her smile a reflection of the way I thought about her, or an artifice of the playacting we had to undertake?

"How do you know about him?" she asked.

I dared a glance at the couples sitting on the grass. Five years ago, that had been us lounging under a tree on a nice day.

"My brother, Charlie," I answered, bringing myself back to the present.

"How does he know him? Charlie, I mean."

"Being the future duke, it's part of his life."

She started to glance back again.

I jerked her against me. "Don't look."

"You really think he'd take a picture of us?"

"Maybe. Maybe not till tomorrow. Just smile."

The warmth of her body through my clothes added to the sunshine threatening to overheat me.

"I like it here," she said as she hip-bumped me.

"I like the company."

"Why didn't you tell me about your parents before?"

I stopped, pulled her to the side of the path, and held her waist. "I didn't keep it from you any more than anyone else." I looked deep into her eyes. "How would you like to go around your whole life wondering if what people were telling you, or how they were treating you, was genuine, or because of who your parents were?"

She placed a hand on my chest. "You could have told *me*."

I moved a hand to her cheek.

She leaned into the touch.

"Some secrets need to be complete."

Her fingers stroked my chest. "Even from those who care about you?" Her eyes held hurt.

I nodded. "It doesn't mean I didn't trust you. Each secret is a weight to carry around, and I didn't want to add to your burdens." Her own family issues had burdened her back then, and defying her mother had taken an emotional toll. "That and, as I said, some secrets shouldn't be revealed to anyone, even family."

"I'm stronger than you think, Ethan."

"I didn't lie to you."

"No, but you weren't completely honest either, and it hurts that you didn't trust me."

She still didn't understand. I couldn't jeopardize the family. This conversation was going the wrong direction. "Then I'll tell you what I can over dinner, and after that we drop it."

"Dinner," she repeated. Waiting wasn't something she did well.

I nodded. "But first we have shopping to do."

CHAPTER 12

Rebecca

"Shopping? Are you kidding? We're supposed to be working."

Ethan pulled me along the path. "This *is* working. And it's going to be fun. You'll see. And if you don't like it, you'll have to turn in your girl card."

"You're nuts, you know that? And it's a woman card."

At the street, he hailed us a cab. "Top of Sloane Street," he told the cabbie as we climbed in.

I buckled up. "What are you shopping for?"

He smiled and raised an eyebrow. "Not me, you."

I had to stop this. "Hold on one minute. I don't need anything, and if I did, the shops on that street are out of my price range." Sloane Street was populated with designer shops, not department stores.

He took my hand.

The heat of his touch had me wanting to protect myself. I couldn't be drawn back into the vortex that was Ethan Blakewell. Not again. I'd barely survived the first time. The look I saw in his eyes, though, kept me from pulling away.

"My girlfriend is going to wear the best. She's going to dress like she's dating the son of a duke."

I pointed at my perfectly presentable business suit. "What is this? Chopped liver?"

He brought my hand to his mouth and kissed it. "This is fine, but we're going for exquisite, even outrageous. We want to be noticed."

I cocked my head. "For the photographers?"

His head bobbed up and down in exaggerated fashion. "Exactly." His boyish grin said he was enjoying this. "Look at it this way… You'll end up with a new wardrobe when this is over."

"I still can't afford the stores on that street."

Ethan pulled out his phone and dialed. "Smithers, we're going to need to spend some money on Miss Sommerset's wardrobe for this. You don't have any problem with that, do you?… You did say whatever we required… Just checking in. Yes… Bye."

My brows went up. "And?"

"Less Sex is footing the bill. I gave him a chance to back away from whatever we required, and he didn't."

"You're sneaky."

"Let's get you some clothes."

We exited the cab, and Ethan's touch startled me as he guided me into the first store. I had to get past that reaction, but every touch had an electric feel to it—dangerously electric.

"I want you to look so gorgeous that when you walk into the room, all eyes shift to you."

I gave him the side-eye. "I'm not some prized possession on display, you know." The words left me before I realized how bitchy they sounded.

He shook his head. "That didn't come out right. You are gorgeous, and I want you wearing something worthy of you."

He was heaping it on pretty thick. "Thank you, I think."

A saleslady started toward us, or rather toward me.

"Remember, being noticed is the strategy."

I didn't get a chance to object before the saleslady was upon us. "My name is Celine. What may I help you locate today?" she asked.

"Just a moment," Ethan told her.

Celine was perceptive enough to back away. Ethan's voice, and the way he carried himself, demanded respect.

"Money is not an issue today. We need stunning," he said loud enough for Celine to hear.

He motioned her back. "We're going to a few formal events, beginning with the Chatterham Ball, and my Rebecca needs a few things to wear."

"So not just one outfit?" Celine asked, no doubt with visions of a big commission.

"Remember, my mother, the duchess, will be in attendance," he told me.

Celine's brow rose almost imperceptibly. "I'm sure we can find you some suitable dresses."

Ethan turned and took a seat. "I'll wait here to see what you select."

Celine urged me toward the back. "This way, Rebecca. Do we have a color in mind?"

I followed her. "Not really."

"American?" she asked as she flicked through dresses on a rack.

"Pretty obvious, huh?"

"Which duchess are we talking?"

"The Duchess of Lassiter." I hoped I got the pronunciation right.

"Ooooh." She nodded back toward the front. "Is that Lord Blakewell?"

She probably meant Charles. "His brother."

She turned to me. "What's the Chatterham Ball like? I've never been lucky enough to go."

"I wouldn't know." Just her suggestion that I looked like the kind of girl who'd attended one made me smile.

"I hear it's magical. Many of the girls are choosing something between red and rose as a color this year."

"Sounds fine to me." Then I remembered Ethan's statement that we wanted to stand out. "On second thought, not a hint of red. I'd rather not be one of the crowd. And, he wants stunning."

"And what is it *you* would like?"

I gave her the simple answer. "He's paying."

"Sexy it is, then."

"Mouthwatering," I added.

Celine continued her fawning. "What's she like, the duchess?" It was an indirect question, the kind I might use in an interrogation.

I hadn't met any of Ethan's family when we were together before. Both times we'd had dinner scheduled, something had come up. "I haven't met her yet."

She picked out a few dresses in various colors, including one in burgundy that I vetoed.

It was hard to ignore the tags. The prices seemed to go up as the amount of fabric went down, but this was on the company's dime. *"Whatever you require,"* Cornwall had said.

After a few swaps, I carried the lot to the dressing room.

This was a young girl's dream come true, an all-expense-paid shopping trip for fairy-tale gowns, but instead I was nervous. I had to model these for Ethan's critique. Would I measure up to his usual dates for these events?

Back in the dressing area, Celine brought in another dress, this one in black. "If this will be the first time meeting his mother, this might be more appropriate." It was basic black, and without the scoop back or a neckline that plunged as far as the others.

I started with that one, and Ethan's response when I walked out was less than I'd hoped for. "That's nice." He twirled his finger.

I circled for him.

"Maybe a little too nice," he said.

"I'm meeting your mother for the first time."

He shook his head.

Celine came to my defense. "If she's meeting the duchess, I think this makes quite the sophisticated impression?"

Ethan nodded. "Perhaps for supper with the family, but not out and about."

I hurried back to the dressing room.

The next one was a blue number. Getting into it, one thing became obvious: This was going to be a new experience for me. I wasn't used to garments this revealing. Every one of the remaining gowns was backless, and half of them with quite low necklines as well.

Tentatively I walked out to be viewed and judged.

Ethan's eyes bugged out when I rounded the corner.

I turned for him. "What do you think?" I ignored my promise to not evaluate his statements and allowed myself the luxury of watching closely as he said the words.

"You look stunning."

Truth is what I saw, and it thrilled me. "You sure?"

"Absolutely." His brows went up with delight. "We need more like that."

Celine perked up at the implication of a higher total tab.

After that I held my own little fashion show—walking out, turning, and earning the glint in Ethan's eye that I relished more each time.

His eyes popped as I rounded the corner. His phrases of appreciation made me giddy. He almost drooled at the sight of me as I bounced on my toes in front of him, jiggling my girls.

I decided against the white one when Ethan's response was polite, but told me it didn't fall into the mouthwatering category.

After a total of four dresses, we bid Celine goodbye.

She urged me to try a few more, but I knew enough to want dresses from more than one designer.

Ethan settled the bill and arranged to have the clothes delivered to his address.

Celine fussed over my fake boyfriend when he produced the black Amex card mortals like most of us never got invited to apply for. "Be sure to ask for me when you return," she said, offering her card. She didn't want to lose a big spender like Ethan.

"Thank you. We will." I took the card from her and claimed my boyfriend with an arm around his waist.

Ethan was patient, but his smile wavered when we walked out of the next two stores without a dress.

I had several brain fog incidents after he put a hand to my back to guide me down the street. Each time he touched me, an electric jolt shook me—a jolt I didn't want to admit meant I hadn't forgotten our time years ago. My subconscious didn't understand that this was different. *This is work*, I kept repeating in my head, but it wasn't getting through to my irrational animal brain.

I let Ethan open the doors for me, as a lady would, although as the day went on, my urges felt less and less ladylike.

I discarded the thought that he was being anything more than gentlemanly, playing the role. That had to explain it. He couldn't help himself. Insisting on opening doors for me, always walking on the street side—he was just following the gentleman's code he'd been taught in whatever boarding school for aristocratic children he'd been sent to.

His words pulled me back to the present. "Should we try in here?"

"Sure."

On cue, he held the door open.

Inside the Prada store, we were quickly met by Fern, and Ethan again explained my quest for a dress to wear to the ball, even though I already had several to choose from.

I followed Fern back to the racks while Ethan again waited up front.

She pulled out several selections that were lukewarm at best. "These would be fitting for a formal event."

I looked them over briefly. "Not quite right."

She tilted her head toward the front. "You don't think he'd like these?"

Like wasn't the word we were going for. "He might, but I don't want him to *like* it; I want him to love it, or better yet, be shocked by it."

She switched racks. "Shocking, huh? Then this might be what you're looking for." She pulled out a bright red example.

I'd wanted to avoid red, but the cut of this dress shouted *stand out* in bold letters. I wouldn't blend in as just another socialite in this.

I emerged from the dressing room almost too embarrassed to walk out to Ethan. The neckline almost reached my navel. "How do I keep from falling out of this?" I asked Fern.

"Same as everyone on the red carpet. We have tape for that. I mean, if the actresses didn't use it, they wouldn't be able to televise anything, now would they?"

I turned around for her.

"You'll also want to go down the street to La Perla for something to go with that." She pointed to my panties showing through the more-than-thigh-high slit. "They'll have a color match for this, no doubt."

I wiggled and pulled my underwear down and off. I didn't want them ruining the effect when I modeled this for Ethan.

∽

Ethan

We were at the fourth store now, and I was ready to call it a day and go with what we had so far.

Each of the rejected dresses at the last two stores had looked beautiful on her, but that was to be expected. Becky could make a T-shirt and jeans look sexy. Still, for one reason or another, she'd decided against them.

She appeared from around the corner. "What do you think of this one?" She twirled in front of me.

My mouth dropped.

She wore a bright red gown with a deep V front showing off her marvelous braless cleavage, and a slit that came almost to her waist, revealing a complete leg with each step, and barely hiding what I guessed was her naked lady parts. Each time she moved, my eyes darted to her thigh, hoping for a glimpse, but I was denied—just barely.

"Well?" she asked, breaking my stare.

I fumbled for the right word. "Breathtaking."

"You think so?"

"Absolutely. Every man in the room will be wondering…" I stopped myself and rephrased. "…how I got so lucky to have you as my date." She would cast a spell on every pair of eyes in the room.

"You're going to make me blush."

"It'll just make the dress look better."

That extra line did draw a blush out of her, and it was cuter than I'd expected.

This latest saleslady was hovering, waiting on the verdict.

I stood and offered her my credit card. "We'll take it."

When Becky returned, she'd changed into her work clothes, and all I could think was how magnificently sexy she'd looked in that dress. My eyes drifted to her chest, imagining the luscious cleavage that had been on display, and that slit—my God, that slit was like a pulse of aphrodisiac with each step, displaying her mile-long leg and all that skin.

This one I insisted on carrying out with us. It would be perfect for this evening. I offered to carry the garment bag. "Shoes next?"

"In a bit," she said. "First we go across the street."

The surprise trip across the road was to La Perla for lingerie.

I pulled open the door for her. "I hope you'll be modeling for me again?"

"Not a chance."

I didn't hide my disappointment well.

"I promise I won't be long." She held out her hand. "Card?"

I surrendered my black Amex card one more time and was relegated to waiting by the front while she and one of the sales staff wandered off.

As additional female customers entered the store, I earned a sideways glance from each—probably wondering if I was a pervert or just a guy too stupid to know this was a designated testosterone-free zone—no Y chromosomes allowed.

Becky reappeared with her purchases concealed in a bag.

"What'd you get?"

"I'm not telling." The girl had me at her mercy.

"Now shoes?"

She tilted her head. "Among other things." She winked. "Just a few more stops, I promise."

Thankfully she knew where she wanted to go for shoes, and we accomplished that with only a single stop.

Next up was a handbag, she informed me.

The woman had worn me out. "Are we done yet?" I complained.

"You're the one who insisted on shopping today."

"True. But I hadn't realized how exhausting it would be."

She took my arm. "You poor baby. Let's get you home."

CHAPTER 13

Rebecca

Ethan pulled the Aston Martin to the curb. "Ready?"

"Not really." The idea of wearing this super-sexy red dress to dinner still had me freaked out.

"It's just dinner," Ethan said as the valet looked at him expectantly through the window.

I shivered. "There's nothing *just* about this."

His hand came across the console to squeeze mine. "You'll be fine."

I swallowed my fear. "Let's do this."

He hopped out of the car, tossed the key to the valet, rounded the front, and pulled open the door for me.

The apprehension I'd felt slipping into the barely-there dress was nothing compared to how naked I felt climbing out of the car. Lucky for me, the slit on this dress was on the inside leg, and I was able to get out without giving everyone a peep show.

I hung on Ethan's arm and still almost tripped on the uneven pavers of the sidewalk.

Ethan caught and supported me.

A few clock ticks later, we were safely inside the door.

"Are you sure this is the best place?" I asked.

"According to Charlie," he whispered in my ear.

"Where is he, by the way?" I asked as we advanced to the maître d'.

"Somewhere in your country, but that's not to be repeated."

It felt good to have Ethan trust me with a secret, even if it was a little one.

"Reservation for Lord Blakewell," Ethan told the man. "Unfortunately the duke will not be joining us, so it'll just be two this evening."

He checked his book. "I certainly hope the duke is not unwell?"

"No, he was merely unable to make it."

"This way, Lord Blakewell." He showed us to a quiet table next to the window, facing the courtyard garden.

Ethan held out the chair for me. He was going to spoil me with all this chivalry.

I waited until the maître d' left. "What was that all about?"

He leaned forward. "Making sure he knew which Blakewell."

"Oh." I didn't get it, but this was his town. "Am I supposed to address you as *Lord* now?"

With a grimace and quick shake of the head, Ethan opened his menu. "You look stunning this evening."

The heat of a blush rose in my cheeks. "I was going for mouthwatering."

His brow raised. "Mission accomplished."

I checked the menu for a few seconds. "You didn't have to take me to a place this expensive."

"Trust me."

"And, we didn't have to drive. A cab would have been fine with me." That was a bit of a lie because it had been my first ride in an Aston Martin. The car oozed coolness.

"A taxi? That would destroy the narrative."

I looked down at the tablecloth. "Right." For a moment I'd forgotten that everything about us being together was playacting. "Can't forget the narrative."

The waiter arrived to take our drink order.

Ethan's lips transfixed me as I watched him speak to the waiter. For a moment I was transported back to our first dinner date. I'd watched his lips all night, wondering what it would be like to kiss him, and by the end of the night I'd learned.

"If that's okay with you," Ethan said, breaking my trance.

"Sure." I'd completely missed what he ordered.

After the waiter left, Ethan reached across to take my hand for the second time tonight. "More importantly, I wanted to impress you."

"What?"

"The car."

The sentiment warmed me, but I pulled my hand back. "I have to admit, the car impressed me. A James Bond car? How could anything be more cool?"

"Maybe another day I'll drive you out into the country, and we'll see if it can run as well as it looks."

"Deal."

I picked up the menu again to peruse it, but more importantly to take my eyes off of Ethan and keep me from blurting out my question again. I had to know what I'd done wrong.

I made it through the appetizer and all the way to having our entrees served. I'd chosen the lamb. But after my first bite, I couldn't hold it in any longer. He'd promised to tell me more at dinner, and the wait had been eating at me all afternoon.

Before I even raised the fork to my mouth, I blurted it out. "You said you'd tell me tonight."

He raised a finger as he chewed his potato. "I did."

I waited while he sipped his wine. "What did I do wrong?"

"Nothing, Becks. Nothing at all. It was all me."

"But I called, and you didn't call back. Not once."

He sighed. "It was a very difficult time for me."

"Me too. I thought we had something special."

For the third time, he offered his hand and I took it. "Believe me, we did. My family was going through a difficult stretch—a very private problem I couldn't tell you about."

"Why not? You could have told me anything, and I would have understood. But shutting me out... That was..."

He pulled my hand toward him and added his other hand. "It had nothing to do with you, or us. It was a family crisis."

"What kind of crisis? I should have been the one you turned to to deal with it."

"I told you that some secrets have to remain absolute?"

I nodded.

"This is one of those. It's not my secret to share."

That finally gave me a clue. He was keeping someone *else's* secret. "Couldn't you have told me that much?"

He shook his head. "Not the way you were. I couldn't lie to you, and I couldn't have you figure it out either."

"But you didn't even tell me that much."

"I didn't handle it well. I apologize for that. It had nothing to do with you, or us. It was a family emergency."

"What kind of emergency?"

He let go of my hand and sat back. "That right there is the problem I was avoiding. You won't let anything go unanswered."

"I'm sorry." I sighed. He was right. I had poor self-control when it came to asking questions—more like no self-control.

"You have to realize that some things are the way they are, and you have to let them be."

I picked up my fork and pushed my vegetables around. "I am sorry." I'd screwed up again by asking a question, or three or four, too many. Exactly what made me good at my job made me terrible at relationships. "No worries, Becks."

That made me smile. "I'll try to be better."

"I know." He sat back. "Enough about that. Tell me what has been happening in your life. How did you end up at Less Sex?"

I let go of my fixation on our breakup and spent the next hour chronicling how I'd stumbled into working as an investigator at Lessex and offering highlights from several of the cases I'd worked.

As I finished up, he cut another piece of his meat.

I watched it travel to his lips, the lips I wanted more than anything to taste again tonight.

The man had a magnetic pull. All during the meal, I'd glanced up to catch a smile on his lips and could only hope I'd put it there, that it wasn't just part of the act.

This might've been a job we were assigned to do, but once I dropped the inquisition, just being across from him had my insides turning somersaults. My feelings from years ago came crashing into my consciousness, refusing to be put back on the shelf of yesterday's memories.

After a day of shopping on probably the most exclusive street in London, I'd been transported here in a car straight out of a James Bond movie. I was having dinner with the son of a duke in one of the most expensive restaurants in town. It was like a fairy tale come true. To top it off, Ethan was every bit as handsome as Bond himself, just as sophisticated, and twice as charming. And he was mine—at least for the duration.

Somehow what was supposed to be simple preparation for an undercover assignment looked and felt an awful lot like a real date. That shouldn't have surprised me. But where did the illusion stop and reality begin? Maybe I just didn't want to see it, but I couldn't tell.

Before I knew it, we'd finished the main course and a glass of wine each.

I took a forkful of the cheesecake and berries we were splitting for dessert. "When do I get to hear about your work at Scotland Yard?"

He looked around. "Shhh."

"Oops," I giggled. He'd warned me earlier that his work was hush-hush, but surely he could at least hint at what it involved. "Maybe a clue?"

He shook his head, taking this secret agent thing a bit too far.

"Is that why you drive that James Bond car? Because you really work for MI-6 and have a license to kill?"

The lady at the neighboring table looked over with concern on her face. She probably thought I was serious. Didn't she understand that the movies were entertainment, not documentaries on the real life of an MI-6 agent?

Ethan glanced toward her table and leaned forward to give me an evil death stare. "This is serious," he said softly. "Do you want to get thrown off the case?"

I felt the blood drain from my face. I'd been joking, but he certainly wasn't. "Sorry," I said, shrinking into my chair. "No more questions. I'll be better. Promise." Somehow I was always asking him the wrong thing.

With gritted teeth, he said, "I'm sure you will."

I cut another piece of cheesecake and leaned over to offer it to him. "How do you put up with me?"

He didn't open his mouth for the dessert. "You can't help yourself, can you?"

Once again I'd asked a question. "Let me try again. I'm glad you put up with me."

He leaned forward, and I managed to get the bite into his mouth without spilling it. His eyes fell perceptibly to my cleavage, which this dress so prominently displayed.

"It's my pleasure," he mumbled with his mouth full.

I decided to own it and pulled my shoulders back, widening the neckline. I caught myself just before asking if he saw something he liked. "I'm enjoying this evening as well." It was the truth and not a question for a change.

Ten minutes later, Ethan handed the valet chit to our waiter. "I'll take the bill, and could you please have the valet pull my car up?"

The waiter turned and promptly pulled out his phone as he walked away. He was out of earshot before he began to speak.

Rationally, I understood the meal had to end sooner or later, but I knew once we passed outside, I'd miss this time with Ethan and yearn for more.

He'd listened so intently, gazed on me with eyes so appreciative, that I'd been on a cloud for the last hour. No questions about a case at work had entered my mind, not once. It wasn't until I realized that fact that the specialness of the evening hit me.

I'd been Ethan's sole focus tonight, and he mine. I hadn't felt like this since, well, since we'd dated five years ago.

I dabbed my lips one last time with my napkin. "Do you think this will... I mean, I hope this works."

"We'll see."

A few minutes later, our waiter returned and handed Ethan back his card and the machine to input his PIN. "Your car is ready for you, sir."

"Thank you very much. Excellent meal, as always." Ethan put bills on the table for a tip and replaced his credit card in his wallet before standing and offering me his hand.

As we walked toward the door, I clung closer to him. We pushed through the door, and in an instant, the flashes started, as did the questions—wanting to know my name, if it was serious, how long we'd been dating, and a half dozen others I didn't catch.

I kept a death grip on Ethan and still almost tripped again as the camera flashes blinded me. I didn't answer any of their questions.

Ethan opened the car door for me, and I slid in—less than ladylike in my hurry to get away from the mob.

My door had barely closed when Ethan raced around to his side, started the car, and punched the accelerator.

After a quick screech of tires, we were away from the mayhem. He turned the corner and slowed down from Mach 1 to merely fast.

Now that I could breathe again, I managed, "There ought to be a law against that." I still had spots in my vision from the flashes.

"Scary, aren't they?"

I shivered. "Insane, if you ask me."

"I'd say that worked."

I nodded. "Better than I expected." We'd wanted to be noticed, but the experience was terrifying.

"They're like a pack of hyenas," he added.

I'd first thought wolves, but hyenas fit them better.

∼

ETHAN

THE PLAN HAD WORKED WELL. MY BROTHER CHARLIE HAD BEEN RIGHT IN HIS suspicion about the staff at the restaurant feeding tips to the paparazzi, probably for a fee.

I glanced over at my date. Even in just the scant illumination coming in through the windscreen, she was gorgeous, and that dress was something else entirely.

She'd claimed her desired effect was mouthwatering, but she'd affected much more than my mouth.

Sitting across from her all night—close enough for a good look, but just out of reach—had been torture. All I'd wanted was to finish the dinner quickly and take her anywhere I could hold her. But that wouldn't have fit the script of a romantic dinner out.

She'd seemed happy and focused on the moment, but how much of that was playing the part, and how much was real?

I didn't have her gift for ferreting out the truth.

"A penny for your thoughts," she said. She'd managed to avoid asking a direct question again. Good for her.

I had misgivings about being honest at this point, but I dismissed them and laid myself open to be disappointed. "I was thinking how beautiful you were tonight, and how hard it was to sit that far away all evening when I couldn't touch you or hold you."

Even in the dim light, the blush that rose in her face was obvious. "I was thinking the same about you." She extended a hand over the console.

I made the decision to take it. The electric feel of her fingers intertwined with mine made my trousers tight, and our situation infinitely more complicated.

CHAPTER 14

Rebecca

As we wound our way back to Ethan's place, the energy that flowed through our interconnected hands was like a life force—invigorating, yet also reawakening a long-dormant wound in my heart.

When I'd left Ethan, I'd had to go back to school in California. My semester of study abroad had ended, and the snow on the ground when I'd left had mirrored my mood.

The professors at Imperial had been generous in their assessments, yet my grades had still been the worst of my college career.

The disappointment in my father's eyes had been palpable when I'd confessed that a boy had distracted me. Stellar grades had always won me his praise and love. But that semester, I'd let him down, and myself.

"I never meant to hurt you," Ethan said as we turned another corner.

"I know." I hadn't known it at the time, and I still didn't understand why some enormous family emergency he couldn't share with me had impacted us as a couple. At the current rate, I'd never know and never feel good about it.

Back in California, I'd buckled down after that semester, not letting the social side of college distract me from my goal. Graduating summa cum laude had been the result, and that distinction had gotten me job interviews galore. That same work ethic had propelled my career since then and would land me that window office soon. I knew it would.

When Mom had married Dad, she'd given up her dreams in favor of family. A couple years ago, my marriage to Wesley had been the expedient way to quell my mother's constant nagging and also experiment with having both—a dream and a family. It had been a means to an end, and not a good one, the way it worked out. Now Mom was trying to find me another man, and my lack of interest was in no way a deterrent.

One failed marriage was enough to convince me to stop trying, but not her. It had only made her more determined to set me up with the *right* man. But as much time as my job took, I wasn't sure there was such a thing as the right man. I wouldn't make her mistake and let a man derail my ambitions.

She'd shown me how that road led to regret.

We'd moved from Missoula, Montana, to San Francisco when I was seven. I'll never forget how excited Mom was to take us to the opera for the first time.

She cried a river at the event, and when I asked her why, she'd said, *"I could have been up there."* It was then I knew she'd given up her dream of opera to be with Dad. For years, she'd dragged me to the opera. She cried every time, and the lesson was reinforced. After all this time, it still hurt her that much.

As we turned the corner, I looked over at Ethan and felt a smile I couldn't contain on my face. Tonight had been magical.

A minute later, he parked the car and turned to me. "Do you believe me?"

"About what?"

"I didn't mean to hurt you."

I thought a moment. Did I believe he hadn't meant to hurt me? "Honest answer?"

"Of course," he answered.

Although he'd said yes, I could read in his eyes the indecision that meant he only wanted to hear good news. I smoothed my hand over my leg. "I'm not sure yet." It was the honest answer he deserved. At the time I'd been angry, and certain he'd done it intentionally. I still didn't understand.

His eyes slid away from happy. He shut down the burble of the engine and opened his door.

I climbed out before he reached my side. I was done doing what was expected of me tonight. I knew what I wanted, and it didn't lie down the obedient, good-girl road.

His hand against the small of my back as he guided me once again sent my hormones into raging overdrive.

It made sense that I was horny around him, didn't it? We'd been great together, right up until the end. Why couldn't we re-explore our attraction? We had to be around each other. Wouldn't it make our act more believable?

Once he closed the door upstairs, I followed him into the kitchen area and closed the distance when he opened the fridge.

"We should discuss the next step," he said, pulling the juice bottle from the top shelf.

I wrapped my arms around him from behind and let my hands roam his chest and my boobs press up against him. His heat was intoxicating. "I know what I want the next step to be."

He pulled away, returned the juice to the fridge, and closed it. "I meant the next step in the case." He turned toward me.

I twined my arms around him and pressed my chest against his. My hand slid down to squeeze his butt. His arms came around and pulled me closer, making Big Ben's arousal in his pants obvious. He and I were on the same wavelength.

"I never forgot you," I told him. There'd been a time I wanted to, but I'd reconciled myself to him being a sad part of my history.

"And I never forgot you either, Becks." He pushed my shoulders back to gaze into my eyes.

I could see it in him. He wanted me as badly as I wanted him. I closed my eyes and raised up for the kiss.

"This isn't right since you don't believe me," he said, pulling away.

"I didn't say that. I meant—" I didn't get to finish the sentence before he turned the corner. I *had* said what I meant; I wasn't sure.

"We'll discuss the next step for the case in the morning," he said from down the hall.

I stumbled back against the counter, unable to pull in air. I closed my eyes. It was a minute before I could breathe normally again.

This was the second time he'd shown me that opening myself up to him came at a cost. As I walked in the slinky dress to the guest room he'd assigned me, I had a new purpose. I would figure him out. All it would take was the right questions and my one-in-a-million skill.

Ethan

I closed the bedroom door behind me and locked it—as much to keep me in as to keep her out. The yearning I had at this moment had to be controlled.

I'd managed to resist Becky this time, but only barely. And I had to. I couldn't endure another bout of leaving her. The only way to prevent it was to keep her outside the wall I'd built since the first time she'd gone. After she'd gone back to the States, it had taken me months to get back to my studies and on with my life the first time. Now I had a job at the Met and people who depended on me. A month or more of self-pity wasn't a luxury I could afford.

Becky's condition of complete transparency had been and still was too high a price to pay to have her in my life. Why couldn't she leave the past alone and let buried secrets remain hidden? Bringing mine into the light could only hurt the people I loved. How could my feelings for her outweigh my responsibility to my family? It couldn't. Any other answer would be rooted in selfishness. I had to be a bigger man than that. I had to be worthy of the Blakewell name.

CHAPTER 15

REBECCA

I HEARD NOISES BEYOND THE DOOR WHEN I WOKE THE NEXT MORNING.

Ethan was up, and doing who knows what.

Did I care? Not one whit. I had no idea exactly how big a whit was, but it sounded cute, and very British.

I would not make last night's mistake again. This was a job, and I always excelled at my job. I'd be the perfect girlfriend in public, get back the necklace—or at least the jewels—get my window office, put the stupid HR complaint to rest with Cornwall's help, and move on with my life. My career would be assured. Nothing else mattered. End of story.

Several minutes later, I let the hot shower water rinse away the guilt I'd felt since last night. It wasn't my problem Ethan was self-absorbed and needy. I knew how to take care of my itch when I needed to, and it involved a bar, a few drinks, and a hotel room. It didn't need to involve some stupid son of some stupid duke of some stupid country where they drove on the wrong side of the stupid road.

Ethan had said we would discuss the next step of his plan this morning, and we needed to do that so we could wrap this up. A quick resolution—that's what I needed to get on with my career, out of this rainy city, and back to where the sun shined. Back to where a stupid son of a stupid duke of a stupid country wasn't a distraction.

Dressed casually in jeans and a T-shirt, I reached for the door knob, but pulled back. After shedding my bra, I pulled the T-shirt on again. With the way he'd treated me last night, I wasn't above being mean this morning. I'd taunt him with what he'd rejected. He deserved it.

I wasn't above admitting I was horny. I'd always been up front with my hookups about things being casual and not leading anywhere. Why did it have to be any different with Ethan? Sure, we had history, but that only meant we could avoid the awkward stage, didn't it? We could have gotten straight to satisfying the itch, if he'd been willing. It made sense to me.

I turned on my phone before heading out to tease Ethan. A few paces out of the door, it beeped at me. A missed call from my sister, Lizzy. I pocketed the device. Her twenty questions could wait.

Bouncing into the kitchen, I found Ethan pulling a big, stainless appliance out of a box. "What is that?"

He turned, and his eyes didn't miss the double-barreled salute my nipples gave him through the thin shirt. He swallowed, then shifted to the machine. "Since you prefer coffee to tea in the morning, I got this for you."

It was a huge, very high-end coffee machine, and brand spanking new.

I checked the time on the oven display. It was barely seven o'clock. "How?" The stores weren't open yet.

He shook his head. "Can't you for once accept something nice without a question?"

His observation hit me hard, because it was spot on. "Thank you, Ethan," was all I could think to say.

"You'll have to help me figure out how to run it, though. I have zero experience with something this complicated. I can barely handle a teapot that whistles."

I moved to the stainless-and-chrome contraption. It was even more complex than the expensive one we had at the San Francisco office. "This is too much." He'd obviously spent a fortune on this.

"My father knows someone at Harrods, and I was able to get this before opening. The man said it was the best."

Naturally when a duke called, the red carpet came out and official store hours didn't matter like they did for the rest of us.

I couldn't resist hugging him. "Thank you." I held him a little too long and felt him tense up.

He pulled away. "You already said that. You deserve it for putting up with me."

I looked through the packaging on the table. "Where are the beans?"

"Beans?" he said. "Sorry, I'm not good at this coffee thing. I guess I didn't think—"

"It's wonderful. I'll get beans later. This is so very thoughtful of you."

That compliment hit the spot, causing the stoic Brit to blush.

I started reading the quick-start guide for the coffee machine. With buttons, knobs, and levers galore, there was nothing quick about it.

This gesture meant my opinion of Ethan had to be reevaluated.

He looked over when the musical ringtone that signaled Lizzy calling started in my pocket.

I pulled the phone out. "Hi, Lizzy. What are you doing calling at this hour?" It was well after midnight New York time.

"My God, why didn't you tell me you were dating a duke's son? You know that could be big for me." As a reporter she was always after the latest gossip.

"I bumped into him and we had dinner is all."

Ethan's brows lifted.

"Well, you could have let me break it," she said.

I stretched the truth. "It just happened, and I didn't know he was related to a duke until we were at dinner."

"Will you be seeing him again?"

"I hope so, but it's not like we're an item or anything serious."

Ethan smirked.

"Okay, but you owe me, so if things change, you'll let me know first, right?"

"Sure. If things get more serious with him, you'll be the first to know."

"Is he a good kisser?"

I turned away from Ethan. "Yes, he's a good kisser. Now I've got work to do. Go to sleep."

"Bye, sis."

"Later gator." I closed off the call.

"Only good?" Ethan asked from behind me.

I turned and glared. "What was I supposed to tell her?"

"You wound me." He staggered back against the counter with a hand to his heart. "I don't know… Super, fantastic, amazing? Anything but *good*."

I moved toward him with exaggerated, bouncy steps.

He was entranced by my boob bounce.

"Sorry to hurt your sensitive ego." I licked my lips and put a finger to his chest. "I think you can do better."

His eyes moved from my chest to lock with mine, and the lust behind them burned. "Is that a challenge?"

The air almost crackled with the tension between us.

Before he could act, I moved back. The closeness had been dangerous. He'd made himself clear last night, and I wouldn't make a fool of myself again.

"Why was she so curious?" he asked.

"It's her job. She works for the *Evening Mail*."

"Could we have used her to spread the news of our relationship?"

I knew better than that. "No way. I've never confided in her. She would've smelled a rat, and this would have been over before it started when she told the whole world it was fake."

Ethan nodded. He checked his watch. "We have an appointment this morning with the Duchess of Lindsley. Since she's in on the inquiry, we can get a statement from her. Anyone else, we'll have to rely on informal conversation."

∽

THE ENGINE ROARED AS ETHAN ACCELERATED OUT OF A TURN ON THE WAY TO OUR interview with the duchess.

"Slow down," I pleaded.

Ethan had let the beast of an Aston Martin loose once we exited the motorway, and every time he stepped on the gas pedal, it threw me back into the seat, only to be almost shoved out the side of the car in the next turn. I'd ridden in a Corvette before, but I didn't remember it being nearly this fast or this scary. This car had proven its pedigree.

Ethan glanced over. "I thought you wanted to see what it could do."

"I've seen enough, thank you very much."

"We don't want to be late."

"If you don't slow down, I'll lose my breakfast, and we'll be very late after going back for a change of clothes."

Ethan gave in to my logic and slowed to a pace that allowed me to relax my death grip on the door. The engine's roar lowered to a growl.

"Thank you. So what's the plan when we talk with the duchess?"

"Simple," he said. "Get what we can from her and swear her to secrecy. Your job is to let me know if there's anything odd in her answers."

"By odd you mean deceitful?"

"Put bluntly, yes."

A mile of silence later, I had to speak up. "Can we talk about last night?"

He didn't look over. "No."

"What do you mean no?"

"No means no. Do you have a different word in American English? We talked at dinner. We are no longer discussing the past."

I looked over in amazement. "It was just last night."

"Past is past."

I crossed my arms. "Right."

I endured a few more miles of silence before his phone rang and he answered it on the Bluetooth speaker. "Hello?"

"Ethan, you really should be more careful when you go out. You and some barely dressed young woman are plastered all over the paper this morning. It's—"

"Mother, stop. I'm driving, and that young woman you mentioned is in the car with me."

It was quiet on the other end.

"And, you should know she's not some young woman," Ethan continued. "She's a very special lady to me."

My eyes widened, and my heart raced as I repeated his words in my head—"*she's a very special lady.*" Once again, I wished I had Brit-speak translator on my phone, although this one was closer to American English than his last phrase had been.

His mother found her tongue. "Then why is it you haven't brought her by for supper? If she's special to you, we really should meet her."

"We will be by when we can. In the meantime, Mother, let me introduce Rebecca Sommerset. Rebecca, my mother."

"Hello, Rebecca, very nice to speak to you. No offense intended. That was a lovely dress."

I deflected. "Ethan picked it out for me."

"No doubt. Now don't let that son of mine delay bringing you out to Rainswood."

"I'll do my best, and I look forward to our meeting, Mrs. Blakewell," I replied. Inwardly, I dreaded the critique I was likely to get.

"Ethan," his mother said. "This does not substitute for a proper introduction over supper."

"Yes, I understand. We have to go now. Talk again soon."

"Bye-bye" she said.

Ethan ended the call. "Well, I guess now we know the papers picked up the pictures."

"She thinks I'm a tramp."

"No, she doesn't."

"That was embarrassing. How am I supposed to meet her and forget what she really thinks of me?"

"She's got more reason to be embarrassed than you do. Trust me, once she realized you weren't a one-night thing—"

"Like a hooker?"

He sneered at my comment. "She's rooting for you. She wants me to settle down. That, and stay out of the papers."

I didn't need to argue the point; her initial words had been plain enough. She wasn't a fan. "Been in the papers a lot?"

Ethan looked down the road and didn't answer.

His words had hinted at something. "When was the last time you had a steady girlfriend?"

"We're almost there," he said without even a hint of a smile.

I didn't press my luck by repeating the question. If he was in the papers a lot, an internet search might net me the answer he wouldn't give. Pulling out my phone, the first thing I found was from this morning.

I smiled at the picture of us. It was as scandalous as we'd hoped, which is why the papers ran with it.

A minute later, Ethan turned down a long, gravel drive and we arrived at a sizable, old house.

We were shown into a parlor by a man I assumed was the duchess's butler. "Her grace will be with you shortly," he said before leaving.

When the duchess arrived, we stood.

"You are looking well, Aunt Helen," Ethan said as she approached.

Aunt Helen?

She took his hand. "Ethan, you're looking more like your father every year." She turned to me.

Ethan touched my elbow. "May I introduce Rebecca Sommerset."

I curtsied. "Your grace."

"Helen will do fine for any friend of Ethan's." It wasn't lost on me that she hadn't suggested the same to my managing director in his office. Her eyes crinkled in recognition. It seemed she'd placed me, even though we hadn't been introduced in Cornwell's office.

She gestured to the sofa on one side of the table. "Please have a seat." She settled in opposite us and smoothed her skirt before turning to the butler, who'd returned. "Martin, tea, if you please."

He disappeared again with a simple, "Yes, mum."

"We're here about the necklace," Ethan began.

"What necklace?"

"Aunt Helen, I've been loaned to the Metropolitan Police to look into the necklace you reported stolen."

Even in saying he'd been *loaned* to the police, Ethan kept his regular work for them secret.

"Tommy Maxwell told me he'd send somebody by. I never would have expected it to be you."

"The two of us have been assigned the case—"

She turned to me. "I knew we'd met. You were with the insurance company, in Joseph's office."

"Yes, ma'am."

"What can you tell us about it?" Ethan asked.

"It was stolen. There's no more to know about it."

"When and where?"

"At a party. I don't know exactly where and when, but all I can think of is it happened in the loo, when I felt faint."

Martin reappeared with a tray of tea, and Ethan halted his questioning.

The duchess poured cups for Ethan and herself.

I declined the offer.

After the butler closed the door, Ethan began again. "You're sure it was at the party and not somewhere else?"

"I'm old, but I'm not senile," she said. "It had just come back from cleaning that afternoon. I put it on for the party, and when I took it off after returning, it had been switched. It couldn't have been anywhere else."

"When you fainted—" I started to ask.

"I said I *felt* faint, a little lightheaded, so I rested for a moment on the sofa. I don't know how long. I lost track of time, but heavens, I didn't fall on the floor or anything."

"And you're certain you didn't take it off at any time?" Ethan asked.

"Being related doesn't give you the right to insult me in my own home. No, I did not remove it at any time."

"No insult intended, Aunt Helen. Just being thorough. You never can tell what small detail might be important."

"Very good. Now her I understand." She motioned to me. "But how, pray tell, do you come to be on this inquiry?"

"We'll be doing this surreptitiously, mingling with the guests at future functions to ascertain how these crimes are being perpetrated," Ethan explained.

Her brows went up. "Covert mission like James Bond? I rather like that."

"Have you mentioned the theft to anyone, anyone at all?" he asked.

"Not a soul outside of the insurance company, and the mayor, and also Tommy Maxwell when he called."

I asked about one person she'd left off. "Does Martin know?" We had to be absolutely certain.

"No, none of my staff," she said.

Ethan sipped his tea. "You mentioned that this may also have happened to Lady Haversom as well."

She picked up her teacup. "Absolutely. Elizabeth lost a brooch at a party three weeks earlier. She was beside herself. The same thing—an almost identical copy replaced it. And before you ask, she told me in confidence, and I haven't relayed it to a soul, although I did tell the mayor I knew I wasn't the first."

I judged her to be telling the truth with that. She'd probably forgotten she'd mentioned it to Cornwall in my presence.

She put her cup down after a sip. "I've told nobody except the list I already gave you, Joseph Cornwall, and Tommy Maxwell."

"Did Lady Haversom mention feeling faint at any time?" Ethan asked.

"She said she felt ill for a bit. At the time I didn't make anything of it."

"We'll need to talk to Lady Haversom as well then," Ethan noted.

"You'll have a long wait on that," the duchess said. "She up and left for India and Nepal. Won't be back for months. Not that I can understand why she'd want to go there."

That left us with only this one theft for clues, and so far only one commonality, the lightheaded feeling.

"Do you know where she lost her brooch?" I asked.

The duchess fidgeted before answering.

I watched carefully for a deception coming.

∽

Ethan

"Same place I lost mine, Rainswood Manor," Aunt Helen finally said.

The answer sucked the breath out of me. My father's home was now a common link between the cases.

Becky glanced over at me, having certainly caught the implication.

"Do you have any questions, Rebecca?" I asked.

"Not at this time," she answered.

"One remaining item, Aunt Helen. This matter and its inquiry is covered by the Official Secrets Act, and nothing we've discussed—or even the existence of our inquiry—may be relayed to any third party."

My aunt nodded solemnly. "Excellent. You have no idea what people would say about me if they learned of this. I'll be the last person repeating a word."

"Very good then. We'll be on our way, and thank you for the tea."

With our goodbyes, Becky and I were out the door. Yesterday's sunshine had given way to a sky that signaled an approaching storm. I got her seated in the car and started the engine. We were off after waving goodbye.

Once we turned down the long drive, Becky spoke up. "You didn't mention that you were related to one of our victims."

I'd screwed up. "Not a close relative. My mother's second cousin. Sorry. I should have mentioned it earlier."

"That's right, you should've."

We were halfway down the drive before I asked the obvious question. "What did your super sense tell you in there?" It was the reason she was on this case, after all.

"She's telling the truth. She didn't like having to confirm that both thefts happened at your family's home, but none of her answers were deceptive or even ambiguous."

I glanced over when I stopped to join the main road. "So all we have to go on is a fainting spell."

"That, and both crimes occurred at Rainswood Manor," she said, stating what I'd not wanted to admit out loud.

Aunt Helen worried what people would think of her for losing the family necklace, but what would people think of my family if it got out that jewelry had been stolen twice while people attended events at our house? My parents would find the shame unbearable.

"You don't think… Your parents?" Becky asked.

"Not for a minute, but they were present," I told her. "They might know something and not realize it. I guess this means we accept Mother's invitation to supper sooner rather than later."

"I'd like that."

When I looked over, I wondered if she was thinking this was overdue because I'd never brought her to meet my family when we were together before.

∽

Rebecca

Back at Ethan's apartment, I looked up from the pen and paper I'd been playing with, trying to figure out ways the heists could have been pulled off. "Maybe we should put it off until tomorrow," I called to him.

He returned from the other room, where he'd been on the phone. "Supper is set for tonight."

"The weather app on my phone says a big storm is coming this evening."

He wasn't swayed. "This is England. Wind and rain are the normal state of things."

I sighed.

"Anyway, Mom is dying to meet you," he added.

I looked back down at my scribbles. I'd scratched off invisibility cape and three other equally ridiculous ideas, so the only thing left on my page was amnesia gas.

"Solve the riddle yet?" Ethan asked.

I held up my paper. "Ever heard of a temporary-amnesia gas?"

"A general anesthetic would cause that, but you wouldn't stay on your feet."

I'd dismissed that already. His aunt hadn't fallen, laid down, or lost consciousness. "Do you have any better ideas?"

"Not at the moment."

My phone rang with Mother's song.

"Dammit," I said, letting my frustration show.

Ethan reached for my phone. "You choose the most interesting ring tones."

I held my hand out, afraid he might answer it for me. "I don't want to talk to her right now." I'd had enough of her meddling. Especially with Ethan in the room.

"It says Mother. Mothers are the most important people in our lives. I'm actually very good with mothers."

"Not this one. Let it go to voicemail."

"Why are you mad at her?"

Somehow he knew.

"It's just…" I didn't know how to explain.

"Never mind. You can and should forgive your mother anything." Instead of handing it over, he swiped to answer and set it on the coffee table in speakerphone mode before he sat next to me. His arm went around my shoulder.

I leaned forward for the phone, but he pulled me back and grabbed my arm.

"Becky? You there?" came from the phone.

"Yes, Mom."

"Did you put me on speaker?"

I struggled against Ethan, but it was no use.

He smiled. Apparently this was a game for him.

"I've got my hands full at the moment," I told her.

"You promised to call yesterday, and you didn't. What am I supposed to tell Bobby Jensen about the opera next week?"

"Mom, I can't. Work has me pretty tied up."

Her side of the line was silent.

Ethan had his arms wrapped around me so I couldn't reach the phone.

"When then?" she asked.

"Mom, I can't talk now. I'll have to call you back another time."

"You'll call?"

"Yes, Mother. Now I really have to go."

"Rebecca, you will call this time?"

Her using my full name was Mom-talk for *you must call*.

"Sure, Mom. Bye."

"She sounds nice," Ethan said after the call terminated.

"Except when she's trying to set me up on some blind date."

"You can forgive her for worse than that. She means well, I'm sure. What's with the opera, though?"

"Mom is always going."

"Interesting."

CHAPTER 16

Rebecca

Three hours later, we were nearly ready to leave for dinner with Ethan's parents.

I twirled for him in the more-conservative black dress I'd picked for this occasion. "What do you think?"

Ethan rubbed his chin. "You really want to know?"

I cringed. That didn't bode well. "Of course," I lied. What I really wanted to hear was *"That's perfect."*

A smirk that hinted at a wise-ass comment appeared. "I think you're overdressed. I like the red one better."

I rolled my eyes. "You would."

Any guy with a pulse would. Where the red dress was daring and mouthwatering, this one was dull and proper, but elegantly so.

"Becky, you look perfect."

"I'm nervous," I admitted. This was a duke and duchess, for crying out loud.

"It's just me mum and dad. They're going to love you."

Not when they find out I'm there to figure out if they had anything to do with the stolen jewelry, they're not. I couldn't voice that without sounding either paranoid or bitchy or both.

Ethan came up and took my shoulders in his hands. "If you feel nervous, just hold my hand and squeeze." His eyes bored into me.

"Squeeze? Like that's gonna help."

"The alternative is you kiss me in front of my parents."

I could feel the blood drain from my face. "Got it. Hold hands. Don't kiss."

He spun me around. "Now, off with you to finish getting beautiful. I have to dress as well."

~

As we headed out on our journey, the rain that had been threatening all afternoon arrived with a vengeance. The windshield wipers worked hard to clear it and were losing the battle.

"We're here," Ethan announced as he turned down a tree-lined drive off the road.

The house came into view before long. The building was larger than the last Holiday Inn I'd stayed at.

"This is where you grew up?"

"Rainswood Manor. It's been in the family for generations, since shortly after the dukedom was created." Ethan shut off the car. "Ready?"

"Do I have a choice?" Looking past him, I could see the tree branches whipping in the increasing wind.

He didn't answer, but instead got out, ran around to my side with an umbrella, and opened my door. He helped me out and kept the umbrella centered over me, exposing one side of him to the huge raindrops.

The tall, wooden door opened as we ascended the steps.

"Good to see you again, Master Ethan," an old man said.

He was trim, with thinning gray hair. He held the door open as we entered. Apparently every duke's house came with a butler.

"It's good to be home again. Winston, I'd like to introduce my girlfriend, Rebecca Sommerset."

Winston bowed his head. "A pleasure, Miss Sommerset."

"Rebecca, please," I corrected him.

"Welcome to Rainswood Manor, Miss Sommerset. May I take your coat?"

I wiggled out of the small thing and handed it to him.

"Your parents are in the library." He started off down the hallway.

Lesson number one: apparently first names weren't appropriate. I swallowed hard and followed Ethan and Winston.

The room we entered was huge—two stories tall—with bookshelves lining the walls and a rolling ladder to reach the upper shelves. There were enough books to keep someone busy for years, if not a lifetime.

"There you are, Ethan. It's been too long," said the man who rose from the chair. "Your mother was worried you might cancel on account of the weather."

His mother and I must have been on the same wavelength about the storm.

"Dad, it's been three weeks," Ethan told his father as they hugged. Ethan also hugged his mother before putting a hand at my back. "I'd like to introduce the special lady in my life, Rebecca Sommerset."

His father took the hand I offered in both of his and squeezed, more than a handshake, and less than a hug. "Welcome to Rainswood, Rebecca."

"Thank you, your grace."

The old man scoffed. "Nonsense. Unless Ethan marries you and you call me Dad, I insist on Carter."

I felt heat in my cheeks at the implication Ethan could feel that way about me.

"Don't be pressuring Ethan now," his wife said before giving me a similar two-handed shake. "You look lovely, dear, and please call me Diane."

"You have a lovely home," I responded, unsure about using the informal names they'd suggested.

"Have you heard from Charlie?" Ethan's mother asked him.

Ethan put his arm around me. "Not for a while now."

"His mobile isn't picking up," she complained.

"He must be back in Africa," Ethan said without a hitch.

I didn't need to see his face to know it was a lie. He'd just told his parents something patently false. Where Charlie had gone was a secret he'd shared with me last night.

"Di, he'll surface again when he's ready," Carter said.

Winston reentered the room. "When would you like supper served, mum?"

Ethan spoke first. "Perhaps I could have a few minutes to show Becky around?"

"Certainly. We're still expecting Winnie and Ophelia back from town," his mother responded as she checked her watch. "Twenty minutes would be good if we could, Winston."

"Yes, mum. I'll tell Karen," he said before retreating.

I looked over at Ethan, who whispered, "Our cook," to my implied question.

"The girls are staying with us for several weeks while their father is traveling," his mother explained.

A minute later, Ethan started our tour and spoke into his phone. "Set a timer for fifteen minutes."

"She said twenty," I pointed out.

"We need to be early."

The penalty for being late to the table must've been something horrendous.

We toured the downstairs first, and Ethan mentioned room after room—drawing room, smoking room, sun room, and two others I didn't catch as I was taking in the size of the place. The ballroom was a name I recognized, and it looked like it belonged in a convention center.

"The parties are held in here," he said.

I was stunned at each turn by the spaciousness of everything from the carved marble fireplace mantles to the vista of grass and woods out the windows in all directions. The estate had to be a hundred acres at least. Only one building was within view. The rain and wind were picking up.

"Who are Winnie and Ophelia?" I asked.

Ethan did his version of an eye roll. "Cousins. The most gossipy girls you'll ever meet." He pointed to the nearby building. "Our stables."

Of course. What English aristocrat's house would be complete without its own stables?

Gossipy relatives could be a problem since we didn't have our act down so well. "Your mother only mentioned the girls' father."

"Yes. Uncle Jeremy."

I guessed this was a divorce situation. "Why don't they stay with their mother when their dad is away?"

"Their mother has been out of the picture for a few years. It's better for everybody that way." He strode toward the stairs.

I followed him up, feeling sorry for the girls I hadn't yet met who had to go through life without a mother. People talked about how boys needed a father figure to emulate, and I felt the same way about girls and their mother.

"And this is my room, or rather *was* my room," Ethan said as he opened another door.

Room wasn't the right description. It was a suite, complete with not only an attached bath, but a sitting room with corner windows, and a small office with a desk.

"Cozy," I murmured. The main bedroom alone was larger than Lizzy's apartment in town.

"If it seems ostentatious, blame my ancestors. It was the style of the time when this was constructed."

I could get used to this style, if it wasn't so far removed from the city. I closed the door to the hallway behind us. "You know this is a problem, right?"

"What is a problem?"

"Your cousins. I thought we only had to fool your mother and father tonight. We haven't rehearsed any of this."

"Just follow my lead."

"It's not that simple."

"Yes, it is." He turned and those eyes looked right through me again. "How do you feel about me?"

I wasn't prepared for the question. "I wish you wouldn't keep secrets from me," I said after a moment.

He pointed a finger at me with a scowl. "Wrong answer. I have great affection for you, Rebecca."

I closed my eyes to block his gaze and listened for the tirade to follow.

"I've missed you since the day you left years ago. But I hadn't realized how much until I bumped into you again. As you Americans would say, I'm head over heels for you. Now, how do you feel about me?"

Confused, I opened my eyes again. Without watching, I hadn't been able to judge those last sentences, but they'd sounded sincere enough for our purposes.

Taking a breath, I started my story. "When I was here at college, I fell for you, but I didn't realize how hard." I hoped I was catching on. "Not until after I left and missed you terribly. I was crushed that somehow we got our wires crossed or I would have been back sooner. Now that we've reconnected, I couldn't be happier. You're the one man who ever made me truly happy."

He nodded. "That's the idea."

The words had been harder to speak than to come up with, because it was all pretty much the truth—all except me not knowing how much I missed him until later. In truth, the breakup had instantly torn me apart. Ethan had taken a long time to get over.

"You can sell that, can't you?" he asked.

I didn't formulate an answer quickly enough.

His phone alarm went off. "Time to go." He strode quickly to the door and held it open for me. "You'll do fine."

I took his arm as we walked down the stairs. All I had to figure out now was what part of his speech had been sincere—if any of it. That, and how much of what I'd said was truer than I wanted to admit.

He led me into the dining hall. Instead of going to the long table and standing by one of the place settings, he took me to the far wall. A large grandfather clock ticked loudly next to us.

"Are we early enough for you?" I asked.

Girlish laughter came from the hallway.

"We're right on time," Ethan said as he backed me up. "Play along."

My back hit the bookshelves on the wall. "With what?"

He came closer and caged me with a hand on either side. "With this." He leaned in.

I closed my eyes when his lips met mine as they had years ago.

He took control of the kiss.

I gave it willingly.

His tongue stroked my lips.

I opened for him and gave him the access he desired. I'd forgotten what kissing him was like. My hands wrapped around him as I pulled him closer for more contact, more warmth.

Ethan smelled of the spice I'd thought I'd forgotten, and I was instantly transported back to a happier time—a picnic on the grass with him on a college weekend. The sound of the clock gave way to the sound of blood rushing in my ears and eager panting as we traded breath.

He pulled me tighter with one hand and the other glided up my side to caress the underside of my breast with his thumb as he'd done so many times before. Such a light touch with such meaning. It had been a language between the two of us back then—a language full of strong feelings and implied hope for the future.

The firmness of Big Ben's arousal in his pants also spoke to his desire for me.

A cough sounded behind him.

He jerked away and wiped his mouth with his sleeve.

I smoothed my dress and patted my lips.

Ethan took my hand and led me toward two young women—who wore grins that meant they thought we were a real couple. "Rebecca, I'd like to introduce my cousins, Winifred and Ophelia."

"Winnie, please," one of them objected.

We shook with pleasantries back and forth.

"Hope we weren't interrupting anything important." Ophelia giggled.

I caught a wink from Winnie.

"We were merely examining some of the newer volumes," Ethan said, waving his hand toward the bookcase that had hosted our make-out session.

Ophelia giggled again.

"Girls, I see you've met Ethan's lady friend," Diane said as she entered with Ethan's father.

In a minute, we were all seated at one end of the long table, which could easily have seated twenty. I sat next to Ethan with Winnie on my other side and Ophelia and Diane opposite us. Carter took the end chair.

Winston and Karen, their cook, brought in the soup to start, and the questioning soon began.

"We saw the morning paper," Winnie said with a grin. "That was quite a dress."

"Ethan picked it out," I told her.

"Is the food there as good as they say?" Ophelia asked.

"I'm not sure," Ethan told her, leaning over to join our conversation.

Ophelia cocked her head.

"I was so mesmerized by Becky all evening, I don't even recall the meal."

My blush matched the one rising in Ophelia.

Ethan merely smiled.

"Carter," Diane said. "You should listen up and take some lessons in complimenting a woman from your son."

"Yes, dear," he said between sips of water.

"Someday I want to wear a dress like that," Ophelia said softly to Ethan's mother.

Winnie nodded along.

Ethan pretended not to have caught it.

We got to the main course before the question of my relationship with Ethan came up.

"I'm back in town on business," I said, answering Diane's question.

"Which business would that be?" Carter asked.

"I'm in insurance."

Winnie nudged me. "I hope it's more exciting than it sounds."

"Sometimes," I admitted.

The plate in front of me held three small, sickly chickens on a bed of rice with florets of broccoli. Maybe the English weather wasn't good for growing chickens? Either that or they didn't let them get full grown.

"Quail," Ethan explained when he noticed my expression.

"Oh."

Ophelia was already devouring her first bird. "What do you do for them?"

I couldn't think of a reason to not be honest about it. "I'm an investigator."

"Investigating what?" Winnie asked.

"Not everyone we deal with is completely honest," I said as I cut into the first scrawny bird on my plate.

"Insurance fraud," Winnie told Ophelia.

"I know that," Ophelia shot back. "And you catch them?"

I nodded as I chewed the first bit of quail.

Winnie raised a brow. "How?"

"She catches the liars," Ethan answered for me. "She can spot a liar at twenty paces."

Winnie persisted. "How?"

I shrugged. "I can tell." I didn't want to get more specific.

Diane rescued me from more interrogation. "Rebecca, is this transfer to London for the long term?"

I hadn't thought this through. "I'm being considered for a promotion that would put me here." At least half of that sentence was correct.

Ethan cocked an eyebrow.

During dinner, Ethan brought up the parties his mother had been hosting, but the conversation got side-tracked.

Karen wandered in to refresh our glasses. Her face was sour.

The answers to Ethan's generalized questions didn't give us any relevant information that I could discern.

Winnie leaned over. "What does he call you?"

"Pardon?"

"What nickname does he have for you?"

I shrugged. "Becks."

She leaned close to whisper to me. "No, I mean the crazy-sweet pet name for you. Mary-Madeline was Sugarplum, Patricia was Cookie, and the girl before her—I forget her name—was Cupcake. What's yours?"

This girl was odd with a capital O.

I had no intention of being a food, if Becks didn't satisfy her. I thought back to our meeting at the hospital. "Sunshine. When he doesn't call me Becky or Becks, it's Sunshine."

Winnie giggled. "That's so sweet."

"What is?" Ethan asked leaning toward us.

"Sunshine, your nickname for me," I told him. "The one that shows you care."

Ethan's hand slid under the table to my thigh. "Right. Sunshine." He grinned. "She wanted to be Snuggle Bunny, but I thought it was too long."

I elbowed him. "I did not." The words were all I could manage as my brain focused on the feel of his hand on my leg.

His fingers hiked up my skirt enough to touch bare skin.

I couldn't control my slight gasp.

"Snuggle Bunny is way too long," he said.

The skin-to-skin contact heated me too much to argue the point. I closed my eyes for a second to concentrate.

"How did you meet?" Ophelia asked.

I blinked a few times, trying to comprehend the question.

Ethan chewed. His nod to me was his suggestion that I answer.

I took a deep breath to clear my head of naked-Ethan thoughts and started. "We first met years ago when I was here at Imperial College for a semester." Just saying that brought back memories of languid afternoons together followed by steamy nights.

Winnie looked up from mangling the bird in front of her. "That long ago?"

Ophelia wouldn't be left out. "What happened?"

Ethan withdrew his hand. "Nothing. The semester was over, and she went back to her school in California."

His answer to her question felt as cold as my leg did now without his hand.

"Did you keep in touch?" Ophelia asked.

Ethan's mother perked up at the question.

His father's wine halted halfway to his lips, awaiting the answer he surely knew.

"No," Ethan told her. "We got our wires crossed, and she was crushed when I didn't reach out." Ethan had remembered my line from up in his bedroom.

I put down my fork and slid my hand under the table to his thigh. Two could play this game. "And…"

Ethan's glance was part interest, part terror. He clearly worried I'd reveal to his family how cold he'd been when we'd parted ways.

I clawed his leg with my nails. "I didn't realize how much I'd missed him until we bumped into each other again. Ethan promised me we'd straighten out our prior miscommunication, and that was all it took to convince me to dine with him again." I dug my nails in harder. "And here we are."

Ethan winced enough for me to catch. "We agreed to clear things up, and here we are."

I released my tigress grip on his leg. I would hold him to his promise of communication.

"She didn't realize I'd missed her since the day she left," Ethan said, smiling at me. "She never knew how much." He leaned over and kissed me. "Now I get a chance to show her."

That forced another blush out of Ophelia. "Getting back together after several years sounds so romantic."

Diane fixed Ethan with a glare. "Think of how much more wonderful it would have been without the miscommunication and separation."

Agreeing with his mother, I patted Ethan's leg and looked up at him with a smile and a nod.

Carter came to his son's defense. "Water under the bridge at this point."

Typical male perspective.

With a bang, the wind propelled something against the window behind Diane, and she jumped in her seat. "Getting nasty out there," she said, looking over her shoulder.

"I'll say," Carter agreed. "Reminds me of the big storm two years ago. Tree branches breaking in the wind everywhere."

Ethan leaned over to explain. "Lost power for two days."

"Not to worry. This old house has seen worse," Carter added.

"Are you sure you want to drive back to town in this?" his mother asked.

"We'll be fine," Ethan insisted. "It's an English car, built for English weather."

The car might keep the water out, but with the way the rain was beating against the windows, I was pretty sure we'd be soaked before we got to it. The umbrellas would be next to useless.

His mother continued, "I was just thinking—"

"We'll be leaving," Ethan said firmly.

His mother's face fell.

"But not just yet. Right, darling?" I looked up at Ethan, hoping he wouldn't screw this up and disappoint his mother.

"Of course not, Sunshine. After a bit."

His mother smiled.

CHAPTER 17

Ethan

Dinner had gone quite well so far.

Becky's performance had been exemplary, fooling not only my cousins, but me as well into thinking for a moment that she still truly cared. Unfortunately, I now knew anger was her predominant feeling. The claws digging into my leg earlier had made that crystal clear.

The wind outside kept up and seemed only to increase. The trip home was going to take much longer than the one here.

Under the tablecloth, I let my hand rest on Becky's leg again.

She glanced my way with a smile I hoped was genuine. She had an easygoing way about her that put others at ease.

I hadn't expected her to win over Winnie and Ophelia so quickly, but she had. Their conversation had drifted to the stables, and the girls had gotten into a long discussion of horses and riding.

All the while, I'd let my fingers rub tiny circles on Becky's thigh. The warm smile on her face when she sent glances back to me was reward enough.

When we'd been together at college, we'd spent the occasional dinner with friends, and each time, she'd been the way she was now: engaging others in conversation on various topics of mutual interest.

Becky put her wine glass down. "Ethan tells me you throw the most marvelous parties here."

Mom's face glowed. "We do try."

Ophelia perked up. "You should come to the next one. Auntie Diane does such a nice job."

Mom did do a fabulous job hosting parties, but Ophelia was laying it on a little thick, no doubt making sure she got invited as well.

Mom looked my way. "Yes, Ethan, you and Rebecca must come."

Becky put a hand on my shoulder and looked up with the most sincere smile. "I'd love to. What do you think, Ethan? Can you spare the time away from work?"

I returned her look in kind. "Certainly, Sunshine."

Becky had managed to get us an invitation without me even having to ask.

"Auntie Diane has more parties here than anyone around," Winnie said.

"Why is that?" Becky asked.

Winnie pointed to her left. "Because Rainswood has the biggest ballroom."

"That must keep you quite busy," Becky said to my mother.

"It's no bother," she answered.

Dad looked out the window, smart enough to keep out of this conversation.

"We only host two of them ourselves," Mom explained. "The other six are put on by ladies who don't have quite the venue we do. We merely provide the location."

That wouldn't be how the press would portray it if the news of the jewelry thefts here became public.

Ophelia added, "The ballroom here is the largest in fifty miles."

"The original duke," Dad began, "wasn't one to be outdone. He nearly went broke in the process of building this place. And now the heating bill alone is enough to make one weep."

"You love it, though," Mom replied.

Dad nodded. "It grows on one." He looked squarely at me. "Passing this place and the land on to the next generation of Blakewells is my solemn responsibility."

Mom placed her hand on Dad's with a loving smile.

"Family is everything, and a family needs a place to call home, a place that provides roots and connects one to history," he said. "This building will last a thousand years and be home to many more dukes and duchesses of Lassiter to come. The Blakewell name will live on. It must. Tradition is what makes this country special."

Inside I cringed. One slipup and he could be the final duke to call this place home.

Becky looked up at me admiringly, not understanding the import of Dad's proclamation. I leaned over. "He means Charlie," I whispered to her.

Her hand on my thigh was warm and comforting. "I'm sure he loves you both the same," she whispered back.

My cousins were oblivious, but Mom nodded, having heard us most likely.

∼

Rebecca

The pain in Ethan's eyes was obvious when his father made the pronouncement.

The elder Blakewell said he would be passing the estate and its grounds on to the next generation of Blakewells.

I kept my hand on Ethan's leg as his father talked. I hoped I could pass some strength to him through my touch.

Since the archaic laws of succession of old England deemed only the eldest male heir to be worthy—even if he was older by just a few minutes—that meant all this would be going to Ethan's older brother. When I'd told him his father surely loved him as much as he did Charlie, to say nothing of his sister, Kelsey, his expression wasn't what I'd hoped for.

That would be another thing I needed to get him to open up to me about, when we got to that point. And it wouldn't be tonight. I just wanted to help him be at peace with it.

Ophelia seemed to sense the unease of the conversation. "Rebecca, maybe we could get together for lunch sometime next week."

Some of the tenseness in Ethan's leg dissipated as she spoke.

I nodded as I patted his thigh under the table. "I'd like that. Then you can tell me all the secrets he's been hiding from me."

When I glanced over, those words had broken the frown from Ethan's face. He waved a finger at his cousin. "I'd be careful, if I were you."

"I've got some juicy ones," Ophelia told me.

"For the price of the lunch, I've got a few too," Winnie offered.

Both girls laughed.

Ethan pulled the napkin from his lap and placed it on the table. "With all the rain, I'm afraid it may be rather slow going getting back to town, so we best shove off now."

"Do you want to borrow the Range Rover?" Ophelia asked.

"Are you sure you won't stay the night?" his mother added. "We could make up some rooms."

Ethan pushed back from the table, and I removed my hand lest anybody see it. "No. I've got work in the morning."

I nodded. "I do as well."

Ethan stood, and I joined him.

Winston appeared out of nowhere to clear the table as we all rose and made our way to the door.

"You didn't bring a heavier coat?" Diane asked as I got into the thin, waist-length thing I'd chosen because it matched my dress. It wasn't going to be much of a match for the downpour outside.

"California girl," I told her. "We don't get many storms like this."

"I'll have to train her," Ethan said as he held the umbrella at the ready.

"Thank you so much for dinner tonight," I told his mother.

I received hugs from his parents, followed by his cousins.

"Drive carefully now," his father cautioned us.

Winnie pulled out her phone and showed it to Ophelia. The girls giggled as Winnie typed something.

Winston opened the door to the gale outside.

Ethan ventured out and opened the umbrella.

I pulled up my collar and followed him. I'd been right about the umbrella. The rain was almost horizontal, and the umbrella barely kept my face dry.

We trotted through the puddles to the car.

Ethan closed me in first and then rushed around to his side. Tilting the umbrella while he opened the door allowed the wind to catch it and turn it inside out. After wrestling with it for a few seconds, he got what was left of it stuffed behind his seat and settled into the rain-soaked leather.

"This is quite a storm."

"A real frog-strangler," I told him, since he liked to learn Americanisms.

"Very apt. You're probably right that not even the frogs are enjoying this." He pressed the start button, and the big engine began its throaty rumble. With lights and full wipers, we began our trek toward the main road.

Totally soaked, I reached for the climate control and turned the heat on my side up high.

"That won't do much until the motor warms up."

"Then heat it up," I complained as I shivered.

"Okay." Ethan sped up.

I couldn't see much out the windshield. Even on high, the wipers were no match for the downpour. "You should slow down."

"The only way to get heat is to put a load on the motor," he said, hunched forward over the wheel.

Once again, going fast turned out to be my fault.

"Shit." He jammed on the brakes, and we came to a quick halt.

A tree showed in the headlights. It lay across the drive, only a few feet in front of us.

"So much for getting back to town tonight," he told me.

"Can we go around it?"

He chuckled.

I didn't see the humor in my question.

"Not in this car. We'd get stuck in the mud." He put the Aston Martin in reverse and started backing toward the house. "I don't even think I'd chance it in the Range Rover tonight."

He backed up a little fast for my taste. I looked behind us, and without a wiper on the back window I could see even less in that direction. "Maybe you should turn around."

"The drive is not very wide."

"But at least you'd be able to see," I argued.

He stopped the car. "Maybe you want to drive?"

I shook my head. "No. I just thought…" I decided against finishing the sentence and getting in more trouble.

He started again, but yanked the wheel to the right, stopped, started forward a few feet turning left, and reversed again.

I smiled, knowing my logic had prevailed.

He turned left again and started forward. The engine accelerated, and the whirring sound of spinning wheels came from behind us.

The car had gotten stuck in the mud and suddenly, my logic didn't look so great anymore. "Maybe you should rock it."

He tried forward and back to no avail. The wheels spun in the mud. He hit the steering wheel. "Bloody hell."

"Sorry," I said sheepishly.

"Not your fault, Rebecca. I'm the driver." He hit the steering wheel again.

Heat had just started to come out of the vents when we got stuck, and we were a long way from the house.

"Now what?" I asked. "Should we call them?"

"We walk back."

"In these shoes?" My question struck me as childish as soon as I asked it, but what was the choice? Barefoot?

He just looked at me and shrugged. "We could spend the night in the car. The heat is working now."

I groaned and waited for him to make the first move.

"We don't have a choice, Sunshine." My new nickname wasn't bringing me good luck. He shut down the engine and opened his door.

I climbed out my side. This was what I imagined it felt like standing under a cold waterfall.

Ethan turned on the flashlight on his phone to give us light to stay on the road back to the house. We were both soaked to the bone by the time we made it to the door. I was freezing cold.

Winston heard us come in and shuffled up. "Master Ethan has returned," he announced loudly. He held his hand out. "Your coat, Miss Sommerset."

"I'll keep it on, thank you, until I warm up." It was sopping wet all the way through.

"Very well, Miss Sommerset."

Ophelia and Winnie were the first to arrive.

"A tree is down on the drive. Nobody is leaving tonight," Ethan said.

Ethan's parents arrived, and Ophelia gave them the bad news.

Diane nodded. "Well, it looks as if you're staying over after all." She turned to Winston. "Is the Green Room presentable enough for a guest?"

Evidently, this house had rooms named for colors, just like the White House.

"Yes, mum," Winston assured her.

Diane looked at me. "Let me show you to your room."

Carter grabbed her arm. "Di, it's the new millennium. Rebecca can stay with Ethan, if she chooses."

They both watched for my reaction.

I couldn't break our cover. I put my arm around Ethan and pulled myself close, signaling my choice. "Thank you."

A night with Ethan and me in the same room with one bed was more dangerous than anything I'd envisioned on this assignment.

My fake boyfriend smiled down at me as he pulled me tightly against his warmth.

Dangerous warmth.

CHAPTER 18

ETHAN

"You two look like drowned rats," Mom said. "You should get out of those wet clothes before you catch your death of cold."

Now I was totally screwed. Our fake kiss to throw off the cousins had gotten much too heated much too quickly. And now my mother wanted me to get undressed with Becky?

Becky's lips were an elixir I couldn't get enough of, to say nothing of the rest of her. She was temptation wrapped in a wet dress, and would be seriously dangerous once it came off.

Even shivering in cold, wet clothes, just the feel of her against me had my lizard brain remembering what it had been like to be with her. Those were dangerous thoughts, thoughts that could lead to passion when instead I absolutely had to keep my wits about me. My secrets were too important to be revealed in a moment of weakness—and around her I was definitely weak.

"I'm freezing," Becky said as those doe eyes looked up at me. She moved toward the stairs.

The cousins started up. Becky pulled me after them.

At the top, Winnie turned and winked at me. "See you in the morning."

"Don't stay up too late," Ophelia added with a giggle before continuing to her room.

When I put my arm around my fake date again, her shivering had worsened. "We have to get you warmed up." I guided her toward my room.

More giggles came from the girls.

I closed the door to my bedroom firmly behind us. "You're freezing."

"That's what I've been saying."

"Into the shower with you." I pointed to the bathroom door.

"That's the best thing I've heard all night."

I followed her into the bathroom. "You'll need help with—"

She cut me off. "If you unzip me, I'm sure I can manage the rest." She turned around, still shivering, but it was her right to be surprised.

I pulled the zipper down slowly. She was icy cold as my knuckles grazed her skin. At the bottom of the zipper's range, I got a glimpse of a pink thong that matched her bra, which sent a twitch to my cock.

She held her dress up at the shoulders "Thank you." She turned toward me when I didn't move. "A little privacy, please." She waved me back.

I turned to leave. "Yell if you need anything."

After closing the door behind me, I started counting the seconds. My mental bet was thirty before she called for help.

I started taking off my wet shoes, followed by my clothes. I got down to my trousers before the yell came from the other side of the door.

"Ethan?"

It was five seconds later than I'd expected. I opened the door and walked in, and the sight was more than I'd expected.

Becky was naked in the glass shower enclosure, covering herself. "I can't get the water on." Her skin was pale, bordering on blue from the cold.

I strode to the shower and undid my belt. "I tried to warn you."

"Can you help me, please?"

I pulled down my zipper and worked the recalcitrant, wet fabric of my trousers down.

"What are you doing?"

"You asked for help, but I'm not getting my clothes any wetter than they already are." I managed to step out of my trousers but kept my underpants on. They were also soaking wet and cold enough to shrivel my balls to nothingness.

She moved aside when I pulled opened the glass door.

"You may want to get out for a second."

She looked at me and shook her head. "No way. Not naked."

I stepped inside and closed the door behind me. "Your choice."

This shower was tiny compared to the one in my London flat, but that's what came with retrofitting running water into a building as old as this.

I grabbed the sticky water control and tried to turn it with one hand. It didn't budge. "These valves are older than I am and pretty stiff."

She just shook her head like I didn't know what I was talking about. "Maybe you need to go to the gym."

When I applied two hands, the handle moved, and water spurted out of the shower head—cold water.

Becky yelped, turned, and jumped away from the cold stream—right into me.

I wrapped my arms around her and pulled her as far from the frigid spray as the space would allow. "It takes a minute to warm up."

"Now you tell me," she mumbled into my shoulder. She pulled her arms from between us and wrapped them behind me to get farther from the cold. "This is even colder than outside."

Slowly the water warmed.

Without letting go of her, I shuffled us back under the stream, giving her all the warm spray.

"That's better," she murmured as I turned us a little one direction and then the other to get both sides of her under the hot water.

She looked up. "You need some too." She tried to turn us farther.

"No. You need it more." I kissed the top of her head.

Big mistake.

She pulled me closer, and her hand behind me moved down, closer to my arse.

Although her chest up against me was ice cold, the feeling of her soft body against mine was perfect, and lighting a fire in me.

I turned us to the side and lessened my grip enough to create space for the water to run between us, and I made the mistake of looking down. I slammed my eyes shut, but it was too late. The image of her knockers up against me had burned into my retinas. I remembered all too vividly how her marvelous boobs felt in my hands. The vision made my cock surge from frozen mini wiener to alive and pressing against her.

She must have felt my reaction and moved her hand down to grab my ass. "You really need the water, Ethan. You're freezing cold."

I opened my eyes, but kept my gaze up. "You're the one who needs it more, Sunshine, you're frigid."

"You're calling me frigid?" Her tone was indignant.

"Poor choice of words. I only meant you need warming up." I turned us again so the water hit from the other side.

"Yeah. You're already warmed up, or is that a banana in your pants?"

I changed our position and put her head under the water for that comment.

She pushed to the side and came up sputtering. "Hey. It's the truth."

I put her head under the water again.

"I get it. Shut up," she sputtered.

With a rocking motion, as if we were dancing, I started us turning under the spray all the way around. The warm water on my back and down my legs was a welcome relief.

I ran my hand up her back as we turned. Her skin had thawed. "Are you warming up?"

She laid her head against my shoulder. "Getting there. You're still colder than me."

"You're the priority," I told her.

Her arms tightened around me. "Can I tell you something?"

I took a chance. "Sure."

We rocked under the water without words.

"I wanted to say…" It took her a few seconds to complete the sentence. "Just, thank you."

I couldn't resist kissing the top of her head again. "For what? Almost crashing into a downed tree or getting you almost frozen to death?"

We made another turn under the water before she answered. "For caring."

The words took my breath away. I did care, and that was a big problem.

I stepped back and turned away. "What would the superintendent say if I let my partner freeze to death?"

I pushed out of the shower and closed the door behind me. My job was done here.

∾

Rebecca

. . .

He closed the glass door behind him and walked to the towels on the rack.

I'd blown it.

Again.

He'd been honest before when he said he hadn't meant to hurt me years ago.

I'd seen it in his face, but instead of admitting the truth, I'd reacted petulantly by saying I couldn't believe him.

He turned to the side, and the erection in his boxer briefs was apparent. I smiled that I could still have that effect on him. He'd had the same effect on me, but he couldn't see the way being held by him had excited me tonight.

My nipples were pebbled as I watched him dry off, and not from the cold anymore. Even freezing cold, in his arms was where I belonged.

He glanced my way as he toweled off his hair.

I turned under the water and made no effort to hide myself. It wasn't anything he hadn't seen before, and there was no reason to hide from him any longer.

A slight smile came across his lips before he looked away.

I'd guessed at his feelings just now, and his reaction to my vocalizing them told me I was spot on. He didn't need to answer in words for me to know I'd been right.

I just still didn't understand what drove him to push me away—back then or now.

A minute later, he was dried off. "Let me know when you're done, and I'll turn off the water for you," he said as he opened the door to leave.

"Thank you," I said as I turned to face him, naked both physically and emotionally.

The door closed behind him, and I was alone again, trying to figure out what had just happened.

Our words could contain lies, or hide the truth, but our bodies had communicated our subconscious feelings for each other in a way that didn't deceive.

At the time, I hadn't been able to decode the kiss downstairs before dinner—how much of it had been real and how much of it had been an act for his cousins and his parents.

Now I knew the kiss had been much more real than fake. I'd sensed it as he held me under the water. His touch had been warm and caring. Our nonverbal communication had been true to our feelings. And I hadn't wanted it to end.

Ethan had been caring, sensitive, even romantic in a crazy way, right up until I'd tried to put words to what was happening. Then he left.

It seemed talking about us in the now was as sensitive a topic for him as talking about our past.

I turned one last time under the warm water before leaving the shower. After drying off, I wrapped one towel around myself and the other around my head to deal with my wet hair.

My dress went on a towel hook to dry before I opened the door to the bedroom. "I'm done."

Ethan was on the far side of the room in a bathrobe. "Feel better?" he asked as he passed me to go turn off the shower.

"Much." I didn't dare use any extra words, lest I admit something I shouldn't.

A few squeaks from the difficult water valves came from the bathroom followed by silence.

Ethan returned to the bedroom. "Sorry about the difficulty with the water. I should mention that to Dad."

"No. I don't want to complain. Let's just agree that it gives the house character." The large bed loomed in front of me.

Before I could even ask, Ethan said, "I'll take the sofa. You can have the bed."

"Don't be silly." I was proud of using the word *silly*. It sounded almost British. "This is your room; you should take the bed."

He huffed and strode over to the couch, where he'd already placed a blanket. "You Americans have the oddest lack of common courtesy. You're the guest. You take the bed."

The couch was closer to a loveseat than an actual couch and couldn't possibly fit him. "That's much too small for you, but I could fit there."

"Sunshine, why do you have to argue about everything?" He said it more as an accusation than a real question.

"I'm just being practical." I put my hands on my hips. "Darling."

"You're being ornery." He picked up the blanket and tried to situate himself on the couch. "Sunshine."

It was comical to watch, and I couldn't hold back my laughter. "I told you." I moved to the bed and sat on one side. "It's big enough for both of us."

"A gentleman would take the sofa."

"And a lady would not let her gentleman be so uncomfortable," I shot back.

"You're still arguing."

"Only because I'm right."

He unfolded from the couch. "Okay, already. If it'll get you to stop arguing."

I faced the next problem. "Do you have anything I could sleep in?"

"Sure." He opened a dresser drawer and threw me a T-shirt. "Will that do, Sunshine?"

"Perfect, darling," I responded before going back into the bathroom to change into it.

When I came out, the bathrobe had disappeared, and Ethan stood in a dry pair of boxer briefs, which showed the outline of him.

"Which side do you prefer, Sunshine?" The sarcasm showed he hadn't completely given up the fight.

I always slept on the left side of my bed at home. "Either. Your house, your choice." I intentionally left *darling* off my response.

He passed me on the way to the bathroom. "Choose."

I climbed under the covers on the left-hand side.

He returned with a rolled-up towel and walked to the door to turn off the lights. With no streetlights this far into the countryside, and the storm howling outside, the room went pitch dark.

The sight of the rolled-up towel sent my mind back five years to me stuffing a towel like that under my hips as he entered me from behind. I almost combusted at the memory.

"Shit." He bumped into the bed. "Shit, shit, shit, shit."

"Don't hurt yourself." His potential injury pulled my mind away from the sensual image I'd conjured.

"Damn. You'd think I could manage my own bedroom in the dark."

I wanted to say something about his mind being occupied, like mine was, but I held back the words. I felt the mattress shift. I considered offering to kiss it to make it better, but thought better of that as well.

He pulled the covers back in the dark.

I shivered with anticipation as I waited for his hand to reach out to me. It didn't.

The rolled-up towel settled in lengthwise against my arm. My longing, it seemed, had been one-sided.

"What's this for?" I asked.

"I thought it would make you feel safer."

Disappointed was more like it, or perhaps *frustrated*. "You didn't need to," I told him.

Ethan had proven himself the gentleman at every turn. Here he was trying to make me feel safe sharing a bed with him while I was fantasizing about how wonderful it would be to have him jump my bones.

"A gentleman should make his lady feel safe," he said.

He didn't realize how unladylike my thoughts had been.

It was now or never. "Ethan, we're both adults here." It was as close to an invitation as I thought I could manage and stay ladylike.

"We're coworkers here," he corrected me. "Sleep well, Sunshine." With those words, he doomed me to a night of frustration.

Fifteen minutes later, by my estimation, his breathing settled into the rhythmic pattern of sleep.

I'd missed an opportunity in the shower to tell him how I felt, and how I believed him when he said he hadn't wanted to hurt me. The more I thought about it, the more I regretted my words.

He'd hurt me before, and my residual anger at that led me to tell him I didn't believe him. But it was my job to detect lies, and he hadn't.

I concentrated on his breathing, and eventually sleep overtook me.

CHAPTER 19

ETHAN

Light filtering in past the drapes slowly woke me, but the hair in my face kept the vision blurry.

I froze when I realized it was Becky's hair in front of me, and I was draped half over her.

The towel between us kept my morning wood from poking her, but I had my arm over her, and that was definitely not good.

Her hand lay over mine.

At least my underpants were still on, and I hadn't done anything more reckless in my sleep than hold her.

Maybe I could get out of this without waking her. I started to pull my hand away.

She pulled it back. "No," she mumbled.

I couldn't tell if she was fully awake or not. "I need my arm, Becks."

"Uh-uh," she mumbled. "Keep warm."

I gave up for the moment and resisted the urge to stroke her through the cotton.

She giggled. "And the name is Sunshine." She'd been playing me.

I yanked my arm back. "Sorry, I didn't mean to—"

"Darling, you're cute when you get flustered."

"I am not flustered. I'm apologizing."

She rolled over toward me. "No need. You kept me warm like a gentleman would."

I didn't feel like a gentleman. I felt like an opportunist.

Suddenly it was her arm over me, pulling me toward her. "I have something to confess."

"I'm listening."

Her fingernails scratched my back the way she knew I liked. "I do believe you."

My brain was still sluggish. "About what?"

She pulled me tighter and moved her face to mine, our noses touching as she looked into my eyes. "I do believe that you didn't mean to hurt me." She moved closer and her lips touched mine in the briefest kiss before she pulled back.

I was tempted to grab this opening as the proposition she probably intended, but I held back. "What does that mean?" I was going to make her be absolutely clear. I didn't want anything that would worsen the trauma I'd inflicted on her before.

Five years ago, outside events had forced my hand and made the outcome unavoidable. She needed to understand my limits before we traveled that road again.

She pulled back slightly and tapped my nose with her finger. "It means…" She tapped my nose again. "That I'm still attracted to you." She tapped my nose a third time. "And I can tell you're still attracted to me."

"Or again," I said.

"Or again." She repeated tapping my nose. "We're both adults here."

"And what does that mean?" Hurting her again due to unclear expectations would be unconscionable.

"Do I have to spell it out for you? Are you dense, or just ornery?"

"Probably both." My cock had hardened to granite. I was already a goner.

"We both know I'm going back to San Francisco when this is over. I don't expect anything more, but in the meantime." Her hand slid down to my engorged cock. "Does Big Ben want to play?" My heart raced at the touch. "Consenting adults can enjoy each other's company…"

My mouth was on hers before she could finish the sentence.

She'd been right when she'd said I wanted her, and I was going to show her just how much. I pulled her hand away from my cock and yanked the towel out from between us to the top of the bed. The feel of her hot flesh against mine was almost too much.

I pulled back from the kiss. "I'm not sure this is a good idea."

"I am." Her nails scratched at my back. "Please."

The feel of her breast in my palm brought back memories of hours with her naked next to me. As much as it would kill me, I would make sure we took it slow. It was what I owed her.

∼

REBECCA

HE WAS SO TENTATIVE WITH HIS SLOW CIRCLING OF MY BREAST AND THUMBING OF MY nipple. He wasn't getting the message that I was ready and more than willing.

I pulled on his hip to roll him toward me. "In case you haven't figured it out, Einstein, I want you to shag me like there's no tomorrow."

His eyes bored into me. "In time, Sunshine. But you have to be quiet."

A hand traveled up my inner thigh. I spread my legs and gasped as his fingers finally parted my soaked slit.

"Quiet," he said as he licked my breast, circling my nipple and blowing little shivers on my wet skin.

I jerked as a single finger entered me, retreated, and moved to circle my clit, sending sparks through my whole body. I gave in to him and scratched his scalp with one hand and his back with the other.

"Still, Sunshine. Stay still," he whispered just before pulling my pebbled nipple into his mouth.

As his fingers played beautiful music on my sensitive little bean, he kissed his way up my chest and neck to my ear. "You are going to come for me." It was a demand.

The words sent a spasm to my core. He licked and then gently blew into my ear, extinguishing any working brain cells. The sensations built as jolts of pleasure rattled from my core to my toes and fingers and back again. Each circle and flick of my clit was another step toward the precipice of my release.

His relentless onslaught continued with renewed vigor as he found exactly the right motion and pressure to make me quiver and take me to the edge of my orgasm. I'd never come this close so quickly before.

I started to shake with all the built-up tension in my body, but he pulled away before I reached my release.

"Please," I begged him.

His fingers darted into me and then back to my tiny bud as he moved his mouth to my breast and sucked in a nipple.

His fingers pressed harder, and his pace increased. "Come for me, Becks. Come now," he said with a jagged breath.

With another pinch of my nipple and pressure to my clit, he pushed me past my limit. I bit down on a mouthful of pillow to hold back the scream. Spasms overtook me as heat exploded in my veins and my body convulsed with pleasure.

"Good girl," he murmured.

"I think I'm wet enough for you now," I mumbled. "I need you inside me." It was the truth. I was dying to feel him fill me. Grabbing the rolled towel he'd shoved away, I pulled it under my hips.

He swatted my ass and pulled the towel loose.

"But you like this."

He slid out of bed.

Not wanting to end it here, I poked my ass up in the air. "Please."

I'd misjudged—he returned with a condom packet and ripped it open. "Roll over, Snuggle Bunny. I want to look into those beautiful eyes of yours."

I grimaced at the name, but turned and spread myself for him. Because of Big Ben's size, I'd had trouble the first few times we'd made love in college and was hoping I hadn't shrunk.

Ethan quickly sheathed himself and slid between my legs. Lifting my ankles over his shoulders, he bent me as he moved into position and pushed in part way.

I was as wet as advertised, and he slid in easily, stretching me with his girth.

"Okay?" he asked softly.

I desperately wanted him to lose the control he was keeping. "I promise I won't break. Now, are you going to fuck me like you mean it or not?" I needed him to want me and take me with abandon. It had always led to the closest feelings between us.

The noise of Winnie getting up next door stopped him for a second.

I scooted toward him, taking more of his shaft. "Chicken?"

The challenge did the trick. "Shhh." He gave me the corner of the towel to bite on.

I took it in my teeth as he bent me farther and began to move inside me.

His eyes drilled into me as we matched our movements and joined as we had before.

His jaw tightened. "You make me lose control," he said as his pace increased.

I was the one losing control. I wanted to see him come for me. I spit the towel out. "That's a good thing," I panted. I took the towel again to hold back the moans.

He rode me hard and fast.

I dug my fingers into his arms and clenched my inner muscles around him in an effort to pull him to the finish line first. I failed as my climax shattered over me. Biting down on the towel stifled the scream into a loud moan.

He pumped harder, arching his back and straining.

I spit out the towel. "Watch my boobs, Cowboy."

His eyes fell from my face to my boobs, which were jostling furiously back and forth with his thrusts.

The visual did him in. He tensed, and his cock throbbed inside me as his tether broke when he went deep. After a few seconds of panting, he let my legs off his shoulders and collapsed on top of me, as spent as I was.

I rubbed my hands over his heaving back. "Thank you."

In return, he raised up to give me a kiss. It was difficult with us both still panting, but glorious still.

"I missed you," I admitted.

CHAPTER 20

Ethan

Ophelia greeted me at the base of the stairs. "You look well…rested."

I nodded. "Thank you. Being in a familiar bed makes it easier." The way I'd woken up had made all the difference.

"I had trouble with all the wind myself," she admitted. "Sounded a bit like ghouls running loose outside."

I followed her into the dining hall where we found Winnie and Mother.

"There you are," Mom said. "Breakfast is ready."

I looked out the windows toward the woods. The wind had made a proper mess everywhere. "Quite a storm."

"Your father is outside organizing the cleanup. You should be able to get on the road soon."

"Good. We both need to be in to work."

Winnie looked up from her toast, but didn't join the discussion.

"After you eat breakfast," Mom said.

"I'm not sure we have the time."

"Breakfast first," she repeated.

"Mother, I'm not ten."

"Of course not. You were better behaved when you were ten."

Ophelia snickered.

Winston appeared from the direction of the kitchen. "Full breakfast for you and Miss Sommerset, Master Ethan?"

"Thank you, Winston," Becky said from behind me. "That would be wonderful."

I turned to see my girl wave me toward the hallway.

I joined her around the corner.

She turned. "Darling, could you help me with the zipper."

The zipper was sticky. I raised it slowly, staring at her bare skin the whole time and wishing I could pull the dress off instead of zipping it up.

She turned and whispered. "Now be nice. Your mother made breakfast. It's only polite to stay for it." She took my hand and started for the dining room.

I understood the point but wasn't going to enlighten her that Mom didn't actually do much of the cooking.

We took the same seats we had last night, next to Winnie.

Winston arrived with plates of food for each of us.

"Thank you, Winston," Becky made a point of saying.

"You are quite welcome, Miss Sommerset."

I added my thanks a second later.

Winston quickly returned with another basket of toast for the table.

Winnie, next to me, was reading the paper on a tablet in front of her.

The picture was from my dinner out with Becky. The headline caught my eye.

Is marriage in the cards for the son of the Duke of Lassiter?

The mystery woman Ethan Blakewell, son of the Duke of Lassiter, was seen dining with has been introduced to the family. Will this beauty succeed where so many before her have failed?

How had they found that out so quickly?

"You look chipper," Ophelia said from across the table.

Becky smiled back. "It's the genes. I don't need much sleep."

Ophelia shot me an odd look.

I went back to cutting my egg. When women were commenting on each other's appearances, it was best to stay out of it.

Rebecca

The drive was cleared of tree branches by the time we finished breakfast. Ethan's car had been towed to the front of the house.

I didn't see any dents in his precious machine, but it looked like it had lost a fight with the mud monster.

"Now don't forget the party Saturday," his mother said as Ethan opened the car door for me.

"You can count on us," I said, settling into the luxurious seat.

Ethan kissed his mother's cheek, and we waved goodbye to the cousins before getting underway.

A mile down the road, Ethan laid his hand on the center console for me.

I took it and intertwined my fingers with his. "You have a lovely family."

"Thank you. We do try. Do you think they bought it? Our cover story, I mean."

"Your parents, yes, but not Winnie." The feel of our hands together brought a warmth to my chest.

"Not Winnie?" He pulled his hand back to make a turn, and I missed the connection.

"You heard her." I'd known exactly what she'd meant by her comment at breakfast.

"Heard what?"

"You heard the comment about how rested I looked. She knew we weren't up all night boinking. I think she suspects."

"She can't know anything. But…" He zoomed past a slower car.

"I tell you, women can sense these things."

"She made a similar comment to me about being well rested when I came downstairs. And she was in the room next to ours."

I slammed my fist down on the center console, angry that I hadn't thought of it last night. "We should have made noise before getting to sleep."

"You mean like banging the headboard against the wall?"

"We should have been loud this morning. If we'd just gotten back together after five years, what would they think we'd be doing?"

He thought for a second. "Not sleeping, that's for sure. As soon as the door closed, they'd expect me to shag you so hard you'd scream my name loud enough for everyone to hear."

"That's not how I'd put it." I was mad we'd lost our chance.

"How would you put it?"

I smiled. "That I took you so high, you screamed *my* name loud enough for everyone to hear."

"That works for me." He laughed. "But, water under the bridge now," he said, echoing his father from last night. "Loud next time."

"You said both of them were big gossips."

"So?" he asked as he sped around a slower car.

The problem was obvious to me. This entire operation depended on nobody catching on to us. "Do you have any idea who the thief is?"

"Of course not, and because of that, we have no way of knowing if Ophelia's gossip would reach the thief and tip him off."

Ethan nodded. "We'll have to do better, be louder."

I extended my hand for him again. "Yes, we will."

He took it.

The connection I felt through his touch calmed me. I could have maybe fixed this by being more assertive last night. We were adults, and friends.

A minute later, I felt I had to be more forthright about my feelings. "I feel great affection for you as well, Ethan," I said, trying on his odd British phrase. It sounded innocent enough.

He squeezed my hand. "Dad-gummit, missy," he said in his version of a Texan accent. "Y'all say the nicest things."

I laughed. "Thank you. But I think you should stick to your version of English."

"Y'all don't like my Texan?"

"It needs work."

He slowed down for a truck.

I was slow this morning, but now I got it. I'd made the mistake of calling him *Cowboy* again in bed—the way I had before—and he was reminding me of that, forcing me to remember how it had been. But those memories were best left on the shelf.

"You can drop me off at my sister's. I need to change for work." I also needed distance. *This was casual,* I repeated in my head.

"Okay. And after work?" he asked.

"I have a lot to catch up on." That was the situation I suspected, anyway. Smithers had said I needed to be available pretty much full time.

"Which means?" He wasn't going to let me off with a simple answer.

"My boss has a lot for me to do at the office. I can get free Friday afternoon, though, to get ready for the party."

My phone rang with the "Stayin' Alive" ring tone I'd assigned to my sister.

Ethan looked over. "That's musical."

"Sorry. It's my sister." I took the call. "Hiya, Lizzy."

"Hey, Beckers."

"Why are you calling me at this ungodly hour?" It had to be way before dawn in New York.

"I'm back in London, silly."

"London?"

"Yeppers, and where the hell are you anyway?"

"I'm driving."

"That's bad. You know you don't have any experience on the wrong side of the road over here."

"To be technical, I'm being driven."

"You had me scared for a minute there. Who's driving you, and you still didn't answer my question."

"Ethan is driving." I reached over to pat his shoulder.

"The hunk?"

"I have to go. Talk later."

"You're avoiding."

"You're prying."

"It's not fair. I had to find him on the web. I told you this could have helped my career. At least now you can give me the inside scoop—like, a play by play, and all the places he's going to take you and shit."

"We can talk about this later," I told her.

"Sure."

"Later gator."

She ended the call.

"We have a ways still to go," Ethan noted. "You could have talked with her longer."

"No. I love her dearly, but she's best enjoyed in small doses. With your family name, her questions would never stop."

"She's still family."

I hadn't expected Lizzy to be back in town so soon. Her call meant maintaining distance from her wasn't going to be in the cards. I sighed. "She works for the *Evening Mail*. She's a bigger gossip with a wider reach than either of your cousins." The problem became obvious. "Shit."

"What?"

"She'll smell a rat for sure if I stay at her place. I guess I'll have to live with you."

He pressed the accelerator angrily as he passed another car. "You say that like moving in with me would be a bad thing."

I hadn't meant to, but I'd obviously hurt his feelings. "Sorry, I didn't mean it that way."

～

When I arrived back at work, Ginny was on me in a second. "Is it true you're dating a Blakewell?"

The internet had certainly done its job spreading the gossip far and wide. I nodded. "I'd rather not discuss it."

Margaret was right behind her. "What's he like? Is it true he only has one testicle from inbreeding?" That last question was a new one.

I couldn't hold back my laugh. "He's very nice." I didn't have to stretch the truth even a millimeter to admit that. "And he has all his parts."

"Mr. Smithers left you this list," Ginny said, handing me a piece of paper.

"Of course he did." I took the list of interviews to critique. The handwritten note alongside said *urgent*.

"Oh," Margaret said. "Also 'he who shall not be named' called again, but I didn't tell him anything."

"Thank you," I said in my most heartfelt voice. I really didn't need to add anything to do with my ex to my plate.

I closed my door and got to work as soon as the busybodies left.

Ethan's call on my cell interrupted the first interview. He sighed. "About having to move in with me—I understand it wasn't what you planned, Sunshine. I can stay in a neighbor's flat one level down if that will make you more comfortable."

His use of my new nickname sent a thrill up my spine.

"Don't you dare. I didn't mean it to sound like that. It will be fine. My main problem now is that my boss here expects me to be able to do our secret job in addition to my regular work, so I'm behind."

"Should I come rescue you from the building later? Or send a car?" Another sweet offer.

Ginny was at my door.

"I can manage, thank you."

"Dinner is at seven, Sunshine. Don't be late."

"Later, gator."

"Ta-ta for now."

I hung up with a contented sigh.

Ginny wore a mischievous grin. "I know that smile. That was him, wasn't it?"

I nodded. "What do you have?"

"Mr. Smithers wants to see you at five."

~

I KNOCKED ON THE DOORFRAME OF SMITHERS' OFFICE AT THE APPOINTED HOUR.

He motioned me in. "Close the door, if you would."

I did and took a chair.

He had the paper open in front of him. "This is your idea of an investigation? What have you accomplished outside of dinner at expensive restaurants and..." He held up a separate piece of paper. "Almost fifteen thousand pounds in a shopping spree?"

I straightened my back and held my chin up. "Yes. You and Mr. Cornwall said the Met had the lead on this, and I'm following their suggestions." I pointed at the paper he held. "The thefts are being held at exclusive parties, and clothes like that are necessary to attend."

I was on a roll and kept going. "We interviewed the duchess at length about the theft of her necklace. We've already interviewed the hosts of the next event over dinner and have secured invitations. The party is scheduled for this weekend." *Hosts of the next event* sounded much more business-like than calling them Ethan's parents.

He waved the piece of paper again. "This better be the end of the expenses."

I whipped out my trump card. "You should be prepared for a lot more. Mr.

Cornwall told *me*," I said with the emphasis on me, "that I would have access to whatever resources were necessary. Has that changed?"

He gritted his teeth but didn't say anything.

I might be the pawn in their game, but with Cornwall's backing, I had the upper hand at the moment. I stood to leave. "Is that all?"

"Remember, we need the necklace back."

"Or the jewels."

He nodded. "Just so we know what success looks like."

"Understood." I closed the door behind me.

He'd just reminded me that even the pawn protected by the king could be sacrificed in the endgame. The pressure was on.

CHAPTER 21

ETHAN

On Saturday, Becky and I had arrived at Rainswood prior to lunch to help with the preparations for the evening. Our plan was also to stay the night, which would be an opportunity to get the cousins on the right page.

"Quite a stroke of genius, offering to supply the photographer," Becky said as she touched up her makeup in the mirror.

"Mother liked the idea when I'd suggested it." Unbeknownst to Mother, the photographer, Julian Waters, was also an undercover Met operative, giving us another pair of eyes at the event.

"You think it'll scare the thief away?" I asked.

She pulled the makeup brush away from her face. "Doubtful. My guess from what little we know from Aunt Helen is that he knocks them out temporarily to change out the piece, which obviously would be in a private area away from photographers in the first place."

But we had yet to come up with a method he could use to do it. Becky's elusive amnesia gas was her best guess, but so far none of the experts I'd asked had heard of such a thing.

She'd suggested everything from hypnosis to an invisibility cloak à la Harry Potter, but none of it struck a chord with me.

Her mobile rang, but not with one of the musical family ring tones I'd heard before.

"It's work," she said.

When she answered it, I left the bathroom to give her privacy.

A minute later she came out. "Smithers wants an update tomorrow morning after the party."

"This is just the first night. There might not be anything to report."

"You try telling him that."

I shrugged.

We headed downstairs after a brief struggle with my bow tie.

"I quite like her," Dad told me when Becky wandered off with Mom.

"So do I." My words sounded pathetic after I said them. My feelings for her ran deeper than that.

Dad cocked his head. "Really?"

I gave him the shortest answer I could. "Quite."

He gestured to the door. "Shall we talk outside?"

A question like that from him was never meant to be ignored.

"Sure." I pulled open the door to the back patio.

He didn't speak until we were a dozen yards from the house. "Why did you lie to your mother at dinner the other day?"

I stopped in my tracks. "What?"

"You said you hadn't heard from Charlie and led your mother to believe he was in Africa. That worries her."

"I don't know exactly where he is."

"Ethan, you should understand that I know everything that goes on in this family. Charlie is in America, and you know that as well as I do."

I pulled out my only defense. "He swore me to secrecy."

"Fine, but don't go upsetting your mother that way."

It wasn't clear exactly what he'd expected me to say instead, but I let it drop. He *didn't* really know *everything* that went on in our family, and that was a good thing.

When we reached the roses, he stopped. "I wanted to talk about the business for a moment before our guests arrive."

That came out of left field. Dad rarely discussed anything so crass as money or business in my presence.

"I'm listening." I'd actually been hoping he would open up to me and Charlie before now.

He looked down momentarily. "The nature of mergers being what it is… I'm afraid I'm going to need to warn you and Charlie." He checked our surroundings before continuing. "People, very powerful people, have not been happy recently."

"About what?"

"As I said, mergers."

Now I understood where this was going. His last several acquisitions had been viewed by some as ruthless, more in the American mold of business than the polite mode of British businessmen.

"It is possible that…some of these parties might want to exact revenge for their perceived slights." His vocabulary spoke volumes about his view of these nebulous other parties' grievances, but didn't get to the point.

"Spit it out, Dad."

"There have been veiled threats."

"And I should watch my back?"

"Exactly. Both you and your brother."

"Dad, I can take care of myself. What about Kelsey?"

My sister's name set him back a bit. "They wouldn't dare," he snarled.

He thought there were rules of gentlemanly conduct even when the stakes were high. I wasn't so sure.

Duels might be out of style in this day and age, but it didn't mean Dad wouldn't get violent if someone messed with my sister. And he wouldn't give them the even chance a duel provided, either.

His overprotectiveness is what had driven her away to the States.

"I'll let Charlie know when I hear from him." That I'd also warn Kelsey didn't need to be stated. It would only remind him of why she'd left.

Dad straightened at that. "Perhaps we should get back inside, then. I just thought you should be aware."

We started back to the house.

"Any name in particular I should be careful of?" I asked.

"Knightley," he said. "Or, Wentworth."

"Is that all?" Kevin Knightley and Jerrod Wentworth were both ruthless, if the business press was to be believed, and both had the resources to cause damage, even to my father.

"Perhaps not, but those two top the list."

"What possible acquisition has them excited?" I used *excited* although I meant angry.

"Hawker Technologies."

"The American outfit?" They were big in jet engines and a host of other things. Hawker would be a large bite for my dad's company to swallow—also a huge accomplishment.

He nodded. "And... Never mind. It doesn't matter."

I dropped the query about other companies. Getting into a long discussion with him about business could wind its way back to what I did and require more lies I didn't want to tell. "Why are you making enemies all of the sudden?" I asked.

He changed the subject. "What do you have going on these days at your work?"

"Just more of the same. Keeping companies safe from cyber criminals." As far as he or anyone knew, I worked for TechniByte, not the Met.

He put his arm over my shoulder. "I don't say this enough, but I'm proud of you. I think your work is noble. Your division should spread the word about the good work you're doing. People should know."

I swelled with pride and found it hard to swallow. "Thank you." He rarely gave out praise. It felt good to hear him say that today.

He gave me a squeeze before releasing me. Physical displays of emotion weren't his thing. "*A cost of the title,*" he'd once told me when I was little.

"It is important work," I said. It was a constant battle to keep my true job concealed from him and Mom, but that was the requirement in my division of the Metropolitan Police Service. We couldn't even tell our family who we actually worked for in our effort to keep the country and its enterprises safe.

His use of the word *noble* had been spot on. It was exactly how I saw the work I did. It was a shame I couldn't tell him the full extent of it.

Once inside, I checked with Winston and Karen in the kitchen.

Four waiters from the catering company were waiting in the corner, no doubt too scared of Karen to venture any closer.

"The food is warming, and everything is ready," Karen assured me. "And before you ask, assure her grace that the quantity is sufficient."

"And we will not want for beverages," Winston added.

He'd probably ordered several extra cases of champagne just to be sure.

~

Rebecca

Ethan's parents strode down the hall toward us as we stood near the front door.

"The first guests are due shortly, your grace," Winston announced with a hand on the front door. He didn't open it. "Yet the Marquis and Lady Chatterham have not arrived."

Ethan's father wore a tuxedo very much like Ethan's, or perhaps it was the other way around. His wife wore a gown more modest than what Ethan had chosen for me, but even more elegant.

The Duke checked his watch. "Five minutes late."

"Carter," Diane scolded him.

Ethan addressed his mother. "Karen asked me to assure you that she has sufficient food."

Diane merely nodded.

My eyes were drawn to the necklace she wore. "That necklace is stunning," I told her. It was a diamond-and-emerald beauty that would make her thief's target list for sure.

She touched it gently. "Thank you. A present from Carter on our engagement."

Carter placed his arm around her waist. "A Blakewell tradition—a pre-wedding gift in addition to the ring."

That tradition I hadn't heard of before.

Diane elbowed him. "And I thought it was because I was special."

"You are, my dear." Carter checked his watch again and sighed.

Winston glanced out the window when a car arrived. "The Chatterhams, your grace."

Carter checked his watch again and nodded to Winston to open the door.

Ethan let go and moved away. "I'll mosey on into the kitchen and see iffen I can rustle up some bubbly for all y'all," he said in his imitation Texas accent.

His mother shot a grimace his way as he left.

Shortly after the Chatterhams joined us at the door, guests began arriving. I stayed next to Ethan's mother in the introduction line to meet them all. This gave me a chance to gauge who might be the most likely target if the thief was active tonight.

I'd lost track of how many guests with titles had arrived when Ethan's mother turned to me. "Lady Montague called to say she couldn't make it, so everybody is now accounted for."

Winston followed us to the ballroom. "A very good turnout, mum."

"Three more than last weekend," she said as I surveyed the very full space.

She leaned in and pointed toward a well-endowed girl in a long, rose dress. "You should go find that son of mine before Christie there latches on to him."

I nodded. "Thank you. I think I'll do that."

"I think she might be the reason he hasn't been to any of these this season," she added.

I started off to the right, looking for my date.

Julian, our photographer, did his part, snapping pictures from around the room.

Noticing Christie wandering the same direction as I was searching for Ethan, I sped up my pace. Finally, I located him at the far end of the room, talking with his father and another man.

He smiled when he noticed me.

I parked myself next to him, our hips touching.

"Jeffrey, I'd like to introduce Rebecca Sommerset," Ethan said to the other man.

"Becky, Jeffrey is the Earl of Sherwood."

After the earl and I exchanged pleasantries, I pulled Ethan aside. "Anything yet?"

"Nothing out of the ordinary, but then what does a jewel thief with an invisibility cloak look like, anyway?"

I jabbed him in the ribs. "Don't make fun if you don't have a better suggestion."

Our plan was simple. Ethan would stay within sight of the entrance to the ladies' bathroom, and I would make the rounds with his aunt Helen. She was the only one here who knew of our investigation, and she'd agreed to introduce me around.

Several of the white-coated waiters from the catering company circulated with hors d'oeuvres and champagne. I hadn't paid attention to them earlier, but staff like them blended in at an event like this. It would be the perfect cover.

"You're checking the catering staff?" I asked Ethan.

"Of course. The full list of names already went to headquarters. A fight or two, one auto theft, but nobody stood out. What did you gather during your stint in the receiving queue? How many targets do we have to watch?"

"Not counting rings or earrings, I think we have your mother, plus four ladies here tonight with valuables that could be targets—three necklaces and one brooch. Not counting your aunt Helen, of course, but the thief already knows that one's not real."

"Okay. Point them out to me."

I nodded to my left. "The lady in yellow, next to the short, bald guy—Lady Swarthmore, if I remember. A very nice emerald-and-diamond necklace."

Ethan took my elbow, and we walked in her direction. He glanced over casually as we passed. "Very nice indeed. Next?"

We continued down the long side of the ballroom. Catching sight of the next one, I prodded Ethan. "Lady Devonwood in the navy blue to your right, a diamond-and-ruby necklace. And the woman in black—I don't remember the name—talking with her is wearing the sapphire-and-diamond brooch."

"That's Ernie Sutton's wife."

"No title?"

"Ernie's a baron."

"Of course he is."

Ethan gave me the side-eye for my flippant remark.

Once again we meandered by them to give Ethan a good look.

By my estimation, the final expensive piece graced the neck of a lady in red at the far end of the room, and it took us a minute to get there casually.

Ethan's eyes darted to his right. "Why not that one?"

An older lady nearby wore a pearl necklace.

"A nice single strand like that is worth less than your car." That was a tidy sum, but nothing compared to the gemstone-encrusted others in the room.

He nodded slowly. "I see. Not topflight."

During the second half of the evening, we'd planned for me to join Ethan near the ladies' room entrance to see if any one of our likely targets entered. This was based on Aunt Helen's feeling that her necklace had been taken in the ladies' bathroom. But that's all the information we had to go on, other than both thefts had occurred here at Rainswood, and both women hadn't felt well.

"Okay, time to mingle," Ethan told me. "Enjoy your time with Aunt Helen."

Without being able to ask probing questions, it wasn't clear how much I'd get out of what Ethan called my "truth-detector mode," but it was worth a try.

Aunt Helen broke away from the clutch of ladies she was talking with when she saw me. "Shall we get started?"

"No time like the present." I followed her back into the crowd.

She introduced me as her nephew's girlfriend from America, which started us off with a few questions coming my way before she asked the other party a few simple questions that allowed me to look for my telltale signs of deception.

A few minutes later, we'd left the first couple behind.

"Is it one of them?" Aunt Helen whispered when we reached the wall, away from anyone.

I shook my head. "No. Not that I can tell."

"Are you sure?"

I didn't want her to feel bad. "Reasonably." I was certain of my ability to detect deception, but with softball questions of party conversation, we wouldn't be putting the thief in a position that required a lie. "That's one down and another several dozen to go."

This was going to take all night, and even then it might not yield anything.

CHAPTER 22

ETHAN

WE HADN'T QUITE REACHED THE MIDPOINT OF THE EVENING.

So far, I hadn't seen anything out of the ordinary. None of our target ladies had had reason to venture toward the women's toilet yet.

I'd kept a half-filled champagne flute in my hand the entire night. And I'd split my time between keeping track of where our suspected target ladies were on the floor and watching Becky work the crowd with Aunt Helen.

Right now I would have given anything to be able to read lips and know what had made her laugh. It put a genuine smile on her face, the kind I wanted to put there with some pithy remark or other.

It brought me back to our time at university. It had been a carefree few months filled with good times—before the DNA results that changed everything for my family.

The secret I carried prevented me from getting that close to a woman again. A slipup couldn't be tolerated. Dad had put it succinctly: *"Family is everything."* And I'd do my part to protect the family.

"Ethan?" Karen said as she offered another tray of hors d'oeuvres from the kitchen.

I'd already devoured several of the delicacies, and this time I chose the caviar-topped deviled egg. "Thank you."

She nodded and moved on.

I watched, and she only made it halfway into the room before her tray emptied.

"There you are, you rascal," a female voice from my left said. It was Christie, whom I'd avoided by ducking into the hallway twice already.

"Christie, I didn't know you were coming." Not a total lie, because I hadn't known ahead of time she'd be here.

The strong whiff of jasmine hit me as she moved close. "You were supposed to invite me the next time you were attending."

Understated had never been her style in the fragrance department, or clothing. Her neckline was the most daring here tonight, and showed off a dangerous amount of her more-than-ample cleavage.

"I don't recall it that way."

She was persistent to the point of obnoxiousness.

"I do, but I forgive you," she said loudly enough to catch the interest of the couple nearby.

I shifted to an open space a few yards away, toward where Becky and Aunt Helen were talking to the Jordans.

"We should take a walk in the garden, just you and I," Christie said.

I caught Becky's eye. A simple head motion asked her to join us. "No, thank you," I told Christie.

"I think we should," Christie repeated loudly.

It was a few seconds before Becky made it to my side.

"Christie Slutter, I'd like to introduce Rebecca Sommerset."

Becky held out her hand. "A pleasure to meet you, Miss Slutty. Ethan's mother has told me all about you."

I swallowed my laugh.

"Slutter," she chided. "An American—I might have known," she added with an upturned nose.

Becky's eyes darkened, but she didn't snap back.

"I'm hungry. Run and fetch us some canapes, if you would," Christie said to Becky with a wave of her hand.

Becky sniffed the air. "Ethan you should have your father check the heating grate…" She pointed to the wall. "Over there. It smells like a rat might have died inside."

"This party is for the aristocracy." She lifted her nose. "I didn't realize we'd admitted any Americans to the peerage yet."

Becky put a finger to her chin. "You are quite correct, Chrissy."

Christie bristled at the misspoken name.

"We haven't had any British nobles on our continent since we defeated the English army at Yorktown in seventeen eighty-one and shipped Earl Cornwallis and his soldiers home to you."

Christie turned toward me. "Ethan, I'll accept that offer of a walk in the garden now."

I pulled Becky to my side. "You can walk yourself. I'll stay with my girlfriend. Rebecca may not have a title, but she has more honor and character in her little finger than you ever will." I leaned down and placed a quick kiss on my girl.

With a huff Christie was gone, and hopefully for good this time.

Becky's eyes were misty when she looked back up at me. "You say the sweetest things."

"I meant every word."

She winked at me. "I know."

I sighed with a shake of my head. "You promised no mind-ninja tricks with me."

"I did, didn't I?"

"I don't know how, but I'm going to get you back for that."

She looked down at the floor.

I touched her arm to get her attention again. "That was quite the history lesson you gave her."

She looked up and smiled. "Daddy drilled history into me, and she deserved it, the snob."

I chanced a glance in Christie's direction. She was already chatting up poor Stanton Hoover.

"Your ex?" Becky asked.

"For one dinner date was all. And even that was too long."

"You sure can pick 'em."

"It was a blind date set up by my brother."

"Was he mad at you for something?"

"Livid." I looked past Becky to see Lady Devonwood returning from the hall that lead to the ladies' toilet. "Uh-oh."

Becky turned to see her. "Did you see when she went in?"

"No."

"Or who went in right before or after her?"

I shook my head. "No. I was busy fending off Christie."

Becky elbowed me. "Keep your head in the game, Blakewell. This is serious." She turned down the hall to the ladies' toilet.

How quickly I'd gone from hero to goat.

She returned a minute later. "It's empty," she said before disappearing into the crowd.

A few minutes later, Becky returned with the bad news. "Lady Devonwood is leaving early. She isn't feeling well." That was a bad sign.

"All we can do now is finish the way we planned and see what happens." I had a bad feeling. Christie might have just screwed up the entire evening by distracting me at exactly the wrong time.

∽

REBECCA

THE PARTY HAD COME TO A CONCLUSION, AND AUNT HELEN'S DRIVER WAITED BY THE door.

She put down the same half-full champagne glass she'd carried most of the evening and said her goodbyes to Ethan's parents.

I accompanied her out the door.

She stopped by the car. "I hope I was able to help."

I smiled and gave her a gentle goodbye hug. "You were marvelous."

"Do we get to do this at the next one?"

"We'll see," was all I could promise. The approach hadn't seemed as fruitful as I'd expected. The only deceptive answers all night seemed to relate to the food or enjoyment of the party itself.

"Thank you for the help, Aunt Helen," Ethan said as he kissed her cheek goodbye. "And mum's the word."

She giggled. "Official Secrets Act—I remember."

Upon reentering, Diane waved Ethan and me over. "Carter and I are going to enjoy another glass of champagne. Care to join us?"

"Maybe later," Ethan told her. "Rebecca owes me a dance."

I did a double take. "Huh?" Then it came to me. He'd mentioned a dance while getting rid of that leech, Christie.

Ethan urged me back toward the ballroom. "I'm shocked you would forget."

"We'll be in the kitchen when you finish," his mother said as she left.

Once inside the massive room, Ethan started a song on his phone and placed it on the table.

A second later I was in his arms and loving the feel of it as we swayed in the emptiness of the large room.

"We should review tonight before we forget anything," he said into my ear. It wasn't a sweet nothing, but with us sharing body heat like this, I'd take any words.

"You say the sweetest things," I chided him.

"I'm serious."

"What did Julian say before he left?" I asked.

"He didn't notice anything, but he'll forward all the photos in the morning for us to review. What did you find out?"

I went back over the evening in my head. "All I learned was that people liked the caviar, but not the smoked salmon."

"And?"

"That's all."

He sighed. "What happened to your super lie-detector skill? You didn't figure out who it is?"

I pulled away from him. "It's not like I could interrogate them. They're not supposed to know either of us is looking into this. I can't ask direct questions about jewel thefts. I can't help it if all they want to talk about is the food and each other." I should have mentioned this problem earlier.

"Well, that doesn't help."

"If Devonwood lost anything, we didn't get a look at who it might have been because you were too busy checking out Miss Slutty's boobs."

"I wasn't checking her out; I was trying to get rid of her."

"And not watching the hallway in the process."

He sighed. "Guilty. I admit I screwed up."

I raised up and kissed him briefly. "That's one of the things I love about you. You're honest." I messed up using *love* instead of *like*, but it didn't seem he'd caught it.

"One of the things? Tell me more."

I rested my head against his chest so he wouldn't see my smile." He was letting his guard down.

Breaking free of him, I turned. "Turn off the music. I have an idea."

He quieted the phone and followed me down the hall toward the ladies' room.

I pushed open the door. "If this is where it's happening, there has to be something about the room."

He stopped at the doorway.

"Come on, help me look around."

"A gentleman doesn't go into the ladies' toilet."

"Pretend you're a janitor, then, instead of a gentleman."

"I'll wait to hear what you find." He let the door close.

The man had the oddest idea of what a gentleman did and didn't do.

I started my survey. It was a large space, complete with a sitting area and even a chair in front of a makeup table with generous light.

I wasn't even sure what I hoped to find. Maybe a nozzle for spewing my fictitious amnesia gas? A scan of the ceiling and walls didn't show any anomalies. Each of the stalls was the same and just what I'd expect to see, except that everything was antique.

The sinks were built into a long vanity with drawers. The first drawer I tried contained an assortment of lipsticks—not something the average person put in their guest bathroom. But then the average person didn't have separate men's and women's restrooms large enough to handle a crowd of a hundred.

Two more drawers contained tissue, eyeliner pencils, and blush. The final one was empty. I pushed it closed, hard, frustrated that nothing here was out of the ordinary.

I pulled the top one out past the latch and peered in.

Lighting the space with my phone revealed the surprise.

The diamond-and-ruby necklace Lady Devonwood had been wearing was taped to the bottom of the counter inside a plastic bag.

My heart raced as I reached in and traced my finger over the gorgeous necklace. Shallow breaths came rapidly. The thief had struck again, and this time I had the necklace to turn over to Cornwall.

I closed my eyes and could see my window office. I could feel the plush leather chair. I imagined breathing in the new-car smell of the company car that came with it. My superiors would be thrilled about this.

Success, thou art sweet.

Opening my eyes brought my brain back online and stopped me before I broke out in a happy dance. Who would leave it here?

When the possibility came to me, I felt queasy for a second and flopped onto the couch. Somebody in the household might hide it here.

His parents?

I raced to the sink and leaned over just in time. My vomit splashed into the porcelain bowl.

This was their house. They'd been present at each of the parties when the thefts occurred. Would I have to ruin Ethan's family to get my promotion?

The sound of a knock at the door stopped my heart.

"Almost done?"

Ethan. I dry-heaved over the sink.

CHAPTER 23

ETHAN

"Not quite," Becky said loudly from the other side of the ladies' toilet door.

I stopped my toe from tapping, something it had started of its own volition. Nervousness did that to me.

The men's toilet that serviced the ballroom and dining room was spacious, built for a crowd rather than a family. The women's most likely was large as well. Even so, Becky had been in there a long time.

"You go ahead. I'll join you in the kitchen," she added. Her voice sounded strained.

I was probably being overly proper about this. No guests were in the toilet, and leaving her to do it all herself wasn't gentlemanly either. "I could help?" I offered.

"No," came the immediate reply, a complete turnaround from earlier.

"Okay, but don't say I didn't offer." I wasn't having this thrown back in my face.

"I've got it. You go ahead. I'll be along."

As the hall opened to the ballroom, I looked to where Christie had cornered me. It had been the one time all night that I'd lost sight of the assignment for even a second.

Becky had been right to chastise me—not for being mesmerized by Christie's jubblies, although they were awesome, but for allowing Christie to get under my skin and distract me.

On my way to the kitchen, I plucked a rose from a vase near the ballroom entrance and nodded to myself. It would make the proper statement.

In the kitchen, Dad was filling his and Mom's glasses from a bottle.

Mom stood across the island from him and saw me first. "Where's Rebecca?"

"She'll be along in a bit," I answered.

Mom cocked her head. "Are you sure?"

"Huh?" Perhaps Mom had already had more champagne than she should have.

"You really think that is going to do the trick?" she asked looking at the rose I carried.

"Do what?" I asked, looking to Dad for a translation.

Dad shrugged. "I didn't say anything."

"I'm ashamed of you, Ethan. You virtually ignored the poor woman all night long, and now you want to make it up with a single rose?"

"Mom, I didn't..." I couldn't explain that splitting up for the evening had been part of the plan.

"You spent more time talking to that...that tart, Christie, than you did your girlfriend."

"She came after me."

Mom didn't stop. "No wonder you can't keep a girlfriend if this is how you treat the women in your life."

"Di, isn't that a little harsh?" Dad asked, coming to my rescue.

Mom narrowed her eyes at him. "Carter, you should know better than to condone such behavior."

Dad and I were both in trouble now.

"I wasn't..." he started before deciding silence was the better alternative.

"I should think not." Mom looked down at my tapping foot.

I stilled it.

Silence fell between us as the telltale click of heels on the floor announced Becky was on her way.

REBECCA

. . .

After dry heaving twice more after Ethan left, I started the water to wash away the gross evidence of my inner turmoil.

I closed my eyes and leaned against the counter. How could I possibly think Ethan's family might be involved in such a thing?

This didn't make any sense. Why would they be stealing from their friends? It wasn't like the Duke needed money. And stealing from Aunt Helen wasn't targeting enemies.

After rinsing my mouth, I pulled out another top drawer and gasped when I looked up inside. Ethan's aunt's necklace and a brooch were taped there.

If not the family who lived here, what thief would take millions of dollars of jewelry but leave it hidden in a bathroom? Not a logical one. Something was off about this whole episode. We had no idea how it was being done, and now the loot was being left at the scene? Nothing added up, yet here it was, ready for me to claim success. I'd really blow them away if I presented two recovered necklaces, completely intact.

I could take the jewelry, turn it over to Smithers and Cornwall, and be on a plane back to California tomorrow. I'd have the managing director on my side to battle HR, and my window office would be within reach.

Reaching my goal would be so simple.

But is that what I'd become? So selfish that with no evidence I'd throw Ethan's family to the wolves for my promotion?

I looked in the mirror and studied the face I knew so well. "Turning in the jewels is the right thing to do," I said out loud.

My bullshit detector went off. I knew my own words were a lie.

Nothing about this—other than the circumstances—said they were involved, but that's not the way it would be viewed. While I cruised at thirty-five thousand feet toward my new future, the Blakewells would be crushed by the circumstantial evidence I'd provided.

A week ago, I'd have already packed the items in my purse and been heading out the door. My career was all that had mattered to me for years.

I sat down on the couch again to think.

This situation is so fucked-up.

Ethan's comments from earlier hit me like a tidal wave, and tears started down my cheeks. Why didn't I care about what was right and wrong, he'd asked. The answer—that it was in the company's best interest not to pursue the wrong-doers—hadn't swayed him, and it sounded equally hollow to me now.

He'd insisted the way we'd done business was morally wrong, and I couldn't fault him now.

I realized he was right. If I turned the jewelry over to Cornwall, it would be wrong. It would taint the Blakewells without any evidence that they'd done anything, and with my clear suspicion that they hadn't. And, equally bad, the real perpetrator would get away. I'd be wronging the man who'd just told Miss Slutty he thought I had honor and character.

This smelled just like the Bergdorf case, where the neighbors had hidden their own jewelry in the Bergdorfs' house and claimed to have seen Mr. Bergdorf steal it.

Why else would the thief not take the goods along?

I hadn't been able to resist grading Ethan's statement to Miss Slutty with what he called my mind-ninja trick, which was actually merely observation. He'd believed every word he'd spoken about me having honor and character. Now, I had to make them true. I had to live up to the way Ethan had described me to his slutty ex-blind-date disaster, and that was a tall order.

Gathering myself, I put the drawers back the way they had been. I couldn't chance making the crook suspicious.

As I dabbed at my eyes with tissue, I realized I now had to do the thing I despised most. I had to lie to Ethan and not tell him what I'd found. Lucky for me, he didn't have my finely tuned truth meter. But it wouldn't be easy to hide my own disgust for my deception.

If I told Ethan, he'd be duty bound to report it to the superintendent, and in all likelihood, that would be game over for his parents. I couldn't do that to them—or to him. That wouldn't be proving I had the character he'd claimed I had.

Putting on my best smile felt like a contortion when I left the bathroom to join him and his parents.

It felt odd to need to prove myself to a man, but Ethan had never been just any man to me. For a few months five years ago, he'd made me feel… I wasn't sure how to finish the sentence because the way he'd made me feel back then had been something I hadn't experienced before or since, until a few days ago. It was the reason being dumped had taken so long to recover from.

As I entered the hallway leading to the kitchen, the muffled conversation halted before I turned the corner.

My smile faltered as the three sets of eyes on me felt like a spotlight highlighting my weakness. "Sorry I'm late."

Ethan's mother nudged him.

He held out a rose for me.

The simple gesture brought back my smile. My heart thudded against my chest as I took it.

CHAPTER 24

ETHAN

THE FEAR I'D SEEN IN BECKY'S EYES EVAPORATED THE MOMENT I HELD OUT THE ROSE for her. "I shouldn't have left you alone all night," I said. "It was inconsiderate of me."

She took it in one hand and reached for my arm with the other, pulling herself up for a quick kiss. "You're so sweet."

I missed her lips as soon as they left mine and wished to hell my parents weren't here right now so I could finish what she'd started—only naked on the kitchen island.

Becky looked at Dad and then Mom. "It was my fault. I'd asked Aunt Helen to introduce me around without Ethan."

Mom's look turned quizzical.

"I didn't want to play on the Blakewell name," Becky explained.

I took her hand. "Sunshine, your beauty this evening would have only enhanced our reputation." I meant every word.

"But I'm American."

"Well, there is that." I laughed.

Dad joined in with a chuckle. "Rebecca, dear, always take pride in your family and your heritage."

I spread cheese on a cracker and handed it to Becky.

Mom poured champagne and slid it toward her. "Join us in a glass."

"Thank you all." Becky swung the glass around to the three of us. "For accepting me so graciously into your home."

Dad lifted his glass. "Ethan, I think she has a future in politics."

We shared crackers, cheese, drink, and conversation for another hour. Every minute had me more amazed by Becky's grace.

In front of my parents, I had to maintain a more civilized distance from my girl than I would have liked. Every touch of her hip to mine brought my cock alive in a way that kept me pressed firmly against the island lest my parents get an eyeful of my feelings for Becky.

Eventually Mom decided it was time to call it an evening. "I think I've had enough excitement for one day."

Dad quickly concurred.

"You go on up," I told them. "We'll clean up down here."

Becky nodded.

∼

REBECCA

"Ethan?" I asked, after his parents had left us alone in the kitchen.

"Yes, Sunshine."

That new nickname warmed me inside and gave me hope each time I heard it—hope that I meant more to him than a means to an end on this mission of ours. There was no denying I hoped to find out if we could have been more, if we hadn't ended the way we had.

I banished the wishful thinking for the moment. "I got the impression your mother doesn't like Miss Slutty."

He choked back a laugh. "Miss Slutty. Good name for her." He started wiping off the island.

"So why was she here tonight, if she's not a friend?"

"Can't keep her away. She's a marquis' daughter, and that gets her entrance to these things. One can't play favorites. It's one of the unwritten rules."

"That rule sucks." I wouldn't be inviting undesirables to one of my parties.

He sighed. "Do you think we messed up with Lady Devonwood?"

I couldn't tell him I knew for sure that we had. "I think so. She said she felt ill, and that's just like the other two instances, so far as we know." I rinsed the glasses in the sink.

"Yeah, I think so too." He sighed. "And you couldn't see anything in the ladies' toilet that explained how this is being pulled off?"

That one I could answer honestly. "No. Whoever this guy is, he's as slippery as a ghost." I turned to Ethan.

He tensed. "It was my fault, letting Christie distract me."

Big boobs had that effect on guys. Any girl who said she didn't at some point wish to have a little more up top was a liar, or was already a double-D.

"So you noticed the cut of her neckline?"

"Her jubblies aren't as nice as yours."

"Jubblies? Really?" I turned the question around on him. He was being entirely too nice.

"Yeah, knockers, tits, boobs. Her big problem, though, is up higher—the emptiness in her head." He moved closer and wrapped me up. "Are you jealous of her?"

"Of course not," I managed to say, although I wasn't as big as her in the boob department. I'd watched the men's eyes track her as she moved through the room this evening. It was like she had man-magnets stuck in her bra. Scratch that, she hadn't been wearing a bra. That had been obvious and part of the allure.

Damn, I was self-conscious, and my denial of being jealous didn't ring true either.

Ethan had taken me to bed frequently since the first morning I'd suggested we could enjoy each other casually. He'd been passionate, but in a gentle and attentive way—not like it had been before. I could sense that he was holding back, and I didn't understand why. But questions were off-limits for now.

He pulled me closer. "She's got nothing on you, Snuggle Bunny."

That name suggested I was soft, cuddly, almost fragile. I wanted to get back to danger and passion.

I nodded toward the island. "Now that we're alone, we could try some of the things on your list."

His eyes went wide. "Not down here," he whispered. "Someone could come in."

"Not up for the challenge?" We'd had a list of things to try back then, and the kitchen counter had been one I'd put on it.

I pulled on his jacket and walked toward the door. "Upstairs then, but louder. We said louder, remember?"

We raced up the stairs—or I raced, and he let me win.

As soon as the door closed, he hiked up my skirt, lifted me up by my ass, and backed me against the door.

I reached over and flicked off the light.

The moon provided a dim glow—enough that I could see the lust in his eyes, feelings that mirrored mine.

Our lips crashed together, and I held on to him with my arms around his head and shoulders and legs around his waist.

He pinned me against the door. "This was on your list, wasn't it?" He lifted me higher and moved to kiss my neck.

I nodded breathlessly. "But not tonight. I want you to take me hard."

He growled.

"Fuck me like you used to, Cowboy." I needed the old, out-of-control Ethan.

∼

ETHAN

BECKY HAD SAID SHE COULD DO CASUAL, BUT I WASN'T CONVINCED. CASUAL MEANT staying in control, keeping to feeling good without adding any damned emotion to the mix to fuck everything up.

But the minute she said she wanted me to fuck her hard like before, my mind went blank. I knew exactly what she meant, what she wanted, what we both wanted. Quiet wouldn't be part of it.

The way she'd said it was more provocative than anything I could imagine right now. I kissed her neck, allowing my teeth to graze her.

Her nails clawed at my back in response, and we were off to the races.

I couldn't resist her magnetic hips. She was going to get the pounding she'd asked for. I picked her up and took her to bed. We could talk tomorrow. Talking was overrated, particularly with a hard-on that could drill steel.

The tigress came out to play as she pulled at my clothes. Her hands and lips were demanding as she kissed me with renewed abandon. She pounced on me and pulled at my pants as I wiggled out of my shirt.

I whipped her around and yanked the zipper down. If it had given me a fight, I would have ripped it. Waiting was not an option.

Her marvelous knockers bounced as she struggled to undress me the rest of the way. What a sight. I couldn't keep from cupping them, supporting their weight, and teasing the hard, pink nipples. The softness of the flesh was such a contrast to the hardness of the tight little nipples that peaked at my slightest touch.

I was ashamed to be a boob man, but hers were perfect—soft, supple, and large enough to fill my hand, full enough to form enticing cleavage, without making her look as slutty as Christie.

I pulled down the thong she'd chosen this morning as she struggled with my boxer briefs. My underpants were not cooperating. "Ouch," I complained.

"Sorry." She'd tried to bend Big Ben in a direction he wasn't going to go.

I took care of extricating myself, and we were naked in the dim light. Pushing her back onto the bed, I kissed a trail up the inside of one thigh to her apex.

She sucked in a loud breath as I breathed over her sex.

"You have a wonderful fanny."

She giggled. "You like my ass now?"

My tongue traveled the length of her slit. "No this."

She speared fingers in my hair and pulled my mouth down on her. "We call this a *pussy*. My fanny is what I sit on."

"Wonderful pussy then." I ran up and down the length again before lapping at her entrance.

She shivered as I circled her clit. Her back arched and her grip on my hair tightened as she pulled me to her.

I dove in and teased her entrance with one finger and then a second as I concentrated on the little bundle of nerves and the groans and moans I pulled from her—not loud yet, but not quiet.

Her taste drove me crazy as I licked and sucked on that responsive little bud. I had her jerking and yelping her way closer to her undoing.

She writhed and ground her hips into me.

I took the direction she gave me via her grip on my hair.

She opened her legs wider and pulled at my head aggressively, rocking her hips into me with each stroke, each suck on her little button. Her sounds grew louder as I gave her a tongue-lashing.

She was a wild tornado when she came with an avalanche of tremors, jerks, and yelps. She found her pleasure and then pushed my head up and away.

After rolling over, she pulled her knees under her, her face down in the pillow, and that beautiful ass up. "I told you what I want, Cowboy…"

She had.

I got up and retrieved a condom. I sheathed myself, unwilling to wait another second, and positioned myself behind her.

With her hand between her legs, she guided me until my tip teased her pussy. She was slick, slippery, and oh so tight as I pushed in.

"I told you before, I won't break," she said, grabbing my balls and pulling me in.

I pushed in farther, but not all the way.

"Is that all you got, Cowboy?" she taunted me.

I grasped her hips and rammed into her, fully to the root.

She cried out, but I knew it was one of her screams of pleasure, and the loud phase was beginning.

I pumped into her and grabbed a fistful of her hair before snaking a hand around to fondle those great boobs.

She rocked back into me in rhythm, with loud moans. "Oh… Oh… More… Yeah… More…"

The tension built in me as her animal desire kept pace with mine.

She was so tight, and her walls constricted around me every time I pulled out. She might not know it, but she had a perfect technique. Her little yelps as I thrust into her were erotic music to my ears.

Her moans increased as she came again, convulsing around my cock, pulling me to my limit as well. Her dirty requests for me to fuck her harder pushed me to the edge.

With one last pump, as deep as I could go, I tensed and came with a shudder, breathless from the exertion. A few moments later, I collapsed forward on her before turning us both to the side.

Still inside, I wrapped my arm around her and held her boob. "Better?"

Her hand found my thigh. "Harder is better. I like it when you lose control."

I'd remember that.

We settled into bed, with me wrapped around her and my cock against her ass. One arm rested above her head, and the other wrapped around her, with a handful of boob.

She had wanted to play hard, and giving in to her desires had benefited us both. Somehow every slap of flesh against flesh brought us dangerously closer to bonding as one. She'd given herself to me fully, as I had to her. It had been exhilarating, yet scary, to progress to a level of passion that was almost like before.

Perhaps it was the time apart, but I valued everything about her even more now than I had the first time. I knew without a doubt that she wasn't drawn to me by my family name and title. That was a rare gift in these days of the connected world where pictures of my brother and me went out onto the internet and could never be pulled back or controlled.

I left the bed to dispose of the condom. On my return, I curled up behind my Sunshine, cupped her breast, and kissed her neck.

Her breathing slowly returned to normal, and her hand moved to trace lazy circles on mine.

It was time to say it. "Sunshine?"

"Yeah?"

"You are the best thing that ever happened to me." I used *are* instead of *were* on purpose.

"You mean that?" This was the question she often asked when she couldn't look me in the eye to judge my truthfulness.

"It hurts that you have to ask."

She pressed my hand against her breast. "Sorry. Force of habit."

I waited for her to say something more. Wasn't this where one's lover reciprocated a kind statement? I would have accepted even an "I like you too," right now.

She breathed in a big breath. "I think we should get engaged."

I couldn't swallow. That wasn't what I'd expected.

CHAPTER 25

Rebecca

He pulled away so fast he almost yanked my boob off.

"Ow." I put my hand behind me to show him what being pulled hard felt like.

He grabbed my wrist before I could yank anything important. "We said casual, not married."

I turned to him and laughed. "Not like that, silly. Fake engagement." I turned away again, missing the heat of him against my back. "Now hold me like you mean it, and listen for a change."

He moved close and put his arm around me again.

I pulled his hand to my breast where it had been, and where it belonged. "And gentle. You do that again, and I'll pull one of your balls so hard they'll hear you in France."

"Sorry. You surprised me."

For a moment, I breathed in and out, relishing the feel of him against me and the way he cupped my breast. "I mean a *fake* engagement. Splitting up to watch the floor tonight didn't work, and you saw how your parents reacted. A couple wouldn't do that, and I can't use the introduction excuse a second time."

"Getting engaged doesn't fix that."

"Watching isn't cutting it. I need to be in the bathroom when it happens."

"So you're going to hide in the toilet all night?"

"I need to be the bait. I need to be the one wearing the jewelry he wants to steal."

"That doesn't sound safe to me." Ethan's voice carried genuine concern.

"As your fiancée, I would receive the kind of over-the-top necklace that would be a target. Your father said it's a family tradition, and that's what makes it perfect."

"We think he's knocking these women out. You'd be a sitting duck. I can't let you do that." He tightened his embrace.

"You'll still be around, and besides, the other ladies weren't expecting anything to happen," I countered. "I'll be prepared. Give me a Taser, and I'll have him writhing on the floor for you." He had to see the logic in my approach. I'd just come up with it, but it all fit together.

"Those aren't legal in this country."

"Then pepper spray."

"Also not allowed."

"Look, I can defend myself. I'll have the upper hand because I'm expecting him. Those other victims weren't."

"I don't like it."

"We have to catch him in the act. Would you rather put CCTV in the bathroom?"

He *tsk*ed. "You know we can't do that either."

"Exactly. We may only get one more chance before this thief moves on, and watching from outside isn't cutting it."

With three pieces of jewelry already stolen and hidden in the bathroom downstairs, I knew we didn't have much time before the thief's trap snapped shut and Ethan's family was ensnared.

"It may only seem that way to you because nothing got pinched tonight. Maybe we could put a camera in the hallway leading to the toilet," he suggested.

"And how would you monitor that? How would we know which woman was being targeted from the outside? They walk out with what looks like the same jewelry as they went in with."

"That could be a problem," he admitted.

"I'd bet money that Lady Devonwood's necklace got *pinched*, as you put it," I told him. "But you wouldn't be able to tell that from a hallway camera you checked at the end of the night." I couldn't reveal that I knew she'd been targeted tonight, but my logic was sound. What he'd proposed just wasn't as good as my plan.

"I can't allow you to put yourself in danger like that."

We couldn't take the chance of being hands-off again. "That's sweet of you, but I'm attending the next one as bait, one way or another."

"That's not your call."

"Sure it is. I'm going to be wearing the ultimate necklace. Your father said it was a family tradition for the men to get their fiancées a necklace. You're not winning this argument, Blakewell. No way." I wouldn't let his headstrong opinions jeopardize his family's reputation.

"I said *no*."

"I'll have your aunt Helen call the mayor, if I have to. Why don't you save us both the trouble and just agree?" I couldn't give up on this.

He sighed. "I'll agree on one condition."

He couldn't see me smile at the surprise. I'd won. "Sure. What?"

"You wear an emergency call button. One sign of trouble, and you press it. I'll be five seconds or less away."

It actually sounded like a good idea. "Thank you for caring. You're going to make a very sweet fiancé."

"You think you have this all figured out, don't you?"

I could feel his hot breath against my neck, and it tickled. "You know I'm right about this." I wiggled my butt against him. "You're going to need to be more attentive than you were at the party tonight, and more touching would be good too."

"I'm English. That's not how we are."

"You need to learn, if you want to sell it."

"I hear you." His thumb began tracing circles on my breast again.

"Not just in bed. In public is what I meant."

"Timing is going to be an issue. We need some time for a proper courtship."

"Trust me, I'm easy." The way his hands on me felt, I was *super* easy tonight. "I don't need much time to be convinced."

"You Americans don't get it. For this to be believable in English society, it has to take some time. You've met my parents, and I've taken you out socially, so some of it is behind us, but I can't just propose to you tomorrow. The people who know me, especially my parents, are going to be a problem."

"Why? Because I'm American?"

"No, not that. But I've been pretty much opposed to having any kind of relationship, so suddenly wanting to get married would be a radical change for me."

"It's not like we just met," I countered. "I thought when you explained it at dinner, the story was convincing. I'll bet your mother is very happy for you."

"Perhaps."

I didn't get why he thought his mother would be any way except over the moon he was getting married. "Anyway, we can worry about the timing tomorrow."

Had I misjudged his mother and she didn't like me? Could it be because I was an American?

~

Ethan

Becky's breathing settled into the slow rhythm of sleep. I lay awake next to her, staring into the darkness. Our conversation rattled around in my brain and wouldn't let me sleep.

Me getting married? People wouldn't believe it.

But her reasoning made sense in terms of catching the thief, so we had to figure out how to sell it.

We couldn't spring it on everyone—*hey, I decided to propose to this woman who just came back into my life. Sure, I said I wasn't settling down for a long time, but there's no time like the present.* Those conversations wouldn't go over well, and for this to work, the thief had to believe us.

This would take some preparation, some time in front of the cameras to sell the illusion. But first I had to sell Mom, and that had to start first thing in the morning.

The second problem with this plan was putting Becky in harm's way as the bait on the end of the hook. We had no idea who the thief was, or even if it was a *he*, or a single person instead of a team. With no clue who the adversary was, the attack could come from anywhere and at any time.

Becky claimed she'd be prepared, but how could she be without any idea who was coming after her?

Now I wished Maxwell had paired me up with a professional from the Met, a woman who'd been trained in taking down criminals and defending herself.

Becky was the perfect partner if we had to interrogate suspects, but that was something we couldn't do on this case. Now we had to rely on our history. People could believe I'd have her with me at these parties, so she could be the extra set of eyes, someone who wouldn't stand out.

But the thought of sending Becky into a dangerous situation made my skin crawl. If I'd known or even suspected we'd be going at it this way, I would have insisted on someone else—a professional I wouldn't have to worry about.

But then none of this would have happened. I thought back through the evening and the past few days. I smiled in the dark. Becky had a pull on me that I couldn't describe or foil. If only she didn't have that damned lie-detector capability, it would be easy to fall under her spell.

She was the reason I couldn't have a long-term relationship.

Dad always said relationships were built on trust, and trust was built on honesty. So, how could I get there with the secret I had to carry? It would pop any balloon of honesty we built between us—or between me and any woman who wasn't a short-term fling.

I thought back to our last picnic in St. James's Park. The vision of that day was one I'd played over many times since then. Tonight, it would be the vision that finally let me fall asleep.

CHAPTER 26

REBECCA

Sunday morning, I stretched my arm out on the bed when I woke, only to find it empty. "Ethan?"

The door to the bathroom opened.

He had only a towel wrapped around his waist, and his hair was wet from the shower. "I tried not to wake you, Sunshine."

I reached in his direction. "I didn't get a good-morning kiss yet." I'd hoped for more, but him up and out of bed already didn't bode well for that.

He ambled over, sat on the bed, and leaned over to kiss me. "I'll see you downstairs when you're ready," he said as he moved away.

"Do you have to leave already?" I pulled the sheet down below my chest, in case my words weren't obvious enough. It struck me how quickly I'd fallen back into an easy attachment to him, as if he hadn't broken my heart five years ago.

His fingers grazed my breast as he got off the bed. "You make this hard."

"Hard is good," I teased.

"I have work to do, if we're going to pull this off."

I gave him a questioning look. I had no clue what he was talking about.

"I have to plant the seeds with my parents if we're getting engaged next weekend."

Understanding now, I blew him a kiss as he backed away. "I'll be thinking of you." I slid out of the bed after the door closed behind him.

In the shower, I wondered about the end of this episode in my life. Years ago, me engaged to Ethan would have been a dream come true. Now the fairy tale would play out only partway, stopping before either of us had to make the hard choices a marriage would force.

But as the water ran down my back, I had to ask what was different now. Why couldn't it be a dream come true?

I leaned back until the water ran over my face and rinsed away the silly thoughts that things could play out any differently for us now than they had before. He remained unwilling to talk about the past or fully share his secrets with me. And besides, I had a job—even a promotion—waiting for me back in San Francisco. Ethan's life was here.

Square peg, meet round hole. Sure, as lovers, our bodies fit together perfectly, but as much as we wished it, our lives didn't mesh. Sufficiently cleansed of irrational thoughts, I wiped the water from my eyes and looked for the shampoo.

∽

ETHAN

STOPPING IN THE LIBRARY, I CLOSED THE DOOR AND DIALED CHARLIE'S NUMBER. AS expected it went to voicemail.

"Charlie, Ethan here. Dad asked me to pass on a warning that either Knightley or Wentworth may be planning something and to watch your back. Give me a call when you get this."

I settled into a chair to see if he was monitoring his mobile or not.

A minute later the call came, but the name on the screen surprised me.

"I see you have a new girl," my sister, Kelsey, said.

"You spying on me from afar?"

"A girl can't check out a news website without finding something about you these days. You're making quite the splash."

I leaned back. "Damned paps are everywhere."

"Tell me about her."

"First, I need to pass on a warning from Dad."

"I don't need it."

"Humor me and listen anyway."

She sighed loudly. "Go ahead."

"He's worried that one of his competitors is about to try to hurt us. You should be careful."

She didn't say anything for a few moments. "What else is new? He's paranoid, and don't you even consider asking me to come home for my own protection." Her voice was almost a yell by the end of the sentence.

"Calm down. I'm just the messenger here."

She sighed. "Sorry."

"This time I think it might be more than that." I couldn't elaborate further.

"Consider me warned…again. Now, tell me about your girl."

I breathed in a big breath. How to start? "Her name is Rebecca Sommerset. We met at university when she was over here for a semester. We hit it off—"

"That Rebecca?" she interrupted. She'd known about our time at Imperial.

"Yes, and she's back in town." I smiled as I said it.

"She made you happy, didn't she?"

The memories of our time together were good. "That would be a yes."

"Well then, don't screw it up this time."

"Got any other great advice?"

A voice on her end called her name. "Just a minute," she told them. "I gotta go. I just wanted to say I'm glad you found someone worth bringing home to Mom and Dad."

"Thanks. She's special. Are you coming back for the holidays?"

She was quiet.

"We miss you."

"I miss you, too. Give Mom my love. Gotta go."

Several minutes later, when I still hadn't gotten a call from Charlie, I headed for the kitchen.

Mom and Dad's conversation stopped as soon as I entered the room.

Dad looked away and stuffed something in his back pocket as I approached.

Mom smiled at me. "You're just in time to join your father on his morning walk."

My empty stomach complained. "I'd love a little exercise to stimulate the appetite," I said anyway.

Dad slid on his cap, and I followed him to the door. "We'll be back in a jiffy," he called to Mom.

"Breakfast will be waiting."

Dad and I walked silently through the garden and toward the woods. The trail led to the Yellow and Red cottages.

I started our conversation. "Any more threats I should know about?"

"As a matter of fact, yes. Karen found a note by the gate when she came in this morning." He pulled the wrinkled envelope from his pocket and handed it to me.

I opened it and removed the note by the corner. The paper looked like it had come off a printer, so tying it to someone's handwriting, or to a typewriter, was out.

You hurt us. Now it's your turn.

The message was sinister in its brevity.

I read it again, and shivered. "Mind if I keep this?"

"Why?"

"Maybe there's a fingerprint on it or something." I knew the Yard's laboratory could find amazing things, if I gave it to them.

He extended his hand. "No outsiders. I'll keep it."

"I know someone—"

He cut me off. "No, I said."

I handed it over, unable to tell him what resources I had at my disposal.

He folded the paper and replaced it in the envelope. "I had the first two analyzed already. They're too cagey to make a simple mistake like that."

"This isn't the first one you've received?"

He shook his head, but offered no details.

"Any inkling of who's behind it?" I pressed.

"Not for certain. Wentworth would be my first guess, or maybe Knightley." His shrug said even those were guesses. "Anyway, that's not what I wanted to talk with you about."

I only had to wait a few strides to learn what it was.

"I agreed with your mother last night," Dad said before we reached the tree line.

"About?" I asked.

"Last night when she said you'd behaved poorly by leaving Rebecca alone most of the—"

I cut him off. "She's more secure than that. She understands how I feel and doesn't need me constantly next to her to reassure her." I thought the best defense here was a good offense.

Dad nodded, but didn't speak again for a few strides. "I was going to say I agreed with your mother, but I liked Rebecca's explanation better."

I'd been chastised for speaking up too quickly.

I went left with Dad when he chose the branch of the trail to the Yellow Cottage.

"A woman that sure of herself and trying to meet others without implying an association with you or our family is a rare find, rare indeed. A fine head on that lady of yours."

"She is quite special." That was something I could say without acting. Becky had never stopped being special to me.

"I'd hoped for years that you two would meet again."

I stopped in my tracks. "What?" He had to have misspoken. I'd never told them about Becky until dinner a few days ago.

Dad stopped and turned. "I thought I was clear. I'd hoped for years that you two would find each other again."

"But..." If it weren't Dad, I'd be calling him a liar or just plain stoned.

"You thought I didn't know? I told you, I know everything that goes on in this family. It's my responsibility to know." He turned and waved me forward.

I went with him. "But how?"

"Charlie, of course. He said he'd never seen you like that with a girl. Your mother and I didn't need to meet her to understand."

"Oh." Charlie had been sworn to secrecy, but I guess it made sense that they'd pressure him to open up. "You never said anything."

"You didn't want us to know, and that was good enough for us."

Us meant more than him. "Mom knew too?"

"Of course. I don't keep anything from her. We can talk about anything with family."

I swallowed hard. What would he say if he knew what she'd kept from him about me—about *us*?

"If you feel the same way you did, you should count your lucky stars that she's back in your life."

The warmth in my chest those words evoked was clear enough. "I do still adore her." I'd never been happier than spending the last few days with her, even if her questions could annoy me.

"My advice is to not let your infatuation obscure the truth," he added. "Be sure she has a good moral compass before you get in so deep that your judgment is impaired. An honest woman is a requirement above all else."

Could he tell that Becky was merely putting on an act? "Do you doubt her?"

"Not in the least, but I know much less about her than you do. What does she value? What does she abhor? What thrills her, and what scares her?"

Becky was the most honest person I'd ever met. It was her devotion to the truth over everything that had made continuing our relationship impossible years ago. She would have dug relentlessly for the truth I couldn't admit to her, and it would have torn us apart.

"She values honesty more than anyone I know," I told him. "That's a certainty."

Dad nodded. "Good to know. You always need to know who you can count on."

Dad's emphasis on honesty could never square with what I knew Mom had done. It would destroy him to find out.

He put a hand on my shoulder. "Have I told you how I met your mother?"

I'd heard it a half dozen times, but I'd let him regale me again. "Not in a while."

"She came up to me in Waterloo Station. She'd just found a man's wallet, and she didn't have time before her train to take it to the lost and found, or to find a bobby. She hadn't even opened it to find out the chap's name because she didn't want to invade his privacy."

We arrived at the Yellow Cottage and stopped outside.

"Turned out," he continued, "the chap had almost a thousand pounds in the wallet. When I located him, he wanted to give her a reward, but she'd run off so fast after her train that I hadn't gotten her name. It took me a week of waiting by that same train in Waterloo to catch up with her again. And she refused the reward —said it wasn't proper to get paid for merely doing the right thing."

He pointed at the cottage. "This place is very special to me. It's where I proposed to your mother—the very same place my father proposed to your grandmother, by the way."

I nodded. It seemed I didn't need to plant as many seeds as I'd thought for our plan, at least as far as Dad went.

"So I had to take the reward back to the chap who lost the wallet. Morty was his name. He was an ornery sort, and he wouldn't take the money back either."

He nodded back down the path. "We should head back."

I followed him.

"I was stuck between two opinionated people who wouldn't take the money," he said. "Morty said if she wouldn't accept it, I should use it to buy her a nice dinner and not take no for an answer. So that's exactly what I did. Had to ask her three times, but it was worth it."

As we walked, I realized how good this story always made me feel.

It was several paces before Dad spoke again. "You shouldn't lead her along this time."

I hated that it was going to look like that to him in the end. "I'm not. I adore her more than you can understand."

"Glad to hear it. You two deserve to be happy." The pat on the back he gave me said I'd made the sale, and he wouldn't be a problem when I announced our engagement.

The hard part would be unwinding it after we caught the bugger who was after the jewelry.

∼

Rebecca

Ethan's mother was at the stove when I found my way down to the kitchen.

"Sleep well, I hope?" she said cheerily as she brought me a coffee.

I accepted the cup. "Very well, thank you." It wouldn't be appropriate to add that her son was the reason.

"Ethan told me you prefer coffee to tea."

"An American weakness," I explained as I took a sip.

She brought two plates over. "Crumpets and eggs. It's just us girls. Carter took Ethan out on a walk."

I nodded.

"What would you like on your crumpets? We've got honey, marmalade, vegemite, or butter, if you prefer."

"Marmalade would be wonderful."

She brought a jar over and opened it. "I'm so glad you and Ethan got back together. He's needed to make it right with you for years, and been too stupid to realize it. I wish I'd been allowed to tell him back then, for both your sakes."

"I'm not following." I scooped marmalade onto a crumpet.

Ethan had told me his parents hadn't known anything about us back then, and our dinner with them had been his first discussion of me.

She spread honey on one of her crumpets. "He tried to keep it from us, but we knew about you and Ethan when he was at Imperial College. Children think they're being so clever sometimes."

"He thinks you didn't know."

She chewed a bite. "We knew, but enough of that. I've waited five years to meet you."

"Well, I'm here now." It was all I could think to say while I waited for the inquisition to start. Sending the boys out was probably her way of getting us alone, but this was part of the job.

"I saw that you managed to get Christie off him last night."

"She didn't seem to like me." I didn't feel comfortable bad-mouthing their guests. That could be full of land mines I didn't understand.

"She is something, isn't she?"

I ventured a minimal distance into the mine field. "She seems not to like Americans."

Diane laughed. "Did she call you a colonist?"

"No. But she did try to tell me to fetch her some hors d'oeuvres."

"Sounds like her."

"You're not a fan?" I tried a question to illuminate her feelings.

"No, not at all." Her response was pure truth so far as I could tell. "That girl is the very definition of a social climber."

Instead of responding, I brought a forkful of eggs to my mouth.

"Ethan was devastated when you two broke up last time." The statement made Diane's agenda this morning clearer. She wanted to keep her son safe and warn me not to break his heart again, as she saw it.

"It was hard on both of us. I feel we both made a mistake, and we've both matured since then." Even though it had been Ethan's fault, I was willing to shoulder half the blame to make his mother feel better.

"He looks at you in a way he doesn't other girls."

That was the invitation for me to tell her how I felt.

"He's very special. As I said before, he's made me very happy, and I wish we hadn't gotten our wires crossed earlier."

Her eyes crinkled in a way that said she didn't entirely buy my line. "Yes, wires crossed. Well, let's hope that doesn't happen again."

CHAPTER 27

Ethan

Monday morning we were back in town, and Becky had gone to check in at her office and pick up files she needed to work on.

At nine, I rang up the Superintendent.

"Anything to report, Blakewell?"

This conversation was going to be a bit touchy. "We attended one of the parties over the weekend and didn't see anything of note, sir."

"And your partner, did she discern anything from the conversations? I'm told she can spot a scammer at a hundred paces."

"There's nobody quite like her, sir. But no, she didn't find anyone dodgy in the crowd."

"And?"

I made a supposition I knew Becky didn't agree with. "Sir, my best guess is that the thief wasn't there this weekend." In the end, my guess was as good as hers.

"Well, that doesn't get us anywhere. And what do you plan to do next besides wait around?"

Attending the parties undercover—as if the thief would be obvious—had been his and Smithers' plan, but I could see where this was going to go if we didn't get any results.

"Sir," I started, "we intend to bring the thief to us by having Miss Sommerset attend the next parties wearing jewelry he won't be able to resist."

"Now that makes more sense than passive observation. Is she equipped to handle a role like that?"

A wrong word from me now could get Becky pulled from this inquiry, and she was relying on this assignment being successful. That wrong word would guarantee her safety, but also her hatred of me.

"She's capable enough, sir, and with an emergency call button, Detective Waters and I will be able to assist quickly." At least that was my commitment to Becky. "Waters will be posing as a photographer again," I added.

"Very well then. Requisition whatever equipment you need, but one question."

"Sir?"

"Who is supplying the shiny bauble you think will attract this bugger?"

That was the one thing I hadn't worked out yet. "Her managing director promised whatever support we needed for this inquiry."

"Well, good luck with that."

He apparently didn't think buying an expensive piece of jewelry was what Cornwall had in mind.

I swallowed as I realized he might be right.

On the way downstairs, I texted Becky.

ME: Lunch 11:30 corner of Horse Guards Rd and Birdcage Walk

Outside I hailed a taxi.
It was time to start being seen.

∼

REBECCA

I DUMPED MY PHONE IN MY PURSE. "I HAVE TO LEAVE FOR LUNCH," I TOLD GINNY AS I slipped back into my shoes. Before I'd left this morning, Ethan had told me to dress up for lunch today, and these were my best heels. This pair looked great, but left something to be desired in the comfort department.

"Don't forget the meeting at one with Mr. Smithers and Mr. Paul," Ginny said.

"And have a fun time with Ethan," Margaret added. She'd been pumping me all morning for more details on the party, and Ethan in particular.

I'd been rather vague.

Her interruptions had only frustrated both of us. Her, because I wouldn't give her details, and me because her interruptions kept breaking my concentration on the interviews. I had to rewind almost to the beginning each time to get the feel of it.

New videos were being added to my list faster than I was getting through them.

Downstairs, after exiting to the street, I checked the time and flagged down a cab. Luckily I was running late, and could use that excuse to avoid the walk to the tube station in these shoes.

At a few minutes before eleven thirty, the cab dropped me where Ethan had asked, but he was nowhere to be seen. Then there was the problem of there being no restaurant in sight either.

My feet rebelled at the mere thought of a long hike in these heels.

A few minutes later Ethan jumped out of a taxi.

He carried a wicker picnic basket in one hand and a blanket in the other. In college, any old plastic bag from the market had sufficed to carry our lunch for a picnic in the park, along with his ratty, old green blanket.

Silly me had thought lunch meant *sit down at a table*, given that he knew I was in heels and a pencil skirt today.

"You know I'm not dressed for this," I said, pointing at the basket.

He put down the basket and in a swift move, pulled me to him.

The kiss he planted on me made me remember why I missed him, and forget the argument my feet were making about the walk.

"I missed you, Sunshine," he said as he nuzzled my nose with his.

My skin warmed. "You should have told me it was a picnic you had in mind. I could've changed my shoes, at least." I shifted my weight to the other foot.

He pulled back and appraised me slowly from head to toe—with hungry eyes. "You look delectable. I wouldn't change a thing."

Whatever liquor he'd added to his tea this morning, I liked the effect. "Tell me again, darling."

"You look good enough to eat." He added a wicked wink that melted my panties. "If you can carry this," he said, handing me the blanket. "I'll handle the basket."

I took the blanket, which was a thousand times nicer than the old one.

He held out his elbow for me to take. "Shall we?"

With my arm hooked with his, we started across the road and into St. James's Park.

"Let me guess, you want to be seen and photographed by that guy with the long-lens camera, right?"

He showed me an ear-to-ear smile. "Beautiful and smart. Quite the package. Not him, but another Charlie told me about."

"We have to make this quick."

"I wouldn't count on that." The arm I had a hold of snaked behind me to pull me close. He adjusted his stride to match mine. "We can discuss that over some bubbly."

"Is this what you call joined at the hip?"

"It's not my preferred way of being joined to you, but will have to do for now."

Heat shot straight to my core. "You sure are romantic today."

"Don't look now, but it's time to smile and giggle."

Without turning my head, I glanced to the right. Sure enough, there he was.

The photographer was playing with his camera and hadn't aimed it at us yet. A few seconds later, it pointed our way.

I giggled. "Why is he hanging out here?"

Ethan laughed. "We're not far from Parliament. According to Charlie, this guy likes to catch the occasional MP walking this way."

"Why would he be interested in us?"

"Do we look like anybody else in the park?"

Of course we didn't. When I glanced around, there was not a suit or a tie in sight, and almost no dresses—certainly not one like mine. We were dressed as if going to a fancy restaurant, and every other group on the grass was in casual attire. We stood out for sure.

Ethan turned me toward the grass. "This should do well."

We had gone a bit beyond Camera Guy, but not out of his sight.

I giggled again for him as my heel sank into the turf. "Hold on a sec."

Ethan held me steady while I pulled off one and then the other shoe.

A dozen yards from the path, he stopped us. "How about here?"

I nodded. "You're the boss."

His wicked grin reappeared. "Just you remember that, Sunshine." He set down the basket, took the blanket from me, and laid it out. Not only was it cleaner and larger than his old one, but it was soft when I settled onto it.

Ethan took the side facing Camera Guy's tree, and I had my back to him.

A nearby couple looked over longingly as Ethan pulled a bottle of Bollinger out of the basket and popped the cork. It went almost straight up, and he had only to reach a little to catch it on the way down.

He poured us both glasses of the bubbly. "To a wonderful week," he proposed with a raised glass to me.

I clinked my glass to his. "A wonderful week."

He leaned back on his elbows. "I think the fresh air agrees with you, Sunshine. You look gorgeous."

The blush scorched my cheeks. "What has gotten into you today?"

"Just stating a truth."

That was right. My radar hadn't detected an ounce of deception in his words, and that realization turned my blush up another notch. "You're embarrassing me." He had to be exaggerating, but that was something I couldn't gauge.

"Okay. Do you want me to promise to only say nasty things about you for the rest of the day?"

"I wouldn't go that far." I laughed and realized some of this was probably to make me smile for the camera. Exaggerate, laugh, and give Camera Guy a show—that was Ethan's gambit here.

He took a sip from his glass and winked. "So far I haven't said anything that isn't true."

"Let me add a truth, then. We'd better get started on lunch. I have to get back to work by one."

"No," was his single-word answer.

"What do you mean, no? I have a meeting with my boss at one."

He took a sip of this champagne and did that thing he could do with his eyes that froze me. "Like you said, I'm the boss. This is more important."

He couldn't just *decide* he was the boss of me. That was a childish way to put it, but exactly how I felt. "Stop trying to get me in trouble." I put my glass down. "Now let's get the food out and make this quick."

"You don't get it, Miss Sommerset. You're the one who said we possibly have only one chance to catch this bugger, and therefore we have to make this courtship look the best we can. Do you agree?"

He had no idea how much I believed we only had the one chance before his family was ruined.

I nodded, though I was not pleased by the demotion from Sunshine to Miss Sommerset. "But I still have other work to do."

He sat up and moved close to take my hand. "You can do that at home with me."

It struck a chord that he'd called his apartment my home. Was I reading too much into it?

"We're playing a love story here, you and me—a believable one with long, romantic lunches, intimate dinners, and every other thing that goes with it. A thirty-minute picnic in the park isn't in the script."

Now we were back to playacting a love story for newspaper consumption. "You don't have anything else going on," I pointed out. "I do."

"Stop. Here's the question you have to answer. Which is more important? Getting this right, or any one of the several other little projects you're working on? And for me the answer is simple. Working with you on this assignment comes first, and everything else is a distant second. You said yourself that this inquiry could land you the promotion you want."

When he put it that way, there was only one answer. He, his family, and this project were all much more important than anything else at the office—not just because this was my ticket to a promotion, but because in the last week, Ethan had become important to me again. And I hoped I'd become equally important to him.

"What'll it be, Sunshine? Are we going to do this right, or not?"

"I'd love a long, romantic picnic." I pulled my phone out and selected Ginny's contact. It went to voicemail. "Tell Smithers I won't be back in today. I'm busy on the Lindsley project," I said after the beep.

Ethan laid back on the blanket. "Good choice."

I turned off my phone and settled against him with my head on his shoulder.

In the distance, Camera Guy took an interest in us.

"He's watching," I whispered in Ethan's ear.

"Then I think it's time you kissed me."

CHAPTER 28

Rebecca (one week later)

Late morning at my makeshift desk at Ethan's apartment, I finished my review of the second of the two interviews from the New York office. I hit send with a satisfying click.

Ginny had sent them yesterday. This constant barrage of work from Smithers was exhausting.

For the last week, Ethan and I had been making the rounds of places his brother had said paparazzi hung out. Picnics in the park and dinners at the right restaurants had resulted in daily coverage in the tabloids. Ethan and I had become the hot new item for the gossip rags. All the while I'd made sure we avoided Lizzy, lest she sniff out that this wasn't real. It wasn't my normal behavior, but it was for the best.

For the first several days, I'd been the mystery woman, and then my name came out. The gossip about us was going the right direction, including marriage speculation. They'd also learned I was from California.

A few nasty comments had been directed at Ethan. Evidently marrying an American would be bad form, in the opinion of some. Diluting the Blakewell line with American blood instead of courting a proper English girl was considered sacrilege.

Ginny and Margaret were full of questions about Ethan when I called into the office, which I'd been doing instead of visiting it.

To the world, we were with each other constantly, out and about on the town. In reality, I was working at Ethan's apartment each morning and late each evening to try to keep up with my work after making our photo rounds for the day.

I'd much rather have spent my evenings relaxing in front of the television with Ethan.

My phone rang with Smithers' name on the screen. Avoiding him wouldn't help.

He started in right after I answered. "I got your latest email with the two New York cases, and I'm wondering where the other two are."

"Ginny only sent two video links yesterday," I said.

"You should check your email more closely, Sommerset. I was copied on it, and all four were attached."

I scrolled to the message and checked.

Bad news. He was right.

"I'm sorry, sir. I didn't see them. I'll get to them soon."

"I'm disappointed, Sommerset, in the way your work ethic has deteriorated."

"I'm working very hard at all my projects," I said.

He huffed over the line. "I can read the papers. It's pretty clear that all the cavorting around town with that Blakewell chap is taking up your entire day. That's not what I call work. I've had about enough of this."

I reminded him of his own words. "You said the Met was in charge, and this is the plan the inspector put together." Me not contributing to the plan's formation was an exaggeration that didn't matter.

"I'm not happy with it. You're needed here."

I'd had enough of *this*. "I'll have the inspector call, and you can hash it out with him."

"You do that. And one other thing, the expenses on this are getting out of hand."

After ending the call, I started on the first of the other two New York interviews. Something about Smithers' attitude bugged me.

Did he want me to fail?

It would take a few direct questions to ferret that out, and it couldn't be done over the phone. I was as useless as the next person when I couldn't see the visual clues.

~

AN HOUR LATER, THE SOUND OF A KEY BEING INSERTED INTO THE LOCK ALERTED ME TO Ethan's return.

"Are you ready?" he asked when he appeared.

I'd been up before six to watch the New York interviews. "A nap is what I'm ready for."

He checked his watch—sure sign that a nap wasn't in my future.

But as impatient as he was, just the sight of Ethan brightened my outlook.

Walking up behind me, he started to knead my sore shoulders. "We have an appointment at the jeweler."

The tightness slowly gave way to his kneading fingers. "Keep that up."

"You can have five minutes; then we need to go."

Today was the day we'd scheduled to look at engagement rings. After Smithers' meltdown over the expenses we'd piled up between the shopping, the dining, and the expensive wines, buying this ring was going to aggravate him even more.

At first it had been something to look forward to, but today it didn't hold that promise of excitement. When we'd initially talked about this, I'd dreamed about how wonderful it would be to go engagement-ring shopping with Ethan, pretending it was five years earlier, before the breakup.

Now, with it written down on a schedule, it had become just another item to cross off the list, another scene in our fictitious love story.

That's what he'd said, after all, at our picnic; we were following the script of a love story, a fiction to draw in the newspaper readers and the thief.

When the shoulder rub ended, I saved my document and closed the laptop lid. "You win."

When I rose and turned, the hurt in his eyes was obvious. "I thought you were looking forward to this." He stepped back. "If you want, I can go pick it out by myself."

"I was... I mean, I am."

He checked his watch again, a reminder that we had to be on time if we were going to get caught by the paparazzi. Ethan was certain the clerks at the jewelry store he'd chosen would pass our appointment time on to one or more of them.

Tossing the phone into my purse, I took his hand and dragged him toward the door. "Let's go. Can't be late."

"Really, if you're too tired, I can do this alone."

My lack of enthusiasm had hurt his feelings. I gave him my best smile.

Ethan locked the door behind us. "You've prepared your family for this, right?"

I turned away with a lump in my throat. "Yeah," I lied.

I couldn't tell Mom this was all for show, and I also couldn't tell her I was engaged and then promptly break it off, even if I blamed it on Ethan.

Mom would die at the prospect of me losing another chance to have the life she had, of mother and wife. It didn't matter that I had a different dream. In her mind, I just didn't know any better.

Dangling a man like Ethan in front of her and then telling her we'd decided not to get married would be devastating. It would also cement my position as loser in her mind—the ultimate disappointing daughter.

"Good," he said as he took my hand. "We'll tackle mine as soon as Dad gets back to me. What did yours say about marrying a Brit?"

I let go of his hand when we reached the stairs and followed him so he couldn't see my face when I spoke. "Mom hopes her grandkids won't end up with your accent."

"What's wrong with my accent?"

"Nothing. I love it." That was the only true thing I'd said since he'd asked about my family. It felt odd to be talking about children when everything about our relationship was a fraud.

∼

ETHAN

MY MOBILE RANG AS THE TAXI WENDED ITS WAY THROUGH MIDDAY TRAFFIC. IT was Dad.

I'd left him a message this morning that we needed to talk.

"I got your message," he said. "Unfortunately, I leave for Heathrow this afternoon. I should be back from Dubai at the end of the week."

That wouldn't work with the timing of our plan.

"I have an errand to run, but I'll be out to the house this afternoon. Can you wait for me?"

"What's so important?"

"I can't talk about it over the phone." Telling him of my engagement plans had to be done in person to be proper, and more importantly, before he heard it secondhand.

"Okay, but I have to leave for the airport by two."

"See you soon."

"Problem?" Becky asked after I hung up.

"We have to hurry out to Rainswood. He's leaving this afternoon. We'll need to be quick."

The taxi made good time, and we arrived at our New Bond Street jeweler on time, in spite of our late start.

The recognizable red motorcycle of one of the paparazzi was parked across the street.

"*Blakewell*." The yell came from our right just as I reached for the shop's door handle.

The sound served its purpose, as both Becky and I pivoted. Catching sight of the paparazzi I'd nicknamed Red, I yanked the door open and urged Becky inside.

"Did I tell you how much I hate that?" Becky asked.

"Only a hundred times or so." I leaned close to whisper in her ear. "Sunshine, we have to do it." It was an important part of the plan. Our plan.

She pulled away. "I hate them. Do they have to be so damn intrusive?"

I was about to explain that it was just their job, but I caught the words in the back of my throat. With her sister in the business, she certainly knew that. And anyway, I knew she was right. I disliked them almost as much.

They were parasitic pains in the ass, and the only redeeming thing about this plan was that we got to use them for our purposes for a change. The tabloids were eating up our story so far. Getting them to back off later might be a challenge.

I followed Becky.

She stopped in front of a display of diamond solitaires.

"May I be of assistance?" a young man asked her as I walked up. The nametag on his off-the-rack suit read *Robert*, not the sales manager I'd scheduled to meet.

"We have an appointment with Mr. Katz," I told him.

He didn't skip a beat. "My manager is busy in back right now. Perhaps I can help you." Robert no doubt worked on commission and hoped for at least a piece of the transaction, if he got us started.

I glanced toward the window. Red was just outside with his camera, watching. "If you'd tell him his noon appointment is here, I'd appreciate it." Dealing with the manager instead of a lowly salesperson didn't matter to me, but would be what Red's readers expected of us.

The enthusiasm drained from Robert's face. "Your name, sir?"

"Blakewell. Ethan Blakewell," I said in my best James Bond cadence.

When Mr. Katz appeared, his appearance didn't disappoint. In a dapper bespoke suit, an expensive Rolex, and with a ring of short, white hair around his bald pate, he was the Hollywood image of a successful jeweler. "Lord Blakewell, it's an honor to serve you." He'd already been clued in as to who my father was.

We shook, and I introduced Rebecca as my soon-to-be fiancée.

She blushed appropriately.

With a whispered command from Katz, Robert scurried off to help another customer.

Katz tapped the glass of the display Becky was perusing. "These are rings for… those starting out."

Translation: he expected a duke's son to be spending more, and his fiancée to be wearing more.

Becky looked up.

Katz moved to our left on the other side of the display cases. "Over here we have others you might prefer."

"Darling," Becky said. "Some of these look quite pretty."

I realized a little too late now that we should have discussed this ahead of time. "Let's come back to those after we see what else Mr. Katz has to offer."

At first the thin line of her mouth indicated she was ready to argue.

"Please, Sunshine," I added. The nickname seemed to always help with her.

Becky's mouth turned up in a smile. "Of course."

Katz started bringing rings up from the case one at a time, each more ornate or with larger stones than the last.

Becky nodded politely. "That is very nice," she said again and again, but each of them only got a shrug or the shake of a head.

Katz put the most recent ring back inside the case. "I'll give you two a moment to discuss what you're looking for," he said before moving away to a discreet distance.

"Which of these do you prefer so far?" I asked.

She leaned close. "They're all too expensive."

"No, they're not. Let me worry about that."

"But Smithers will blow a gasket."

"Smithers?"

"He's all over me about the expenses."

I had to chuckle at her misunderstanding.

"It's not funny. He's really mad."

I tapped a finger on her nose. "Look at me and read my lips."

Her eyes narrowed at the challenge.

"I am buying you a ring."

"But—" she instantly responded.

"But nothing. I'm asking you to marry me, Rebecca. My job is to buy the ring and ask the question. Your job is to say yes."

"Or no." She giggled.

"To say yes," I repeated. "And to proudly wear the ring I have given you so everyone knows you're taken. This is a gift from me to you. Do you understand?"

Her eyes misted up, but she didn't say anything.

"And it won't be one of those that you Americans would say came out of a cracker box. Do you understand me?"

She nodded. "Yes. And it's Cracker Jack box."

"Whatever. I'm glad we understand each other now." I waved Katz back over. "We'd like to see that one." I pointed to the ring on the end.

"An excellent choice, sir. This is our best diamond ring at the moment."

Becky gasped when he brought it up on the velvet.

"It's a Princess Diana style," Katz said. "The center stone is five point one carats, flawless, and color D—a very rare find indeed—and each of the twelve smaller stones is a flawless D to match."

Becky blinked rapidly and wiped her eye. "May I see it?"

"Of course." Katz handed it to my smiling girl.

Her face said it all. This one was perfect. She slipped it onto her finger and admired it with wonder in her eyes.

She handed it back to Katz and sucked in a breath. "Ethan, it's too much, way too much."

"I say it's perfect."

"No," she repeated. "I think something smaller would be better." She placed it back on the velvet.

"You're worth it."

Katz backed up a step.

She shifted down to the discount end with the smaller stones. "I'd like to see that one."

Katz brought the ring I liked over to where she stood, and laid the simple diamond solitaire she'd indicated next to the one I preferred.

Becky held it up and tried it on. "This is the one."

I put my finger on the counter by the larger one. "This is more appropriate for my fiancée."

She straightened up. "I've already been mugged once in this city. I'm not wearing that and making myself a target." Her eyes narrowed. "You brought me along so I could choose."

She had a point there. The memory of her in the hospital rushed back and sent a chill through me. I looked to Katz.

"She is correct, sir," he started, "It is customary to allow the lady to choose if you bring her along."

"We'll take it," I told him. "The one she prefers." When I checked behind us, Red was still at the window.

Becky rose up, wrapped her arms around me, and gave me a photo-worthy kiss.

Red would be inside two minutes after we left to find out from Katz what we'd been shopping for.

"Can I wear it?" Becky asked while Katz was running my credit card.

"No. I haven't asked the question yet."

Her face screwed up in frustration. "Now you're teasing me."

"There's a sequence to things."

She pouted, but didn't say anything.

Five minutes later, we left with the ring box in my pocket and smiles on both our faces.

CHAPTER 29

ETHAN

An hour later, we were in the Aston headed for Rainswood. An accident on the motorway had messed up our timing, and it looked like we might miss Dad.

Becky braced herself as I darted right and punched the throttle hard to round the slower car in front of us.

"I want to live long enough to wear that ring," she said.

I slowed a bit once we passed the Peugeot, ashamed that I'd frightened her. "Sorry. We have to get there by two."

She checked the time. "Maybe we should have met him at the airport."

"Wouldn't work. This isn't an airport discussion."

She gripped the console. "Then you'd better step on it, Mr. Bond."

And step on it I did, mashing the throttle to the floor to pass the next four-wheeled obstruction.

When we arrived, Dad was just inside the door with his suitcase nearby. He checked his watch nervously. It was ten past two. "What is so bloody important?"

The hallway was crowded, with Mom, Karen, and Winston waiting around. Word had spread that I had an emergency.

I opened my arm toward the library. "Perhaps in private."

Dad followed me in, and I shut the door behind us.

"I plan to ask Rebecca to marry me," I said with my back to the door.

His mouth puckered, and he nodded slowly. "Isn't this a bit rushed?" *A bit* was an intentional understatement.

I'd thought through my answer, and it resonated with me because it was so close to the truth. "She's the one. I've known it since college. But I wasn't smart enough to acknowledge it."

If I were going to get married at this point, she'd be my obvious choice. Obvious if I were willing to ignore the elephant in the room every time we were together: the secret she had to know and I couldn't reveal.

His eyes narrowed, taking my measure. "You've thought this through?"

I'd thought of nothing else in the last week. "Absolutely." Conviction wasn't something I had to fake.

"And what does her father think of it?"

How could I be such a fool? That was something I hadn't considered. "I don't know."

"Yet." Dad's voice had turned harsh. "No son of mine is going to ask a woman for her hand in marriage without first consulting her father. It's just not done in polite circles."

I hadn't built this part into our plan, and it wasn't anything Becky had mentioned either. It was going to put a serious crimp in our timing.

Dad caught my look. "I'm surprised you hadn't thought of it. I raised you better than that."

"Yes, you did," I admitted. Shame flooded over me. "But she's American. Things are different over there. She's prepared her family for it…"

"Bollocks."

"I should—"

"Damned right you should have. Good manners are universal."

"I—"

"It's expected in polite company. Even in America."

"Yes, sir."

"Before you ask her," he stated.

"Yes, before."

"See that you do."

"I will."

Done berating me, his face morphed into a smile before he took me into a hug.

"In that case, you have my blessing. We think she'd be a wonderful addition to the family."

"Thank you."

He released me and reached for the door handle, but paused. "Where will you hold the wedding?"

"We haven't discussed that yet."

"While it is the bride's family's choice, I do hope you will consider Rainswood."

"I'll suggest it."

He opened the door to the hallway.

I took in a lungful of air and followed him a second later.

Mom's look was inquisitive.

Dad strode up and kissed her. "I'll be in touch when I land."

Her glance shifted from him to me and back again.

"No worries. We're all good," Dad told Mom.

Her features softened. She had complete faith in him. My eyes shifted to Becky. Would she be as trusting?

"Well?" Becky asked when we were back in the car. "How did he take the news?"

"I fucked-up."

Her head snapped to mine. "How?"

"He gave me his blessing, but…"

She waited a second before asking, "But what?"

"He pointed out that I've skipped a step." I turned onto the main road. "I need to ask your father."

When I looked over, her jaw had dropped open. "That's not necessary."

"It is in my family. No Blakewell man has ever taken a wife without asking her father for her hand. I don't intend to be the first."

"That's so eighteenth century."

I slowed for a lorry ahead. "We'll need to catch a flight tomorrow morning."

She slumped back in the seat. "That could be a problem."

Rebecca

. . .

"Be a problem how?" Ethan asked as he waited for a chance to pass the truck ahead of us.

Now I was caught between the proverbial rock and a hard place. I looked out the window on my side of the car. But the answer wasn't out there, and stalling wouldn't save me. "They won't be ready for us to visit."

He drove to the right and looked around the truck for a second before rejoining the lane behind the slow mover. "They don't need to be ready. We won't take much of their time, just pop in long enough for me to have a chat with your father. Maybe take them out to supper. We couldn't dally even if we wanted to. We have to be back here for you to be seen with the necklace."

If I wasn't in such a jam, I would have made fun of his use of the word *dally*. How was I going to explain this? I decided on simple and direct. "I didn't tell them anything about us, or a possible engagement."

Ethan's knuckles turned white as he gripped the steering wheel. He pulled the car off the side of the road and stopped before turning to me.

I shifted toward the door, backed up by the intensity of his gaze.

"You said you'd told your mother."

I shook my head. "I couldn't."

"But you told me you did."

His sharp words cut me with the criticism I deserved. I shrugged. "But I didn't."

"And what happened to our honesty pledge?"

This was what embarrassed me most. "I screwed up. I meant to tell her, but I couldn't do it."

"Becky, are you that ashamed of me?"

"How can you even ask that?"

"What choice do you give me when you won't explain yourself? You're the one making a big deal about having no secrets."

I deserved all that he was laying on me, and I couldn't feel any worse about having let him down. "I screwed up. There's no excuse for it."

He held his hand out on the console for me.

I shied away like it was a snake ready to bite.

"I forgive you."

I placed my hand in his, and his gentle touch meant more to me than I could express. "I'm sorry."

"You owe me two things now."

I'd have agreed to anything to erase the shame I felt for letting him down. "Okay. What?"

"First you need to promise to give me the benefit of the doubt when I ask for it. I'm destined to screw up at some point and need it."

That was simple enough. "Okay, I promise."

"I'm serious. I'm a man, and at some point I'll do something stupid and need a do-over, no questions asked."

I giggled. "You got it. What else?"

He checked his mirrors and pulled back onto the road.

"You need to explain why you felt you couldn't tell your mother about us."

That was what I'd expected his first request to be, but I wasn't prepared for this discussion. "Mother thinks I should settle down and have a family."

"There's nothing unusual about that coming from a mother."

"No. I mean she *really, really* thinks I need to get married."

"Let me guess. You don't want to get her hopes up?"

I nodded. "She'd be devastated if I told her we were getting engaged and then a couple weeks or month later called it off. I figured… Well, I guess I really didn't think it through."

Ethan finished the thought for me. "You thought if we finished this assignment quick enough, she'd never even know you'd had an engagement?"

I squeezed his hand. "Exactly."

He zoomed around another truck. "We don't want her to be disappointed."

"Right. I still think my idea of not telling them is better."

"Not an option. I promised Dad to ask your father for your hand, and that's exactly what I intend to do."

That settled that.

"The solution is simple," he said.

My face twisted up in confusion. "How?"

"When we need to end this, I can become such a complete wanker that your mother begs you to call it off."

"I guess that could work." Although I didn't see any way that Ethan could be that bad.

"Sunshine," he said, looking over briefly, "first we have to get your father to agree."

"Do we have to tell them?" I asked one more time. Keeping this whole episode from them would be so much more convenient.

"I have no option. Good manners require it."

I pulled my phone from my purse. "I better warn them." I didn't say that I also hoped they'd be out of town and we could avoid this trip.

He nodded.

I dialed Mom.

She started as soon as she answered. "I was about to call you again. I miss my little girl."

"I miss you too, Mom."

"Any idea yet how much longer that project you're on is going to last?"

"No, not yet, but I am going to be able to get back to see you."

"That would be nice," she said. "When?"

"I fly out tomorrow."

She squealed with joy. "Wonderful. I knew you'd come to your senses about meeting Bobby. His mother was considering setting him up with Sharon Montrose. You probably remember her. But it doesn't matter. I'm pretty sure that date hasn't happened yet, so I think he's still available. I'll call tonight to check."

I had to wait for Mom's matchmaker monologue to finish so I could get a word in. "That won't be necessary."

"Well… I guess you could call him. That would probably be very well received. Yes, I like your idea better."

"No, Mom. Drop the idea of Bobby. I'm bringing someone with me."

There was silence on the other end.

"A man," I added.

"That Mr. Smithers, by any chance? He sounded quite sophisticated."

"No, Mom, not him. His name is…" I stopped myself. Going any further would turn this into a three-hour phone call. "Never mind. You'll meet him tomorrow."

"Rebecca, don't be a tease."

Mentioning Ethan's name would poison this before it even started. "Mom, I have to go. I'll text you tomorrow when I have some idea when we'll get in."

"Is that really all you're going to tell me?"

"See you tomorrow, Mom. Love and kisses."

She tried three more times to get a name out of me before finally giving up and ending the call.

Ethan's questioning look was obvious.

"What?" I asked.

"Why didn't you want to tell her my name? Are you ashamed of me?"

It was the second time he'd asked that.

I gave it to him straight. "She would've recognized the name, and the way things ended between us… Let's just say she wouldn't start off with a wonderful impression of you tomorrow."

His face showed the pain my words had delivered. "You know I didn't mean to hurt you."

I nodded. "That may not be what you intended, but I can't change how I felt at the time, and she knows it."

He nodded slowly. "So I have a shit reputation to overcome."

That was about the size of it.

I dialed Lizzy to swear her to secrecy if Mom called.

CHAPTER 30

Rebecca

The next morning, we wended our way through the terminal to the British Airways counters.

I followed Ethan into the first-class line with my little roller bag. The sign didn't say *aristocracy enter here*, but I probably didn't know the rules.

"Blakewell and Sommerset on flight two-eight-seven," Ethan told the lady behind the counter.

We both handed over our passports.

Ethan then opened up his police credentials for the agent.

"Very well, Inspector. I'll add it to the notes for the flight crew."

We got our passports back a moment later.

"You're all set," the agent told us as she handed two boarding passes to Ethan. "Gate B thirty-six, and you best hurry. Boarding begins in forty-five minutes."

As we walked away, I asked, "What was that about?"

"In the event there's a disturbance aboard, they'd like to know if there are any coppers around."

I had to ask the other question on my mind. "Do you get first class because of your father's title?"

He laughed. "No, Sunshine. As you Americans would say, his title and five bucks will get him a cup of coffee. We're traveling in the forward cabin so you get a lie-flat seat. It'll give you a chance for the sleep you didn't get last night."

I'd been restless all night over the prospect of seeing—and deceiving—my parents, but it wouldn't be any easier to sleep on the plane. "I don't need—"

He stopped abruptly and turned to me. "You need to stop complaining when I do something for you. It's not polite."

"It's just that—"

He silenced me with a pointed finger. "Hey, little missy," he said with his Texas accent. "What there part of no complainin' didn't y'all understand?"

I fumed silently. Appropriately chastised, I followed him to security without another word. Ethan breezed through as soon as he flashed his police identification. I still had to go through the whole gamut of checks.

When we finally approached the gate, we were coming up on the boarding time we'd been told about. I could see the board behind the gate agents as we arrived.

> British Airways Flight 287
> San Francisco
> On-time

There was no avoiding this now.
I had no idea how I could soften the blow for Mom.

～

IT WAS THE MIDDLE OF THE NIGHT LONDON TIME WHEN WE LANDED IN CALIFORNIA. I notched a major victory of sorts when Ethan gave in and let *me* rent the car for our trip south to San Jose. "A lady should be driven," he'd complained, but he had limited experience driving on the right-hand side of the road, and he gave in when I pointed that out. I was tired, but at least I wouldn't zig left when I should zag right.

He started tapping and scrolling on his phone as soon as we got on the freeway.

"Important work?" I asked.

A grunt came back and finally, "Important, yes."

An hour later, I turned the rental car off Highway 85 at the expressway toward home. Rush hour traffic had been manageable.

I'd gotten maybe an hour or so of sleep on the long flight, and Ethan had kept me awake on the drive down to San Jose with a constant series of questions.

"Are we getting close?" he asked.

"Yup," I said, conserving my words.

I stopped at the second red light in a row on the expressway.

"Why do they call it an expressway if it moves so slowly?"

I shrugged.

"You shouldn't be afraid, Sunshine."

"Easy for you to say." Showing up at my parents' doorstep with a freshly minted fiancé wasn't the way I'd been brought up.

"They love you dearly, and at the end of the day, nothing you do can change that. I'm the one they'll be judging, not you."

I sucked in a deep breath, realizing how self-centered I'd been. Ever since leaving Ethan's parents' yesterday, I'd been focused entirely on the downside for me and completely neglected how hard this had to be for him.

He looked out the window. "The hills here are gigantic."

I pointed to the right. "Mount Umunhum there is about thirty-five hundred feet. If you want to see big, we have to go east to the Sierra."

"That's taller than anything in England, but I can't say I care for the name."

I removed my hand from the wheel and slid it over to him. "They're going to love you. You having great affection for me goes a long way."

He took my hand. "That I do."

His squeeze reassured me. When I glanced over, my heart did a little flip.

His eyes echoed his words. "I truly do."

After the series of turns that took us to my parents' street, I stopped in front of our house. "We're here."

It had seemed plenty big enough growing up. Today it looked positively tiny compared to Rainswood Manor.

Ethan let go of my hand and unfolded from the car to run around and open my door.

"We're in America. That's not necessary here," I told him.

"Nonsense. Good manners are universal, or so I've been told."

I'd texted after we'd cleared Customs, and Mom was outside the door as soon as I shut down the engine.

I waved.

She smiled and waved back.

Ethan pulled our bags from the back seat.

Mom took me into a tight hug when I reached her. "It's so good to see you again."

"Mom, I'd like to introduce my boyfriend, Ethan."

Mom's brows went up and her smile widened at the word boyfriend. She seemed not to have caught his name.

Ethan extended his hand. "It's a pleasure to meet you, Mrs. Sommerset."

Mom took his hand. "Oh my, an Englishman." She shook his hand with renewed vigor. "Welcome to California, Ethan."

I went around them and opened the door.

Ethan and Mom followed.

Dad arrived from the back of the house with an extended hand. "Dan Sommerset."

"Ethan Blakewell, Mr. Sommerset. A pleasure."

Mom's brows drew together, and she shot a puzzled look my direction when she heard Ethan's family name. She'd connected the dots, but at least we'd gotten a cordial greeting in first. "Blakewell, is that a common name in England?"

Ethan didn't miss a beat. "Not very. Blackwell would be more common, and before you ask, yes, I am the Ethan Blakewell from Imperial College in London."

Mom's face hardened into something approaching a scowl.

Dad looked on without the attitude.

"I'm incredibly sorry that Becks and I got our wires a bit crossed at the time. I've missed her terribly since she left, and I feel incredibly fortunate that we were able to reconnect now."

"A bit?" Mom asked, not letting go of her anger.

I wrapped my arm around my man. "Mom, Ethan and I have worked through that and are very happy now. I didn't understand what he was going through at the time."

Mom's face softened.

I pulled myself closer to Ethan to emphasize the point. "Every day, I feel better about it as he explains things and I understand what he faced." I wasn't letting this opportunity to paint him into a corner go to waste.

Ethan changed the topic. "You have a wonderful view here."

Our house backed up against the sixteenth fairway of the golf course.

"It beats looking at a fence and someone else's house," Dad said.

Mom moved closer to Dad. "You must be hungry after that long flight. I'll have dinner ready in a little while."

"That sounds lovely," Ethan told her.

"Daddy, why don't you take Ethan over to the club for a game of pool while Mom and I fix dinner?" That would give Ethan a chance to talk to Dad, which was the whole purpose of our trip.

"I'd be honored," Ethan said with a quick smile in my direction.

I winked back.

It only took a few minutes after the door closed behind the men for the questions to start.

I washed the potatoes while Mom set an onion on the cutting board.

"Are you gonna tell me why you're back with him?" she asked.

I didn't know where to start. "Because he's a wonderful man." I thought that said it all.

She sliced into the onion she had skinned. "And what about the way he treated you last time?"

I used our standard answer. "Like he said, it was a misunderstanding."

She glared and pointed the knife at me. "Don't give me that, young lady." She waved the knife. "Refusing to take your calls is not what I call a misunderstanding."

I put the potato I'd been scrubbing to the side and grabbed the next. "Mom, that's behind us."

She carved a few more slices off the onion. "And you think he's changed?"

"I know he has." I still might not know what had happened between us back then, but I knew for sure he wasn't acting like that now. The Ethan I knew now was a man I wasn't ashamed to bring home.

"I wouldn't trust the leopard to change his spots. I'd be careful, if I were you."

I put the third potato to the side and turned to her. "You don't know anything about him."

She stacked the slices and started to chop. "I know he hurt you once, and that's all I need to know. I wouldn't trust him after that."

"I do trust him. He's never lied to me." Even though I didn't know his secrets, I knew he'd never lied. This was possibly the one time I didn't regret my gift when it came to a relationship.

"Are you certain?"

I faced the sink and scrubbed the final potato. "Sure enough that we plan to get engaged."

She was silent behind me.

I turned to catch wetness in her eyes. From the onion or emotions, I couldn't tell.

"Engaged? This is so sudden." At least questioning the timing was better than questioning my judgment.

I nodded. "He's going to ask Daddy's permission. He says it's required of a gentleman."

She blinked back tears. "You're sure about it this time?"

"Wearing his ring will make me the happiest girl in town." I sniffled and blinked back tears matching hers. The words flowed naturally, and the emotion didn't require work. I'd fallen for him. Again.

She rounded the island and held out her arms for a hug.

We embraced, and my tears started for real. "I love him, Mom." It scared me a little to realize I'd admitted out loud how I felt. It was a feeling I'd kept repressed and not even admitted to myself.

I'd convinced myself we were playacting for the cameras, but my smiles hadn't been forced. Every meal and every outing with him had made me happier than the one before. Even when arguing, we clicked somehow.

Mom held me for a whole minute, telling me how happy she was.

When I'd suggested the fake engagement, it had sounded simple, like crossing the street. But with Mom's words of joy filling my head, I feared unwinding this would be an even harder task than I'd thought. We couldn't simply turn back across this street. The breakup we'd scheduled would devastate her if I didn't prepare her somehow. Worse, I was pretty sure it would also devastate me.

She released me and wiped at the moisture under her eyes. "Soon you can quit that horrible job of yours and start a family."

I turned back to the sink. "Not right away, Mom."

I'd vowed I would never repeat her mistake, but that wasn't an argument for tonight.

"Is he going to move here?" she asked.

Reality crashed my fairy tale to the ground. "No, but I'm working on a transfer to the London office." The lie flowed smoothly over my lips. It fit the act we were playing and highlighted another reason things couldn't work between Ethan and me in the long term.

"But you'll be so far away..."

~

ETHAN

I HELD ON FOR DEAR LIFE AS BECKY'S FATHER TOOK THE FIRST TURN AS FAST AS THE little electric golf cart would go. With the Aston Martin at least I had a seatbelt and two tons of steel, aluminum, and carbon fiber between me and the roadway.

Becky had been right about me not driving. I felt almost ill as the little plastic cart hurtled down the wrong side of the road and a big American car came around the corner toward us.

"You play pool much in your country?" Dan asked as he cranked the wheel hard the other direction for the next curve.

"I've played billiards a few times."

"Eight ball is a whole different game. I hope you don't expect me to be easy on you."

"Wouldn't think of it, sir."

"Dan will be just fine." He turned up the drive to a large car park.

"Wouldn't think of it, Dan."

He pulled the electric cart into a space. "Best country club in the south bay, if you ask me. If you golf, maybe we could squeeze in a round tomorrow."

I slid out and followed him toward the large building. "Sorry to say that's a game I haven't picked up yet."

I also didn't want to spend an extra day here. Becky and I had to be visible in London with her necklace before the party at Rainswood.

"Too bad. A few hours of smacking the hell out of a little ball is a great way to relieve your tension."

I wondered if he sensed my apprehension about our upcoming conversation. "Perhaps one day, but I'm not ready to embarrass myself just yet."

He held open the door for me to enter. "Down and the first right."

The sign said *Men's Lockers*.

"It's a humbling game," he said as we passed through the locker room and showers. "Golf," he added.

We reached a door that read *Men's Lounge,* and he pulled it open.

The lounge had plush seating, racks of books, two billiards tables, two poker tables, and a large-screen television that was thankfully off. One older man sat at the far end reading a book.

"You can break," Dan said as he arranged the balls in a wooden triangle.

I'd seen enough American pool in movies to not embarrass myself by asking what he meant. I pulled a cue from the rack and found chalk on the edge of the table. "You play this often?"

"No. Only occasionally." He finished positioning the triangle of colored and striped balls. "So, Ethan, what do you do for a living?"

The vetting process had begun.

I lined up the cue ball and shot. Balls went scurrying in different directions. "I'm in IT consulting." Eventually, the five ball disappeared down a pocket.

"You've got solids, it seems."

I nodded and lined up a shot at the three ball.

"And what does that mean? IT consulting?" he asked.

I shot, but the ball banked off the edge and missed the pocket I'd meant to put it in. "We help keep companies safe from cybercriminals, help them protect their systems and their data."

He walked around the table to line up a shot. "Are you any good at it?"

It was a very American question, not one I'd been asked before. "Good enough." That sounded to me like an American response.

He shot and dropped a ball in the side pocket. "How did you meet up with Becky again after all these years?" So he did remember my name.

"She asked for me."

He made another shot and pocketed another striped ball. "Asked for you?" He shifted position to make another shot.

"From the hospital," I explained.

His head shot up. "Hospital?"

I'd thought for sure Becky would have told them, but apparently not. There was no sugarcoating the truth. "She was mugged."

He straightened up. "Mugged? When? Was she hurt?"

"It happened just after she got to London. She was lucky. A bump on the head was all. I checked her out of the hospital and took her home to watch over her."

After a few seconds contemplating what I'd said, he went back to the ball he'd been lining up. "Thank you for taking care of her. I guess it doesn't surprise me that she didn't tell us. Becky has always been very self-reliant." He shot and pocketed the ball quickly. "I wouldn't mention that to her mother."

I nodded and watched as he circled the table, looking for his best opportunity. He stopped and rested his cue. "Tell me, what is it you wanted to talk about?"

Unprepared for his bluntness, all I could manage was a blank look.

"Rebecca obviously sent us out of the house to get us alone."

He'd seen right through her.

Direct seemed the only way. "I would like to ask for your daughter's hand in marriage."

He chuckled. "You're asking the wrong person. Over here, we don't give away our daughters. For better or worse, they decide on their own who they want to marry."

I tried again. "I didn't make myself clear. I'd like your permission to ask her is what I'm trying to say."

His eyes narrowed. "And if I say no?"

CHAPTER 31

Rebecca

Ethan gave me the good news when he and Dad returned, and we were a go on our plan to get engaged.

The news truly thrilled me, as if it were real. But after a few seconds of glee and a sensual kiss—once we ducked around the corner from my parents—the guilt hit me.

My emotions bounced from elated to worried and back again as the dinner progressed. Ethan kept the conversation going with ease, charming my mother with his accent and his easy manner. Daddy was harder to read. His gaze kept traveling back to me with an implied question. But each time I let my attention move to Ethan, my smile came naturally.

"Do you really have to leave so soon?" Mom asked, looking between me and Ethan.

Ever the gentleman, Ethan took the blame. "I'm afraid I have an urgent matter at work that I need to get back to."

I moved my knee under the table to make contact with his, and gave him an appreciative smile when he looked over.

Mom wasn't about to give up so easily. Her gaze settled on me. "Maybe you could stay a day or two longer?"

Dad put his fork down. "Tracy."

Mom turned to him. "I was just asking."

"Sorry, Mom, but I had trouble getting even a day off. I've got to get back too."

Mom shook her head and sighed. "I just think it's sorry that you let work dominate your life like this."

"Tracy," Dad said, louder this time.

"Well, it is." Mom always insisted on getting in the last word.

Was I like that?

No. I couldn't be. If I were, I'd recognize it.

Ethan finished a sip of water and surprised me with an arm around my shoulder. "We can't stay, but we would like to make this short visit special."

I shifted my smile from Ethan to Mom and Dad, as if I knew what he was going to say. But he was off script, and I had no clue.

Ethan pulled me a little closer. "If you two are free tomorrow morning, the opera has a matinee scheduled."

Mom's eyes widened.

"I've reserved tickets. Third row."

My mouth dropped open. I recovered as soon as I realized it.

Mom was so busy saying yes to Ethan three times that I don't think she caught my shock.

Dad merely forked another bite of his food and nodded. "Sounds good."

After Mom's reaction, what else could he say?

Mom gushed about the opera for fifteen minutes, and Ethan eventually put his napkin on the table. "It's been a very long day for us."

I nodded and followed his lead with my napkin.

Mom assigned Lizzy's old room to Ethan, and I got mine.

I didn't complain, and neither did Ethan. We could do this for a night.

Mom was on the phone while Ethan and I worked on the dishes. He'd volunteered to help. She was loud as always in the next room.

"Yes, Becky and her new fiancé are taking us to tomorrow's matinee of the opera. Isn't that thrilling?… Yes, ten thirty… Great. Lunch sounds good… Let me check."

Mom poked her head around the corner. "Do you have time for lunch with us tomorrow?"

"If it's quick," Ethan answered.

She disappeared around the corner again. "We'll have to be quick. They have to catch a flight back to London."

I returned to the dishes.

"I know," Mom continued on the phone. "A one-day visit is way too short, but you know how kids can be."

Ethan and I finished up the last of the dishes, and I grabbed the detergent packet from under the sink.

Mom got off the phone. "That was Rosemary," she told Dad. "I set up lunch with them for tomorrow."

I dropped the packet on the floor when she mentioned the name. The last thing I needed was lunch with my ex-husband's family.

I pointed an angry finger at Ethan. "Ethan, since our flight is international, are you sure we have time for lunch?" I shook my head vigorously, hoping he'd play along.

"Yeah, maybe not," he said slowly. "Sorry, Mrs. Sommerset. Maybe not," he yelled into the other room.

I smiled at my man as I breathed a gigantic sigh.

Mom appeared in the door.

"With the slow security, we really don't have enough time for lunch," Ethan added.

Mom nodded. "Okay. I'll make your excuses to the Strouds tomorrow."

As if I needed an excuse to not meet up with my ex's family.

How could Mom be so clueless? She'd been friends with Rosemary Stroud forever and had even had a hand in setting me up with Wesley back when I thought he was a nice guy.

A few minutes later, I followed Ethan up the stairs. I waited until we were out of earshot. "Why didn't you ask me about the opera tickets?"

"I thought it would be a good surprise."

I shook my head. "When did you do that?"

"On the drive down. What's the problem?"

I sighed. "We'll talk about it later."

"She seemed thrilled," Ethan said before giving me a chaste goodnight kiss. "Sleep well, Sunshine."

It was too late to do anything about it, and Ethan meant well, so I'd have to endure another of Mom's crying sessions at the opera.

Ethan

The next morning, I woke to a persistent knock at the bedroom door.

"We don't have a lot of time," Becky said through the door.

I rubbed at the sleep in my eyes. "I'm up."

The noise of water running began in the bathroom next to the bedroom I'd been assigned. A quick check at the window showed the sun had been up for a while, and my watch on the dresser confirmed it.

While I waited my turn to use the bathroom, I pondered last night's opera reaction. Becky hadn't explained why the opera tickets were a bad idea. I'd thought it was a nice gesture since she'd said her mother liked to attend. I'd fallen asleep without a clue and had nothing better this morning.

Becky's bedroom door had closed behind her by the time I opened mine to shave. A shower could wait a day.

Downstairs, I was the last one to the breakfast table.

"I hope you like waffles," Becky's mom said.

"Sounds splendid." I gave my girl a kiss on the cheek as I sat.

Becky graced me with a smile under eyes that said she hadn't slept well.

"Sleep okay?" her dad asked me.

"Better than I expected with my body clock way off."

Breakfast went quickly as I fielded questions about what my work entailed at TechniByte. Becky was spared having to lie about what she was working on at the moment because no questions about her work came up.

We took separate cars since we had to go straight to the airport.

After we got on the road, I finally had Becky alone to ask what the problem was.

"No problem," was her curt answer.

"Missy, that there is a load of bullcrap," I said in my Texas accent.

"It's bullshit," she corrected me.

I reverted to my native tongue. "You're deflecting. What is your problem with taking your mother to the opera?"

"I said I don't have a problem."

"I don't have to have your gift to know that is a fucking lie."

She scowled at the road ahead.

"Do I need to ask her?"

"Don't you dare," she spat.

I looked out the window.

She glanced over a few seconds later. "Can we put this off until the flight? Please?"

I didn't understand, but if it was that important to her, I could wait. "Sure thing."

"It was sweet of you to think of it."

"Sure. That's me. Mr. Sweet." Now I *had* to leave it alone. I was a sucker for a compliment from her.

∼

Rebecca

We were just past the second intermission of *La Traviata* when Mom's tears began again.

Ethan didn't notice at first, but a few minutes later, he leaned over to ask me softly, "Is she okay?"

"She always cries at these," I whispered back.

"It is a sad story."

I nodded, not daring to explain the real reason in this crowd.

When the end came and the applause began, Mom was the most enthusiastic among us, as always.

I'd never asked Dad if he realized how lucky he was that Mom had given up so much for him. Looking past her to where he sat, I knew I never would. The question would hurt too much.

It had been Mom's decision. She'd made that clear enough.

Why she came here to remind herself over and over again was a puzzle I'd never understand.

We made our way outside, swimming in the sea of people.

Once past the doors, the crush of people dispersed and we had a chance to stop.

Mom hugged Ethan with still-wet eyes. "That was wonderful. I'm so glad you suggested it."

"It was Becky's idea," he said.

Mom's look my way said she wasn't buying that. "You take care of her now."

"I will," he assured her.

Ethan and Dad shook while I exchanged a goodbye hug with Mom.

"You still should call more often," she said.

I grabbed Ethan's hand. "We need to get going so we can stand in line at the airport forever." I tugged him back toward me. The last thing I wanted to do was encounter Wesley's parents because we'd dawdled.

After a quick goodbye, Ethan and I turned toward the car.

I felt safe once we turned onto the cross street.

I was wrong.

"There you are, dear." Suddenly Wesley himself stood in our path.

I gasped and tripped, I stopped so fast.

Ethan grabbed me to keep me from falling. "Careful."

Wesley extended his hand toward Ethan. "You must be Blakewell."

I shivered, speechless.

Ethan took it. "And you would be?"

"Wesley Stroud," he said as he nodded his head toward me. "Rebecca's husband."

Ethan's eyes narrowed as he pulled his hand back. His questioning look settled on me a second later.

"Ex-husband," I finally got out.

"Separated, not divorced," Wesley said.

The air left me like I'd been hit by a train. "Ex," was all I could get out.

Wesley smiled as he looked between us. "You should have answered my letters or taken my calls so we didn't have to hash this out in public."

"But—"

"You didn't tell me you were married," Ethan said, with hurt in his eyes.

"Was," I said.

"Are," Wesley said, almost giggling.

Ethan backed up.

My eyes pleaded with him. "I was going to—"

"Rebecca," Ethan said. "You and Weasel here obviously have things to discuss." He turned and strode off.

"It's Wesley," my stupid ex called after him.
Ethan didn't respond. He kept walking.

CHAPTER 32

Ethan

Married? To Weaselface?

I didn't see that coming.

And to not tell me? How could she?

Last night things had been going so well, and now everything was a total fucking shitstorm.

When I reached the main street, I pulled out my phone and summoned an Uber.

At least Weaselface had shown up before we announced our engagement back home. How would that have gone over? To find out she was still married when Mom and Dad were entertaining their guests at our engagement party? I shivered.

The Uber app notified me that my driver was arriving. No doubt a fare all the way to the airport was a juicy one they pounced on.

I opened the back door to the little Prius when it pulled up.

"Blakewell?" the guy driving asked.

"That's right. SFO."

"Meeting someone?"

"No. Leaving."

He gave me a questioning look in the mirror. "No luggage?"

Shit. In my haste to leave, I'd left my luggage in the rental car. "My girlfriend is meeting me with it." *I don't really know that, but it's better than explaining the truth.*

"English?" he asked after a minute.

Rather than answer, I grunted and looked out the window.

He got the hint.

∼

THE TEXT ARRIVED BEFORE WE MADE IT TO THE AIRPORT.

BECKY: You fly ahead. Will follow when I can.

I cursed under my breath and shut down my phone. I had my wallet and my passport, so I wasn't physically stranded, but mentally, I was in never-never land. I had no idea what had just happened, or how we'd gotten to this place.

Becky had to have known this would be a problem. Why didn't she tell me?

Once at the airport, the agent at the counter questioned my lack of luggage, just like the Uber driver had.

At security, there was no queue for first-class screening. But taking that route turned out to be a mistake.

The lack of even a carry-on bag got me pulled aside for special screening. Everybody had a backpack, or bag of some sort. Everybody but me.

"No carry-on, sir?" the officer asked.

"It was a one-day trip," I explained.

"Irish?" he asked.

"British. Going home."

"Stay here," he said as he called over his supervisor.

They chatted for a minute as another officer watched me.

A police officer with a gun was summoned as well.

That's when I recognized the severity of my situation. I fit their profile for a terrorist: traveling alone with no luggage.

The policeman kept his hand on the butt of his gun.

I pulled out my credentials for the supervisor when he approached. "Detective Inspector Blakewell, Scotland Yard."

He took my identification and squinted at it. "I'll need to check this out, you understand."

"Certainly." Getting testy with these blokes would backfire. I checked my watch. Still plenty of time before departure.

It took twenty minutes for him to come back—no surprise, given that it was late evening UK time. "Inspector, sorry for the wait. I hope you had a pleasant visit." He returned my credentials. "You understand we have to be careful."

I nodded. "It pays to be vigilant."

The cabin crew finally closed the airplane door, and the seat beside me was still empty. I resigned myself to a long flight, just me and my doubts.

A few hours ago, I'd looked forward to this flight. But ten hours with my girl to plan our engagement had now become a very long flight with nothing but doubts about Becky, doubts about the assignment, and doubts about my future.

Married?

How had that slipped her mind?

~

Rebecca

"You're a fucking asshole," I told Wesley loudly enough to garner stares from the people walking by.

"Calm down, Becky—"

"Rebecca to you, asshole."

"The deal isn't good enough anymore, and if you're going to be a complete bitch about it, maybe we should have the lawyers hash this out," Wesley said.

We didn't need lawyers mucking around and running up bills. "There's nothing to discuss. We're divorced, and I'm not changing anything. You agreed. We are not revisiting it. End of discussion."

His evil grin appeared—the one I should've known meant not to marry him the first time I saw it. "I didn't file the papers."

I felt ill as I looked over to find that Ethan had disappeared around the corner. "What the fuck?" I yelled. "You agreed. I even saw you sign. Now leave me alone. I have a plane to catch."

"Yeah, well, I got delayed." He pulled a thick envelope from his back pocket.

"That was eight months ago."

He reached for me. "We should sit down and talk this out."

I pulled back. "You touch me, and I'll scream."

Wesley looked around and took a half-step back. "Is that any way to start our negotiation, Sweetcakes?"

I'd never cared for that name. "Rebecca to you, and there is no negotiation. We already settled everything."

The evil grin reappeared. "I saw online that you're dating that sissy English dude. Excuse me, *rich* English dude." He cocked his head in the direction Ethan had left. "So the price just went up. Meet me at my place in a half hour."

I wasn't going anywhere near his apartment. "No. It needs to be in public." I picked the safest place I could think of. "The sandwich shop on Fifth." It was across the street from the police building, and cops were always in and out of there.

"I don't think so."

He was being a dick as always. I took a chance that he was desperate for whatever he wanted. "The sandwich shop on Fifth, or I'm getting on a plane to London and you can meet me there." I turned around and started walking.

"Okay," he called.

I stopped and turned, giving him my best icy stare. "See you there in a half hour."

"Actually, I can't make it that soon. I'll see you at six."

It was just like Wesley to fuck with my plans for getting back to London.

Without another word, I started for the rental car and gave him the finger over my shoulder. "Asshole," I said under my breath.

Once inside with the door locked, I started the engine and turned on the air conditioning. After a half hour of feeling sorry for myself, I typed the text I owed Ethan.

ME: You fly ahead. Will follow when I can.

I touched the scar on the back of my head—my reminder of the mistake I'd made with Wesley. Unable to deal with the embarrassment of admitting my situation to my parents, I headed for my favorite Mexican hole-in-the-wall to hide out until six. This was going to be a very long afternoon. In the meantime, I had to change my flight to tomorrow. No fucking way was I letting Wesley waste any more of my time, any more of my life. We were settling this tonight, once and for all.

CHAPTER 33

Ethan

I'D BEEN HOME A DAY. I HADN'T GOTTEN MUCH SLEEP ON THE LONG FLIGHT, NOR MUCH last night. Thoughts of Becky and our recent time together kept intruding.

My memories of the meals, the walks, the picnics, and our times at Rainswood had been punctuated by that one horrible statement outside the opera.

"*I'm Wesley Stroud, Rebecca's husband,*" he'd said. What a kick in the balls.

My initial confusion at the situation had been replaced with anger. I hadn't suspected, and I hadn't asked the question, but it wasn't the kind of thing one kept from one's boyfriend, and that's what I'd thought I'd become. What I'd *hoped* I'd become. Where I stood now, I had no idea.

Had I been wrong about Becky's feelings? Had the intimacy been fake, or merely one-sided? Had my feelings warped my perception so badly that my read of her had been all wrong?

I was as angry at myself for being gullible as I was at her for hiding her marriage. I should have known better, and now the whole operation was in jeopardy. Screwing up my one and probably only assignment in the field didn't sit well with me. All because I hadn't read her correctly.

Since returning to London, I hadn't heard a peep from Becky. Not a text, not a voicemail, not even a missed call.

I jumped up when my mobile rang, and raced to the counter where it was charging.

Dad's name graced the screen.

"How did the trip to California go?" he asked ten seconds into our conversation.

"Her father said yes." Elaborating about the current twist wasn't something I would broach today.

"Excellent. Do you have a ring?"

I nodded, even though he couldn't see. "I do."

"Then what remains is for you to pick out a fitting necklace."

In my funk about our relationship status, that task had slipped my memory this morning.

The superintendent had already given me a card for the purchase from Becky's company. *"The card doesn't have a limit,"* Maxwell had told me. "They suggested keeping the expense down, but that would defeat the purpose of attracting the thief, in my opinion."

I agreed with him.

"I'll pay ninety percent of the cost," Dad said, bringing me back to today. "The rest is up to you."

"That won't be necessary."

"Nonsense. It's tradition. My father did the same for me. One can't go upsetting a Blakewell tradition."

I sighed. This argument couldn't be won. "Yes. Tradition."

I'd have the insurance company buy it, and return it after the assignment was done. As far as Dad needed to know, it would be on loan to see if Becky was comfortable with it.

"Any suggestions as to where I might find something suitable?" I asked.

"I would suggest the same place I purchased your mother's, The House of Stafford, jewelers to the royal family. You could try another shop, but you're likely to find pieces they make by the dozen. Your fiancée deserves something unique."

The word *unique* hung in the air. Becky was special, and unique it would be. If this was still on.

"Thanks, Dad."

He rang off shortly after that.

I called into Molly at the Yard and gave her a task.

Ten minutes later, she rang back after having checked the flight manifests from San Francisco. Becky was due in this morning.

∽

Twice since her scheduled landing time, I'd picked up my mobile and considered ringing her, but decided against it.

She needed to make the first move, and she hadn't called.

When the knock sounded at the door, it didn't surprise me.

She could have gone straight to her sister's flat, but retrieving her clothes had to be done at some point anyway.

When I opened the door, she looked even worse than I felt.

"May I come in?" she asked.

I stepped aside. "You could have used your key." I'd given her one the first day we'd become a pretend couple.

She walked in, her eyes on the floor, and her shoulders slumped. "Do you want it back?"

After closing the door, I opened my arm toward the great room. "No. I'd rather hear the truth for a change."

"That's not fair."

I started toward the room. "You're the one who's always put total openness and honesty as the first requirement, but it seems that only goes one way."

She followed. "I know that's true, but…"

I sat.

She took a seat on the wingback chair across from me. "But nothing. I'm sorry."

I didn't have much more to say, so I waited.

She wrung her hands. "I can understand it if you're angry."

"If?" I raised my hands. "I asked your father for your hand in marriage, and you forget to mention you were already married. Would you call that a small thing?"

"I meant to tell you I had been married, but—."

"It just slipped your mind?"

"I thought it was in the past." She huffed. "Damned Wesley. I thought it had been finalized."

"Little bit of an oversight, huh?"

Her eyes hardened, and she leaned forward. "He screwed me. He signed the papers and was supposed to have filed them. He didn't, and I never knew. Until yesterday."

"You still should have told me."

She raised her voice. "I was going to tell you, but things moved so fast I never got the chance, and it didn't seem important."

I raised my voice to match hers. "'Hey, Ethan, I just wanted to tell you I was married once before.' Would that have been so hard to say?"

"This is Wesley's fault, not mine."

"Sure, blame it on the guy not in the room. It could have blown the whole operation. You needed to tell me."

"Hey, that's not fair."

∼

REBECCA

"WHAT'S UNFAIR ABOUT IT?" HE ASKED.

He deserved an apology, and I'd come to give him one. But I didn't deserve to be treated like this. He didn't know it, but since I'd already found the stolen jewelry, I could've been out of here and on to my promotion, leaving him and his family to deal with the aftermath. I was the one keeping the investigation from blowing up in his family's face.

I took a deep breath. It was time to set the record straight. "I'm just following your rules."

"Bull fucking shit."

"You told me, and I quote," I said, making air quotes. "'*No dissecting the past. We need to focus on the case.*'" I held my eyes on him.

His mouth fell half-open. I had him on this point, and he knew it. "That's not the same."

"I'm calling bullshit on that."

He took a deep breath and leaned back into the sofa.

"Look, Ethan, let me be honest here. This last little bit since I came back to London and met you again…" My eyes watered. "…have been the happiest days of my life." They truly had.

"Including the mugging?" he asked.

"Okay, all except that part... No, I take that back. Without that you wouldn't have come back into my life. It was a small price to pay for—"

He leaned forward. "I—"

I raised a finger. "Let me finish, please. I know this whole thing with Wesley was my screwup, and I'm sorry about it. But I'm back here with you because this is where I want to be. Can we please just focus on the case? Just as much as you, I want to close this out without having any negative fallout for your family." That was as much as I could tell him about that.

He smiled quietly and blinked a few times.

"I want to go back to how we were before Wesley showed up." I'd laid myself bare to him, and my future was in his hands now.

"Tell me what Weaselface said."

That wasn't the answer I'd hoped for.

"Why?" He still hadn't answered my question.

He stood. "Stand up." His voice was firm, demanding.

I stayed seated. If he was going to throw me out, I wasn't going to make it easy. I'd have the last word in this argument. "Why?"

CHAPTER 34

ETHAN

"Why is everything an argument with you?" I stepped forward and offered my hand. "Sunshine."

The nickname did the trick, and a tentative smile appeared. She took my hand. I pulled her into my arms and held her tight. "I want to fix this."

"I'm sorry. I screwed everything up," she said into my shoulder.

I stroked the back of her head. "Sunshine, I could never stay mad at you. I want to fix this for you." Holding her in my arms again, I knew how true my statement was. I couldn't stay mad at my woman.

"You can't fix it."

I relished her soft, warm form against me. "Tell me everything he said and did."

"Why? It doesn't matter anymore."

"Really? Another question?"

She gave me a half giggle and relaxed into me.

"I want to know so I can give him the right amount of arse kicking."

The next giggle was better. "Can I watch?"

"That's another question."

"Sorry." The word came out muffled against my shirt.

"That word is another thing we are going to scrub from your vocabulary. Now, start at the beginning. Tell me about Weaselface."

It took her a half hour on the sofa to describe the marriage that shouldn't have been, the breakup that came later than it should have, and the divorce papers she'd seen him sign and promise to file.

She took in a breath. "I should have insisted on doing that part myself."

"Don't fret about that. What did Weaselface want yesterday?"

She shook her head with a snort. "He saw pictures of us online and decided he wanted to change the split of assets. He hadn't filed the papers. I had to agree to give him the Lexus and thirty thousand more."

"That's giving in to extortion."

"No. It's being practical. It's over with him. I gave him what he wanted. He signed, and I filed the papers myself. The divorce can't be stopped now. It'll be final in six months. We're getting engaged to catch this thief. Wesley is just asshole enough to splash my married status all over the tabloids to punish me, punish us, and blow the investigation to hell."

I took her hand. "It's still not right."

"It's called expedient. He's running for the Board of Supervisors next year and wanted money."

"When this is over, I'm going to teach Weaselface the cost of messing with my girlfriend."

She smiled and gave my hand a squeeze. "Is that what I am?"

I pulled her over to me. "Can't you tell?"

The kiss she started answered that question.

She took control of the kiss, and I gave it willingly. My Sunshine was back.

I pulled her against me, having missed the heat of her breasts against me and the comfort of her in my arms.

She squeezed my arse and broke the kiss, moving away enough to start pulling at my shirt. "Your girlfriend has had a shitty day, and you should take her to bed."

"Is that right?" I scooped her up and carried her toward the bedroom. "How can I make it better for you?"

I kicked the door closed behind us and deposited her on the bed.

"I need you, Cowboy." She started pulling off her clothes.

I struggled out of my shirt. "I'm a comin', missy." The last button took too long. I ripped it loose. I was hard as a rock. "You have no idea what you do to me,

Sunshine." I shoved down my boxers and trousers and moved onto the bed. I pulled to spread her legs.

She resisted, clamping her legs together. "Hold me first."

We'd moved from fast to slow in an instant. I moved up alongside her and pulled her to me, her head on my shoulder.

"Talk to me, Sunshine."

She ran her nails over my chest. "I want..."

I waited.

"I want it to be special tonight."

I kissed the top of her head. "You're always special," I told her.

She was silent for a moment, her hand circling my nipple.

I moved a finger to circle her nipple as well. "I'll give you a tongue-lashing you won't forget."

"I don't want..." She didn't finish her sentence.

I had no idea why this had come to a halt, but she'd certainly had a rough time with Weaselface. "We can just snuggle then." It was time to suck it up and be a gentleman.

"No," she said slowly. "I want skin."

"You mean no..."

"Yeah, Big Ben without a condom."

The thought made me even harder. "You're sure?"

"I don't have anything, and I'm on the pill."

"I'm clean too. But I have to warn you, I might not last very long."

She rose up and straddled me. "Another thing, I want to be on top." She leaned over and playfully licked the tip of my nose.

I could enjoy that, watching and feeling her breasts. "Sunshine, whatever you want." I palmed the weight of her marvelous breasts, soft mounds topped with those responsive pink peaks.

She rubbed herself over my length, slowing down as her clit ran over my tip. Each trip forward brought a moan as she pleasured herself on me. She increased the pressure, and her wetness built.

I shuddered every time she rode over my sensitive tip.

It took all my concentration to resist the urge to lift her up and take her as she vulva-fucked me. I let her choose the rhythm as she glided her hips over mine.

Little moans escaped her lips as I attended to her breasts, holding their weight and circling her nipples with my thumbs, letting her murmurs be my guide. I looked up into her closed eyes as she came ever closer to the end of her rope. Her ragged breaths told me how close she was as she increased her tempo. Her hand went to mine, squeezing it against the warm softness of her breast.

Suddenly, she lifted up, guided my cock with her hand, and slid down on me. I slipped in easily and arched up into her.

She was so wet she took me to the root, lifting up and sliding down first slowly, then more quickly. Straightening up, she leaned back and braced her hands on my knees.

The sight of her wonderful breasts bouncing every time she came down on me was too much. I closed my eyes and concentrated on holding off long enough to satisfy her.

I grabbed her hips and pulled her down hard. Every stroke made it harder than the last to maintain control. I nearly exploded when she reached around to hold my balls. I retaliated by moving a thumb to her clit.

She ground forward and back against the pressure of my thumb as the words spilled out of her between quick breaths. "Oh God…I'm gonna…come… Oh…my God… Holy shit…I can't."

With the next rock of her pelvis, I rubbed her clit hard, and she went over the edge, tensing, shaking, and leaning forward to claw at my shoulders.

She shuddered—convulsing around me as she rode the wave down with several gyrations forward and back—and then collapsed on top of me, her breasts hot against my chest.

"My God, Ethan," she said over and over again. "I had no idea."

She rolled off, panting to regain her breath. "Your turn." She put her head on the pillow and poked her butt up. "Ride me, Cowboy."

I didn't need any more encouragement. I got behind her and let her position me with her hand before I pushed in—hard.

She moaned. "That all you got?" she asked with a giggle.

I grabbed her hips and dug my fingers in, pulling her to me, seating myself fully, and holding her there. She was so fucking wet and so deliciously tight that I couldn't hold back.

"Harder, Cowboy," she urged.

I knew she said it for my sake, not hers, but I gave her harder. The sound of flesh slapping against flesh filled the room as I thrust again and again.

"I want you to lose control."

And, I did. The pressure that had built behind my balls was too much to hold back. I shot my load with a final thrust, tensing up and holding her hips tightly to me, welding my cock inside her. Slowly, the throbbing eased. I pushed her forward onto the bed and lay half off of her, sparing her my weight as I panted.

She angled her head to give me a kiss. "That's what I call special."

"Yeah." I ran my hand over her back.

After a minute I got up to wipe off and returned with a warm, wet washcloth for her.

Our sweat mingled as I curled up behind her, cradling a breast with my hand. She was mine, and I wasn't letting her go.

CHAPTER 35

Rebecca

Later that afternoon, Ethan put on his coat to leave for his errand.

"Are you sure you don't want me along?" I asked.

"That's not how this works. I'm getting you a present. That means I select it, and you *ooh* and *aah* when you get it…or not."

He was off to buy the expensive necklace I'd be wearing to attract our thief. Everything rode on this being something the thief would covet.

Ethan had told me about the card my company had provided him to purchase the bait necklace. I'd fantasized about spending the company's money on myself, even if only for one night.

I handed him the list of jewelers. "Get it from one of these four."

He opened it and read the names. "Setting conditions?"

"I'm just helping. I know they'll accept the company credit card."

Smithers had provided this list of four jewelers. Lessex insured each of them. That meant he and Cornwall felt confident they could reverse the sale when this was over with the application of a little leverage, and the net cost would be zero. They were probably right.

Ethan kissed me, and the door closed behind him a minute later.

I opened up my laptop to continue grading interviews for New York. Sitting idly waiting for him to return would drive me nuts.

∼

Ethan

I located The House of Stafford with only a little difficulty. The shop was clearly old, with understated signage—nothing like the bawdy, large displays of the modern jewelers on New Bond Street. Pushing in, I entered what easily could have been the shop as it was a hundred years ago. A bell jangled as the door opened. No electronic beep in this store.

The space was empty of customers as I perused the first display case.

A door at the back of the shop creaked open. "Good afternoon. Welcome to The House of Stafford. My name is Martha. How may I assist you today, sir?"

I turned in her direction. "Martha, I have an appointment with Mr. Stafford."

She paused and the briefest hint of recognition crossed her face. "Who may I tell him is here?"

I must have gotten her expression wrong. "Ethan Blakewell."

"I will let him know," she said as she disappeared once more into the back.

I peered in the display case, which housed some magnificent engagement rings while I waited for the shop's namesake. This would have been the perfect place to bring Becky for her ring, but that time had passed, and she would have refused the nicer ones regardless.

Martha returned with an older gentleman. "Mr. Stafford, may I present Ethan Blakewell, son of his grace the Duke of Lassiter." I hadn't mentioned my father, but she'd probably read the papers.

The older man extended his hand. "Yes. You are right on time, a quality in short supply these days."

"I try," I said as we shook.

Martha stood back.

"I've sold your father several things over the years, including making the necklace he gave your mother on their engagement."

I nodded, but it wasn't something I'd heard from Dad. "You created that?"

"One of my more exquisite efforts at the time. Your father demanded something unique. But enough of the past. What can we help you with today?"

"Actually, I'm getting engaged myself."

"I see, and you require a ring." He started toward the first display case I'd scanned.

I didn't follow him. "No. I have that covered. What I'd like is a necklace also. Something unique."

He laughed lightly. "Ah, yes, the Blakewell tradition. I wish I had more customers like your family." He turned to Martha. "Mrs. Marston, a pad and pencil, if you please."

She hurried to the corner.

"It was fortuitous that you came by today," Stafford said. "If we come up with a sketch, I can get started on it as soon as I return next week."

I shook my head. That timing wouldn't work. "I'll need this quickly. I don't have time to commission a custom piece."

"And, what budget are we considering today?" Stafford asked, slipping into salesman mode.

"I don't want to skimp." That was as specific as I cared to get.

He nodded and moved to a different display case. "In that event, we should start here." He put his hand atop a case near the wall.

I followed him. The display contained simple necklaces and pendants set on fake velvet necks. The jewels weren't modest, but the pieces lacked heft. "Something more substantial, I think." These were not inexpensive, but didn't rise to the level we would need to attract the thief.

He moved to another display and unlocked the back. This case held better prospects.

Stafford brought up a nice multi-strand pearl piece.

"Too bland," I said.

The next one down the line was more impressive, with a half dozen nice rubies each surrounded by diamonds.

It didn't strike me as special or unique enough. "This is closer to what I'm looking for."

He left that one out while pulling up the next from below the glass. "When exactly do you require this?"

"Her first function as my fiancée will be at an event my family is hosting next Saturday, and of course she needs to be wearing the engagement necklace."

"Of course. Pity, that is a bit too soon for a fresh creation."

He showed me another three, and that exhausted the contents of the display. Scratching his chin, he asked, "Would you like to re-examine any of these?"

None of them quite compared to the necklace I knew Aunt Helen had lost, and we needed something of that caliber.

I shook my head. "The lady is very unique." I used Dad's word. "And I'd like to get her something worthy of her."

"Perhaps the Overdale necklace," Martha offered from her perch two cases away.

Stafford's brow lifted. "It is vintage, and rather expensive," he cautioned.

"Let's have a look," I said.

I followed him to a case, which had a note in gold lettering.

From the collection of the Duchess of Overdale.

Among the earrings, pendants, and smaller pieces was the most magnificent necklace in the shop.

He unlocked the case and lifted its display to the counter.

A smile crept across my lips as I took it in. This was what I was looking for—over-the-top gorgeous, almost extravagant beyond reason. This set of jewels would have every woman in the room envious, and the thief salivating. "Tell me about this one."

Stafford beamed. "This piece was created by my father for the duchess. The vivid yellow diamond is a flawless seventy-seven carats and extremely rare in its own right. The strand is adorned with another eighty-one carats of colorless D stones, each of which is also flawless. I dare say you will not find a finer piece currently available anywhere in the world."

I moved closer to examine the large, yellow pendant stone. "May I?"

"Certainly. It is meant to be worn."

I gently lifted the largest diamond I'd ever seen. "This is stunning." The bright yellow was surreal.

Stafford nodded with a wide grin. "The color is fancy vivid, quite rare." He'd sized me up as a possible buyer at this point.

"And how much, exactly, is 'rather expensive'?" I asked, releasing the large jewel.

"The estate has set the price at…" Stafford took in a breath. "Eight million pounds."

Instead of the insurance company card, I removed my own black card from my wallet. "Place ten percent on this, and if you ring my father, he will commit to the balance." At least I hoped he would.

We hadn't discussed a limit, and this was probably at least ten times what he was expecting, but he's the one who'd made the commitment, and standing by one's word was more sacred to him than anything.

Martha looked on with a smile while Stafford made a call in the corner.

I watched his expression as he talked to my father. Having this turned down would be the ultimate embarrassment.

Stafford smiled my direction before ringing off and running my card. He returned with the machine for me to enter my PIN.

I'd never tested the card to see if the claim that it didn't have a limit was true, and I was relieved when the small machine beeped its approval. I would have to sell some shares to raise the amount to cover this bill.

"Mrs. Marston, would you please box this for us?"

She disappeared into the back with the necklace still draped around the display.

"I'm so pleased," he said, "that it is finding a proper home." He leaned closer. "It is a pity to see many of our finer pieces leave the country."

My guess was that he was more pleased about the sales commission he'd just earned.

Martha returned a moment later with a blue leather box embossed with *Overdale* in large, gold lettering, and *House of Stafford* under the name. She opened the lid to show me the necklace. "I expect your fiancée will be the hit of the evening wearing this."

I accepted the box gingerly. "I'm sure she will be."

"Mr. Stafford," Martha said. "In examining this, the clasp appears to be in need of repair."

Stafford held his hands out. "May I?"

He took a quick look inside. "Yes, it does." He closed the box and checked his watch. "This happens on occasion with these vintage pieces. It would ruin the value to replace the clasp with something modern. I'll need to fashion one to match the original. Unfortunately, I don't have time today. Are you able to leave it with us for the repair?"

This was a kink in my plans. "I was planning on giving it to her today."

He handed me back the closed case. "It can be worn as it is, if you are careful, but I wouldn't delay. I'll be back in town by next Thursday, and we can repair it then."

I nodded. "I'll bring it by." That timing would allow us to be seen around town with it enough to be in the papers and be sure the crook knew Becky would be wearing it.

∼

Rebecca

I'D GONE THROUGH TWO INTERVIEWS DURING ETHAN'S ABSENCE WHEN THE SOUND OF A key turning in the lock signaled his return.

I pretended to be engrossed in what was on my computer screen as he walked in.

The smile on his face was Cheshire-Cat wide as he approached with his hands behind his back.

I stood quickly and bounced on my toes like it was Christmas morning. "Did you find anything?" A stupid question given the way he was acting.

"Close your eyes, Sunshine."

"I'm not a little kid."

He shook his head. "No. You're worse when it comes to following simple directions."

I huffed my displeasure. "You're being mean."

"You're being difficult."

I gave in and shut my eyes.

"Rebecca Ellen Sommerset, will you marry me?"

I opened my eyes to find him on one knee in front of me, holding open the box containing the engagement ring we'd picked out. "Now you're being silly." I was disappointed that he'd come back without the necklace.

"Is that a no?" He looked hurt.

I could play along. "Okay, I'll marry you." I'd thought we agreed on a public proposal over dinner, but this was his show.

He pulled the ring from the box and slipped it onto my finger.

I looked down as he slid the platinum band with the large stone into place. If only this were real. I blinked back a tear. It was such a silly thought.

"Close your eyes."

"I've already seen it."

His glare said what he didn't have to repeat.

"I know. Shut up and follow orders." I closed my eyes again, but not before painting on a pout.

"What do you think?" he asked.

I opened my eyes and was faced with a royal blue House of Stafford box he'd opened to reveal the most magnificent jeweled necklace I'd ever seen. Then it dawned on me; I'd seen this before. "You went to Stafford?" It hadn't been on the list of jewelers I'd given him.

"For my Sunshine."

I blinked back tears of joy at the gorgeous diamond necklace and huge, yellow pendant stone. It was the necklace from the Overdale collection I'd seen my first day here. "This is overkill."

"Only the best for my fiancée."

I couldn't hold back the tears any longer and wiped under my eyes.

"Stafford said his father made it for the duchess."

"It's beautiful." I didn't deserve to wear something like this, but I knew I'd have a hard time giving it up when the time came. I should have been focused on how lucky I was to wear it for even one outing.

"We have to be careful with it. They said the clasp needs to be repaired, whatever that means. I'll take it back in next week for that."

"Is it safe to wear it?"

"So long as you are careful, he said. Now, get ready for dinner. We have more paparazzi to entertain."

"I hate this part."

"It's advertising. Just remember, we're using them as much as they're using us."

I knew we had to do it, but I didn't have to like it. "The next time one of them puts the camera right in my face, I'm going to punch him."

"I know how you feel, but it's not a good idea to be saying that in front of a police officer."

I waggled my eyebrows. "Detective Inspector, are you threatening to put me in handcuffs? Because that could be fun."

"Stop delaying." He took my shoulders and turned me around. "Go get dressed. We have a reservation."

I stopped and turned after a few steps. "I want to wear the ring."

I knew what was coming from his expression before he even said it.

"That's tomorrow night, remember?" He was sticking to the script.

Tomorrow night we had a reservation where we knew the paparazzi could get pictures through the window, and tonight we didn't, but we knew they'd be outside.

I took the necklace case with me into the bedroom and set it on the counter while I dressed. After tomorrow night, I'd get to wear it out.

In the middle of finishing my makeup, a question came to me. Pulling the jeweler's loupe that Stafford had given me from my purse, I opened the case and began my inspection.

I was giddy when I found the tiny HS on the fourteenth link, and also on the clasp. It was just like Stafford had said.

After replacing the necklace, I pushed the top of the box down to go back to my makeup. It slid on the counter and dropped to the floor.

"Fuck," I yelled. I had the worst luck.

"You okay?" Ethan called from the other room.

"I'm fine. I just missed with my mascara brush."

I lifted the blue case gingerly and opened it. I let out a gigantic breath once I'd determined the necklace didn't look damaged. The case itself, though, had a small dent on the corner where it had hit the marble floor.

I moved the blue case to atop my dresser where it would be safe and tapped the Overdale lettering on the top. "So sorry, your grace. I'll be more careful in the future." I don't know if she heard me, but it felt like the right thing to say.

Going back to my makeup, I realized this would be my last dinner as Ethan's girlfriend. Starting tomorrow night, I'd be on his arm as his fiancée.

That thought thrilled me.

CHAPTER 36

Rebecca

Late the following morning, Ethan drove us back home after seeing his parents.

Everything was unfolding according to plan. We'd just told them the good news that Ethan was proposing, and we had it scheduled for dinner tonight where we could be easily photographed.

I still couldn't get over this compulsion to ask and inform everybody in the families before popping the question, but he knew I planned to say yes regardless.

It was all backward. Our families knew, but I hadn't been asked yet, and instead of it being a private moment between us, it would be choreographed so photographers could catch it. Ethan had confided in his cousin, Ophelia, and just like the last time, after our first dinner with the family, either she or Winnie had been a pipeline to the paparazzi.

The countryside whizzed by in a blur of green. My phone rang with the "Stayin' Alive" ring tone.

Ethan looked over. "Your sister again?"

I nodded and took the call. "Hiya, Lizzy."

"Hey, Beckers. Why did I have to find out from Mom that you're getting engaged?"

Telling her would be like painting it on a billboard. "He hasn't asked me yet."

"So when?"

"I can't talk about that right now."

"He's there, isn't he?"

"He's driving."

"Put her on speaker," Ethan said.

I shook my head and mouthed *no*.

"Yes," he insisted.

I did. "Lizzy you're on speaker with him now."

"Hi, Ethan," Lizzy said.

"Hello, Lizzy. How are you?"

I had no way now of warning Ethan the dangerous waters he was wading into.

"Fine," she said. "I was calling to ask you two to lunch."

Ethan shot me a quizzical look.

I shrugged. I couldn't avoid her forever.

"Okay," Ethan answered.

"Great. Shall we say Mortinson's at noon?"

"Sounds good," Ethan answered. "Right, Sunshine?"

"Yeah, noon," I said.

"I'm really looking forward to meeting him. See you at twelve."

"Later, gator."

She ended the call. "I'm not sure this is a good idea."

"We don't really have a choice. She's your sister, and we're just being sociable. Your boyfriend would be sociable, wouldn't he?"

"She knows me better than anyone. What if she sees through us?"

"I'll see that that doesn't happen."

~

Ethan

Telling my parents our plan to get engaged had gone more smoothly than I would have guessed, and the rest of the drive into the city had been uneventful.

I knew parking would be a problem near the restaurant Lizzy had picked, so we stopped by home and took a taxi to our lunch meeting.

As soon as I stepped out near the restaurant, the problem began. "Put your hand up to shield your face," I told Becky before she exited the taxi. I shielded my face as well.

That didn't stop the annoying photographers from snapping dozens of pictures and lobbing questions our way.

I urged her to keep walking, and I pushed away one of the paps who got too close.

"I don't understand," she said as I pulled her along to the restaurant's entrance.

She'd barely been able to handle it when we knew they'd be around. Being surprised made it ten times worse. I pulled open the door for her.

"They're terrible," she complained as the door closed.

Once inside, the harassment ended.

"How did they know—"

"Your sister." It was obvious to me.

Becky's expression showed disbelief. "She wouldn't do that to me." She looked around the room. "There she is." She pointed to a woman alone at a table on the side.

The woman waved.

I looked back toward the street. Through the darkened glass, I could see the photographers lurking outside to ambush us on the way out.

I urged Becky ahead of me. "You say hi. I'm going to use the toilet for a second." I waved to her sister and headed for the back hallway.

I found a waiter exiting the kitchen. "Is there a back door?"

He shook his head. "Employees only, sir."

After retrieving my wallet, I counted out three fifty-pound notes. "I'll ask again. Is there a back door?"

He took the money and pocketed it. "Yes, sir. This way." He waved me toward the door leading back to the kitchen.

"Not yet. I'll let you know when."

He nodded. "Very well, sir."

I waited in the hallway for a half minute before returning to the table where Becky and her sister sat.

I offered my hand to Lizzy. "Hello, I'm Ethan. You must be Judas."

Her expression darkened, and she pulled back her hand.

I sat down and motioned to the street. "That was uncalled for."

"I don't know what you're talking about."

"The paps. You called them."

"You're the son of a duke and a public figure. It's the name that attracts them, most likely."

I sat opposite her. "Becky is not, and she doesn't deserve to be treated that way."

Lizzy gave up the pretense. "It's my job."

"Fine. I have a meeting to get to." I stood. "Becks, I'll catch up with you later." This way she didn't need to worry about our act being adequately convincing.

Becky was frozen, with that deer-in-the-headlights look.

I patted her shoulder. "You should stay and enjoy lunch."

I waved to the waiter I'd paid.

He ushered me through the kitchen and out the back.

A minute later, I was safely in a taxi without the photographers out front being any the wiser.

I gave the driver my TechniByte address.

Lizzy certainly was a piece of work, to call the paps on her own sister.

But then I knew firsthand that there was more than one way to be betrayed by a family member.

∽

Rebecca

"It's my job," Lizzy had said. Her deception at first had been easy to read. She couldn't keep anything from me.

I watched Ethan storm toward the back until he was gone before turning back to her. *Should I have supported him and left as well?* "Your job sucks. How could you ambush us like that?"

Lizzy shook her head. "He knows the score. It's an act."

Ethan's tells were second nature to me, and he'd been honestly incensed at what my sister had done. "It was not. You don't know him. I do."

She tilted her wine glass up for a gulp. "Whatever. They all act like that, but they don't mean it. They love the attention."

From the sound of her words, it wasn't her first glass of wine. I ignored the comment and picked up the menu.

"Look," my sister said. "It goes with the territory. He doesn't have a choice. It's just the price of hanging out with that crowd."

I cocked my head. "Maybe I should try slugging a paparazzi or two?"

The waitress came by and took our lunch orders.

"He's stuck with it because of his name. The public has a right to know."

"Bullshit. It's not news. It's private. You guys just do it for the clicks."

"You're going to get engaged, right?"

"Yeah, but—"

"No buts, Beckers. You're the one who's always on the truth kick. If it's the truth, it's fair game."

"Doesn't he, don't we, deserve at least a little privacy?" Now I was firmly on Ethan's side about this.

"You're the one who doesn't think anybody should keep secrets."

"I said *privacy*, and you guys are just doing it to make money, not for some greater good."

She ignored the slight and kept going. "We're in business, just like everybody else. If you want to hang out with him, being subject to the spotlight is the price you have to pay. So, what are you going to do?"

I sighed. This is where our cover story and my own feelings actually merged. "I'm sticking with him. He's a great guy."

"Between you and me..." She leaned forward. "I think he's one hell of a catch. How did you meet him?" Her eyes gave her away. She didn't mean what she'd just said, and I could expect to see whatever I told her in the paper, attributed to *confidential sources*.

In spite of the intrusiveness, I realized it was a chance to solidify our story and maybe use her to feed the necklace details to the one we were after.

I twisted my wine glass and smiled. "I met him at school five years ago during my study-abroad semester. We were both at Imperial College."

Her eyes went wide. "He's that guy from college? You never told me he was a duke's son."

I shrugged. "I didn't know at the time either. He never mentioned it."

"No way. You're blowin' smoke up my ass."

I put up my hands. "Honest to God truth. I had no idea until I returned here and we met again."

Lizzy held off her questions while our waitress brought the sandwiches. "Go on," she said once we were alone again.

"I'd just gotten here, and I went to the automatic teller for some money." I swallowed. This was the hard part to admit. "I got mugged."

Her mouth dropped open. "Bad?"

"I ended up in the hospital." I touched the back of my head, which still sported a bit of a lump. "I still have a bump on my noggin, but nothing serious."

"That's good, but that still doesn't explain him." Her mouth turned crooked at the word *him*. She didn't like Ethan, most likely because he'd had the audacity to call her on her shit.

"The nurse asked who she could call, and you weren't here, but his name came to mind. He took care of me, and it just went from there. It was like we were never apart."

She didn't look convinced. "Weren't you pretty pissed at him back then?"

"Yes and no." I remembered our lines on this. "We got our wires crossed. Big miscommunication. I longed for him after I went home, and it turned out he'd felt the same way."

"You sure can screw up your life," she lamented.

I added Ethan's mother's line from last night. "Think of how much more wonderful it would have been without the miscommunication and separation. That's what his mother said."

"You only have yourself to blame," Lizzy mused. She picked up her phone and started tapping. "And now you're getting engaged. Wow, you move fast. What are the duke and duchess like?"

"Normal, just a family."

"There's nothing normal about living in a castle on that much land." She scrolled her phone and turned it toward me with a picture of the manor. "Big enough to be a castle."

"It's not a castle."

"Says you."

I sipped my wine. "It's been wonderful—like we were never apart." And in my mind, that's how it felt. Maybe not to Ethan, but to me at least.

"I still don't see how you screwed it up five years ago."

Like everyone else, she saw the title and the family, not the man.

"Well, that was a long time ago." I couldn't go into what had really happened, especially not with her.

"When do you think he's going to ask you?"

"Any day now. We just told his parents this morning."

"No shit?"

I nodded. "And you're not going to believe this part."

She leaned forward.

"The tradition in his family is to give a ring *and* a necklace as engagement presents."

"This just gets better and better. Bet you're really kicking yourself now that you dumped him back then." Once again, my sister's crasser nature showed through. "Is it going to be a good one?"

"A necklace from the Duchess of Overdale's estate." I widened my eyes. "It is just gorgeous."

"Expensive?"

I sipped some water to make her wait for it. "Keep-it-in-a-bank-vault expensive."

"This I have got to see." She switched gears quickly. "Any way maybe you can introduce me to his brother?"

That last question managed to surprise me, because it wasn't a joke. "He's not in the country."

"When he is?"

"That's enough about me." I ignored her question about Charlie. "So, besides checking out my boyfriend, how's work going?"

We managed to finish lunch without having to revisit my relationship with Ethan again.

When we'd finished, I still had to brave the stupid photographers outside to get to a taxi.

CHAPTER 37

Rebecca(One week later)

The engagement had gone off without a hitch, and pictures of the proposal had made all the papers the next day.

Now it was Thursday, two days until my evening as bait at the party. We had been officially engaged for a week, and Ethan was off retrieving the Overdale necklace from The House of Stafford where it was being repaired.

It had done its job at each of our dinners since our official engagement. It attracted the paparazzi like flies after Lizzy's story had hit the pages of the *Evening Mail*.

I hated that I couldn't even leave the apartment now without them shoving cameras in my face and following me through the city.

Because of it, I'd had to stop going into the office at all. One or two of them were always around, like stink on shit.

I checked my watch.

Ethan was due back soon, and it couldn't be soon enough for me. I was trying to stay awake through another interview Smithers had thrown my way. This one was from Edinburgh, and I had to go slower and rewind on occasion to understand it all with the accents.

When my phone rang with Lizzy's ringtone, it was a welcome interruption. She started with her usual. "Hey, Beckers."

"Before you ask, no, I will not be set up for another paparazzi ambush."

"Would I do that to you?"

"You did," I reminded her.

"I meant a second time."

"What can I do for you?" She'd already asked for a picture of the Overdale necklace her paper could use, and I'd sent one.

"I need some help on a story I've been put on."

"I'm listening."

"I hear there's been a string of high-value jewelry burglaries in the city." She was fishing.

I stood to relieve some of the tightness in my shoulders and shrugged even though she couldn't see me. "News to me."

"Being in the insurance biz, I figured you'd know something about them."

I didn't like where this was going. "You give me too much credit. Mostly they've had me analyzing New York cases from over here. Nothing much local. Workload shuffling." That was mostly true.

She didn't have my gift, but she could still smell bullshit if it was deep enough. "So you haven't heard anything?"

"Nothing about jewelry burglaries. What do the police say?" I'd been careful to use her term of *burglaries*, which made my sentence true.

"That's the problem. Nada, zilch, nothin' from them, which is odd."

I started walking around the room. "So if they're not your source for the tip on this string of burglaries, who is?" I asked.

She paused before responding. "Anonymous. My guess is a cop who doesn't like that the brass is keeping a lid on it. Says the whole gang is going to be taken down on Sunday."

Her words worried me. "That sounds like it has to be someone inside the police then. So what can I help you with?"

"My source said there'd been at least three big jobs already, but the brass is keeping a lid on it so as to not alarm anyone."

I cut the corner, and my foot hit the coffee table. "Shit." I jumped on one foot, yelling some more. "Shit. Shit."

"What? The cops?"

"No." I hopped again. "I stubbed my fucking toe, and it hurts like a mother." I slumped into the couch and grabbed my aching foot.

"Sorry."

I checked, and at least I hadn't broken the nail. "Damn, that hurts. You were saying?"

"None of the cops are saying a thing."

I didn't think staying quiet was right. "If they think they're close to cracking a case, they might handle it that way." I got up and waddled on my good foot and the heel of the injured foot to find some aspirin.

"Could you check with your industry contacts? I'm looking for some corroboration, maybe the size of the burglaries?"

"Before you publish?" I asked as I checked the cupboard. I found the pain reliever the hospital had given me.

"Yeah—you know, expand the story, give it more depth."

I read the label and tried to remember. "Hey, you live here. What's Paracetamol?"

"That's Tylenol."

"Thanks." I popped open the bottle and took two tablets. My mouth was dry, and I couldn't swallow them, so I spit them into my hand. "Hold on." I waddled toward the kitchen. "If they're sure they can roll up this guy or guys this weekend, why are they telling you now?"

"This guy promised me the inside story on the takedown when it happens."

I pulled open the fridge, popped the pills in my mouth again, and swallowed them with a bit of orange juice, which went down the wrong way and made me cough.

"What's going on there?"

I recovered after a bit. "Sorry. Had trouble swallowing the stupid pills."

"You should try not kicking the furniture."

I huffed. "Smart-ass."

"Dumbass."

I sighed. "Look, I don't have anything for you on this, but I'll let you know if I hear anything."

"Thanks, Beckers. Hey, is Ethan's brother back in town yet?"

I didn't bother answering that. "Later, gator."

After we hung up, I slumped into the couch. My sore toe was the least of my problems now.

Whoever was setting up Ethan's family had to be the source of her story, and they planned to give the police a convenient tip on Sunday that would lead them to the missing jewelry. If we didn't catch whoever it was at the Saturday party, I had a terrible choice to make.

I could either tell Ethan and make him turn in evidence that would implicate his own parents, or move the items out of the house without telling him and become complicit in the thefts at some level.

If I didn't do either of those things, the fix would be in. The cops would get the tip, search the house, find the jewelry, and the trap would be sprung. It would be too late.

I laid back on the cushions and contemplated my next move.

The clock was ticking, and I didn't have much time. *We* didn't have much time.

The Saturday party where I would be the bait was three days off. But, my inability to tell Ethan without putting him in an ethically awkward spot meant I had to figure this out on my own.

∽

ETHAN

I PUSHED INTO THE HOUSE OF STAFFORD FOR THE THIRD TIME IN A WEEK. I'D DROPPED the necklace off for its repair early this morning.

Stafford's saleslady, Martha, was with another pair of customers, so I waited and reread the text I'd gotten. It put a smile on my face.

> Kelsey: Congratulations on your engagement. Stop by sometime. I'd love to meet her.

Of course that would mean flying to the States.

She finished with the other couple and smiled at me. "I'll retrieve your necklace and be right back." She left through the door to the back and returned quickly.

When she opened the box for my examination, the necklace looked just as stunning as it first had, maybe more so.

She read from the note. "Clasp replaced with an identical replica of the original and cleaned." She handed me the paper. "You'll want to retain this for your records, should there be any questions. Mr. Stafford said it's as good as new."

I took the paper, closed the lid, and stowed the valuable box in my briefcase. "Thank you, and please thank Mr. Stafford for me as well."

"I will. And…"

I stopped.

"I must say, your fiancée looked stunning wearing this."

She must have seen the papers.

"Thank you. I thought so." A minute later, I was on my way. Not wanting to walk the streets with the necklace, I'd asked the cabbie to wait for me.

Dad's call arrived on my mobile before we'd made it five blocks.

"Ethan, are you alone?" he asked.

"I'm in a taxi on the way back to my flat."

"I'll be brief then. You need to be careful this weekend."

After several seconds of silence from his end, I asked, "What makes you say that?"

"I have it on good authority that Wentworth is planning something," he said slowly.

"And how is it you've come to know this?" I had to be careful about the words I spoke inside the taxi.

"I have my sources."

I nodded. Of course he had informants embedded within competitors. He'd always said knowledge was king and the key to success.

"Do we know any more about this?" I asked.

"Only that he expects good news by the end of the weekend."

"And what makes you think this has to do with us?"

"I can't be certain, but he's been focused on revenge for several months now."

"I'll be careful."

After he rang off, I couldn't help but guess that it might mean another theft planned for this weekend at Rainswood. All it would take is for the papers to get a tip about jewelry thefts occurring at my family's parties, and the implications would be devastating to Mom and Dad.

Wentworth, if he was behind it, could seed the story with enough facts for the papers to check that we would be guilty in the court of public opinion within a week. The damage would be done.

There wouldn't be any way for Dad to tamp down the scandal. One couldn't prove a negative. The papers would be full of it until a bigger scandal came along to distract them.

Aunt Helen wouldn't be able to deny it if asked publicly, and probably the same for Elizabeth Haversom. Open and shut, as far as the press was concerned, and perception would become reality.

I seethed as the taxi made slow progress toward my flat.

The pressure on Becky and me had just been upped tenfold.

∼

"I'm back," I called out when I returned.

I didn't get a response.

Becky was pacing the top-level patio when I saw her through the glass. Something was clearly wrong. I stopped and watched. She paced to one end, talking to herself, and then back to the other, shaking her head the whole time.

I yelled again, "Becky."

This time she heard me through the glass. The pacing and talking stopped instantly. A timid wave was my greeting.

I opened the door.

The traffic noise of the city was louder than her greeting. "Did you get it?"

"Yeah. What's wrong?"

"I'm nervous about Saturday."

I closed the distance between us and took her into my arms.

She was shaking. "We may only get one chance at this."

"I know. I'm nervous too." I rubbed her back to relieve the stress. "You'll do fine. Let's get you inside." I pulled her toward the door.

She only resisted for a moment. "How did it go?"

"Good as new, they tell me." I opened the door for us and closed the street noise out once we were inside. "I made us a reservation for tonight at Sabatini's."

"You said we were done after last night."

"You love the food there."

"That's not an answer, and I hate the photographers."

"Like you, I'm nervous, but let's give them one more show." I pulled the necklace from my briefcase and offered it. "One more dress-up?"

She took it from me. "But no table by the window. It's like being in a zoo when we do that."

"Table in the back. They'll get arrival pictures, and we can even sneak out the back when we're done."

"That won't work." She poked a finger to my nose. "They've figured you out, Detective Inspector."

She had me there. That trick hadn't worked the last two times we'd tried a back-door escape.

I moved toward the fridge. "Want a glass before we leave?" Last night the wine before we left had steadied her nerves.

She followed me. "Sure." She kneaded my shoulder muscles when I stopped in front of the refrigerator. "You're tense. What happened?"

I pulled out the almost-full bottle from last night. "Nothing." I wasn't ready to tell her about Dad's call yet.

When I turned to get the glasses, she jumped in front of me. "Tell me that again."

"Nothing. I picked up the necklace."

"Liar. What is it?"

I'd fucked-up again by giving a specific answer while facing her, rather than evading. I'd set off her lie detector. "You agreed to not pull that stunt on me."

"And you agreed to tell me the truth so I wouldn't have to evaluate you."

"Okay," I said as I moved around her to the glasses. "Dad called."

She pulled glasses down for us while I uncorked the bottle.

"He has a warning." I poured the two glasses. "Let's sit."

She accepted the glass. "You're scaring me."

I started as soon as we sat down. "He is concerned that a few of his competitors are out to get the family."

"Why?"

"They're not happy with his business practices, but *why* is not important."

"Who, and what does he mean by 'out to get the family'?"

I sipped. "A while ago, he told me to watch my back and to warn Charlie that either Wentworth or Knightley—those are two business competitors—might try something to hurt us."

"Like, physically?"

I gulped down more wine. "He doesn't know."

After a pregnant pause she asked, "And what was today's call about?"

"He has an informant near Wentworth that told him Wentworth is expecting something to happen this weekend."

She put her glass down, and the blood drained from her face. "And you think this jewelry-theft business might be the something?"

I nodded and finished my glass. "It fits."

She picked her glass back up and downed the contents. "Then we need to put on another show tonight." She stood and retrieved the necklace box before turning for the bedroom. "I'll get beautiful."

"You're already beautiful," I called after her.

"I need to be camera ready for the mug shot after I slug one of those fucking photographers tonight."

"That's not in the script."

"Then keep them out of my face." The door closed behind her.

CHAPTER 38

Rebecca

When he'd told me his father had heard something would happen this weekend, I'd almost fainted. It fit perfectly with Lizzy's tip.

Saturday was going to be our one and only chance to catch this fucker. Whoever was pulling the strings on this planned to spring the trap on Ethan's family before the weekend was out.

I did my face before stripping down and going through the closet. I found the red dress that was even more scandalous than the one that had upset Ethan's mother the first time we'd ended up in the papers. This was the dress for tonight.

As a general rule, I'd been toning it down for these evenings as Ethan's fiancée, and I'd let the necklace and ring do the talking. But if we were going for maximum exposure in the papers, that meant I had to expose the maximum amount of skin tonight.

Pulling it on, I felt barely dressed, yet confident this would draw male eyes from a mile away. Turning in front of the mirror, I saw a problem. The high slit on the thigh exposed my *knickers,* as Ethan would call them.

I pulled them off and found a pair with a higher waist. Still not high enough, was the mirror's verdict.

I gulped and slid them off. That was the draw of this dress. It made it obvious that I was braless and panty-less, a thought that would fry the brains of the men watching.

Time to own it, girl.

I stood tall and turned once more in front of the mirror. Sex on a stick. No wanna-be actress with a short skirt was drawing more camera flashes than me tonight.

The Overdale necklace took my breath away when I opened the case, as it did every time. I'd nearly fainted when Ethan admitted how much it had cost. I figured I'd hear Cornwall's head explode all the way over here when he got the bill.

The clasp felt secure when I put it on, and it looked marvelous. The large, yellow center diamond hung at just the right level to draw the eye to my cleavage.

I closed the case and noticed something. Turning it over and around, I double checked.

The small corner dent on the case from that first night was missing. This had *Overdale* printed on the top in gold the way it should have, but it wasn't the original case.

Taking off the necklace, I pulled the loupe Stafford had gifted me from my purse. The fourteenth link didn't have the HS engraving it should have had, nor did any of the others I checked.

HOLY FUCK.

I paced the room. Now I knew how they did it, and it hadn't involved an invisibility cloak after all.

It was the perfect crime, because the jewelry had been switched *before* the party, at The House of Stafford. We'd never gotten the *where* of the theft right—nobody had. And without the where, the who was impossible.

I stopped and sat. That was only half the story. They had to get the real one into the hiding space in that bathroom at Ethan's family estate. The frame job wouldn't work any other way.

It was brilliant. Make a replica, switch it when the owner brought it in for cleaning or repair, and plant the real one in Ethan's family's house. Then, call the cops with a tip, and it didn't even require the owner to know she'd lost the item. She could be notified after the jewelry was found.

Knowing the missing jewels had all been present at a Blakewell party recently, and finding the real ones hidden on the premises, there was only one logical explanation when looking at the situation from the outside: someone in the household had stolen them at the events.

It wouldn't matter that there weren't witnesses or fingerprints or anything like that. The real thing had been stolen and found in the Blakewells' possession. The thief didn't need to chance trying to fence the jewels, and time was on the thief's side. He could stash the real thing at any time during the party or even a later one.

Simply brilliant.

If I hadn't noticed the changed case, even I would have fallen for it. But now it was game on.

I had the advantage, because he didn't know I knew. In fact, he'd surmise we didn't because nothing had been reported stolen or found.

I had to catch the person planting the real necklace at Rainswood.

Ethan had just dropped the real Overdale necklace at Stafford's shop this morning. We had to get to Rainswood before the thief did, and reverse the trap.

I dialed the office.

Ginny answered on the second ring. "Hello?"

"Ginny, I need several things, and I need them right now. Take down this list."

When I finished the call, I changed out of the sexy dress. It would have to wait for another night. After reclaiming my bra, I chose the pink thong Ethan liked, then slid my comfortable jeans and T-shirt back on.

The plan was simple. Get Ginny's delivery from work, then get us quickly to Rainswood Manor and beat the crook to the bathroom jewel stash. Set the trap and wait. It might be a long two days.

This would all still have to be done solo, I decided. Telling Ethan what I knew would end badly. He couldn't catch on until I'd snared the culprit and it was obvious none of his family was behind this. Then he could honestly tell the people he worked for that he was as surprised as everyone else.

If what he'd told me was true, this would probably lead directly back to his father's nemesis.

Pasting on my battle face, I opened the door.

CHAPTER 39

Ethan

I was still fiddling with the bow tie that never wanted to stay straight when Becky came out of the room.

She'd done her face, but was in the same jeans and shirt she'd gone in with.

"I thought you were getting ready."

"Work is bringing by some things for me."

"But we have to go out."

"No. Not tonight."

I didn't understand what had changed. "We agreed that we had to get out in front of the cameras again with the necklace."

"Is that all I am to you? A rack to display a stupid piece of jewelry we don't even own?"

I hadn't seen that coming, but clearly the water had just gotten a whole lot deeper in here. "You know that's not true." I moved toward her. Revealing the truth about having bought the necklace outright could wait for a time when she wasn't so volatile.

She backed up—a bad sign. A very bad sign.

Now I was in deep shit with no compass.

She looked down at the floor. "I told you the cameras scare me."

"I said I'd keep you safe. And, you agreed to go to dinner one more time."

"Because it's what you wanted, but I'm done doing it just because you want to."

"I thought the assignment was important to both of us." Decoding her sentence had taken me too long. "I mean, I guess we don't have to."

"You guess?" she hissed.

I put my hands up. "You know what I mean. Of course we can skip it."

"I want to get away from those damned paps. I can't stand another day of being locked in here, afraid to go out because of the camera assholes. Let's go to your parents' place."

When in doubt, Dad always said, *"Tell a woman she's right before you say anything else."*

"You're right, Sunshine," I said.

Her face softened.

"A break from here would be good."

She came toward me, lifted up on her toes, and gave me a surprising kiss. An instant later, she backed away. "Thank you for understanding. I'll pack."

The woman was a study in contradictions.

∼

When the doorbell rang a half hour later, Becky jumped up to get it. "That's probably my work stuff."

I shrugged and went back to reading the paper on cybersecurity that I was only a quarter through. It was a tough slog because the author thought long-winded passages were better than simple ones.

Becky reappeared with a metal briefcase. "We can go now."

Checking my watch, I didn't even need to look at the traffic app on my phone. Right now would be a terrible time to leave. "We should wait until the traffic dies down." I went back to my paper.

She left the metal case of work papers and a moment later came back out of the bedroom with her suitcase. "Let's go."

"I told you, there's a lot of traffic on the motorway this time of day."

She huffed. "This is what I mean. How come we can't do something I want to for a change?"

That came out of left field. We'd done picnics, shopping trips—a ton of things she wanted to do.

"*Don't argue*," Dad's voice told me. "*Lead with, 'You're right, honey'.*"

I rose from my seat and smiled. "You're right, honey."

She turned on her heels. "Don't you honey me." She grabbed the Aston key fob from the bowl where I kept it. "Since it's too much trouble for you, I'll drive myself."

That was a seriously bad idea. Leaping to my feet, I tried to recover. "You're right, Sunshine. We can leave right now." I didn't dare ask why the timing was important. Now was not the time for rational questions, or questions of any kind. Somehow everything I said made my situation worse, so I shut up.

Women.

She handed me the key fob. "Probably better if you drive."

I didn't even dare agree.

Ten minutes later, we drove through the line of photographers and turned west. A light rain shower had started.

At the first stoplight, I picked up my mobile and selected Mom's contact.

Becky sent me a questioning look.

"My mom," I explained. "It's polite to give her some warning."

She accepted that and craned her neck to look behind us. "They're following."

While the line rang on the Bluetooth speaker, I checked the rearview mirror. Two of the paparazzi cars we'd seen before were behind us, but none of the motorcycles—probably because of the rain.

"Ethan," Mom said. "According to the papers, you certainly are showing Becky the town."

I silently shook my head. Discussing the papers with Becky here wouldn't go well. "Mom, Becky's with me, and we're driving to join you now to get out of town and away from the cameras."

"Oh," she said.

The light turned green, and I started.

"We're having a small dinner party this evening," Mom continued. "Will you be in time to join us? I'm sure the Wentworths would love to meet Becky."

The Wentworths? Why?

When I looked over, Becky's mouth had dropped open, also not a good sign. "There's a lot of traffic. We may not—"

"We'd love to," Becky said cutting me off. "We'll hurry." That was another in this afternoon's string of surprises.

Becky looked back again. "They're still following."

They probably would all the way home. I saw a gap in the traffic ahead just big enough. "Hold on." Cranking the wheel over and accelerating, I dodged across traffic just ahead of a bus and onto the cross street.

Becky braced herself and didn't look back until we were halfway down the block. "That was close."

Even my heart was thundering after threading the needle through oncoming traffic. "Well, you wanted to get rid of them."

"I want to make it in one piece too."

"Sorry if I scared you." Three turns later, we were back on the original road with no sign of pursuers. I slowed to a sedate pace.

A minute later, Becky surprised me again. "Why are you going so slow? We have to get there in time to meet the dinner guests."

I couldn't figure her out today, and didn't bother asking another question that would mark me as dumb. "You're right, Sunshine."

As the minutes ticked by, I tried to reconcile Dad inviting the Wentworths to dine with them, given what he'd told me about Wentworth or Knightley possibly planning something. It didn't make sense to invite the enemy inside our walls, but Dad obviously felt differently.

Halfway home on the motorway, Becky checked the time on her phone. "Can't you go any faster?"

I looked over, but didn't ask.

"I have to pee."

"If you can hold out, there's a petrol station ahead."

"Yuck. No way. Just get me to Rainswood as fast as you can."

I pushed the accelerator and let the big engine do what it was built to do.

Becky braced herself, but didn't complain. Instead she pulled out her phone.

"Using that might make you carsick," I said as I passed another four-wheeled obstruction.

She ignored my suggestion.

A minute later she asked, "Didn't you say Wentworth was the name of your Dad's competitor?"

I nodded. "One of them,"

"Why are they coming over?"

"No idea."

She went back to her phone.

Nearing the house, I slowed to avoid becoming another statistic at the tricky corner with the old oak. Looking over as we passed the tree, I could see it still bore the scar from the crash when Billy, one of our groundskeepers, had lost his life. The little MG never stood a chance against the hundred-year-old oak.

Billy would have been twenty-eight this year.

I accelerated again when the road straightened.

∼

Rebecca

Hearing that Ethan's parents had invited the Wentworths over for dinner scared me. Was it them? What if the person planting the evidence would be there tonight, instead of attending the party, and he beat me to the bathroom? If he got the real Overdale necklace planted before we got there, it was game over.

Telling Ethan I needed to pee got him to speed up. The downside was he scared me so much I almost soiled my pants.

Several strange cars were parked near the house when we arrived.

"We're here," Ethan said as he brought the car to a skidding stop near the front door of Rainswood Manor.

I didn't wait for him. Instead I let myself out and hurried up the steps, turning back at the door. "Can you bring the luggage in?"

"Of course," he said.

Once inside, I hurried down the hallway, turning right at the ballroom and right again toward the ladies' restroom.

The bathroom was empty, and I took the precaution of locking the door.

Gingerly, I pulled out the drawer and looked up under the empty space. The two previous pieces of jewelry were still taped under the counter, but not my necklace. After checking above the drawer on the other side, I could finally breathe easier. I'd made it in time. My necklace, the Overdale, hadn't been hidden here yet.

This last week I'd come to think of the Overdale as *my* necklace. I needed to do a better job reminding myself I'd have to give it up when this was over and content myself with pictures of me wearing it. The memory of the weight of it around my neck still made me smile.

A knock sounded on the door. "Becks, you okay?"

I jerked up and yelled, "Just a minute."

I went into one of the stalls and flushed the toilet and followed by running the faucet while I replaced the drawers.

After a few calming breaths, I unlocked the door and exited.

Ethan was at the end of the hall. "I was worried about you."

I smiled and took his hand when I reached him. "I'm good now."

"Mom told Winston and Karen to hold off serving for a few minutes. They're all in the dining room, sucking down cocktails and waiting on us."

We met the Wentworths, Jarrod and Alicia, who offered perfunctory greetings and well wishes on our engagement. The news had spread widely.

His mother called us to the table, and Ethan and I were seated next to his father and across from Mr. and Mrs. Wentworth. Ophelia and Winnie sat on opposite sides of the table.

As the meal began, I couldn't follow the conversation Ethan's dad and Mr. Wentworth were having in hushed tones.

Since I'd spent all my time in the bathroom looking around before I was interrupted by Ethan, now I really did have to pee and excused myself.

Ethan had left my metal work case by the door.

I picked it up and made my way back to the bathroom to set my trap.

CHAPTER 40

Ethan

I couldn't believe Dad had invited Jarrod Wentworth and his wife to dinner.

The man was a snake, and if Dad's information was correct, he was about to try something this weekend, which I guessed had to do with the jewelry thefts happening here under Dad's nose.

The setting didn't allow an opportunity for me to ask Dad what had possessed him.

A moment ago, Becky had pushed her salad away, half eaten. "I have to go to the little girl's room," she'd whispered in my ear.

As white as she'd been while I drove us here, I wondered if her stomach might still be roiling. She really couldn't handle the speed.

A minute later, Wentworth caught my attention. "Ethan, I understand you'll be presenting your fiancée at the ball Saturday. She's quite lovely."

I nodded. "I will, and she's so much more than merely beautiful." I could have gone on, but it would have been wasted on the man.

"Of course she is," his wife answered for him.

Wentworth ignored her and said something I didn't catch to Dad. He was on his third wife, none of them lasting longer than ten years.

I wondered if wife number three, who'd just stood up for him, realized the clock on her stint as Mrs. Wentworth was rapidly winding down toward zero.

"She's an investigator," Winnie said.

"And she can spot a liar at twenty paces," Ophelia added.

"I don't believe that can be done," Wentworth mumbled softly toward Dad.

His wife's smile hardened into a thin line, but the poor woman kept her thoughts to herself.

Winnie caught Wentworth's comment and came to Becky's defense. "Perhaps you should test her?" she said to the toad.

"Perhaps." He nodded. "I enjoy magic as much as the next man."

"It's not magic," I said.

The smile that had left his wife's face returned. She must've been interested in seeing the slob taken down a notch by my Becky.

Dad's eyes settled on me with pride. He was too courteous a host to challenge his guest directly.

Wentworth ignored my comment and gulped down his wine.

When Winston and Karen came to clear the salad, I let them take Becky's, figuring if she was spending this much time in the toilet, she probably wasn't going to want to finish it.

Five minutes after the main course had been served, Becky still hadn't returned.

I blotted my lips and rose. "I'm going to check on my fiancée," I told Mom.

Dad gave me a nod as I left, still listening to Wentworth. Their conversation hadn't provided any information about why he was here.

When I didn't get an answer at the small toilet adjacent to the dining room, I moved on to the larger toilets off the ballroom.

I knocked. "Becky?"

"I'll just be a minute," she yelled from beyond the door.

"Can I help?"

"No. I'll be right out."

When I noticed my foot tapping, I halted it.

Soon, the sound of running water announced her imminent return.

"You didn't have to wait for me," she said as she exited.

I took her hand, and we started back. "I promise to drive slower in the future."

"Huh?"

"I didn't realize my driving scared you this much."

A step later, she squeezed my hand. "Ethan, you're so considerate."

Back at the table, nobody mentioned Becky's absence.

She ate slowly, watching the interplay between Wentworth and my father.

Winnie nodded toward our guests. "He doesn't believe you're any good at what you do," she told Becky.

Wentworth caught the comment and interrupted his argument with Dad. "No, I said there's no such thing as a human lie detector."

My woman just shrugged. "Maybe not."

"Show him," Ophelia urged.

Becky picked up a forkful of rice instead of responding.

Wentworth wiped his mouth. "In my experience, Americans exaggerate everything." That made the hair on the back of my neck stand up.

I glowered at him. "As do certain Englishmen." I added as much snarl as I could manage.

Mom's mouth dropped open.

Becky's eyes shot daggers at Wentworth, but she kept her mouth shut.

"I think she's the real thing," Winnie said.

"Prove it," Wentworth said to Becky.

I put a hand on her arm. "She doesn't need to."

"Jarrod," Wentworth's wife said. "Perhaps we should drop it."

"No," he told her. "I've been challenged."

Becky laid her fork down. "Very well. Mr. Wentworth, tell me four separate things, and make one of them a lie." Her voice was calmer than mine.

Wentworth huffed. "My oldest son's name is Edward. I had sausage at breakfast. My secretary's name is Edith, and I had kidney pie yesterday." He puffed up and sat back.

Becky smiled. "You didn't have kidney pie."

Wentworth shook his head. "Lucky guess. That doesn't prove anything."

"You don't need to believe me," Becky said as she picked up her water glass.

I admired her coolness under his attack. I moved my hand to her thigh and patted it.

She gave me a simple smile.

"My birthday is April third," Wentworth said, taking another try at it. "I traveled to France last month." He paused. "My oldest son's wife's name is Marie, and I ate at a French restaurant last night."

Becky sipped her water.

"Well?" Wentworth asked.

"You tried to cheat," Becky told him.

His brows drew together.

"Those four things were all true," she added.

"Diane, how many people are you expecting this weekend?" Mrs. Wentworth asked, shifting the conversation.

Wentworth didn't take the escape his wife had offered. "I'll figure out the magic trick later," he said before turning back to Dad and asking him something about Norway.

Becky didn't respond to the toad's dig at her skills. My woman had class.

I missed the other conversations that sprouted up to fill the awkward void as I patted Becky's thigh again and looked over. *Good job*, I mouthed silently. She'd taken the windbag down a notch.

She leaned over to give me a soft kiss.

The rest of the dinner proceeded with little fanfare.

Winnie, Ophelia, and Becky started a conversation about horses, which I listened in on. That led them to invite Becky to ride in the morning.

"I'm afraid I can't tomorrow," she told them. "I need to stick around the house and be available for a call at a minute's notice."

Dad and Wentworth discussed politics of the EU.

Mom and Mrs. Wentworth had decided the vile state of the tabloid press in the country needed to be controlled by better laws.

Eventually, Winston cleared the dinner and brought out crème brûlée for dessert.

After an appropriate wait, I leaned close to Becky. "We could take an evening stroll."

She shook her head. "Not while we still have guests." She was showing Wentworth much more courtesy than he'd shown her.

∽

REBECCA

WINSTON BROUGHT THE DESSERT WITHOUT KAREN THIS TIME.

I closed my eyes for a second and let the tasty concoction slide down my throat.

Karen really was a wizard in the kitchen. The silky sweetness made me forget tonight's tension for a moment, but only a moment.

Leaning toward Ethan, I asked what I'd wondered several times. "Why does Karen always look sad?"

He put his spoon down. "Her fiancé, Billy, died in an auto accident a few years back. Grief takes longer for some to process, I suppose."

"Maybe if she sampled her own desserts it would help her mood."

Ethan chuckled. "Suggest it at your own peril."

That put that suggestion to bed. I'd seen grief morph into anger more than once.

After finishing the last of it, I eyed the Wentworths across the table. Would one of them make a move tonight? Or would they wait until Saturday night, where the crowd of the party would make their movements less obvious?

When we got up from the table, that would be the test. Would one of them head to the convention-sized ladies' bathroom where my trap was set?

Winston cleared my dessert plate after I set my spoon down.

"Please tell Karen that was superb," I told him.

"Karen needed to attend to a family matter, Miss Sommerset. I'll pass it on tomorrow when she returns," Winston replied.

"Becky."

"Yes, Miss Sommerset," he repeated.

Ethan cocked a brow and smiled at my failed attempt to train Winston.

"Give her my compliments as well," Mrs. Wentworth added.

Winston cleared Ethan's plate. "Very well, madam."

Alicia Wentworth was a puzzle. She'd come to her husband's aid more than once during the meal, as the peacemaker. Was she truly fond of him, or was it the price of enduring the time until her prenup matured? If the online rumors were true, that was the end of this year.

I'd looked up Jarrod Wentworth and his third wife on the drive over, and Ethan had been right, looking at my phone had made me nauseous. But only half my discomfort had been from the jostling of the car as Ethan shifted it into hyperdrive. The rest was a result of the articles I found about Wentworth's business practices.

Jarrod Wentworth was more adept at making enemies than friends. And something like framing Ethan's parents as jewel thieves didn't seem out of character for him.

"What do you say we adjourn to the library?" Ethan's father suggested to Wentworth.

He clearly had an agenda if he wanted to spend more time with his enemy.

Ethan's mother suggested we ladies join her in the kitchen for a little champagne, her standard place to unwind, it seemed.

Ethan mumbled something about too much estrogen and wandered upstairs instead of joining us.

After adding the first glass of champagne to the wine the other girls had drunk at the table, my companions were getting a little lubricated.

I'd been careful to limit my intake, and only sipped a bit now in the kitchen.

By the second glass, I decided I liked Alicia when she let herself relax, and I settled in to observe her.

"Jarrod works long hours," she said at one point. *True.*

"We met in Zermatt, skiing." *True.*

"I enjoy our dinners at home." *Lie.*

Why not? I wondered. Not an easy thing to figure out.

"I'm really looking forward to our anniversary next year," Ethan's mother said a little while later.

"Yes, me too," Alicia agreed. *True.* Maybe that was when some other part of the prenup kicked in..

"I thought it was sort of rude that your husband didn't believe Becky," Ophelia said.

Looking around at the others, I seemed to be the only one of us shocked by what she'd said out loud, probably because I was the only sober one.

"He doesn't mean to be rude," Alicia said. *True.* And, that was a surprise. "He is just too outspoken for his own good." *Another obvious truth.*

Maybe the rumors of her waiting out the prenup were just that, rumors.

∼

Ethan rubbed my shoulders after we closed the doors on the Wentworths. "You're tense."

I felt like saying, "No shit, Sherlock," but I held it in because I couldn't admit what I knew and what was underway. I'd spent the meal awaiting a move to put the Overdale in place, in case they'd decided on tonight, and I'd kept my eyes and ears open long after the meal.

"It's been a difficult week," I told Ethan.

"We could still go on that evening stroll."

"Not tonight." I pulled away from the neck rub. I couldn't venture far from the trap I'd set in the downstairs ladies' bathroom off the ballroom. "I have work to look over."

Now that the Wentworths had gone, only Winston was left to be careful of in the house, unless I included the cousins as possible suspects. I'd been fooled before and had learned to not exclude anybody.

"I think I'll work for a while in the library," I added. If the perpetrator was in the house this evening, I couldn't wander far from my bathroom trap.

Two hours later, after I was sure everyone else had retired for the night, I slipped into Ethan's bedroom. My phone's volume had been turned up high to wake me if the alarm on my trap sounded, and I placed it on the nightstand.

I slipped under the covers with Ethan and stared at the ceiling for the longest time. I wondered if I'd made the right choices.

Instead of turning in the jewelry the first night I'd found it and claiming my promotion, I'd gone off script completely. I'd not told my partner, Ethan, to protect him and his family, but did that make it worse if my current plan failed? Probably.

I'd already lost the Overdale necklace. The one I had with me was a fake, and delaying reporting it missing meant I had no chance now of convincing anyone it had been switched by Stafford.

As far as anyone looking at it from the outside was concerned, I could have switched it myself and hidden the real one to sell off the diamonds later and retire rich. I now realize my plan had a dozen serious holes and that in many ways it could end up with a terrible result for me, as well as the Blakewells I'd meant to protect.

After the way Ethan had been with me, he didn't deserve that.

He rolled over and snuggled up against me. "Don't be worried," he said, softly nuzzling me.

"I thought you were asleep."

His arm came over me and pulled me closer. "How could I sleep without my snuggle bunny?"

"I wasn't worried." The warmth of his body next to mine gave me strength—not enough strength to tell him the truth, though.

"Liar."

He was right.

Stay strong, I reminded myself. I was lying to protect him. "No, I'm fine."

"I can hear the stress in your breathing. Don't worry." He kissed my ear. "I'll protect you."

Tears formed. I'd never needed anyone to look out for me before. Was it wrong to appreciate his caring?

He kissed my ear again. "It'll be okay. I won't let anything happen to you."

"Love you too." The words came out spontaneously, and everything changed. I'd violated the rules.

He kissed my ear again, offering no other response.

Now I was in way over my head. I'd told him the truth, a truth I hadn't even dared admit to myself.

As I lay awake, I added the words I'd just spoken to my list of worries.

CHAPTER 41

Rebecca

I ROSE AT THE ASS-CRACK OF DAWN—TECHNICALLY WAY BEFORE DAWN—AND SLID OUT of bed before Ethan woke. This would all fall apart if I wasn't nearby when the alarm sounded. I desperately needed this to work. *We* needed this to work.

The unknown creep working with Wentworth had to plant the Overdale necklace in the bathroom either before or during the party. If I didn't catch him in the act, the Blakewells' goose would be cooked. The totality of the circumstantial evidence would indict them.

After padding into the bathroom, a sense of dread washed over me. What if it had already been placed? I hadn't checked last night before coming to bed. What if the bugger had worked around my trap? Leaning over the sink, I prepared for the puke session that threatened.

Two minutes later, the feeling had passed without any actual upchucking, thank God. I slipped on a bathrobe and headed downstairs with my phone. The phone's light saved me from tripping in the dark.

After grabbing the inspection mirror from my case in the library, I proceeded to the big bathroom. I opened the first drawer only halfway to avoid tripping the dye pack, and checked under the counter with my mirror.

The first one was good, and after the second was also the same as I'd left it, I reclaimed the ability to exhale. The tension was going to give me an ulcer.

Looking down at my bathrobe, I realized my predicament. I wanted to restart my work in the library, which was my best guard spot, without waking Ethan and enduring questions I'd have to lie to answer. But I couldn't do that and then desert my lookout post to take a shower after he got up. That would be stupid timing, when people were up and around.

Upstairs, once my phone's light was extinguished, I couldn't see squat. My night vision had been destroyed by the bright light. Slowly, I felt my way through the bedroom to the bathroom and gingerly closed the door behind me. When I turned, I ran smack into the human wall of Ethan.

"Shit," I screeched into the darkness.

He grabbed my shoulders and steadied me. "Hey. It's just me."

"What are you doing up?" My mouth filter failed me.

"It's called a piss. How long have you been up?"

He'd figured out I'd left the bed.

"Just a few minutes." At least that wasn't a lie. "I couldn't sleep, worrying about a work issue, and I had to check it out." Also not technically a lie.

"At four in the morning?"

I shrugged. "Dedicated workaholic, what can I say?"

His arms enveloped me. "Come back to bed, and I'll fix that."

The contact tested my willpower, but I had to be strong, at least until the trap sprung shut on the bad guy. "No. I'm going to shower and get a start on the day. Smithers has buried me in work." Also only stretching the truth.

~

ETHAN

AN EARLY START? AT FOUR A.M.?

Becky was certifiable, but I had to admire her work ethic and dedication. I'd been such a dick last night. When a woman professed love, she deserved more than a kiss as an answer, but I hadn't been prepared. While I'd lain there, wondering how to respond, her breathing had slowed to the rhythm of sleep and it became too late.

"It's important," she said as she pulled away toward the bedroom.

I kept a hold on one hand. "Can't it wait?" I had to try.

"Please?" she countered. "This is important to me."

The dim moonlight entering through the tiny window was enough to show the lack of a smile on her face.

"Up to you," I told her. I could be adult enough to lose this debate and let her chart her own path. My feelings shouldn't bugger up the career that was so important to her. "Anything I can help with?"

"No. I have to do it myself."

I moved to the shadow that was the door to the bedroom, and opened it. "See you at breakfast."

A sliver of light came from under the door after I closed it, and the sound of the shower followed that. She'd been able to manage the recalcitrant valves once she learned to use two hands.

The temperature in the room hadn't changed, but my bed wasn't as warm without her in it. For a moment, I considered joining her in the shower, but wordless shower sex wasn't the way to deal with her profession of love. Neither was pulling her away from the work that had dragged her out of bed this early in the morning.

Our discussion should be the two of us alone, and that meant outside in the garden or the woods—far enough away to be private and uninterrupted.

I feigned sleep when the bathroom light went dark, and she tiptoed out of the room.

CHAPTER 42

Rebecca

While working at my laptop in the library, I'd heard the house wake as people came downstairs and morning activity began.

It was seven thirty when Ethan's distinctive steps approached. "Morning," he said in greeting. "How about a little breakfast?"

I paused the video and took off my headphones. "Sounds great." I'd been waiting hours now for some time with Ethan. After standing, I rubbed my sore butt before waddling his way.

"What's wrong?"

I pointed. "That chair is hard as a rock." I rubbed the sore spot some more.

"I can massage you to fix that…"

I followed him out into the hall toward the kitchen. "Can you now?" Any other time I would have taken him up on that, but not today on guard duty.

"Yesiree, missy," he said in his Texas accent. "I done took a class in that, I did. Ya see, it's all in da thumbs."

"Thumbs, huh?"

He led me into the kitchen. "Yesiree, missy. I shit y'all not."

Winnie turned from the counter. "And what kind of accent is that supposed to be?" Ophelia stood next to her.

"Don't y'all like my Texican?" he asked.

"Don't give up your day job." Ophelia laughed.

I joined her. "It's not going to fool anybody."

Ophelia picked up her purse. "We're going into town for a stroll and a little shopping, if you want to come along."

"Thanks, but I can't today—too much work to finish."

"You sure?" Winnie asked.

"Some other time. Thanks."

Ethan closed the fridge he'd been searching. "Where are Mom and Dad?"

Winnie put her phone in her purse. "They went on a walk. Something about spending the morning at the Yellow Cottage."

A minute later, his cousins had gone, and I was alone with Ethan.

He backed me against the counter. "It's just the two of us," he said as he leaned in seductively.

"And Winston and Karen," I reminded him.

"Just Winston." He pushed a stray hair behind my ear. "Karen comes in late the day after a dinner party." He pressed in closer. "I could take care of that sore spot for you."

This close, my man's scent was tempting as hell, but I had to stay strong. "It's still one set of ears too many." I pushed back on his chest. "Maybe later. What are you making me for breakfast?"

He let me go.

After he suggested a ham, cheese, and spinach omelet, I settled on a stool to watch him cook. "What did you make of your dad inviting his enemy over for dinner last night?"

He moved a cutting board and knife in front of me. "Make yourself useful. The spinach is in the bottom drawer."

It only took me a minute to chop up enough for both of us and bring it over to the stove, where he was busy with the eggs in the pans. "About your dad and Wentworth?"

Ethan turned down the heat. "Not a clue, but Dad doesn't do anything without a reason."

"Do you think Wentworth is the one who's going to make a move this weekend against your family?"

He turned to me. "Dad certainly thinks so, and he's the one with the inside source."

"Like, an informant?"

Ethan took the spinach I'd brought over and split it between two pans on the stove. "Someone like that, or perhaps more than one someone."

∼

Ethan

After breakfast, I joined Becky in the library.

She'd been right that the chairs at the table she was using for her work were hard to sit on.

I chose to work with my laptop on my legs in a more comfortable wingback—at least that was the reason I gave her. The fact that it gave me a perch from which to watch her as she worked also had something to do with it. The silhouette of her chest from this angle was perfect.

I heard the front door open and close. With the sound of a single set of shoes coming down the hallway, I knew it wasn't my cousins.

Karen peeked in.

I checked my watch. Nine forty. "You're early."

She adjusted her backpack. "Yeah. I wanted to get started on preparation for Saturday."

Becky looked over. "Karen, I just have to say, the crème brûlée last night was wonderful."

My woman was courteous to a fault.

"Why, thank you. That's very nice of you." Then she was off down the hall.

Becky turned my way. "What's her normal time?"

I shrugged. "Usually about ten thirty on a day like today, after a dinner party."

Five minutes later, there was a loud bang somewhere out in the house.

Becky's phone screeched.

Becky shot out of her chair, ran to the door, and turned left down the hall.

It took me a second to get out of the chair and untangled from my laptop. I raced after her. "What is it?"

Becky disappeared around the corner in the ballroom. By the time I got there, she was turning down the other hallway.

As I approached that turn, I heard the commotion before I saw it.

"Stop right there, Karen," Becky yelled.

I raced toward them.

Karen was just beyond Becky at the door to the ladies' toilet. She was covered in blue and frozen in place. She dropped a box.

Becky held a baton, of all things, in her raised hand.

"What the hell?" I yelled.

"She's the thief," Becky said, panting. "I set a trap, and she fell for it."

Karen only sneered at us. "You can rot in hell," she hissed at me. "And your whole fucking family. Stealing from all your friends. You're going down for this."

I was totally confused now.

I heard loud footfalls coming our way.

"Master Ethan, what is going on?" It was Winston behind me.

"Check her for weapons first," Becky told me. "Then have Winston hold her so she can't get away."

"Put your hands up," I told Karen.

"Make me," she snapped back.

I grabbed a wrist and twisted her around, bent the arm behind her, and forced her against the wall in a move I'd learned in training.

"Let me go. That fucking hurts, you arsehole," she screeched.

"Then don't struggle." Running my free hand down her side and over her pockets, I determined she didn't have a weapon, unless it was tucked in her bra. I didn't check there.

"Master Ethan, what is going on?" Winston asked again.

"She's been planting jewelry in the bathroom to make it look like your parents stole it," Becky told me.

"Fuck you, cunt," Karen threw at Becky.

"Quiet." I twisted Karen's arm more to shut her up.

She yelped.

"What on Earth?" Winston asked.

I didn't understand either. "A little explanation?" I asked Becky.

Winston seemed agitated. "I demand to know—"

"Shut up," we both said.

Becky motioned to the toilet. "I found Aunt Helen's necklace and Haversom's brooch in there, under the counter."

"When?" I demanded.

Karen struggled again. "Because your fucking family stole them," she hissed at me.

"Nonsense," Winston said.

Becky grimaced. "The night of the first party, along with Devonwood's necklace."

"You are so going down for this." Karen laughed.

"Shut the fuck up." I twisted her arm a bit.

"So I rigged the drawers," Becky continued. "With dye packets to see who would try to stash my, I mean, the Overdale, necklace here to frame your family for stealing it too."

I wasn't following her story. "But you have that upstairs. I saw it this morning."

Becky shook her head. "It's a fake. She's framing you and your family."

"How could you? After all this family has done for you?" Winston asked.

He was normally quiet, and that's the Winston I wanted right now.

I pulled Karen away from the wall and pushed her past Becky to Winston. "Can you handle her?"

"I was in the Royal Marines." He said this like it explained everything, and took a firm grip on her.

I'd forgotten that about him.

Karen tried to wriggle loose.

"Struggle any more, and I shall be forced to tie you up, Miss Dirks," the old Marine said.

Becky pointed to the box Karen had dropped. "She was going to plant that." Her eyes lit up as she motioned to me. "I'll show you how it worked." She pushed open the door to the ladies' toilet. "Get your pansy, British ass in here," she added when I hesitated at the door.

I followed.

Blue dust was everywhere. One drawer was on the floor, along with Karen's backpack.

"Look under here, Inspector." Becky shone the light from her mobile in the opening where the drawer had been.

I gasped. Up under the counter, plastic bags with the jewelry she'd mentioned were taped—or at least what looked like them, pending closer inspection. "What the bloody hell?"

"Somebody at the jewelry store," Becky explained. "Someone has been switching for fakes so good the customers don't notice, and…" She nodded toward the door. "*She* hid the real ones here, just waiting to be found after a convenient tip was phoned in to the police."

My brain was going a mile a minute as I grasped the conspiracy Becky explained. It would have been impossible to refute if a police search had turned up the stolen items here before this.

I stood. "How did you—"

"When you brought back the Overdale from being fixed, I checked it, and it was fake. It wasn't the one you'd taken them that morning."

I waved over the counter. "Why didn't you tell me when you found these?"

"Think about it, Mr. Detective. Ethically, you'd've been forced to report it. Game over for your parents. That would only have snapped Wentworth's trap shut sooner than he planned."

"You think it's him?" I followed her back to the hallway.

"Turn that over," she said, pointing at the box Karen had been holding. "See what's inside."

My eyes went wide when I opened it to see the sparkling beauty of a necklace I'd bought her. "Holy fuck."

She laughed.

"What?"

"You just swore. Twice."

I shrugged. "I know how. I merely prefer to maintain control."

"I'll remember that." She closed the box and handed it to me. "You hold on to this. It was found in her bag. The blue dye and drawer on the floor prove she was accessing the bags under the counter. I think you have your case, Detective Inspector. So get your ass moving."

I agreed with her assessment. This would be a certain conviction. "We still have to tie her to Wentworth."

She poked a finger in my chest. "You. Not me. I'm only assigned to the jewels, remember?"

My cock stirred as I caught a whiff of her shampoo. I grabbed a fistful of the hair behind her head and pulled her closer. "You can't get free of me that easily, my beautiful, smart partner." She had solved this and saved my family.

She pushed at my chest. "Stop distracting me. You have work to do, copper. Put her ass in jail. I'll be waiting for you."

CHAPTER 43

Rebecca

Ethan took the angry bitch to another room to ask some questions after making a call to his Met backup, Julian, who had been staying in a hotel nearby to be ready for another stint as the party photographer.

Winston looked in the door to the restroom. "Quite the mess."

"Do you have anyone who can get this cleaned up in time for the party tomorrow?"

He pulled a phone from his pocket. "Indeed I do."

"But not until the police have taken their pictures and whatever."

He smiled. "I will see to it, Miss Rebecca."

I patted him on the shoulder as I passed. "Thank you very much for all your help, Winston." I'd probably committed another social misstep by touching him, but he'd started it by using my first name. I'd broken through, and I smiled at my accomplishment.

When I reached the room Ethan had chosen for his questioning, I opened the door.

Karen sat across the table, a blue mess with her handcuffed hands on the table.

"You deserved it," she spat. "All of it. You killed him." Intense anger radiated from her.

Ethan turned back for a second. "You probably shouldn't be in here," he said.

"I can help," I told him. A lie-checker could speed up his interrogation.

"Not until I get you clearance," he said with a hand flourish indicating he wished it weren't so. The rules apparently dictated his words to me.

Nodding, I left and closed the door behind me. I'd seen and heard enough. Karen thought she was avenging a death, clearly the death of someone she cared about. Each of her three short sentences had been true, as far as she knew. True *to her* was the important distinction. Some people could honestly believe something that was not factually correct, but was true in their experience or worldview.

I'd seen my share of crazy, but the way Karen had looked at us across that table had been scary. Sloughing that thought away, I texted my analysis to Ethan. He could figure out if it was useful to him or not. As usual, the punishment aspect of the crime was not for me to be concerned with.

The kitchen was my first destination. A stoppered, half-full bottle of champagne sat in the fridge. I poured myself a self-congratulatory glass and downed half of it on the way back to the library, and I brought the bottle with me.

Instead of the hard chair in front of my laptop, I chose the soft cushions of the couch, and after topping off my glass, I dialed in to the Lessex office.

"Mr. Cornwall's office," his assistant, Emily, said.

"Emily, this is Rebecca Sommerset. I need to speak to him."

She sighed. "I'm sorry. He asked not to be disturbed for the next several hours."

"He'll want to talk to me."

"He was very firm about it," she argued.

I sighed loudly into the phone. "Okay. If he doesn't care about saving ten million pounds, I guess that's his problem, not mine. Bye." I hung up.

It only took twenty seconds for my phone to light back up with the return call.

"What is this about ten million?" Cornwall asked as soon as I answered.

"We solved the case, sir."

An audible gasp came across the line. "So I won't have to pay that awful duchess another three million pounds? What makes up the rest of the ten million?"

"Sir, do you know if we insure Lady Devonwood's jewelry?"

"Yes, I believe we do. Why?"

"She may not know it yet, but her necklace was also stolen. We recovered that, as well as the Haversom brooch and the Lindsley necklace."

"Excellent work. I knew I was right to put you on this."

Since I'd been successful, it seemed he'd rewritten history to him having drafted me for this, instead of Smithers suggesting me.

"Are you bringing them back to the office today?"

That would be a problem. "Sir, I can't. They're evidence, and in the hands of police."

"Why? If you found them, you should have brought them straight here rather than get the police involved." He'd managed to forget that I'd been told the Met was in charge. "This is not acceptable. They should have been brought here, so I can restore them to their rightful owners."

"Yes, sir."

The issue was obvious now. He didn't want to be cheated out of his moment of personal triumph when he personally returned the valuable pieces to his customers. It was all about him.

In the end, that didn't matter to me. I had my bargaining chip. I'd pulled his gonads out of the fire. The king owed the pawn a favor, in this case.

"This isn't right," he said. "Where are they now?"

"As I said, with the police. You'll have to talk to them."

We got off the phone shortly thereafter, once he finally understood I couldn't fix this for him.

Once I hung up, I realized the sleepless night and constant worrying about my trap had taken its toll. Now that the adrenaline of catching Karen was wearing off, my eyes fluttered closed. With a start, my head jerked up as it became apparent I had to choose between a mega dose of caffeine or a nap.

I passed Winston and trudged upstairs for the warmth of Ethan's bed.

～

ETHAN

FINISHED WITH MY PRELIMINARY QUESTIONING OF KAREN, I LEFT HER IN THE LIBRARY, secured with handcuffs Julian had brought.

She was not happy to have failed in her attempt to bring my family down, and she had said entirely too much to me for her own good.

I'd recorded it with my phone, and it was too late for her to recant.

She'd be charged, and the evidence was overwhelming, or at least I thought so. The trial would be a formality.

"Miss Sommerset retired upstairs," Winston told me when I asked where Becky had disappeared to. "For a nap, I assume."

I found Julian in the kitchen, cleaning the blue off his shoes.

"Are they done?" I asked. I'd left him to supervise the Scenes of Crime Officers investigating the room I feared we might need to relabel the Blue Toilet.

"They left five minutes ago." He wiped at his shoes. "This shit is some kind of nasty." He patted the evidence bags on the counter. "I've got the jewelry to log back at the Yard. Just waiting for a car to pick me up. I'm not carrying a million pounds' worth in by myself."

"Try about ten million," I told him.

He drew in a deep breath. "Holy fuck. That's one hell of a heist."

I shrugged. "But we stopped it."

He nodded and continued working on his shoes.

"Why don't you take her with you for charging?"

His face lit up. Being lower in rank, he'd assumed I'd want to bring her in. But he deserved the lift this arrest would bring.

I hadn't told him how the real conspiracy had been to frame my family for the thefts.

"I'll take the evidence in," I told him. "But first I intend to confront the jeweler."

"You're sure he's in on it?"

"He's one of the players, for sure."

Julian disposed of the dirty paper off the kitchen roll and put his shoes back on. "That does it for now."

Winston appeared. "Constables are at the door. Shall I see them in, sir?"

"No, Winston. Tell them we'll be right out." I patted the evidence bags. "You take her in," I told Julian. "I've got this handled."

"Thanks, Inspector," he said with a big smile.

I went with him to release Karen from the chair and escort them to the waiting car.

A minute later, crazy Karen was out of sight, the bitch. I spat on the ground, returned to the house, and gave Winston the okay to bring in the cleaning crew.

∼

"What happened?" Mom said loudly from around the corner.

I hadn't heard them return while I was busy in the library. I looked at my watch and realized I'd been in there for hours. I came down the hall to find Dad looking on while Mom interrogated poor Winston.

"We had a mishap," he said. Noticing me, he passed off the explanation. "Perhaps Master Ethan should explain."

Mom turned to me. "Well?"

I motioned toward the other hallway. "We should discuss this in the library."

Dad stopped Mom. "Di, let me talk with Ethan first. Get yourself a glass of wine in the kitchen."

"I want to—"

"Diane, after a glass of wine," he said, pointing toward the kitchen.

Dad urged me toward the library, and Mom followed.

"I'll not be left out of this," she said to him at the door.

Dad sighed, waved her in, and closed the door behind us. "Well?"

I didn't know where to start. "Perhaps we should sit."

Mom took a seat.

Dad didn't. "I'll stand."

I sat opposite Mom. "First, I need to explain something."

Dad's brow lifted just a bit. She merely waited.

"I have an admission to make." I looked between them and couldn't figure an easier way to say it. "I work for the Metropolitan Police Service."

Dad's expression morphed into a smile. "We know."

My mouth must have dropped open. "You know?"

"I told you I know everything that happens in this family. Of course we've known. I understand that you can't discuss it, but I'm very proud of the work you do."

"We both are," Mom added.

I took a deep breath. That was a load off my mind and made this easier to explain. "You both knew and didn't say anything?"

Mom smiled. "We don't keep things from one another."

Dad sat beside Mom and took her hand. "It's the secret to a successful marriage."

This wasn't the time to ask about the exception dealing with his business, or Mom's secret I carried. As happy as they seemed together, that wasn't a subject I'd ever broach.

"Now, what happened while we were gone?" Dad asked.

I started at the beginning. "There have been some jewelry thefts, and they were purported to have occurred here."

"Nonsense," Mom said. "Nothing has gone missing here."

I explained how Rebecca and I had been brought in on the case, what we had learned from Aunt Helen, and how we'd messed up at the first party.

"Go on," he said. "How does that bring us to today?"

I explained how Becky had noticed the switch of her necklace and how she'd set the trap that had snared Karen. "And the mess in the ladies' toilet is left over from the blue powder that marked her and made it impossible for her to deny being in there."

"Why would she do this to us?" Mom asked. "It makes no sense."

"She's unhinged," I said with a shrug. "She kept going on about how we were to blame for Billy Marston's death."

Dad shook his head. "Poor girl."

I balled my fists in frustration. They didn't get it. "Poor girl? Don't you understand what she was trying to do to us?"

Dad put his arm around Mom's shoulder. "You don't know the whole story, and neither does she."

"Then enlighten me."

Mom said, "Billy Marston committed suicide."

That didn't fit the reports I'd read. "I thought it was a mechanical failure, a stuck throttle in the automobile."

Mom patted Dad's leg. "Why don't you explain it. I think I'll check on the cleanup."

Dad stood. "Follow me."

He led me toward his office, while Mom continued down the hallway.

Inside his office, Dad sat at the desk and unlocked a drawer. "This is the note he left in his room." He handed me a folded piece of paper.

> Mom, please forgive me. I can't go on living a lie. I know I can never be with Daniel, but marrying Karen will only ruin both our lives, and I won't do that to her.

I refolded the note and offered it back. "Who is Daniel?"

"His lover."

"You should keep that to explain to her," Dad said.

"Explain what?"

"We carry life insurance on all our staff. It doesn't pay in the case of suicide, however, and for that reason, I thought it best the family not see these. He ran into the tree full throttle on purpose."

"But I heard that the accident report—"

"That was what I told everyone. I… I persuaded the authorities to keep the real one filed away for the sake of the family." The way he said it implied I shouldn't ask for any details. "I gave his mother an altered report. I thought that with the check, it would give her some peace."

"What check?"

He continued. "The insurance company knew the truth and wouldn't pay, so I paid the company one hundred thousand pounds, which they forwarded to his parents and Karen, whom he'd named as beneficiaries, along with the appropriate paperwork. They never knew the truth."

He sighed. "I know that doesn't compensate them adequately, but it's a fair sight better than losing him *and* knowing he killed himself. I, we, thought a mechanical-failure explanation would lessen the burden on everyone involved."

In his opinion, they had done the wrong thing for the right reason to help Billy's parents and Karen.

In a way I was proud of him for attempting to help, but at the same time dismayed that he cared so little for the law. But, that was in the past and not today's issue. "Do you recall the mother's name?"

"Martha, and the father George. They were the only ones affected."

"Except for Karen."

Dad wrung his hands. "I stand by my decision. I know I didn't follow procedure, but I did it to help the family."

Now this made sense, or as much as it could. Martha Marston at the jeweler's had worked with our Karen, both of them trying to punish us for poor upkeep of the car they thought had taken Billy's life. It had never been Wentworth.

CHAPTER 44

ETHAN

Reaching the Aston, I turned on my mobile, which I'd switched to silent for interrogating Karen. It rang as I finished setting my bag with the jewelry evidence in the passenger seat.

Ignoring it, I buckled in and started down the drive, fast. The speed was exhilarating after being cooped up in the house all morning. Getting to The House of Stafford in time to nab the other part of the team in this conspiracy was paramount—and it had to be before Karen was able to make a phone call to warn her.

Once on the main road, the car surged forward as I mashed down the throttle. My mobile started up again, and I answered it on the Bluetooth speaker.

"Blakewell, I've been trying to reach you." It was Superintendent Maxwell, no doubt wanting to congratulate us and ask how we'd done it.

"Yes, sir. I take it you heard of our success."

"Blakewell, I got a call from the assistant commissioner, who got a call from the mayor, who got a call from some duchess or other, who no doubt got a call from that fucking insurance company you're working with. They knew you'd recovered the jewels, but I didn't get a call from you, and I'd like to know why the fuck not."

"Sorry, sir. Things have been moving rather rapidly here. I have the jewelry in my possession, and I was just about to call. We nabbed a suspect. Detective Waters is on the way in with her now."

"Bringing her in? Why?"

"To charge her, sir. I thought Julian—"

"No, you fucking well didn't think. I want you to call him and get him turned around right fucking now, and explain to the constables that it was just some kind of response-timing test or some shit like that. Under no circumstances are we making an arrest."

"But, sir, we caught her clear as day."

"You must have your head up your arse. Didn't I instruct you on day one that there would be no record of this inquiry?"

Ahhh... In my zeal to punish those who'd tried to frame my family, I lost sight of the big picture from the mayor's perspective, which had become the commissioner's perspective, and thus affected my orders from the superintendent.

I had fucked-up. "Sorry, sir. I thought—"

"Since you're not doing it well, stop fucking thinking and follow orders for a change. Cut the suspect loose. We'll deal with her later."

"There's a second one as well that I'm on my way to talk to now."

"No, you're not. You are to deliver the jewelry to your insurance company partner and let them handle returning it to the owners."

"Yes, sir." Now was not the time to suggest alternatives. I slowed and pulled to the side of the road for a chance to reverse course.

"On second thought," he added, "when you cut your suspect loose, make it fucking clear that any hint of this in the press or on social fucking media or *anywhere* will force us to reopen the inquiry, and you tell her that your boss's boss's boss's boss will come down on her like a meteorite and turn her life into a fucking smoking hole in the ground. Are you understanding me now, Inspector?"

"Absolutely, sir." It was a simple translation. If I fucked-up the fear factor with Karen, I'd be on the receiving end of the meteor.

∼

REBECCA

"WAKE UP, SUNSHINE."

I rubbed my eyes and was greeted by Ethan's lovely face. But he was sitting on the bed rather than lying in it, which I would have preferred.

"Beauty sleep is over. You have a task."

I rolled away and closed my eyes again. "We caught her, and that's enough for today. Wake me at dinnertime."

He pulled at the covers.

I grabbed them tighter.

"You have to take the jewelry in to your boss," he said, still pulling on the covers.

I turned back to him, clutching the sheet to my chest for warmth. "Smithers?"

"Cornwall."

This morning's conversation with Cornwall came back to me. "I already told him I can't because you have to process them as evidence." I was pretty sure I'd made that clear, but maybe not.

"Not anymore. We're not charging."

"Who? Karen?" I needed to slow this conversation, so I dropped the sheet.

Ethan's eyes drifted down to my boobs and his mouth stopped.

I wiggled side to side, and his eyes followed.

He blinked. "It's complicated."

Having some fun, I slid out of bed and bounce-walked up to his gaping mouth. "Didn't we already have this conversation? You're the one who told me it was immoral to let the guilty off the hook."

He nodded.

I bounced on the balls of my feet.

He blinked. "Sorry I said that." He tried to look away, but his eyes drifted back when I bounced again. "It's complicated. Orders from on high. This time, I'm the one who doesn't get a vote."

I cocked my head, still bouncing. "Now you see my side of the situation?"

He swallowed hard. "You do that one more time, and your boss's boss will be mad because you didn't make it into work on time."

"Killjoy." I turned to get my clothes.

"Practical. As it is, we don't have a lot of time to get the jewelry into town."

I went to the closet for the work-appropriate attire I'd brought along. I wasn't giving Cornwall any way to ding me on this assignment. Makeup could wait till we were in the car.

Once we were on the road, Ethan drove like an old lady. It made the makeup easy, but a check of the time meant we needed to go faster.

"Why are we going so slow?" I asked after I put my mascara wand away.

"After upsetting your stomach the last time, I promised to drive slower, remember?"

Maybe I was a better actress than I gave myself credit for. "I wasn't sick. I needed time to rig up the dye packs in the drawers without you being suspicious."

He sped up, but thankfully not to warp speed.

After pulling my little cardboard scent strip from my purse, I opened the baggie, but closed it again without sniffing the smell of the new company car I deserved. All of a sudden, I didn't want to.

Looking over, my stomach turned as I realized I might have a choice to make soon between Ethan and my promotion. I looked out the window. I'd never really discussed the promotion with him. It had been my goal for so long that I hadn't considered that there might be anything else. I wondered now if a future with him could be an alternative.

His rule about not discussing the past had kept us from talking about it, and kept me from exploring it. *"I have great affection for you,"* he'd said. But when I'd slipped and told him I loved him the other night, he hadn't said a thing. I looked out the window again.

We passed another car. The woman inside laughed at something the man said. They looked so happy. Was there a future like that for me? For us?

"What's got you down?" Ethan asked, patting my shoulder.

I put my hand over his to draw on the strength that always flowed to me through his touch. I needed it now. "I'm worried about…" I didn't know how to finish the sentence, and it wasn't a discussion for the car. Maybe if we had more time together, things would be clearer. We could try dating without all the pretending…

He patted my shoulder again. "No need to be worried, Becks. Whatever it is, we got this."

I pulled out the one statement I knew to be true. "I've really enjoyed doing this with you." Saying the words brought a threatening tear.

"Me too. Whatever has you worried, we can talk it out tonight when you're finished with work."

I struggled to lean over the console and kiss my man.

"Smithers has been keeping me up to date on your undercover adventure," Cornwall said as we waited for Smithers to fetch the gemologist, Grinley, from downstairs.

I waited for Cornwall's assessment.

"This Blakewell chap seems to have shown you quite a good time."

I couldn't read whether he shared Smithers' take that it had been too extravagant. "The photographers tended to make it difficult."

"In the pictures, you two look like quite the couple."

"We get along very well, sir."

He looked down. "I see you're still wearing his ring."

Smithers appeared with Grinley in tow, as well as Emily, Cornwall's assistant.

"You're sure these are the original items?" Cornwall had asked when I arrived. With false bravado, I'd assured him they were. I'd removed the three items from their evidence bags and displayed them on the conference table. Ethan and I had kept the Overdale necklace in the safe at Rainswood, as it wasn't related to Lessex.

Smithers beamed. "I'd say this is a good outcome for everyone."

Cornwall remained pensive as Grinley started his examination.

The room fell silent.

Grinley looked up after finishing with the last of them, the Haversom brooch. "I concur," he said. "These are authentic."

I let out the last of my held breath. I'd checked for the mark I knew would be on the Lindsley necklace, but didn't know how to authenticate the other two before bringing them in.

Cornwall was beside himself. "All three items undamaged. I never thought... This is fantastic work."

I smiled with the official word that I'd succeeded beyond his expectations. The pawn had saved the king in this chess game. That had to be good for something.

Cornwall turned to Emily. "Set up a meeting with the Duchess of Lindsley tomorrow morning at ten."

"Where?" she asked.

He thought for a second. "Make it here. Tell her we have recovered her necklace. I want that damned three million pounds back."

"Would you like me to convey that, sir?" Emily asked with a smirk he didn't catch.

"No. No. I'll enjoy telling her myself."

Ten minutes later, Emily had been assigned all the client meetings, Grinley had been sent back to his office, and Smithers had taken the jewelry to the vault.

Cornwall moved behind his desk. "Have a seat, Sommerset."

I sat and smoothed my skirt.

"I understand you're interested in the head of investigations position in San Francisco."

This was it—the promotion discussion all of this had been leading to.

I smiled and nodded, trying valiantly to not seem overexcited. I began the spiel I'd prepared for this moment. "Yes, sir, I am. I was thinking that I—"

He raised a hand to stop me. "No sales speech necessary, but first…"

I waited for the other shoe to drop. *But* was never a good word in a situation like this.

"Another matter has been brought to my attention by HR in San Francisco."

I failed in my attempt to avoid slumping with that news. Fucking Miriam in HR had never liked me, and she had obviously been working behind the scenes to sabotage me, even as I was providing more value to the company than she ever had.

He pulled a paper out of an ugly, gray envelope that suspiciously resembled the awful HR one in my purse. He opened the letter and read it to himself. "This letter seems to imply that you have a problem playing well with others." He looked over the paper at me. "How did this come about?"

Fucking Jackson and fucking Miriam. They were both fucking up my best chance for that office.

I took a deep breath and decided on what I'd always cherished, complete honesty. I would not go down without a fight.

"In your own words," Cornwall urged.

"A coworker of mine lied, and I pointed it out. He didn't like that, so he complained that I was creating a toxic work environment." That was all true and the simplest explanation.

"And that was all?"

What else could he be fishing for?

"There wasn't anything personal going on between you two?" he asked.

I huffed. "If you knew him, you'd understand how preposterous that question is. He asked me out a few times, and I declined. Nothing was going on between us and never will be." That was probably oversharing, but he'd asked as if he was accusing me of sleeping with the turd.

"You're an attractive woman, Miss Sommerset."

I didn't understand where that came from and fingered my engagement ring.

He placed the letter back in the envelope. "I suspected as much and asked HR to investigate. Your coworker admitted wanting to spite you for your rejection, and this matter has been put to rest. I've already recommended you for the position."

I closed my eyes a moment. I wasn't fired, the HR complaint was history, and I had the promotion. But... My way forward was no longer clear. Could Ethan and I make it work across the distance? Or did he even want to try?

Cornwall slid an envelope across the desk. "If you'd like it, this is your travel itinerary. You fly out Monday to your new job."

The tempting envelope disappeared into my purse in seconds. "Thank you."

"Or..."

Had I been too eager? The wait for the next words was torture. I could have the promotion or what? Maybe he intended to pay me off with a big bonus.

"There is another alternative. We could promote you to Smithers' position here."

I almost fainted at the suggestion that I could have everything—the promotion and be able to stay here.

"And," he continued, "we could send Smithers to California."

Suddenly all the possibilities lay before me.

He stood. "Before you ask, Smithers would be delighted either way." He'd apparently set this up before I walked in.

My heart leaped out of my chest as I stood and started jabbering. "I don't know how to thank you, Mr. Cornwall."

He extended his hand. "Take a day to think it over, and let me know your choice."

I shook his hand vigorously. "I will. Thank you again."

As I floated out of the office, I had to pinch myself to make sure this wasn't a dream. Stopping at Emily's desk, I pulled out the foul, gray HR envelope and handed it to her. "Please shred this."

CHAPTER 45

ETHAN

WITH CHAMPAGNE IN THE FRIDGE, ALONG WITH THE FLUTES, I WAITED AT MY FLAT FOR my woman to return. Sunshine had become the perfect name for her; she'd brightened my life since returning.

It was time to celebrate, and time to thank her. Without what she'd thought to do, this could have all turned out terribly different. It was also time to ask her the important question. We'd had a wonderful time together so far without dredging up the past. Why couldn't that continue? Mom and Dad proved that not all secrets needed to be shared, and their relationship was strong. Maybe I could convince Becky of the same.

There were roses in the vase on the table, and I'd picked up food from her favorite Indian cafe on the way. The containers were staying warm in the oven as the minutes ticked by.

Finally, the key sounded in the lock, and I sprang to my feet.

The gigantic smile on her face telegraphed the outcome of her meeting with her bosses. "You won't believe it," she exclaimed.

I swung her around as we hugged. When I let her down, I claimed my kiss before hearing any of the details. If she was happy, I was happy. The equation was that simple.

She sniffed the air. "What is that I smell?"

I guided her toward the kitchen. "Just your favorites from Karimi, and the champagne is cold."

She toed off her heels. "You're not going to believe what happened." She hoisted herself up on the stool at the island.

I opened the oven and the delicious smell wafted out. "Let's get this served first." I needed to get her to agree to accompany me to the ball tomorrow.

In two minutes, the food had been plated and the bubbly poured.

Raising my glass, I toasted. "To the premier insurance investigator."

She clinked with me and took a sip.

"Now tell me about it."

She sipped again. "It's perfect. Cornwall fixed the HR letter, and—"

"What HR letter?" We hadn't discussed any problems she had at work.

"Just before I came out, one of my coworkers… Forget it. The short story is that I had this complaint hanging over me, and it's gone now." She spooned some curry into her mouth and mumbled, "This is sooo good."

I scooped up some of my curry with a piece of naan and joined her.

"And…" She lifted her glass. "I'm getting the promotion I wanted."

"Great."

She'd told Mom at dinner that she was in the running for a promotion here, and I'd wondered if that was real or part of our undercover story.

"I was up for a promotion in San Francisco if this went well, and I got it."

My heart fell. Her dream job was thousands of miles away, and that would shoot my proposal all to hell.

Without skipping a beat she added, "Or, it can be here, if I want."

Those words saved me from the heart attack that had threatened. "That's terrific. Is that what you want?" *Say yes*, I chanted in my head. *Say yes*.

Hesitant eyes looked back at me. "I don't know. What do you think I should do?"

This wasn't a time for hesitation and half measures. I reached for her hand across the table.

She gave it willingly.

I hoped the connection of our hands would let me feel her response. "I think we should go to the ball tomorrow as a real engaged couple."

Rebecca

My mouth dropped open and my heart raced. Where was that Brit-speak translator I needed? I pulled strength from his touch. "Are you asking me what I think you're asking?" *Why is it we can't speak the same language?*

He squeezed my hand lightly. "I'm saying that I honestly missed you when you left."

Of course he didn't answer my question. Against my promise not to, I let myself truth-judge him. He meant it—he had missed me. But that still didn't answer my question.

He blinked back wetness in his eyes. "I regret terribly that we got our wires crossed, and now that you're back in my life, you've made me incredibly happy. I don't want to let you go again. I want to marry you."

We hadn't gotten our wires crossed, but his last few words fixed that detail.

His words rang true to me, and my throat constricted. This was too fast—way, way too fast. "But…" I had so many questions and didn't know how to organize them. "We haven't talked. I have so many things to ask you."

Confusion filled his face. "Those can wait. I'd like an answer to my question." He pulled his hand back.

"You didn't ask a question." I regretted the words as soon as they came out. I'd fallen into arguing with him again.

He sucked in a ragged breath. "Rebecca, will you marry me?"

He'd laid out the problem a second before. He thought my questions could wait, and I had to decide about marriage without understanding what had happened to us before, what it was that had torn us apart.

"Will you answer my questions?" I asked.

He nodded. "The ones that I can."

That sentence would lay out the ground rules of our relationship. Unable to breathe, my complaint couldn't get past the lump in my throat.

"Some secrets aren't mine to divulge," he added.

Mom had been right. I couldn't count on the leopard to change his spots.

How could I navigate the future if I couldn't understand how to prevent our past from repeating? He wanted a relationship I couldn't enter into, not like this.

I finally heaved a breath and said the hardest words I'd ever muttered. "No, Ethan."

His face fell.

Gathering up my courage, I put my stake in the ground. "We can't do it like this. It won't work if you keep things from me." I wouldn't chart a course that guaranteed our marriage would be shattered by secrets, as my first had been. I loved him intensely, but I couldn't put us through that. I wouldn't, when I knew it would only hurt us both.

He reached for me. "Don't say that. I told you I'd tell you what I could."

I pulled away and stood. "You can't keep things from me. How do you think that makes me feel?"

He stood as well. "I don't have a choice."

"Yes, you do." I clarified my thoughts for both of us. "And you made your choice." When I turned to leave, my tears began.

He rushed ahead of me. "Sunshine, please don't go like this."

I sniffled. "I can't stay. I have to go."

He stood in front of me. "I just asked you to marry me."

I straightened up. "I heard that, but maybe you didn't hear me. I said no."

"Please don't leave like this."

"I have to." I didn't have any choice.

He moved aside. "I love you."

He'd finally said the words I would have killed for last week, and it was hard to walk past him after judging those words to be true. I didn't echo the statement. I loved him, but this couldn't work. I would get over it in time. I had to.

"Don't hate me," he said as I reached for the door handle.

I made the mistake of looking back.

His face was tortured, and I'd done that to him.

Looking away, I pulled open the door to the rest of my life—a life without him, which wasn't what I'd wanted this morning or any day since I'd returned to London.

When I closed the door to his apartment behind me, the tears I didn't want to show him began in earnest. Sunshine had been a prophetic name. Sunshine only lasted for a time before it was extinguished. The brave way to look at things was simply that the sunset of our time together had come. I was determined to be brave.

On the street, my phone buzzed with a text

ETHAN: I love you

It was followed by another

ETHAN: I always will

And another.

ETHAN: You love me too

And then another.

ETHAN: Deny it

Albert Einstein once said the definition of insanity was doing the same thing over and over again and expecting a different outcome. This wouldn't work, and I wasn't insane. That left me no choice. I couldn't be dragged back into a losing situation.

I'd thought Ethan had been the best thing to ever happen to me—twice, but now it was over.

He'd chosen his secrets over me, and that was that. At least I hadn't lost years of my life before learning his priorities.

I dialed the number I needed to call.

CHAPTER 46

ETHAN

Becky didn't respond to the texts I'd sent.

She'd left, and when the door had closed behind her, it was over.

I'd fucked-up my chance once more.

Five years ago, fate had intervened in the form of that fucking DNA test. Dealing with the aftermath had required me to cut things off with Becky.

This time, I thought I'd helped her understand that what she wanted to know threatened my entire family. I'd thought that explanation would suffice, but I could see now it never would.

Becky's price had been too high.

Dad had drilled into us that family mattered above all else. Being a Blakewell meant understanding that and living it, as he did.

She didn't understand that I couldn't betray my twin brother, and I couldn't explain it to her properly without putting Charlie's future at risk.

My phone buzzed with an arriving text, which I eagerly checked.

It wasn't from my woman.

Christie: Will you be at the party Saturday?

I ignored it.

Becky had been my chance to avoid another Christie type.

Although, unlike Becky, Christie wouldn't demand what I couldn't give.

That thought was too painful to contemplate.

This called for a glass of Macallan. Tonight was not a time for half-measures. I filled the tumbler and drank.

∼

Rebecca

The desperate need to pee woke me the next morning, and getting some fucking pain reliever was my second order of business. The birds trying to peck their way out of my skull were angry.

The mostly empty bottle of tequila next to my bed brought back last night's mistake.

Why couldn't Lizzy stock something better than her rot-gut tequila?

Tequila and I had not been well acquainted, and after this morning, it was going on my just-say-no list. Last night, getting shit-faced had seemed like the right way to wash away the memory of walking out on Ethan. This morning, not so much.

After washing my hands, I didn't find anything for my head in the drawers of the tiny bathroom, so I padded my way to my sister's kitchen.

"Hey, what are you doing here?" she screeched as I turned the corner.

I stopped, not wanting to get any closer to the noise. "Can you pleeease keep it down?"

"Sorry," she said. "Looks like someone had a good time last night." She moved aside as I made my way into the kitchen. "Or a bad time."

I shook my head as I shuffled to the cupboard where I'd last seen Advil. But all I saw inside were vitamins. "Advil?"

"One to the left."

One over, the shelf held the little bottle I craved.

"Here," Lizzy said, holding out a glass of water. "Drink the whole thing. It'll help."

I downed the pills and kept drinking, with a vision of flooding the damned birds out of my head.

"I got in late last night," Lizzy said. "Didn't know you were here. What's up?"

I slumped into the hard, wooden chair next to the tiny breakfast table. "We broke up."

She sat down across from me. "I'm sorry. Want to talk about it?"

I'd expected her to rant that I'd made a terrible mistake—that the son of a duke was a rare catch, one I shouldn't let get away, no matter what. My sister's usual dating advice had all the depth of a piece of paper.

"Did he hurt you?" she asked.

My hand went instinctively to the scar, but I knew she didn't mean it that way. "I broke up with him." I picked up the glass of water and took another deep swallow.

"That must have been hard," she said with uncharacteristic empathy.

Where was the argumentative Lizzy of the last few years?

I looked up. "Who are you and what have you done with my sister? Aren't you supposed to be giving me a hard time?"

"I'm just envious. I wish I had somebody who made me as happy as he makes you."

"Made," I corrected her.

He *had* made me happy, which is why I'd felt so terrible walking out.

"Why?" was all she said.

It had seemed so clear, so simple yesterday, and I guess it still was. "He has a secret, or secrets—I don't know which—and he wouldn't commit to telling me. He said some things aren't his to reveal. He won't promise to be open with me. You know how that turned out last time."

When I'd married Wesley, I'd made the mistake of dropping issues he didn't want to talk about, and look where that had gotten me.

She stood. "Want some tea?" She'd lived here long enough to be converted.

"No thanks." I rechecked the directions on the bottle in front of me. The birds were still clawing at my skull. It said only two tablets. *Fuck it.* I loosened the lid and poured out another one.

"Maybe he's protecting somebody he cares about, and it has nothing to do with you."

I popped the additional pill and washed it down with the last of the water. "How can I know if he won't tell me?"

"It's okay to have some secrets."

"Says the girl who's paper makes a business of splashing people's secrets all over the page."

"They're no big deal. They don't hurt anybody."

I knew better. "What about the MP's affair you guys outed last month?"

That shut her up.

I stood to get more water, and the angry birds complained that I'd moved too fast.

"So you told him why you divorced the dickhead?" She hadn't used Wesley's name since the day I left him.

"No."

The horror of it being spread around had kept me from confiding in Mom or Dad either. Lizzy only knew because she'd taken me to the emergency room. If she hadn't been driving up to the house when I walked out that day, nobody would have known my shame.

The ER doctor had been a little suspicious at first, but telling him I hit my head while under the sink to fix a leak had worked. Admitting to clumsiness was a lot better than the alternative. The bruises on my arms and my chest had been hidden by my shirt.

"When did you plan on telling him?"

I hadn't.

My sister hadn't changed; she had only changed her tactics. "Why can't you ever see it from my perspective?" I asked. It hurt that she never took my side.

"Because you can't ever see both sides of the issue without arguing it out. Don't you remember what you said to me that time you got back from Cabo with the douchebag?"

I'd blocked the weekend I'd discovered the real Wesley from my memory, but my head hurt even more when I realized what she meant. "I called you the worst sister ever for not talking me out of marrying him." I shook my head in shame. "I'm sorry."

She nodded. "Fuck it, you were right. I never trusted the shithead, and I should have at least said something, since Mom was no help."

Mom had been a cheerleader from the day I'd told her of his proposal. All she could see was the wedding bells she'd wanted for her daughters since forever.

"It's not your fault. I'm the one who let him fool me."

"Hey, next time we're home, let's let the air out of his tires or something."

"He doesn't deserve the attention."

"I'll do it for you then." She blew on her teacup to cool it. "Hey, do you realize how few dukes there are in this country?"

My sister was back in form, and the razzing about my decision began in earnest.

CHAPTER 47

Ethan

Midday, I sat on the steps of the Yellow Cottage, far from the prying eyes of my family, with my head in hands.

Looking out at the woods, I couldn't see nor hear another soul, and being alone is what I wanted right now. Trying to sleep last night had been an exercise in futility. My last words to Becky would be forever ringing in my ears: *"Don't hate me."*

Pathetic.

Why hadn't I said something more memorable, like, "I'll never forget you" or "You'll always own my heart"?

If only things could have been different. If only I could have confided in her. If only I didn't owe it to Mom, to Charlie, and yes, also to Dad to keep the truth from ever being discovered, I could be sitting here with her now and looking forward to a life together.

The loneliness of this space in the woods reflected what my life was destined to be. Companionship of the female variety would be limited to the empty-headed Christie types.

She and her like would be demanding on the monetary front, but easily accepting of my need for secrets.

I'd escaped into the woods before running into Dad.

Explaining this to him would be harder than telling Mom. She'd listened and merely said we'd talk later after I sorted out my feelings sufficiently.

When that would be was a puzzle to me. I knew I hated how this had turned out, but she'd implied there was more I needed to understand.

Dad would probably tell me I'd jinxed it by not proposing to Becky at this cottage. Breaking tradition had done me in, he would most likely say.

Not one for prolonging the inevitable, I stood, brushed off my pants, and started back to Rainswood. There was a party to prepare for, and I'd promised Mom I would attend—that was non-negotiable at this point.

∽

An hour before guests were due to arrive for the evening, I'd just finished inspecting the preparations in the kitchen when Dad found me.

"Join me for a walk," he said.

The door had barely closed behind us when he spoke. "We should talk."

I'd been dreading this. "About Wentworth?" Diverting the conversation was worth a try.

He huffed. "You've been thinking about her all day, haven't you?"

Denying it would be pointless. "Yes, I have."

"Tomorrow you will go and fix it."

I stopped on the path. "It's not that simple." He couldn't say that. He had no idea what our issues were.

"Look at me," he said.

I did.

"It isn't as hard as you think."

I breathed in, but bit back my argument.

"Her gift for ferreting out lies is not a mere party trick, is it?"

I was losing track of the conversation with his topic shifts. "No, it isn't."

"I have a similar gift, if you will."

Now I had no idea where this was heading.

"I can size people up and know who to trust and who not to." With a hand to my shoulder, he urged me to walk with him again. "She is one you can trust—no doubt about it. There is no greater gift than finding a partner in life you can trust with all your fears. Do you understand?"

I tried the simple explanation. "We don't see eye to eye on everything."

"Your mother has a gift as well," he said. "She can see that Rebecca loves you with every cell in her body."

I laughed. "She's just saying that."

"She thinks you're an idiot for letting her get away."

"Is that why we're out here?" I asked.

We went a few strides before he answered. "Not exactly. I think your fear is misplaced."

I hadn't talked about being afraid of anything.

"You are afraid of her gift, aren't you?"

"She can be intimidating," I admitted. That was as far as I was willing to go about my fear of exposing my secrets to Becky.

"Marriage is a big step, but it's a partnership. You need to trust each other implicitly. Can she trust you?"

"Sure." I would never let her down.

"What makes you fear trusting her? That's the question you have to answer. Tell me what she's done to make you unsure of her."

I couldn't think of anything.

We had reached the tree line.

He stopped. "Well?"

"It's not that simple." That was the only explanation I could give him. Telling him I was protecting the family would open the door to a series of questions I couldn't answer.

"We should head back."

I walked with him back toward the house, relieved that this was over.

"Since you can't come up with a reason not to trust her, the solution is simple."

I'd misjudged the situation. He wasn't done. "How so?"

"Did you love her when you asked her to marry you?"

I wasn't expecting that question, but there was only one way I could answer. "Yes."

"And does she love you?"

"Right now, I doubt it."

"Don't be smart with me. Go back more than a day. Did you believe her when she said she loved you?"

I sighed. "Of course."

"Then go get her back, and trust that she will not let you down."

We continued on in silence.

I didn't commit to his course of action, but he had given me things to think about.

What had Becky ever done to make me suspect I couldn't trust her with my fears? Substitute *secrets* for fears, and I had the real question. Why did I suspect I couldn't trust her?

When we reached the house, Dad asked, "A lot to think about, isn't it?"

He knew it was.

I nodded. "Yeah."

"First we have your mother's party to attend to." He pulled open the door to the house.

Winston better have ordered a lot of champagne for the evening.

I was going to need it.

∼

Rebecca

Saturday night, I finished my third glass of wine. Or was it my fourth? Fuck it. It didn't matter.

The important thing was I'd learned my tequila lesson.

"This is a good part." Lizzy turned up the volume on the movie she'd selected —*Casino Royale*, the new version with Daniel Craig. The dark, black-and-white opening fit my mood.

I took another sip of my forgetting potion. "If you say so."

I'd vetoed all the sickly sweet romcoms she'd suggested. Tonight, I couldn't stomach a silly story with a ridiculous happy ending totally devoid of reality. But as the evening unfolded, I realized we'd made a good choice. This Bond film was gritty and real, including the ending. Instead of riding off into the sunset with fake smiles, the heroine ends up dead, and the fantasy ending is destroyed, just like in life. My life. I was dead inside.

No doubt, Ethan would be at his party now, cavorting with Miss Slutty or some equally buxom high-society type who'd be offering to suck Big Ben on the patio or something.

Gulping down the last of my glass, I poured another.

"You might want to slow down on that." Lizzy pulled the bottle away after I put it down.

"I need this." I didn't care if she took this bottle. I had another two stashed in my room if I needed them tonight.

"Only if you want to feel as shitty tomorrow morning as you did today."

"That was the tequila. I'll be fine."

"You miss him, don't you?"

"Fuck no." I would be fine without him. I'd gotten over him before, and I could do it again.

"That's not what your drinking says."

I took the remote and upped the volume.

"You know I'm right," she said, taking back the remote. She readjusted the volume to something that wouldn't upset the neighbors.

I drank some more.

CHAPTER 48

ETHAN

SUNDAY MORNING, I WOKE WITH A HEADACHE AND A CARDBOARD TONGUE.

After padding into the bathroom, two ibuprofen tablets preceded my struggle with the shower valves. The warm water slowly cleared the cobwebs, and moving carefully helped with the nausea.

In spite of numerous glasses of champagne last night, I hadn't been able to fall asleep as I worried my way through Dad's question. The clock had read four o'clock the last time I remembered looking at it.

I knew for sure this morning that life without Becky sucked. By not allowing discussion of the past, all I'd done was fall into the delusion that it could work with her.

My refusal to increase the circle of people who knew our family secrets had run smack into her requirement for total openness. Immovable object, meet irresistible force. One of us had to give, and neither of us was willing.

Downstairs, Mom was at the cooker when I entered the kitchen. She turned. "How do you feel this morning? I'm fixing scrambled eggs, if you'd like some."

I waddled in slowly. "I'm fine, but I'm not very hungry."

With a hand on her hip, she pointed the spatula at me. "You do know lying to your mother is a bad thing, right? I saw how much you drank last night."

"Sorry. I'm paying the price this morning, a little."

She shot me a disapproving stare. "A little?" She pointed to the far cupboard. "Ginger tea will help."

I shuffled over to the cabinet. "I don't like ginger."

She shrugged. "It's up to you. Which do you hate more, the hangover or the tea? And, have several cups. You're surely dehydrated."

After a moment, the tea won out. I added the water from the teapot, followed by an ice cube to keep from scalding myself. Then I sat on one of the island stools.

Mom stirred the pan. "I saw Christie hanging on you last night."

That was a question masquerading as a statement.

Christie hadn't been even vaguely tempting, rubbing her breasts against my arm at every opportunity and giggling incessantly. That double-D distraction didn't hold a candle to the woman I wanted to have with me.

I sipped my tea. "She was annoying. I told her Charlie liked her."

"I think Christie and Rebecca make an interesting comparison, don't you?"

Christie wasn't in the same universe as Becky, but Mom knew that and was only trying to provoke me.

I avoided a response and sipped more tea.

"It would have been better if you'd gotten Rebecca to join us." Another implied question: *Why didn't Becky come?*

"We had a falling out, as I told you. I don't expect her back," I said.

"Falling out over what?"

I'd stepped right into that one. I sipped my tea slowly, concocting my response. I should have practiced an answer to this. "She expects more openness than I've been offering." That was a polite, nonspecific way of putting it.

Mom lifted the pan and scooped the eggs onto two plates. "I feel sorry for you."

After sighing, I sipped the last of my tea, happy to finally get some compassion for my predicament.

"It's a sad state of affairs," she added, bringing me one of the plates. "More tea and these eggs will help."

"Thank you." I stood to refill my teacup. The ginger had settled my stomach somewhat.

"Very sad indeed that you'd choose a life of loneliness," she continued.

I added water to my cup. "I'm choosing no such thing."

"Any relationship you have with a woman that doesn't include openness won't last. You should know that." She put the other plate of eggs in the oven.

Making my way back to the table, I picked up the plate. "I think I'll finish in my room."

"Sure. Get used to eating alone, as you'll be doing a lot of that in the future."

I wanted to argue, but no words came out.

"The only difference between being happy and unhappy is the determination to make your life what you want." She turned. "I'll go see what's keeping your father. Very sad indeed, but you're old enough to make your own choice."

Putting the plate down, I forked in a mouthful of egg.

"I thought we'd taught you better than that," she said loudly from down the hall.

Clearly, I hadn't heard the last of this.

∼

Rebecca

Sunday afternoon, I was several miles into my walk. Thinking while walking had always been my best way to noodle through a difficult problem. Something about the fresh air outdoors brought me clarity.

The choice I'd been given—working in San Francisco or here in London—had been unexpected. The corner office in the San Francisco building had always seemed to be my path.

The California job would come with a company car, so I'd no longer have to sniff my fragrance packet to envision it. That office had the benefit that I knew the players well, but the downside that one of those was lying Jackson. He wouldn't be happy now that his revenge had been thwarted by Cornwall.

The whole episode had also taught me that Miriam in HR was the opposite of a fan and not an ally.

I had no idea if she was like that with everybody, but she'd certainly been hostile to me.

On this side of the pond, I would most likely continue to have Cornwall's active support, which could be a big deal. But the other major players in the office were unknown to me.

Would Zander Paul be upset, given that he'd obviously been Smithers' pet? He might have thought the position should have gone to him.

I probably wouldn't be happy, if it were me in his shoes.

A San Francisco posting meant I would be closer to Mom and Dad, but I'd see Lizzy less often, if at all.

Reaching St. Luke's, I turned back toward the apartment to look for more pros and cons. Because I hated retracing the same streets, after a while I ended up on Piccadilly and passing St. James's Park. This route had been a bad idea.

My mind went back to the picnics Ethan and I had shared—both years ago and recently. Those had been happy times that wouldn't come again.

∽

"I'M BACK," I CALLED TO LIZZY AS I OPENED THE DOOR TO THE APARTMENT.

When I returned from the bathroom, she halted the TV show she had on. "So, what did the great outdoors whisper to you?"

I'd decided for the unknown of the London office, without the known enemies I'd certainly have back in California. "Here."

"I knew it," she shrieked as she sprang from the couch and rushed to me.

I gave her back only half the massive squeeze she gave me.

She bounced away. "I was hoping you'd say that. We can do all kinds of stuff together."

"Yeah," I said. "You know I'll have to spend a lot of time at the office...at least at first."

"Whatever. It'll be great. You'll see."

I wandered to the fridge for something to drink. "Of course." I hadn't decided whether I would get my own apartment here, one with space for a desk when I brought work home.

She turned back to the television.

With a cider in hand, I plopped on the couch and picked up her laptop. "What's on?"

"*Friends with Benefits.*"

Not a great title given my recent experience.

I ignored the TV and opened the laptop. After signing on, the screen went to Lizzy's paper's website.

There it was, in stunning color. A picture of my Ethan staring down Miss Slutty's dress. The next picture had her draped over him like a blanket. I stopped reading the text when it mentioned our broken engagement. It had been one day, and already I had to see pictures of him with another woman on the internet, to say nothing of my private life being made public.

I hated breaking Lizzy's heart, but I realized I needed to recalculate. Seeing Ethan in the local papers every few days would be too hard to stomach.

At least in California, I could open a newspaper or visit a news website without being smacked in the face with what I no longer had.

CHAPTER 49

ETHAN

The light streamed in Monday morning, and once again my mouth felt like I'd chewed on a squirrel all night. I rolled out of bed and headed for the ibuprofen.

For four hours last night I'd lain in bed, unable to sleep a wink. Then I'd given up and started downing Macallan until my eyelids got heavy. This morning I was paying the price again.

After downing the pain tablets, I tried to brush the squirrel fur off my tongue. Squinting at the mirror, there was no way to call the visage that looked back anything but horrid.

A stint under the hot shower loosened my brain enough to figure out that I needed a plan for how to deal with work.

Airline pilots couldn't fly drunk, and in my current condition, I'd be just as mistake-prone. That wouldn't be tolerated, regardless of the reason.

A walk in the woods to the Yellow Cottage would be a good-enough distance to make a plan for dealing with work.

Downstairs, I didn't quite make it to the door before being intercepted by the inseparable duo of my cousins.

"Don't have work today?" Winnie asked.

"I don't feel like it today," I said, although the modifier of *today* didn't really fit. I wasn't certain I'd feel like it again for a long time after losing Becky.

"Is that Christie Slutter too much woman for you?" Ophelia asked.

I didn't see a way to get to the door without this discussion. "She's not anything to me."

Winnie cocked her head. "That's not what it looked like Saturday night."

"That was her, not me," I shot back. "I'm not interested, and there never was a thing between us."

Ophelia moved forward. "How are the pictures in the paper going to look to Becky?"

"Pictures?" I hadn't bothered to follow the tabloids since she left.

"Bet she pukes," Winnie suggested.

"Or comes back here with something sharp," Ophelia added with a laugh.

I didn't care for either of those thoughts. "She doesn't care, because we're not a thing anymore." I couldn't bring myself to say *engaged*, because in reality, we never had been.

Ophelia huffed. "I guess you never did change."

"From what?" I asked, unable to let the implied insult lie.

Ophelia sneered. "From a shag-her-and-dump-her kind of guy."

Winnie turned to Ophelia. "I told you she was just another of his short-term sluts."

My temperature rose. "She is not a slut."

"Then what was wrong with her?" Winnie asked.

I sighed and admitted the truth. "I'm the one who's not good enough for her."

Winnie shook her head. "You should let her decide that. But you have your head so far up your arse you can't see how much she fell for you. Whatever you did to push her away was a big fucking mistake."

I'd had enough of this and moved for the door.

"Go ahead, run away. That always fixes things," Winnie said.

"You look like shit," Ophelia added. "That means you didn't sleep because you know you're wrong."

I felt like shit, and I hadn't slept, but I gave her the finger over my shoulder anyway before I reached for the door.

"You know it," she called after me.

All the way to the cottage, I thought about the words of advice and arguments I'd had with my family. None of them thought I was doing the right thing, but they also didn't know the whole story—and I couldn't tell them.

But with each stride I took and each argument I considered, my resolve faltered.

What if they're right?

I turned back when I reached the steps of the Yellow Cottage—the place I probably should have proposed to Becky, instead of that fishbowl of a restaurant.

My mobile rang.

It was Superintendent Maxwell. "Where are you, Inspector? Molly said you left a message about not coming in until later."

"I'm not feeling well, sir."

"Get whatever you need from the doctor, then, to take care of it, but get your arse in here. Not coming in is not acceptable. There's a situation to address."

I stopped walking. "What kind of situation?"

He hesitated before answering. "Not on the phone. See you this afternoon to deal with your mess." He hung up before I could tell him I couldn't in my current state.

My family had certainly concluded that I'd fucked everything up, and now Maxwell could be added to that crowd. I would be walking from one shitstorm into another at the Yard.

Mom's words that I was choosing "a life of loneliness" hurt, but if the hole in my heart wasn't loneliness, what was?

Ophelia's taunt that all I could be was a "shag-her-and-dump-her kind of guy" bothered me because of how true it would seem if Mom was right and it wasn't just Becky. Mom thought this would be true of any woman I wanted to get close to in the future.

Shag her and dump her? Is that who I'd become? That thought was depressing.

Mom had said I had the power to choose to be happy or not.

Dad had been confident that I'd be able to trust Becky with my "fears." Again I realized that if I changed that word to *secrets*, I had what I needed.

A rustling in the bushes made me look back. I stumbled.

"Fuck." I hadn't seen the branch in the path, and I ended up on the ground, spitting out a twig.

I got up and brushed myself off, just as Dad had always taught me to do, both literally and figuratively.

I'd face-planted by trying to go forward while looking back—the definition of stupid.

I sucked in a breath of courage. I couldn't move forward with Becky because I'd been looking backward, back to the day I'd found the DNA test. Focusing on the history behind me made me blind to the path forward.

Ophelia had been right. I hadn't slept because deep down, I knew the path I'd chosen was the wrong one. It was time to look forward and choose happiness, as Mom had said—assuming Becky would take me back, of course.

Winnie had been the one to point out this wasn't entirely up to me.

It was time to take Dad's suggestion and trust Becky with the burden I carried with me every day: the secret that could destroy our family. It was time to make her mine, time to trust her with my future.

Pulling out my mobile, I selected her contact. My finger hovered over the call button, but I pulled it back. Giving her a chance to put me off over the phone was a losing strategy. This had to be in person.

I dialed her office instead, to verify where she was.

This would be face-to-face with no avenue of escape. She'd have to listen to me—have to give me a chance, give us a chance.

While it rang on the other end, I cringed with the awareness that this was a high-stakes game. Becky still had the choice of whether to believe me or not.

"Lessex Insurance," the lady answered.

"Mr. Cornwall, please. Detective Inspector Blakewell calling." He was the one person in her company I'd sworn to secrecy.

"Inspector, what can I do for you?" he answered a few moments later.

"I need to know if Beck—Miss Sommerset is in the office today."

"I'm sorry to say, in the end, she chose the San Francisco office over us here."

It wasn't computing for me. "Pardon?"

"I thought you knew, after the very successful conclusion of your inquiry. Thank you, by the way. She's been given a well-earned promotion, and she chose the position in San Francisco over the one with us in London. Family issues perhaps, but with Americans, it can often be difficult to truly know."

This was bad news, very bad news. "Is she in the office today, though?"

"No. She flies out of Heathrow today. The California team is quite eager for her to start. They've had the opening—"

"What flight is she on?" I asked, cutting him off. I didn't give one shit about what the California office wanted.

"Well, I think it's this afternoon, why?"

I started running. "I need to talk to her."

"If you hold the line, I'll find the fight number and time."

I increased my pace as much as I could while holding the mobile to my ear.

A minute later he came back on the line. "British Air two-eight-seven at two fifteen is the information we have."

I thanked him and calculated in my head that she'd still be at her sister's apartment if I hurried.

Luckily, the roads were dry and the Aston had a full tank of petrol.

I hit redial as soon as I turned onto the main road.

CHAPTER 50

Rebecca

I checked my watch. A half hour until my ride to the airport was due and my suitcase wasn't cooperating. Kneeling on it got the two halves to almost, but not quite, meet. Something had to come out if I was going to ever get it closed.

I'd stopped by Ethan's apartment to pick up the clothes we'd bought me for the assignment. I was taking at least a few of them back with me, come hell or high water.

Lizzy brought out a black dress and held it up. "Can I wear this one, please?"

"I already told you, feel free to wear any of them." It was the least I could do for her. She let me stay here whenever I was in town for only the cost of groceries.

She held it against herself and twirled around.

A knock sounded at the door.

"Tell my driver I'll be a minute," I said.

Lizzy pranced out, still twirling around with the slinky dress.

I heard the door open.

"Guess who's here?" Lizzy called.

"Tell him to give me a few minutes. He's early."

"She says she's busy," Lizzy said in the other room.

After removing two more shirts, kneeling on the stupid suitcase got me tantalizingly close to being able to close it.

"Let me help."

Startled, I looked up to find Ethan in the doorway.

I froze.

He pushed at my shoulder. "Let me try."

I moved off without a word.

In a few seconds, his weight got the case to submit, and it was closed. He lifted it and placed it on its wheels. "We need to talk." His hand rested on the handle.

"We did." I put my hand out. "Thank you. I need that." I didn't look at his face, lest I give in to the pull he still had on me.

He rolled it toward me and let go. "I was wrong."

I grabbed my purse. "News flash, that's nothing new. I have a plane to catch."

He stood in the doorway. "You have a choice."

Lizzy was quiet in the other room, not coming to my defense.

"You made your choice, and I made mine. End of story," I said as I took the carry-on in my other hand.

He still hadn't moved. "You can talk to me now, or I'll follow you to California and camp out in the hallway of your flat until you do."

"I rent a house." I kept my eyes down.

"Fine, on the pavement in front of your house, until you let me explain."

I shook my head. "Move before I call the cops."

"I am the police."

Lizzy giggled, still not helping.

"I'll drive you to Heathrow. We can talk on the way," he offered.

"Sounds like a good compromise to me," my traitorous sister said.

"Will you promise to get me there on time?" I raised my eyes to his face for the response.

"I will." He was telling the truth.

All I had to do was endure him for the time it took to drive to the airport. He would have to be watching the road, and I didn't have to look at him either, a better situation than here where he could advance on me until I was backed against the wall.

"If she's going to keep being bitchy about it, Ethan, I'd love a ride in your car," Lizzy said. She was probably serious. "I've got a super dress to wear out to lunch."

Ethan didn't answer.

I sighed. "Okay already."

He put his hand out for the suitcase, and I let him wheel it, but I kept the carry-on.

I didn't say any more while we made our way down to his car.

At the street, he stopped suddenly and turned.

I bumped into him and immediately felt anxious at the heated contact. It threatened to derail me from my careful plan to extricate myself from his life.

He backed away. "Sorry. This isn't going to work. We need to do this upstairs."

"I want to be early." I should have said *need*.

"Upstairs. You need to look into my eyes when I say what I have to say."

Was he really asking me to truth-judge him for once?

"I'll still get you to the airport in time."

I shook my head. "I can listen fine in the car."

His jaw tensed. "Upstairs. You need to believe me. Then, if you still want to leave, I'll take you, and you won't be late."

Since he was asking to be judged, I knew that to be true.

As much as I didn't want to, I huffed and turned around. "I'm still leaving."

"It was always your choice."

∼

ETHAN

"Did she decide on the Uber instead?" Lizzy asked as I opened the door. Her head cocked when Becky followed me in. "What's going on?"

I hitched my head toward the door. "We need some privacy." I wasn't expanding the circle of people who knew the secret by two.

"I have some bread in the oven," Lizzy said.

"We'll take it out," Becky offered.

Lizzy looked at me. "Am I still going to get a ride in your car and a lunch?"

I hadn't agreed earlier, but I nodded anyway. "Sure."

She looked tentatively at Becky, who said, "I'll be fine."

I set the backpack down, and a minute later we were alone. I motioned toward the table so Becky could see my face when we talked. I needed her to believe me.

She followed and took a chair across from me.

"I didn't call you back then…" I started.

She watched me intently, the way I normally didn't want her to, but needed her to now.

"…because I'm a bastard."

"I'd use a stronger word," she said.

"You don't understand. I'm literally a bastard. I'm not my father's son."

Confusion filled her face. "Say that again."

I laid out the dangerous truth again. "I'm not my father's son." My future, and my family's future, was now in her hands.

"I didn't know who your father was, and I wouldn't have cared. I like your dad, but I don't give a shit that he's a duke."

That was just one of the things that made her the perfect woman for me.

"You don't understand. My mother had an affair, and Charlie and I are the result. This fact getting out could destroy the family—not just my parents' marriage, but the dukedom and family name as well."

"Are you sure?"

"Yes. This is a secret only three people in the family know: Charlie, me, and Mom, of course. Those two don't even know I know." Today I'd expanded the circle to four.

Dad had warned me that the only way to keep a secret was to keep the circle small, and I'd violated that dictum, but he'd also been the one to tell me I could trust Becky, that I *should* trust her.

She'd been silent too long when she finally stood. "I'm not doing this anymore."

Fuck.

I'd lost her, and the secret was loose as well.

Double fuck.

CHAPTER 51

Rebecca

I could sense the pain in his voice. He somehow thought not being the duke's son would have mattered to me.

Sitting across the table from him was too clinical, too much like one of our interrogations.

I rushed around the table and wrapped my arms around him when he stood. "The boy I fell in love with back then was a college kid. His name was Ethan, and his last name didn't matter, not even a little, not one bit."

His grip on me strengthened. "I never stopped loving you, Sunshine." Strong hands rubbed my back. "You have to believe me."

Looking up into his eyes, I told him, "I've always believed you."

"Except when I told Cornwall I was with the Met."

I hugged him tighter. "Moment of temporary insanity. Do you know who your biological father is?"

"He died in a car accident a few years back."

I felt him shiver. "Who was he?"

"His name was Covington, from Los Angeles. Wendell Covington."

"How can you be sure?" I snuggled my head against him. This was hard for him, which made it that much more special that he was telling me.

"Charlie got a visit from a Yank, William Covington, who had a DNA test. I overheard their conversation. The test confirmed they were brothers, which means me too, since we're twins. They agreed to not tell the families, and Charlie threw the test paper away. I retrieved it from the trash and looked him up. His father was Wendell, and I have a few other half-brothers and a half-sister."

"Do you think you'll want to meet them?"

"No. It would be too dangerous. Charlie was right. Nobody can know."

After listening to his heart as he talked, I looked up. "And that's why you broke it off and wouldn't take my calls?"

"That meeting was the day before you left. I couldn't deal with the shame, the fear that what I'd learned would bring down the family. That day, I couldn't trust anyone with the secret that Charlie and I were the result of Mom's affair."

"You do know there are two ways you could be half brothers. It didn't have to be your mother." He hadn't considered that his father could have strayed.

"Dad had never been to the States until I was five."

"Oh." I looked up and asked the hard question. "What changed from five years ago to today?"

"I want you to marry me."

My heart tripped a beat with the words. He'd said them before, but this felt more real, more raw.

"And I want you to know I won't have any secrets. I trust you completely, and I won't keep anything from you."

I could have closed my eyes and still known he meant those words with his whole heart. I remembered his last text to me, and I hadn't answered because I couldn't deny that I loved him. I snuggled against his firm chest and the heart he was pledging to me, with the secret he'd entrusted to me. "I love you too."

He let me go. "Even if I'm only half Blakewell?"

I nodded, but couldn't speak when he produced the ring, the diamond ring that last week I'd wished were real.

I held up my hand. "Stop," I squeaked. I couldn't let this be one-sided.

His hands fell to his side, and he visibly deflated.

"It's only fair that I tell you my secret before anything else."

His eyes narrowed. "Nothing you could say will make me love you any less."

"I'm an abuse victim." There. I'd gotten it out.

His countenance hardened. "Who?" he growled. "Weaselface? Did you get the police involved?"

I nodded. It had been Wesley.

He pulled me to him again and rocked me, lending me his strength through touch. "There's nothing for you to be ashamed of."

"His previous conviction for assault had been sealed, and I didn't know about it when we married. He wouldn't talk about his past, and I let it slide."

"You don't need to say any more."

But stopping wasn't an option now. Ethan needed to know the rest of the story. "One night, he got drunk—super drunk—and let it slip. I couldn't believe what I was hearing and tried to leave. That's when it happened."

"Becks, it's not your fault."

"Remember…" I sniffed. "…when I told you about the dry cleaner who burned down his own business, and you said it was wrong not to tell the cops?"

He scratched my back. "Yes."

I sniffled. "I said the arson case wasn't up to me, but this one was. I'm ashamed to admit I didn't press charges."

Ethan kissed the top of my head. "Don't worry about a thing. I'll make him pay." It came out as a growled promise.

I pushed back to tell him the bad news. "No. You can't. He's dangerous. He has a gun."

"Nobody gets away with hurting you. Not ever."

I fisted his shirt. "I'm serious. Leave him alone. I can't have something happen to you."

"I can handle a punk like him."

"Promise me you won't confront him." I tightened my grip on his shirt and pulled him closer. "Promise me."

He put his hands up. "For one year I won't confront him. I won't even travel to his city. That's all I can promise right now."

I relaxed when I knew I saw the truth. "And after that?"

His previous scowl morphed into a grin. "Forget him. We have other things to talk about." He held out the ring. "Hold this for a second and close your eyes."

"No. Why?"

"Why do you have to be so argumentative?"

I sucked in a loud breath, stung by the truth of his words, grabbed the ring from him, and closed my eyes.

"No peeking."

I shifted to the other foot. "No promises after five seconds. I get dizzy." I heard rustling in the space, but it didn't give me a clue. "Five... four... three... two... one." I opened my eyes and gasped.

Ethan held out the open Overdale case. "Will you marry me? After your divorce is final, of course."

The necklace seemed even more beautiful than the last time I saw it.

I could breathe again when I figured out it had to be the copy. "It looks so real." Even if it was the replica, it was gorgeous.

"Stop answering a question with a question." He snapped the lid closed. "I'm insulted. A Blakewell would never offer his fiancée costume jewelry."

I had to pick my jaw up off the floor. "It's the real thing?" My throat dried up.

"Yes, and before you ask, I bought it with my own money. Well, Blakewell money. When I saw it, I knew I had to get it for you."

Stunned didn't begin to describe how I felt. "You're sure?"

He shrugged. "I was, but I didn't expect an argument." He set the case on the table. "I was hoping for an answer. But if you're not sure, maybe Lizzy—"

I jumped up and wrapped myself around him, arms and legs. "Yes. A thousand times yes."

He stumbled back a bit before supporting me by my ass and taking my mouth with his. He drank me in, exploring all the curves and crevasses of my mouth, my tongue, my lips. Then he carried me over and set me on the cold counter. I held onto him as our tongues dueled for position. His spicy scent transported me back in time—to picnics in the park, as it always did. His mouth moved to the sensitive skin of my neck as he kissed his way down from my ear.

I arched my neck to the side to give him more space. I could take this all day long, but I guessed we might be about to cross the kitchen counter off our naughty list.

His hand ran up under my blouse to my breast, and he traced the underside before moving to circle my nipple through the bra.

A knock sounded on the door. "Ms. Sommerset, your ride is here. Do you need help with your luggage?"

"Shit," I said.

Ethan kissed my collarbone and fondled my breast.

"We have a problem," I told him. "My job is in San Francisco."

The driver knocked again "Ms. Sommerset? You in there?"

Ethan's mouth had traveled down between my breasts. "No, you have Smithers' job here. Unless you don't want the necklace," he said into my cleavage.

"What?"

"Ms. Sommerset," the driver yelled again. "I'm going to need to be paid for the waiting time."

Ethan pulled away and smiled. "I fixed the job with Cornwall on the drive in. You might not be able to take the necklace with you if you left."

"The necklace?" I asked.

"It could be considered a cultural artifact of Great Britain."

I pushed at his shoulder. "Pay the man. I'm staying, but only because you can't go to San Francisco. You promised."

I had my man, my job, *and* my fairy-tale necklace.

Sliding down from the counter, I located a big-enough dish towel and folded it over to provide cushioning. Jumping back up, I waited for Ethan's return.

CHAPTER 52

ETHAN

BECKY AND I STOOD OUTSIDE THE CONFERENCE ROOM ON THE THIRD FLOOR OF NEW Scotland Yard, ready to bring this whole episode to a close. "Are you ready for this?" I asked her.

"The question is, are *you* ready for this? It's your family they're threatening."

"For once will you not answer a question with a question?"

She shrugged. "Depends on the question." She held up her ring finger with the sparkling diamond that claimed her as mine.

I opened the door for her, and we joined the four seated across the table, Karen, Martha Marston, her husband, George, and the man I assumed was their solicitor.

The fourth man stood and offered a card. "Derrin Thompson, solicitor for the Marstons and Ms. Dirks," he said.

Becky and I introduced ourselves and exchanged cards with him.

"As no charges have been preferred against my clients, we are here merely as a courtesy," Thompson stated.

I kept my laptop closed for the moment. "And we appreciate that."

Karen sneered at Becky. "What is she doing here?"

"She represents the insurance company involved," I answered.

"I don't see why that's relevant," Karen replied.

I didn't enlighten her. Instead, I pushed across the charging summary I'd prepared. "This is the offer."

Thompson picked it up.

Martha looked on defiantly.

Her husband shifted to peek at the paper Thompson was reading.

"We are willing to forgo major charges and reduce this to simple conspiracy for Karen and Martha," I began. "And nothing for George."

A slight smile manifested on George Marston's lips. He was getting off free. "I didn't know nuthin'."

"Fat chance," Martha said. "I didn't do anything."

"The Crown Prosecution Service is willing to stipulate to three months confinement and a five-hundred-pound fine," I continued.

Karen looked to Martha.

"We're going to blow wide open your family's involvement in the thefts," Martha said. "We have an interview with the *Evening Mail* tomorrow, and you can't stop us. It'll serve you right."

That confirmed what we'd heard from Lizzy about the timing of their meeting with the paper, which gave us only today to head this off. It was the reason Maxwell had signed off on us threatening to charge them if they didn't take the deal.

Martha crossed her arms. "You're trying to save your rotten family's reputation, but it won't work."

Thompson spoke up. "I understand that you first arrested Ms. Dirks, and then declined to charge her due to lack of evidence."

Karen smiled, obviously thinking she was safe.

"That was then; this is now," I said.

"No way," Martha said.

Karen nodded her agreement.

I pressed send on the text I'd composed before entering the room.

Thompson added the papers to his portfolio. "It would seem we are done here."

"Not quite," I told them.

The door opened behind me.

"Sorry I'm late, Inspector," Maxwell said.

He offered a card to Thompson. "Superintendent Maxwell." After getting one from the solicitor, he took a chair next to me. "So are we all settled?"

"No," Thompson said. "The inspector is clearly biased in this case, and without better evidence, I don't see this going anywhere in court."

"Let's clear that up right off..." He checked Thompson's card, then leveled a stare at the poor man. "Darrin, I'm handling this case. Are you implying that I'm biased?"

Thompson wilted under his glare. "No, of course not."

"Good," Maxwell said. "As for evidence..." He turned my way. "Inspector, didn't you show them what we have?"

I opened the laptop. "I was about to." I started the video loops and turned the screen toward them. "We have video surveillance from the jewelry shop that clearly shows Mrs. Marston switching the items in question."

Martha shrank a bit as the videos played.

I slid the papers across to their solicitor. "And we have a statement from Yoram Krause that says he was commissioned by Mrs. Marston to create replicas of the stolen pieces based on photographs she provided. Along with payments from Mrs. Marston to Mr. Krause, I think it paints a rather convincing picture."

The blood drained from Martha's face.

Karen looked down at the table.

"Martha, is this true?" her husband asked.

She didn't respond.

Maxwell pointed the solicitor's card at him. "Darrin, I'm a busy man. If your clients accept this offer today and save me the effort, I'm all for a deal. But if I'm forced to devote scarce time to this, I'll have them arrested tomorrow on theft and conspiracy, and recommend the maximum punishment to the Crown Prosecutors. Do you understand?"

Thompson nodded. "Completely."

Maxwell rose. "Then you can finish up with the inspector, and I'll be off."

Thompson nodded again, like a bobble-head doll. "Thank you."

Now it was up to us to apply the rest of the pressure.

After the door closed, Becky spoke up. "Karen, as co-beneficiaries, you and the Marstons each received fifty-thousand pounds on the death of William Marston."

George nodded.

Karen smiled.

Becky slid papers across to each of them. "I've highlighted the relevant sections of the agreements you signed when you accepted the money. You agreed not to disparage the duke, his family, or his household in any way."

Karen silently mouthed the highlighted words as she read.

Martha ignored the paper as her husband read it.

"Mrs. Marston, you mentioned a meeting with the *Evening Mail*."

Martha grinned, not realizing what was coming. "Tomorrow."

"Given the evidence the MPS has assembled," Becky said, "any publicity you might initiate in this case that disparages the duke or his family will trigger these clauses and force us to demand repayment of all the funds distributed."

Karen's mouth dropped.

"You can't stop us," Martha said.

"We won't be meeting with 'em," George said. He looked over at his wife. "That's me retirement money."

"But they killed our son," she shot back.

If they'd only taken the deal I offered, I wouldn't have to go this far. I looked to Becky for confirmation.

She nodded. "Tell them." We'd agreed not to bring this up if the matter could be settled without it.

"Tell us what?" Martha demanded.

"We weren't at fault in the accident," I told her.

"Says *you*," Karen said.

I slid the report across to them. "Here is the official accident report. There was no maintenance issue." I followed it with Billy's note. "He left this behind. Billy meant to run into the tree."

"That can't be," Karen said, picking up the paper in front of her.

"His father," Becky said, pointing at me, "funded those payments to you by himself, and kept the suicide note secret to save you the anguish."

"Who the hell is Daniel?" George asked his wife as he read.

"His lover," Martha told him.

Red filled George's face. "He was gay?"

"Marrying Karen was going to fix that," Martha said.

"How could you not tell me?" Karen asked Martha.

I closed the laptop and stood. "Mr. Thompson, I'll be expecting your clients' response shortly."

He nodded.

Becky followed me out of the room. "You didn't tell me it was only going to be three months," she said after the door closed behind us. "That's almost nothing for what they did."

I urged her down the hall. "The knowledge that they contributed to Billy taking his life is going to punish them for a lot longer than that."

A half hour later, Thompson delivered the signed agreement. "You should mention to the Crown Prosecutor that this was Mrs. Marston's idea. She convinced Ms. Dirks that the family was to blame and recruited her into this plan a year ago. Perhaps the sentencing should reflect that."

"I'll pass that on," I assured him.

This episode was done. They were opting to keep the money, rather than go public. The courts would be spared the expense of a trial, and the mayor wouldn't have the reputation of his city tarnished. Lizzy and the *Evening Mail* would just have to get over it.

CHAPTER 53

Ethan(5 days later)

Saturday morning, I ate another mouthful of eggs.

Mom was at the cooker, fixing more eggs for Dad and herself.

Becky and I had arrived at Rainswood last night for a weekend in the countryside, away from the photographers who had camped outside my flat.

Enjoying the freedom being away from the city provided, Becky had joined Winnie and Ophelia on a trip to the market, which was a task Karen had previously attended to.

I swallowed another bite of eggs. "How is the search for a new cook coming along?"

"Winston is previewing candidates, and says he'll give me some to consider next week."

Dad came in from his walk and took off his damp coat.

"Get wet?" Mom asked.

"It's just enough to clear the air." He made his way to Mom and kissed her cheek. "Looks good."

"Sit down, and it'll be ready in a second."

Dad poured himself some tea from the pot before joining me at the table. He opened the paper and scanned it. "Only one picture of you today."

I shrugged. "They're a pain."

Mom scooped the eggs onto two plates and brought them over. "I'm certainly glad it wasn't like that when you were courting me." She looked over at Dad with a smile.

Dad put down his teacup. "They had more manners then than they do now." He continued leafing through the paper.

Mom lifted her fork. "You know this all could have been avoided if you two hadn't—how did you put it? Gotten your wires crossed. You'd be married already."

"Water under the bridge," Dad said, as he often did.

I didn't add anything to that.

"Still, what was it that was such a huge misunderstanding back then?" Her eyes remained on me as she chewed her food.

"It was my fault." I searched for a way to finish the sentence.

Mom's eyes lingered as the silence wore on.

"The first time Becky called after leaving, I told her I was too busy to talk at the moment. I guess she took me to mean I didn't care. She didn't call back. I should have taken the initiative."

Mom's eyes betrayed her. She didn't believe me. "Yes, you should have."

Dad closed up the paper. "So far, no sign of scandal."

"It'll probably stay that way," I told him. "They probably won't chance losing the money." I was happy to be off the topic of Becky and me.

He put the paper down. "Let's hope not."

Mom sipped her tea. "Speculate all you want, but it's not always up to us what secrets get revealed."

Dad put his tea down. "Now that this affair is wrapped up, are they sending you back to TechniByte?"

I nodded. "Started back there Thursday."

"Is that where you want to be?" Mom asked.

I'd thought a lot about that the past few days. "I'm good at it."

"I can put in a good word," Dad offered.

"No," I said quickly. "No, thank you." I had gotten this far on my own merits and intended to keep it that way.

Upstairs in my room after breakfast, I pulled the paper with the DNA results from its hiding place under the drawer and smoothed it out on top of the chest of drawers.

> Subject 1: Covington, W, and Subject 2 Blakewell, C

And further down.

> Certain familial match, common paternity

Those were the important words among the numbers and scientific gibberish. Putting the shameful paper down, I went to the window and looked out on the cloudy horizon.

Would a day come when our secret was discovered and this land was no longer the Blakewell dukedom? Mom had said at breakfast that it wasn't always up to us what secrets are revealed. All I could do was my part to keep the secret, preventing it from destroying our family.

"I'm ashamed of you," Dad said from behind me.

I turned, not having heard him enter.

He stood next to the chest of drawers and the paper I'd foolishly left out.

"For what?" I managed to croak.

"Lying to your mother. You have to learn that you can trust family. You should have told her the truth."

I wanted to tell him I had, but the look in his eyes argued against it.

"I know you never talked to Becky after she left Imperial, and you refused to take her calls multiple times."

Charlie had probably shared that nugget with him.

Before I could move to retrieve it, he picked up the DNA test. "Where did you get this?"

My mouth was too dry to answer.

He motioned toward the sitting area. "We should talk." His reaction to the paper wasn't surprise, as I'd expected.

I followed and sat across from him.

"When did Charlie tell you?" he asked.

I shook my head, too ashamed to admit I'd stolen this from Charlie's trash after he'd specifically decided no one else in the family should know.

"Charlie and I talked about this," he said, holding up the paper. "But I didn't think he'd given it to you yet."

The pit in my stomach grew.

"Bill Covington brought him this news." He shook the paper. "And he came to me with it. I told you I know everything that goes on in this family."

Those were words I wouldn't question again.

The mention of Covington had me trying to formulate the question that wouldn't come out—when had he found out we weren't his sons?

"When the affair happened, it was a different time." With his words, he was forgiving Mom.

I wasn't buying that. Affairs were never okay. "That doesn't make it right."

He cut me off with a raised hand. "Let me finish." He took a breath. "I confronted your grandfather. He wasn't proud of it, but he acknowledged what happened. Bill's father and I are half brothers."

Slowly the words sunk in. "So William Covington is my…?"

"Cousin," he finished for me. "This was confirmation that Wendell and I are both sons of your grandfather."

I grabbed the chair back to steady myself. All this time, I'd had it wrong. I'd been a generation off. Charlie and I were his—we were Blakewells.

"Your grandfather was a man of a different era. He fathered Bill's father, Wendell, who has since passed. Dad never even hinted at it, and I never had a chance to meet Wendell."

I confessed my crime. "I pulled this from Charlie's trash."

"You and he didn't talk about it?"

"No. It's actually the reason I broke it off with Becky. I couldn't have her learn about it."

"Didn't I tell you that you could trust her with your fears?"

"I did. I do. She knows now."

He stood. "Now you know the story of our family scandal."

I'd thought it was a different scandal, but I wasn't about to admit the thoughts I'd harbored for five years. I couldn't believe the magnitude of my error, all the needless harm I'd caused by being rash and inflexible.

"Since Wendell is gone, it's for your generation to sort out," Dad continued.

"For the sake of the Covington name, as the eldest, Charlie gave them our word we'd not talk of it." His eyes held mine firmly. "You need to honor that."

"I will."

He patted my shoulder. "Good." He shook the paper once more. "I'm going to take this and burn it before it causes any more problems."

When the door closed behind him, I took a deep breath and went back to the window.

The light rain had stopped, and the sun peeked through the clouds. Sunshine. I'd be marrying my Sunshine soon, and now without the worry of the secret that had almost destroyed us.

I could almost hear her chastising me, but no matter. It was a new day, and an incredible load had been lifted from my shoulders. Becky would no doubt tell me I wouldn't have had the load weighing me down if I'd opened up and talked to my brother five years ago.

And the worst part? She'd be right.

CHAPTER 54

Rebecca (one week later)

At Immigration, I went through the non-citizen line with Ethan so we wouldn't be separated. I couldn't contemplate doing what I had planned alone.

He was my rock.

Ever the British gentleman, Ethan had wanted to roll both our bags himself. I'd refused, because I needed the strength I always drew from his touch to get through this. I wasn't letting go of his hand.

We walked together down the final hallway and out into the international arrivals hall. The chauffeur's little card read *Sommerset*.

I pointed. "That's us."

I waved the driver over, and he put his card away. "Ms. Sommerset?"

"Yes." I happily gave him the handle of my bag.

"Follow me," the driver said. "My name is Amir."

"You're not driving?" Ethan asked me.

"Were going in style," I told him.

In reality, I'd expected not to be able to sleep on the plane, and I didn't trust myself driving in San Francisco traffic as a half-asleep zombie. I'd been right about the sleep.

"What are your parents going to think?"

"I'll tell them you're rich and you insisted."

"Are we parsing half-lies now?"

"And I thought I might be too tired."

He squeezed my hand. "I think that one's better."

"First time to the city?" Amir asked.

"Grew up here," I said. "But I'm dead tired."

"And you want to buy a car?" he asked.

"It's just a stop on the way," Ethan told him.

We climbed into the back of the town car while the bags were loaded, and I rested my head on Ethan's shoulder, still clutching his hand.

His thumb ran calming circles over my skin. "I've got you, Sunshine. It'll be over soon."

I closed my eyes against the afternoon sun. "Wake me when we get there." I couldn't sleep, but I also couldn't converse with Ethan right now without the possibility I'd talk myself out of it.

When I felt the car exit the freeway, I knew we were close. The day of reckoning had come.

A few turns later, the car stopped and Amir said, "We're here."

I opened my eyes and had to blink to adjust to the brightness.

"Do you see them?" Ethan asked.

"No." I hit call on the number I'd saved.

"Hello, Ms. Sommerset," the man answered.

"I'm here. We just parked out front in a black town car."

"I saw it. We're in the brown sedan parked three cars ahead of you."

"Okay." I hung up the phone and opened the door. "Wait for us," I told Amir.

"You got it," he said.

I pulled at Ethan and climbed out of the car. "Three cars up."

After pushing the car door closed, we started down the sidewalk. I opened the back door of the brown car when we reached it, climbed in, and slid over.

Ethan followed and shut the door.

"Detective Gates?" I asked.

"I'm Gates," the driver said. "This is Delgado."

Delgado passed a clipboard with papers over the seat. "Paperwork first."

I took it. "This is my fiancé, Ethan Blakewell."

"Hi," they said in unison. Gates followed with, "You'll need to stay out of the way."

"Understood," Ethan said.

Gates nodded toward the showroom building. "We verified he's inside."

"You'll need to sign the statement at the bottom and initial each page," Delgado told me.

Ethan looked over my shoulder as I read through, initialed, and signed my statement. "Our paperwork is shorter."

I nodded.

Gates turned farther around. "You understand your husband's lawyer will make the trial difficult for you?"

"Soon to be ex-husband," I shot back. "And yes, I know what to expect." His lawyer would try to drag me through the mud, but that was the price to be paid for doing the right thing.

Ethan put his arm around behind me and pulled me close.

"Also," Gates said, "we're barely inside the statute of limitations as it is. Getting a protective order this late isn't likely."

"I've got protection," I answered, smiling up at my man.

"Detective Inspector, Scotland Yard," Ethan announced, pulling out his identification.

I signed the final page and handed the clipboard back to them.

"Let's do this, then," Delgado said.

"Can I watch? I mean *we*?" I asked.

"Up to you. Just stand back and out of sight. I hate runners," Gates answered as they opened their doors.

Ethan opened the curbside door, and we followed the two policemen toward the building.

Inside, they asked for Wesley.

Ethan noticed him before I did and motioned.

Wesley hadn't seen us yet, so I pulled Ethan to a halt.

Then, I heard the most wonderful words spoken loudly: "Wesley Stroud, you're under arrest for corporal injury to a spouse. Put your hands behind your back."

"What the fuck?" Wesley spat. His eyes found me just before the detective spun him around and forced him down over the hood of a car.

I smiled as I held Ethan's hand, the hand that I hadn't let go of since we left the police car.

The detectives began reading Wesley his rights, and Ethan pulled me toward the exit.

As the showroom door closed behind us, Ethan asked, "Doesn't it feel better to do the right thing?"

"I couldn't have done it without you here."

His arm around me tightened. "You know the detective was right. The testimony at trial will be difficult."

"I have to. A smart Brit I know once told me it was immoral to not prosecute the bad guys."

He stopped us, turned me toward him, and kissed my forehead. "You have no idea how much I love you."

"Enough to take my mom to another opera tomorrow?"

He pulled me into an embrace. "If we can keep it to one, that would be good."

The door to the showroom opened behind Ethan, and Wesley's yell reached us. "You fucking bitch. You'll pay for this, you fucking bitch."

Ethan held me tight. "Ignore him. He's not worth it."

Corralling the urge to yell back, I snuggled into Ethan's warmth.

As Wesley's taunts continued, his anger and threats only made me more sure I'd done the right thing today.

It was hard, but it was over. Wesley was guilty, and he'd have to account for what he'd done. This arrest and hopefully conviction would be one he couldn't hide. It would also put a stop to his ambitions of getting elected to the Board of Supervisors, which was probably a good thing for the city.

The detectives had warned me that at trial, these cases could go either way. But allowing that to deter me would be rationalizing not doing the morally right thing. Ethan deserved a wife who made the right choices, and I was determined to be that woman.

When we reached the town car, the detectives drove away with their cargo: my pissed-off ex.

Ethan opened the door for me. "Well, that was fun."

I nodded and slid into the car.

Ethan followed and closed the door behind him.

"Now the San Jose address," I told Amir.

Ethan put his arm around me. "I'm proud of you, Snuggle Bunny."

"Love you too, Cowboy." I rested my head against him. "Wake me when we get there."

My man's arm was around me, and all was well with the world.

EPILOGUE

BEING DEEPLY LOVED BY SOMEONE GIVES YOU STRENGTH, WHILE LOVING SOMEONE DEEPLY GIVES YOU COURAGE. — LAO TZU

Rebecca

Saturday morning, when the light woke me, I checked the clock. I should have set the alarm—or I shouldn't have agreed to meet Ophelia and Winnie this early. I moved to slide out of bed.

Ethan's arm around me tightened. "No you don't, Sunshine."

"I have to meet your cousins to go riding."

"You can ride me first."

I turned to face him and grabbed Big Ben, who was hard and ready, as he always was in the morning. "We don't have time."

"I can be quick."

I laughed. "Since when?"

"Since today, if that's what it takes." He pulled my face to his and his mouth claimed mine. Our tongues intertwined in the dance of love and lust as well-seasoned lovers.

I closed my eyes and gave in to his control. I was the comet caught in Ethan's gravitational pull. The man tasted like the desire I felt for him every day. In his arms was always where I'd been meant to be.

Liquid heat pooled between my legs as I pulled on Big Ben and envisioned riding him. Ethan moved down to my breasts, where he began kissing, licking, and sucking.

After mentally calculating the time we had, I pulled away from Ethan's lips. "Only if you do what I say." Riding him would take too long.

His eyes held a mischievous sparkle when he looked up. "Taking charge, are we?"

I let go of Big Ben. "Deal or no?"

He nodded and returned to sucking on a nipple and teasing my other breast with his hand.

"In the bathroom," I told him as I moved his head away.

He followed me, with Big Ben swinging as he walked.

Just the sight excited me. I closed the door and grabbed a towel for under my elbows before leaning on the counter. "Show me what ya got, Cowboy." I wiggled my ass.

"Yesiree, missy," he said in that stupid *Texican* accent.

I spread my legs a little wider as he positioned himself behind me and teased my entrance, running his tip between my folds and up to my clit. Each pass sent a tingle through me. "You said you could be quick." I loved that he took his time with me, but not this morning.

Holding my hips, he pushed into me a little at a time, pulling back and going deeper to lubricate his length. This proved he didn't understand *quick*.

I pushed back onto him, hard, and was rewarded with one of his man-groans as I took him to the root.

He began to move with purpose, and the sound of flesh against flesh soon filled the tiny room.

I'd learned that deeper was as good for him as it was for me, so I pushed back into him each time he thrust forward. "Fuck me harder, Cowboy." My little bit of dirty talk also excited the stiff Brit.

"Be careful what y'all ask for there, missy," he said as he thrust faster and harder.

The sensations of him inside me built with each push, and looking to the side to watch us in the mirror on the door accelerated my climb to my climax. I committed the sight of him pushing into me to memory for later recall.

He leaned forward, and a hand circled around me to find my clit. His masterful teasing flooded me with electric shocks. He knew exactly what to do and how to do it.

I'd thought I was in charge this morning, but I was at his mercy. "Fuck... Yeah... Oh my God... More... Right there... Oh fuck..." With another pump into me and a tweak of my love button, I went crashing through to my convulsions.

I locked my knees. When I looked over at the mirror again, Ethan's teeth were gritted as he pumped into me. "Look in the mirror, Cowboy, and come for me," I panted.

My boobs flopped back and forth with each thrust.

I watched him in the mirror and rocked back into him hard every time he thrust into me.

The visual of my boobs swinging did him in quickly. He tensed and shuddered his release with a final push, holding my hips against him, planted as far as he could go.

He straightened up, still panting. "Are you sure you have to go?" Big Ben throbbed again.

"I have to."

My man always gave me his best, and soon he'd give me his name. It had taken me a second try to find a good man to make my husband, but this time, I knew I'd gotten it right. I wasn't keeping my maiden name.

He was good for me in so many ways, and he'd helped me be a better person.

∾

ETHAN

LATE SATURDAY MORNING, I WATCHED THROUGH MY UPSTAIRS WINDOW AS DAD WALKED out of the woods and toward the house with his arm around Mom's waist. They stopped to kiss, and he whispered something in her ear.

She smiled and giggled, poking him in the side before continuing, and I saw what I'd missed.

For years, Mom and Dad had invariably avoided much in the way of displays of affection. That had been obvious to any of us watching.

For the last five years, I'd attributed it to my mistaken belief that there had been a rough patch in their marriage—a patch so rough that Charlie and I were the result. But I'd been wrong about my parentage, wrong about Mom, wrong about everything. Now I saw I'd been wrong in another way. I'd forgotten the times I'd walked in the woods as a child and seen them on walks to the Yellow Cottage, where their stay sometimes lasted hours.

Each time, they'd left with a glow in their cheeks and their arms around each other. This was a sight I hadn't seen since leaving Rainswood to attend university. Nothing had changed, except I hadn't seen them alone together in years. Dad was his same old-fashioned self, keeping up respectable appearances with people around, and only letting himself go to be the loving husband he'd always been when they were alone and thought they were out of sight.

How much of an idiot could I be?

"What are you watching?" Becky asked from behind me.

My first instinct was to say *nothing in particular*, but my pledge of honesty to her precluded that. I waved her over and pointed.

"Your parents?"

"Yeah, don't they look happy together?"

Dad kissed Mom's ear as they walked.

Becky laced her arm behind me and snuggled close. "I hope we're that close when we get to their age."

I pulled my woman near, watching Mom and Dad make a turn toward the door of the house. "We will be. I know their secret."

Becky looked up at me. "What?"

I chuckled. "Later."

She hip-bumped me. "Now."

"Later."

"You said no more secrets," she protested before pulling away. Her smirk gave her away though.

"Surprise, not a secret." I reached over and tapped her nose. "Later, I promise." I planned to show her the bed in the Yellow Cottage, and the drawer that Mom and Dad had stocked with long, silk scarves.

Winston rang the bell that indicated food was ready.

Becky had suggested it would be easier than running all over the house, searching for people.

Winston had adopted it with only a few comments about loss of tradition.

I followed Becky out of the room to the meal.

Saturday family brunch around the kitchen island had been a Rebecca innovation as well. It had been interesting to see her convince my parents to try something new—something new-world, in a way. Mom had liked the suggestion, probably because it was similar to her late-night, after-a-party champagne-and-cheese sessions in the kitchen.

Our family was something of a holdover from historical times, lots of tradition with links to a long-ago England. But we still had to adapt, even if slowly, to a more modern country.

After having parted company with three different cooks since Karen, today's meal was part of another trial run on the fourth contender for the job. The final decision was Mom's, and so far I'd stayed out of the chef controversies.

~

Rebecca

Ethan and I started down the stairs, toward the sound that had announced brunch.

The size of this huge house—castle, manor, or whatever—still awed me. We passed portraits of previous dukes and duchesses as we descended, which spoke to the rich history of the place.

"I like Yasmin. Do you think your parents will keep her?" I asked when we reached the base of the stairs.

"I think," he said slowly, "that they'd be fools to not listen to your opinion." The words comforted me. "I thought Lizzy was coming?"

Lizzy had planned to join us to support her friend, Yasmin, the cook on probation. Today marked the end of her one-month trial period.

None of the others had made it beyond this point.

Staying at Rainswood on the weekends had become the new normal for Ethan and me. The respite from the bustle of the city—and more importantly the annoying paparazzi—had been the initial lure, but it had also become a place to recharge and relax.

Ophelia and Winnie were with Aunt Helen outside the closed kitchen door when we turned the corner.

"Winston won't let us in yet," Winnie complained.

As if on cue, he came out and closed the door behind him again, blocking their entrance.

"The bell is supposed to mean the food is ready," Ophelia told him.

"It awaits us," Winston told her.

"Don't you want to be polite?" Aunt Helen asked her.

Ophelia looked down.

Winston spoke up. "Which means, Miss Ophelia, that we wait for her grace before proceeding."

I turned at the sound of Ethan's parents approaching, which meant the impasse would be broken.

The girls got the hint and stayed quiet.

Winston opened the door, and we followed Ethan's parents inside.

Yasmin stood by the island with the food she'd prepared. She'd been apprenticing at Mortinson's before trying out here.

The door gong sounded. "That would be Miss Elizabeth," Winston guessed as he checked his watch.

"Get used to it. She's always late," I told him as he passed.

His reaction was a mere cock of the head.

Lizzy was likely to get an earful from him at some point.

After the hellos, Lizzy slid over next to me. "Is he always this grumpy?" she whispered.

I leaned close. "All you have to do is be on time."

She shrugged. Taking advice wasn't her strong suit.

The food was excellent, and the conversation around the island flowed freely.

"I heard from Kelsey," his mother announced. "She's doing well, but not sure she can make it for the holidays."

Disappointment crossed Ophelia's face. "I miss her."

"We all do," Ethan's father added.

I made a point of not assessing anyone while they were speaking. It had become easier, with time, to turn it off when not at the office.

Concentrating on only one of the person's eyes, instead of taking in their whole face and neck, made it possible to turn off my ninja power without looking away and appearing rude.

"Anything juicy happen that we're about to see printed?" Winnie asked Lizzy.

With a shrug, Lizzy said, "Wouldn't know."

"But your paper tells us all that stuff," Ophelia said.

Lizzy picked up her glass of water. "I'm done writing intentionally embarrassing things that hurt people," she announced. "I'm going back to school to finish my nursing studies."

"Wow," was all Winnie could say.

Lizzy finished her sip of water. "I want to help people instead of writing drivel that only tears them down."

I put my arm around my sister and hugged her. "That's fantastic." I couldn't have been more proud.

When she'd left her nursing program to earn money writing, Wesley had been a champion of the idea. I'd let my sister down by not arguing for her to stay in school—just another way Wesley had screwed with us. But that was over.

A round of congratulations and affirmations for her choice followed. It would be a good change for her. The best part was now I could invite her here to stay on the occasional weekend. It wouldn't have been received well by Ethan's father while she worked at what he referred to as *"that rag."*

At a lull in the conversation, I realized nobody had mentioned anything about Charlie. "What do you hear from your brother?" I whispered in Ethan's ear.

"He's doing a job for Dad in the States."

"Can we visit him?"

Ethan looked toward his father before whispering his answer back. "Too early to say."

The meal was wrapping up when Aunt Helen wandered to our side of the island. "Did Joseph come around to your way of thinking?" she asked me.

The first time it came up, Cornwall had been resistant to passing on the information we'd learned in one of our recent investigations to the police—another look-the-other-way incident. He'd reluctantly relented after I pushed, but it had been obvious my credit would run out with him if I pushed on too many.

"Yes. I think he sees the light."

"Just let me know if that changes."

Aunt Helen had also talked to him after the incident, and since then he'd been a pussycat on the subject. Whatever she had on him was strong.

"That was wonderful," Ethan's mother announced as she finished her meal and stood up from her stool.

Yasmin beamed. She'd done well again and deserved to be proud.

That was our cue that we could leave the meal, if we wished, and Ethan stood. "I've got something to show you, if you'll walk with me."

Ethan's parents caught us before we escaped the hallway. "Rebecca, one more thing, if you have a second."

We stopped.

His mother touched my shoulder when she reached me. "Do you think we should take on Yasmin full time?"

"It's not for me to decide," I said.

"Nonsense. You're a part of the family now; I trust you to make the right choice."

I swallowed hard. "But—"

"We're leaving this with you. Let us know this evening," his father said before taking his wife's elbow and walking away like it was nothing.

I practically lunged for Ethan's hand and the strength I drew from his touch. He pulled me toward the door to the back. "This way. It's your surprise."

Once outside, I asked, "What was that about? She'll be working for them, not me."

He put his arm over my shoulder as we walked. "You heard them. You're a part of the family, and they trust you."

"They barely know me."

"I said they trust you; it's what family does. You've spent some time with Yasmin."

"A little," I admitted.

"Now that you're in the family, it's a choice they trust you to make."

I sucked in a ragged breath. "Okay, I say we keep her." I pulled myself closer to my man, realizing I'd used *we* instead of *they*.

As we walked toward whatever Ethan's surprise was, I couldn't have felt any happier. I'd gained not only a man in my life, but a family.

THE FOLLOWING PAGES CONTAIN A SNEAK PEEK AT THE NEXT BOOK IN THIS SERIES, **THE Rivals**(Charlie and Danielle's story), which follows Ethan's brother Charlie

SNEAK PEEK: THE RIVALS

CHAPTER 1

Charlie

I'd entered the breakfast diner and exited through the back to lose the thin man tailing me. It would have been exhilarating if there wasn't so much on the line.

After all the turns I'd taken, I didn't think I'd been followed. A casual look both ways yielded only, a lady and child, a teenage couple, and a woman with grocery bags.

I passed through the store's door and looked around.

The girl behind the counter glanced up. Her look said she didn't judge me to be from this part of town. "Can I help you?"

"I'd like to purchase a mobile—sorry, a cell phone."

She pointed to my right and smiled. "Over here."

I followed her to the counter display.

"You're British?" she asked.

I nodded. "London, nearabouts. Is that okay?" The accent gave me away.

"Sure, so long as you have American money." She stroked stray hair behind her ear. "Calling home?"

"Me mum." Already I was making more of an impression than I cared to. Memorable would be bad.

"A lot of people like this one." She pointed out a simple smartphone.

"If you say so. I'll also need a card—let's say fifty dollars."

That earned me a smile as she pulled the box from under the glass.

She totaled it up, and I paid with bills instead of my card.

"Would you mind if I unboxed it and set it up here?"

She shrugged. "Be two dollars for the trash."

I reached for my wallet again.

"Just kidding ya." She laughed and handed me scissors. "Here."

Ten minutes later, I walked out with the phantom mobile in one pocket and the charger in the other.

A block away, I dialed Dad's number.

It went to voicemail.

"Dad, it's Charlie," I said. "I've picked up a fresh mobile for security. Call me back on this number when you get the message."

Twenty minutes later, I exited through the front door of the same breakfast diner as before with a growling stomach and turned right.

After two blocks, I spotted Thin Man again. Skipping the meal had been worth it to procure the mobile without alerting him. Now I had an advantage that whoever he worked for wasn't aware of.

∼

Danielle

My phone rang as I walked up to the conference room for Daddy's weekly company staff meeting. It was my brother, John calling.

"For once you have your mobile on you," he said.

He'd switched to calling a cell phone a *mobile* in deference to our London officemates. He'd even picked up the accent of a local, mostly.

"Hey, big brother, find any cute babes out there?"

He'd been gone over a week now on the latest acquisition Dad was pursuing.

"Very funny, Dani. I need you to talk to Dad about calling off this deal."

SNEAK PEEK: THE RIVALS

"You're the one he listens to."

"I'm serious. This doesn't feel right, and I think we shouldn't do it, but he's ignoring me."

I ducked in the empty copy room and closed the door. "What's the problem? And what can I do about it? He didn't want me to go along with you on this anyway." Actually Dad hadn't let me participate in any of our merger deals—yet.

"This negotiation process smells to high heaven, and I don't trust them. Maybe you can ask Dad a few questions and get him thinking about it. This time his only focus is on winning. It's not like him."

The last time I'd asked Dad if I could join John on one of these, his answers had ranged between *"it's rather technical"* and *"you're needed here."* But I knew my time would come if I kept at it. I was only a year younger than John.

"Okay, if you think it will help," I said.

He sucked in a loud breath. "This feels wrong, so I appreciate the help."

"The staff meeting's about to start. I'll talk to him after that."

"Thanks." We hung up.

When I entered the conference room, Dad hadn't arrived yet, and my brother John's normal seat on Dad's right was empty, so I claimed the power chair.

The room quickly filled, with the other arrivals electing to sit farther from my end of the table, probably to avoid the occasional lightning bolts that emanated from Dad when he was displeased.

Dad arrived promptly at ten and started the meeting.

∽

AFTER THE MEETING, I MADE A CUP OF TEA BEFORE HEADING TO DAD'S OFFICE.

He looked up with the phone to his ear as I reached the door.

When he finished the call, I entered and closed the door behind me. "Are you sure this deal John's working on is worth the worry and effort?"

Dad nodded with a knowing smirk. "He talked to you too."

I laid out my brother's message plainly. "John has a bad feeling about this one."

He steepled his hands and nodded. "This is a difficult one."

"Maybe I could go out and help him. Two heads are better than one." The saying was one of his favorites.

"He has it handled for now. I have faith in him."

I stood and walked to the door. With my hand on the handle, I turned. "If you have complete faith in him…" I opened the door. "Why ignore his advice to drop this one?"

The door closed behind me before he had a chance to answer. John's message had been reinforced, and Dad could stew on his own words.

CHAPTER 2

Danielle

Alicia's brow rose as she sipped her tea. "Do you think he's going to ask you at dinner tonight?" That was not a question I'd expected this morning from my third stepmother.

We got along well, but Alicia was every bit a busybody and definitely of the a-woman-should-get-married-and-prioritize-the-home camp. She graded each of my boyfriends on her own marriage-material scale.

Gerald had rated highly in her eyes as stable and reliable.

I put my tea down. It was hard to fault her for those observations; he was both of those things. "We're not at that stage."

"Sometimes they can surprise you."

I turned the page of the newspaper. "Uh-huh." I wasn't in a hurry to get on the marriage train. Things were comfortable as they were, and Daddy was beginning to take me seriously at the company.

My phone rang. "Speak of the devil."

"Hi," I answered as I rose from the table.

"Hey, Sugarplum. I missed you."

I walked to the window. "Miss you too." I hadn't seen Gerald since he left for Paris last week.

"Don't forget dinner tonight at Dunbar's."

I checked my watch. Luckily I had just enough time to get ready and make it. "Right, Dunbar's."

"See you at seven, Sugarplum."

I let out a relieved breath. "Okay, see you there." I hadn't remembered the time, and he usually liked to eat at six when we went out.

Alicia eyed me. "Forget again?"

I shrugged. "We set it up over a week ago."

"What does that tell you?"

"That I need to set better reminders on my phone."

She shook her head. "No—that he scheduled a dinner ahead of time at a very expensive restaurant?"

It *was* a little out of character for Gerald. Our normal dinners were at simple, local places without crowds or leather-bound menus. "It's probably because he forgot our anniversary." We'd been going out for just over a year now.

I hadn't said anything about it until two days later.

"It seems like just yesterday you accepted my first invitation to a date, Sugarplum," he'd said. A sweet thought, two days late.

"You should dress up," Alicia said.

"I always do."

Daddy strode in. "Always do what?" He leaned over to give me a kiss on the top of my head. "Good morning, Precious."

"I always dress appropriately," I answered.

Daddy leaned over and traded a brief kiss on the lips with Alicia. "And a double good morning to you, Darling."

A blush actually rose in Alicia's cheeks. They were sweet together.

When Natalia had become stepmother number two ten years ago, I'd learned to accept that one of Dad's faults was his inability to make a marriage last.

Alicia was wife number four, having replaced Natalia almost five years ago.

Daddy's taste in women had always been good. While the stereotypical replacement wife was a pretty young thing who was dumb as a rock, none of his had been. Like Alicia, the others had been gorgeous, but also smart and very nice as well. Somehow Daddy always picked nice women—so nice, in fact, that we all got together at the holidays. Why it never worked long term for him was one of the mysteries of the universe.

Faults be damned, he was my daddy, and I was his little Precious—and apparently doomed to stay that in his mind.

∼

My cab pulled up in front of Dunbar's a few minutes before seven.

Inside I waited against the wall when I didn't see my boyfriend anywhere.

Gerald arrived ten minutes later. "There you are, Sugarplum."

I smiled and leaned in for my peck on the cheek.

"You look beautiful tonight," he said.

"Thank you." I followed him to the maître d's podium.

We were shown to a table near a window looking onto the back courtyard.

The waiter was on us immediately, and Gerald sent him away with an order for a bottle of cabernet.

"How was your trip to Paris?" I asked.

"Good. Well, as good as a trip to Paris can be."

"I thought you liked the city."

"The city, yes, the people not so much. The day clerk at the hotel didn't speak a word of English. You'd think with all the tourist business they get he'd spend a few minutes learning the most rudimentary phrases."

We'd been over this before, and at least part of the problem revolved around Gerald not wanting to make the effort to learn any French.

He shook his head. "I'm staying at a different hotel on my next trip."

The wine arrived, and after pouring, he raised his glass to me. "To the most beautiful girl in this restaurant."

I blushed and raised my glass to his.

He talked about Paris, and we ordered our meals.

The conversation came back to my work a bit while we ate.

"How is John?"

Asking about my siblings was one of Gerald's nicer qualities.

"In the States," I told him. "Working on an acquisition."

He cut a piece of his meat. "Hawker?"

"I'm not sure." I shouldn't have let it slip earlier.

Gerald's brows creased. "Sugarplum, you can tell me anything."

"It doesn't matter."

"It does too matter. You should be able to tell me anything and everything."

I nodded. "You're right." This wasn't worth the argument.

"And Mark and Esther?"

I recounted what I knew about my other brother and sister. It felt good to have a man who cared about my family.

A little while later, I cut the last of my fish and looked up.

Oh my fucking God.

Gerald had a box in his hand. As our eyes met, he opened it. "Sugarplum, I want you to take this ring, and take my name."

Blinking back the tears that formed, I looked at the ring that sat in the box and didn't know what to say.

He hadn't asked a question. He shoved the box toward me.

The room had become quiet, and I could feel the stares of those at neighboring tables.

Gerald urged the box toward me again. "Go ahead, take it."

I sniffled and accepted it.

Polite clapping began from the nearby tables.

Our waiter arrived with a bottle of champagne.

Somehow Alicia had been right about tonight.

"Try it on," Gerald said. "I hope I got the sizing right."

I pulled the diamond solitaire from its box and slid it onto my ring finger. It was a little tight, but I got it on.

"It looks perfect on you," he said. "I was thinking next summer. What do you think?"

I nodded on autopilot. Summer was always a good time for a wedding.

The waiter poured flutes of champagne for us.

I couldn't hold back my tears. I was engaged. I'd looked forward to this moment since I was a little girl. I had the man and the ring, and I was fucking engaged. I'd reached another one of my life's goals, and it had snuck up on me.

"Don't cry, Sugarplum."

I wiped under my eyes with my napkin. "I'm sorry, I'm just so happy."

How had Alicia seen this coming and I'd missed it?

"To a long life together," he said, lifting his glass.

I emptied half my flute. This was all happening so fast.

SNEAK PEEK: THE RIVALS

Charlie

This afternoon, I was done being passive.

Downstairs in the fitness center, I dialed Bill Covington's number on my spare mobile. This room wouldn't likely be bugged.

"Hello?" the voice from years ago answered.

"Bill, this is Charlie Blakewell. Do you have a few minutes?"

"Sure, hold on a second." He spoke to someone else on his end. "Can you give me a minute? Family business. Thanks." The sound of a door closing came through the phone. "Yes, cuz, what can I do for you?" We were cousins, but it was a connection only a few people knew.

I walked toward the window. "I'm in a bit of a bind, and I need your help."

"Sure. Anything for family. What can I do?"

I breathed easier. Calling him had been taking a chance, and I'd hoped he would help. "I'm in Boston, and I need someone who can check for bugs."

"I've got a top-notch firm out here, but for resources there, you should ask Vincent Benson. He's in your town."

I wasn't keen on involving anyone outside the family. "I'm not sure—"

"Don't worry. The Bensons are close friends of the family. I'll send you his contact info. He owes me. Tell him you're a friend of mine, and he'll fix you up with someone you can trust."

I looked out the window. Somewhere out there was the enemy. "Thanks, Bill. I appreciate it."

"No thanks necessary. It's what we do for family."

We rang off after I assured him he could count of me for anything he needed in the UK.

The contact information for Vincent Benson arrived a moment later, and after calling him, I had a commitment for a visit from his chief of security within the hour.

Ben Murdoch arrived forty minutes later with a finger to his lips and a card that read:

> Hallway—close the door behind you

I did.

Vincent Benson's director of security looked the part: small eyes, a head of hair—if you could call it that—trimmed to a quarter inch, and a scar through one eyebrow.

Once the door was closed, Ben introduced his helper, Milosh Nikolic, who carried a small suitcase.

"Keycard," Ben said, obviously a man of few words.

I handed it over.

"Make yourself scarce. I'll text you when we're done."

After wandering down and out to the street, I purchased a cup of Earl Grey from the nearby Starbucks.

The text he'd promised arrived before the tea was cool enough for my first sip.

When I returned, Milosh carried the aluminum suitcase same as before, and Ben had a sheet of paper in his hand.

"No video, but three audio devices," he told me, pointing to one of several red Xs on his hand-drawn map of my hotel unit. "One under the nightstand to the left of the bed." He moved to the next X in the suite. "One next to the couch, here, and another under the desk." He looked up. "How do you want to proceed?"

"Pardon?"

"We can either remove them, which I don't recommend because it alerts the other side." This was all a game to him. "Or just feed them what you want, and only say the rest outside in the open."

He handed me the piece of paper and a business card. "Mr. Benson said anything you need. Call me any time, day or night."

They were gone a second after I thanked them, and I owed my cousin Bill thanks as well.

I slid the cardkey in, reentered my suite, and put the paper down. I looked over at the hotel phone I'd used to call Dad on the desk. A listening device there explained a lot.

SNEAK PEEK: THE RIVALS

I LEFT THE NEXT MEETING WITH THE HAWKER PEOPLE LATE IN THE DAY, AND THE situation had been bad.

I dialed Dad on my secret mobile once I reached the street.

When he answered, I gave him the bad news. "Whoever the third bidder is just upped the stakes ten percent."

I'd already increased our bid to the maximum Dad said we could afford. This would put us out of the running, and I'd be coming back empty-handed.

"That's not good," he said.

"You said we couldn't afford more, so do you want me to withdraw or keep our offer in play to see if the other guy fails somehow?"

He sighed audibly through the phone. "I don't want to let this one go, and there is one other alternative. I'll be in touch tomorrow morning."

"What other alternative?" I dreaded that he might suggest additional borrowing.

"I'll have to make a call or two. I'll let you know."

We rang off, and I decided on some exercise in the fitness center followed by a late dinner.

CHAPTER 3

CHARLIE

Dad's call came the next morning before I made it to breakfast.

"We're going to do this as a collaboration," he said.

I stopped walking and leaned against the wall to listen. We didn't do joint ventures.

"I don't understand." I'd expected him to say something about increased leverage, maybe allowing them to maintain board seats and a minority position, or perhaps making some of the purchase price contingent.

"I was right about Wentworth," Dad said.

I dreaded what he might say next. Losing to them would put Dad in a bad mood for a month.

"I talked with Jarrod, and he and I have agreed that this deal is too big for either of us alone, so we're going to do it together—and screw whoever that third bidder is."

His sentence blew up my whole understanding of the dynamics here. Our families had once been close, even vacationing together, but all that had changed, and we'd been fierce rivals for over a decade now.

"I'm not sure I heard you correctly," I ventured. Nothing could have surprised me more than to be working *with* instead of *against* the Wentworths."

Dad laughed. "Yes, I surprised him as well when I suggested it. But it's time to heal the rift. Neither of us wants to pass on this deal, and this is the only way to get it done. You and his son, John, are going to put together a joint offer."

"But—"

"No arguments. Jarrod and I agreed. I'll leave it to you two to work out the details together." He gave me John Wentworth's mobile number.

"Are you certain?"

"Yes. Just get this done."

∽

By three in the afternoon, I hadn't heard back from Wentworth. When I called the Hawker people to tell them I needed a one-day delay to put together another proposal, I didn't tell them how different it would be.

If Wentworth didn't get back to me by tomorrow, I'd know that Dad's idea had died the horrible death it deserved.

∽

Danielle

Near the end of the day, I was in the small conference room, going over the German market numbers with Carlson Gartner, who handled the western half of the continent, when Jenny burst in without a knock.

"I looked all over for you. Your mother needs you. She tried your mobile, but you didn't pick up," she panted.

It was odd for Alicia to call work, but it was true. I intentionally didn't have my phone on me so we wouldn't be disturbed. "I'll call her in…"

"Fifteen," Carlson said softly.

"Say fifteen minutes," I told Jenny.

"She said it's urgent," she insisted. "It's your brother."

I bolted for the door.

Slamming my office door shut behind me, I pulled up Alicia's contact. My fingers shook as I punched *call*. "What's happened?" I asked as soon as the ringing ceased.

"There you are. John has been in an accident. Your father is in the air on his way to Hong Kong."

I collapsed onto my chair. "What happened?" She wouldn't be calling unless John was hurt.

"Auto accident, in Boston."

"Is he okay?"

"He'll pull through, it appears, but he's in serious condition right now. It seems he broke a lot of bones, probably going too fast."

Alicia had always complained about how fast John drove.

"I'll leave for the airport right now and be in touch with you as soon as I can," I told her. I didn't need to be asked. "I'll take care of him."

"Thank you. I'll be waiting to hear—any time, day or night."

I pulled my small, emergency roller bag from its temporary spot in the corner. It was always in my office for sudden, unscheduled trips. The bag contained enough for three days on the road, and had come in handy twice already.

"I'm on the way to Boston," I told Jenny on my way out. "Pass any emergencies to Carlson."

She nodded. "I'm sure he'll pull through."

"He better. He owes me money." The joke was my only defense against crying.

∽

My plane arrived just before eleven in the evening Boston time.

Although I'd used my US passport to get through emigration, I flashed my UK one as I tried one more time to get past the nurse blocking my way at the hospital.

"Visiting hours ended at nine o'clock," Nurse Leslie repeated.

"But Leslie, I couldn't get here earlier. I just flew in from London."

"The only exception is end-of-life care, and your brother is not in that situation. You can come back tomorrow morning at eight."

Bureaucracy sucked.

"I'd like to see your supervisor."

She rolled her eyes. "I *am* the supervisor on this shift. If you don't turn around and let me get back to our patients, I'll be forced to call security."

I let out a heavy sigh. "No need. Please take good care of him."

"We do that for all our patients."

I turned rather than piss her off further. "Thank you, Leslie."

Once downstairs, I called Alicia to give her the quick status, but I got voice mail.

"They won't let me see him until tomorrow. I'll call you after that."

Then I sent her a text as well.

ME: Can't see John until tomorrow - will call after I do

Then it was off to the hotel to check in and get some sleep, seeing as it was now five in the morning, London time.

CHAPTER 4

Danielle

The next morning, I returned to the hospital just before eight after a restless night with little sleep, only some of which I could blame on jet lag.

Upstairs, I switched off my cell phone as the sign instructed.

Evil Nurse Leslie was gone, and in her place was a less frosty nurse by the name of Wendy.

When I entered the room, I had trouble swallowing the lump in my throat.

More machines than I'd ever seen beeped. Dozens of wires and hoses snaked their way to my brother, John. It was all a bit Frankenstein-like. A bruise covered one side of his face, but I couldn't see any of the rest of him.

I approached. "John, I came as quickly as I could." I reached for his hand.

"Don't," the nurse said and pulled me back. "He only just got to sleep and desperately needs the rest. He'll wake up soon enough, and you can talk to him then."

"Can I stay?" I asked.

She motioned to the chair in the corner. "Until the end of visiting hours, if you like."

I backed away from the bed. "What are his injuries?"

"He has a broken left leg, pelvis, ribs, collarbone, and his left arm. Also he has a back problem you'll need to talk with the doctor about."

The bad scenarios running through my brain quickly gave way to worse ones. "A broken back?"

"It's a disc issue, but as I said, you'll need to discuss it with the doctor. From the condition of the car, they tell me he's lucky to be alive."

I wiped a tear from my eye. How could this be happening?

She moved to the door. "The doctor should be by in a half hour or so, and you can discuss the treatment options with him."

"Will he be able to talk?"

"Yes, but he'll have substantial pain."

I waited in the corner and listened to the beeps and chirps from the machines.

Doctor Chen arrived even earlier than Wendy had predicted.

"He is stable this morning," he said after examining the chart that hung on the end of John's bed. "The good news is he doesn't seem to have suffered any head trauma."

"How long does he need to be here?" John hated hospitals and was convinced they were where people went to die.

"If he keeps on this track, probably another two days to be safe before we move him downstairs." He laughed. "With as many broken bones as he suffered, he'll be quite immobile and will need to be heavily medicated for a while. Luckily, no internal injuries means his prognosis for a full recovery is excellent."

"And his back?"

"That is a question mark at this point. He could end up needing anything from physical therapy to spinal fusion. It will take time to evaluate."

"Can you tell me what happened?"

He shook his head. "Car accident is all I know. For more details you'd need to talk to the police with the accident report."

John was still asleep when the doctor left.

I settled into the chair and reclined it to rest.

∼

I WOKE TO ONE OF THE MACHINES BEEPING ANNOYINGLY.

"What the hell?" John said weakly.

I pulled my stiff body out of the chair, grasped my brother's hand, and squeezed. "John, I'm here. You're in the hospital."

He closed his eyes and opened them again. "Dani?"

"It's me."

The nurse rushed in.

"He just woke up," I told her.

She repositioned an apparatus on the end of his finger, and the noisy machine quieted. "You can't go yanking things off."

"I can't move my leg," my brother said.

"That's normal. You've had a nerve block. Otherwise, how is your pain level?"

"It hurts to breathe, but I've been worse."

A normal response from my brother.

"I can up the pain medication for you," she said.

"No. Move it down. I need a clear head."

"Your choice." After a minute of checking things, she stopped at the door on her way out. "If you pull anything else off, I'll be forced to tie you down."

John nodded. His breathing was irregular as he looked around the room.

"Do you remember anything about the accident?" I asked.

"They ran me off the road."

That brought me fully awake. "They what?"

"What day is it?"

"Thursday, but don't worry about that. You need to rest."

"Get my mobile. I have to call Dad."

"You need to rest—doctor's orders."

"My phone. The deal. I need to call Dad."

"It can wait."

"My fucking mobile. I need to call Dad."

"I'll call and tell him how you're doing."

"Now. I hope it's not too late."

Extracting my phone from my purse and powering it on revealed almost a dozen missed calls from Alicia and Dad.

I started by returning Dad's call.

After listening to my status update on John's condition, Dad asked to speak to him.

I put it on speaker.

"Did you get with young Blakewell yet?" Dad asked.

SNEAK PEEK: THE RIVALS

"No." John smiled in my direction. "Dani will have to deal with it."

"I'll send Ellis over," Dad said.

My father's words didn't surprise me.

John grunted out a breath. "I don't trust Ellis with this."

My heart sped up with John's words of support.

Dad hesitated. "I'm not sure—"

"I am," John said quickly.

Dad was quiet for a second. "Okay, until you're ready to get back into it." He was still reticent to give me a chance. "Precious, I have to go. John will fill you in."

A second later he was off the line.

"So what's going on?" I asked.

"We're going in together with the Blakewells to get this done."

My expression surely showed my surprise. "But Dad hates them."

"I had the same reaction, but he insists it's what he wants to do. You need to call and meet up with Charlie Blakewell right away. His number's in my mobile."

The lump in my throat threatened my breathing. "Charlie?"

"Yes, right away."

I hadn't seen Charlie Blakewell since the summer I was sixteen. I almost hadn't survived the crush I'd had on him.

Printed in Great Britain
by Amazon